EMPIRE KNIGHTS

EMPIRE KNIGHTS

The Legendary Aubrey Durrell

TONY BYRAM

ARPress
45 Dan Road Suite 36
Canton MA 02021

Hotline: 1(888) 821-0229
Fax: 1(508) 545-7580

Ordering Information:
Quantity Sales. Special discounts are available on quantity purchases by corporations, associations, and others. For details, contact the publisher at the address above.

Printed in the United States of America.

ISBN-13   Softcover   979-8-89356-263-7
                    Hardback   979-8-89356-193-7
                    eBook   979-8-89330-286-8

Library of Congress Control Number: 2024903343

IN MEMORY OF MY TWO FAVORITE UNCLES:
AUBREY BYRAM AND DURELL MOORE

INTRODUCTION

What's in a name? Well, in the case of Empire, Georgia, the name suggests intended greatness. And indeed, originally that was the case. Back in 1885, a man named Jim Few erected a sawmill on the location of the town, which is about thirteen miles northwest of the county seat of Dodge County, Georgia, a city called Eastman, Georgia. Empire sits in the northwestern most corner of Dodge County right on the Dodge and Bleckley County line. In 1886 two men—-John Anderson and John W. Hightower bought the sawmill and named the location "Empire". These men had great plans and a vision of economic greatness for their venture, but like a lot of other endeavors, the Great Depression took care of a lot of these plans. Nevertheless, there was a bank in Empire and a thriving turpentine industry with a railroad running through the center of this community. A depot was built and a post office in 1887. In 1888 Empire, Georgia became one of, if not the first town in Georgia to install electric lights and a deep well provided a good water system for the town. By 1890 there was reportedly approximately 500 employees in all the mills and railroad business in Empire. The town was thriving and in 1911 was incorporated and elected a mayor, a Mr. P.J. Etheridge and a Mr. R.H. Beauchamp was elected clerk.

A school was established some time either in the late 1800's or early 1900's. Most of the small communities had their own schools during this time such as Empire, Roddy, Union Hill, Chauncey, Chester, etc. This is the basis of our story. I started to wonder how it would have been had these small communities still had their schools during modern times and how things would be so different growing up there. The story will be told through the eyes our fictional hero, a young man by the name of Aubrey Durrell. A great athlete, he grew up in the fictional Empire, Georgia but some of the things he experiences as a youngster are the same things the author experienced growing up in the real Empire, Georgia. Our story focuses on the athletic endeavors of Aubrey and his Empire teammates as they compete with the other small communities for athletic dominance, especially with their archrival—-Union Hill High School. Aubrey falls in love, gets hid heart broken and experiences success and hardships all the while trying to remain true to his upbringing as a good Christian and a true citizen of the greatest place on earth to be from. The story follows Aubrey to college and his marriage to a girl he met there. But no matter where he goes or what he does, Empire is never far from his mind.

Though it is not much to look at now, nor has it ever been much for outsiders to look upon with envy, Empire is a special place to all of us who were fortunate enough to call it home. The bank left years ago and the school ended operation in 1943. There is only approximately 400 citizens (which probably includes dogs and cats) and one lonely caution light that lets you know you are there, but it is rich with tradition and blue-collar values that stay with you throughout your life no matter where you end up. And the sound of that lonesome night train is something that you never forget. In telling the story of Aubrey Durrell, I hope to convey the sense of belonging to someplace special. I am sure that most people have their own Empire that they can go to in their mind if not physically. It is for these small communities and the people that call them home that I dedicate this book.

CHAPTER ONE

This is the story of a young man who was born in 1961 in rural Georgia and grew up to be a fantastic athlete and later a great football coach at his alma mater—Empire High School in Empire, Georgia. Aubrey Durrell's life was seemingly touched by the hand of God. He was not only a talented athlete (playing football, basketball, and baseball) but he was also an honor graduate, as well as a talented singer and guitarist (playing completely by ear) a talent discovered when he began playing and singing in church at the age of 10 with his cousin John Robert "J.R." Durrell; himself a talented athlete as well. One might think that with all he had going for him that Aubrey would have to be a cocky unlikable jerk but that would be wrong as there has never been a humbler superstar and a more likeable fellow. Standing 5'10" tall and weighing 190 pounds by his senior year; with hazel eyes and light brown hair he was a stunning specimen of a young man. However, his charmed life was not without turmoil. As you see everything that glitters is not gold.

This is also the story of a community in middle Georgia that a group of investors intended to become a rich and influential city when it was founded in 1911 around a large sawmill operation but the great depression took away that potential. Nevertheless, Empire, Georgia managed to hang on and developed into a little town of approximately 3500 people and the lumber industry, turpentine production, and cattle farming saved the town economically. Empire High School was established in 1925 and a few short years later in 1931 the Empire Knights started an athletic program that would be the envy of small communities in the state of Georgia. just a few short years later they won three state championships in football (1952, 1957, and 1958) as well as a basketball state title in 1961 under the leadership of Coach "Dixie" Dan McGee all before integration. Meanwhile, the local black high school—Frazier High was winning their fair share of games and championships as well. While Empire High School enjoyed their heyday in the 1950's, the Frazier Wildcats ruled the 1960's winning three state titles in basketball (1963. 1967, and 1968) and two more in track and field (1967 and 1968) under their great coach Arthur Chambers. The greatest athlete during this run was Cedric "Sugar Bear" Watson who lit up the scoreboard to the tune of 36 points per game to go with 12 assists and 5 steals per game for his career. He also ran the 100-yard dash and the 4 x 100 relay and high jumped for the Wildcats track team. He left Frazier on a basketball scholarship to Grambling University and later played for the Baltimore / Washington Bullets in the NBA for 4 seasons as a reserve guard. He also played for the Harlem Globetrotters for a few years after his NBA career ended. Until the arrival of Aubrey Durrell, he was without a doubt the greatest athlete ever produced in Empire, Georgia.

During the 1960's the Empire Knights were mediocre at best and "Dixie" Dan McGee was let go after a 2-8 season in 1965. The promotion of assistant coach Vernon McRae did little to change things. It was all made worse by the fact that their biggest rival the Union Hill Barons were winning region titles in every sport and when they were not winning the title, the Chester Tigers were. Chester won the state championship in basketball in 1965 and finished runners up in baseball in 1968. Union Hill could never quite get the coveted state title in football losing in the championship game in 1968 to the Hartford Red Devils and losing in basketball to the Chauncey Comets in the 1966 championship game. All these schools were located within 60 miles of one another making this the toughest region in the state and all roads to a championship in any sport ran through one of these middle Georgia communities during this time. Empire only made the playoffs in football twice in the 1960's and had only three winning seasons in basketball during the decade. Baseball was never any good never making the playoffs during the same period.

Integration came to Empire High School in 1970, the elementary school had been integrated for about three years already and the leaders in the Empire community knew that this could be a great boon to their athletic fortunes if they hired a coach that could handle problems that might arise because of this situation. That man was Jerome Kelly, a Viet Nam veteran and former high school star from Atlanta who had been coaching the defense for the Gresston Dodgers for three years and had helped transform them into a playoff contender. He was also African American. Some of the old heads had a problem with the hiring of a Black head coach but they were mostly ex-players of "Dixie" Dan McGee who still had heartburn over his firing, so they were basically ignored. Besides, 39% of Empire's population was African American and it was a popular move in that community. Most white citizens just wanted to win, and they did not care what color the coach was if he was good at what he did. Coach Kelly knew that he had to blend the black and white athletes together into a cohesive unit to have success and he knew he would not be given the luxury of a lot of time to prove himself. He brought in a new coaching staff that included three white coaches (defensive coordinator Jerry Lord—an old Army buddy and offensive line coach Don Rainey—with whom he had worked with at Gresston, and Trey Jones a running backs coach from South Carolina who had met Coach Kelly at a coaching clinic a couple of years earlier) and two black coaches (offensive coordinator Dale James and defensive backs coach Prentis Wilson) who had been high school teammates of his, all of them dedicated to making Empire a powerhouse again. In 1971 this group of men started the transition of the Empire Knights.

In his first two seasons he managed to finish with 5-5 records—improvement no doubt, but still no playoffs and probably worse than that; he had yet to beat Union Hill losing 35-6 his first season and 21-10 his second year. He had one upset win over Chester in his second campaign and had defeated Gresston twice and Chauncey and Rhine once each. He defeated the Roddy Pirates and the Dubois Lions both seasons. His greatest victory came in the last game of his second season—a thrilling 22-21 win over Hartford in overtime on the penetration rule. This win set the stage for the third year when Empire returned to winning form going 7-3 and making the playoffs for the first time in a decade with their only regular-season losses coming to Union Hill, Hartford and Gresston. They were put out in round one in a regular season re-match with the region champs Gresston, but everyone could see that the program was on its way back to prominence.

Meanwhile, Coach Jerry Lord had the basketball team winning again winning the region championship over the Chauncey Comets in 1974 and Coach Prentis Wilson had the baseball team winning more than they lost on a regular basis and making a playoff appearance in 1975. Boys' sports were fun again at Empire High School and the girls were winning as well. Coach Kelly was named region Coach of the Year in 1972 and 1973—the first two of many awards that would eventually come his way.

Coach Kelly had been monitoring a group of young athletes that had been dominating recreation league and middle school sports for the last four years and in 1975 this group would be his freshman class at Empire High School. This group of athletes included Darcy Williams at quarterback, a natural athlete who also pitched and played shortstop in baseball and was a smooth shooting guard in basketball; Stevie Wilbur a speedy defensive back; linemen Teddy Robertson, Lamar Pruitt, Howell Emerson, Kenny Dudley, and Melvin Hendrix. Twins, Josh, and Lester Beasley played fullback and tight end respectively, Ashley Stacey a speedy tailback who would become a team leader as a young freshman. But the best of the bunch was the Durrell cousins— J.R. and Aubrey. J.R. was the toughest kid in Empire and had proved it many times when people wanted to fight him and lived to regret that decision. He was easy-going and never looked for trouble, but he never ran from it either. He was a tight end and punter. Aubrey Durrell was special. He was a running back who ran over, through and around opposing defenders. It was just a matter of proving himself at the high school level and that would happen very quickly. The Durrell boys also played basketball and baseball with Aubrey playing point guard in basketball and second base or shortstop in baseball when Darcy Williams pitched. J.R. was a power forward in basketball and a first baseman with a sweet left-handed and powerful swing in baseball. Empire was about to make history!

Aubrey Durrell was born to Wyll and Pattie Durrell in January of 1961 and had been an only child until the age of four when his little brother Kelsey was born. Two years later a sister arrived—Paula Durrell so Aubrey would be a great help in raising the younger siblings and would be a terrific role model in the coming years. When he was around twelve years old, he began working in the family garden pulling a plow. His Dad threw a rope around his waist and off they went. Some may think this was abuse but Aubrey loved the challenge of finishing his task when every muscle in his body ached and told him to give up. He never gave up and kept pulling even as his legs ached and burned. Little did he or his dad know that this would be the reason for his incredible speed and leg drive as an athlete they just knew that the family had to have the garden to eat, and this was good enough for Aubrey. Occasionally his cousins J.R. Durrell and Stevie Wilbur would show up to help him pull the plow but most of the time it was just Aubrey. During summer months the boys loaded watermelons for local farmers which also enhanced their strength and athletic ability. On a single day in the summer of 1976 the Durrell cousins and Stevie Wilbur along with J.R.'s younger brother Donnie Durrell cut, stacked, and loaded 1,472 watermelons. They were convinced that they had an unofficial record doing it all for $2.00 per hour.

The Durrell boys were raised to be tough but also were taught that Jesus was the answer to all problems. They were in church three times per week—twice on Sunday and every Wednesday night at prayer meeting. Aubrey and J.R. had begun singing in church around the age of 10 and were good by the time they got to high school. Aubrey would sing and play his guitar and J.R. would sing the lead. Their favorite gospel song was "Mansion just Over the Hilltop". Later, much to the consternation of the congregation, they played some rock and roll or the "devil's music" as the older church members called it as part of a band, they formed with some high school buddies. They never forgot to pray and thank Jesus for their blessings or ask forgiveness for their sins. For Aubrey, his nightly talks with Jesus were something that he made a commitment to for the rest of his life.

CHAPTER TWO

As the Empire Knights boarded the team buses heading to camp at Rock Eagle State 4-H Camp to begin the 1975 season optimism was high in the community. Coach Kelly was optimistic as well though he kept his optimism well hidden. He knew that he had a chance to be good if the freshmen could contribute just a little bit. After two days at camp, it was obvious that they would contribute more than just a little bit.

Two of the senior players did not think much of the newcomers and set out to establish the pecking order early at camp. Defensive tackle Tony Finch and linebacker Jamie Dickinson were tough guys but seemed intent on bending rules to suit themselves. They had drawn the ire of Coach Kelly many times for late hits and personal fouls which drew fifteen-yard penalties and had literally cost Empire a chance to finally beat Union Hill the season before. They did not care so long as they got personal satisfaction and built their reputations as bad asses. This season they had decided that all players would shave their heads whether they wanted to or not. When the knock came on the door of the Durrell cousins, Ashley Stacey, and Teddy Robertson, they did not anticipate the response they received. J.R. spoke up and told them that they were not going to make him shave his head and he would like to see them try to make him cooperate. Ashley Stacey seconded that motion, and the fight was on. Aubrey and Teddy cleared out of the way just in time as Jamie Dickinson pounced on J.R. but before he knew what hit him J.R. had flipped the script on him while Ashley Stacey took on Tony Finch. When the dust cleared, Finch and Dickinson were bloodied and battered and humiliated. When the Durrells, Robertson, and Stacey walked into the commons area of the cabin and saw the rest of their freshmen with their heads shaved, Aubrey grabbed the clippers and handed them to J.R. who proceeded to shave Aubrey's locks. In turn, each of the boys shaved their heads in support of their fellow teammates. It was not the hair that was the issue, but the idea of hazing that the boys had rejected and had fought to prevent. As for Finch and Dickinson they were a lot quieter but still plotted their retribution.

During scrimmage later that day they both took cheap shots and late hits on Aubrey Durrell, but he just got up and said, "Good hit man", and kept on running the ball hard. In Coach Kelly's Power-I offense, Aubrey was the power back and sometimes lined up at wingback. That meant most of his yardage would come between the tackles on quick traps, power plays, wingback counters, and an occasional quick pitch to the outside. On a 2nd and 4 yards to go for a first down during the night scrimmage, the call came into the huddle for "0 quick trap". Aligned at left power back, Aubrey Durrell would score the first of many touchdowns for Empire as he took the handoff and went 48 yards for the TD. On the play left guard Lamar Pruitt executed a nasty trap block on none other than Tony Finch who never saw it coming. Pruitt nearly broke Finch's hip and right tackle Kenny Dudley and right end J.R. Durrell unleashed a brutal double-team block on linebacker Jamie Dickinson which left him stunned and stumbling around with his helmet on crooked at the end of the play. Aubrey simply had to secure the handoff and run for daylight which he did quicker that any of the coaches had ever seen a high school kid do it, especially a freshman. By the end of camp, the coaches were all in agreement that the freshmen needed to start. They knew this was a special group that would not be intimidated by the bright lights of Friday nights. If they made mistakes, they would make them at full speed and learn from them immediately. This may not sit well with some of the older players or their parents but so be it. The risk was going to be worth the reward.

The season began on September 6 in Eastman versus a non-region opponent from a higher classification the Eastman Wildcats who happened to be a double-digit favorite in this game. Aubrey would run for 189 yards on 16 carries and three TD's. Ashley Stacey would add 98 yards of his own with one TD while QB Darcy Williams would go 7 for 9 passing for 108 yards and a TD pass to J.R. Durrell covering 35 yards. J.R. would catch 3 passes for 62 yards. Left end Lester Beasley would catch 4 passes for 46 yards. The freshmen played so well that even Finch and Dickinson were impressed. Eastman had a high-powered offense itself and managed to outscore Empire in a shootout by a score of 38-35 but Empire got the attention of the region with this performance.

In game number two Empire hosted another AA team, the Jeffersonville Rattlers and gave the homefolks a lot to cheer about completely dismantling the Rattlers by a score of 42-6. Aubrey would be the leading rusher again with 210 yards on 19 carries and 3 more TD's. Ashley Stacey would add another 122 yards on 14 carries and 2 TD's and fullback Josh Beasley ran for 68 yards on 8 carries and 2 TD's. To Aubrey, so far, the game came easy, after all, the linemen were doing all the work; he just had to run through the holes they opened and manage to hang onto the ball.

The next three games were all blowout wins for Empire as they trounced Roddy 56-14; Dubois 49-0; and Chauncey 26-3. Aubrey was the leading rusher in all three contests with 586 yards total for the three games combined and 9 TD's. That gave him 985 total yards and 15 TD's after five games. The tough games were ahead of Empire however with home games versus Chester, Gresston, and Rhine. But the toughest one would be on the road versus Hartford and game number ten at Union Hill. If the freshmen were going to crack, it would be under the pressure of this next stretch of games.

CHAPTER THREE

The first of the murders' row games was a home contest versus the Chester Tigers. Empire would lead by six points 34-28 with three and a half minutes left to play when Chester got the ball for one last drive after J.R. punted them deep inside their own 10-yard line. Chester proceeded to drive down to the Empire 22-yard line with 54 seconds left to play and no time outs remaining. On 4th down and 10 yards to go for a first down, Stevie Wilbur stepped in front of the Chester receiver for the apparent game-saving interception except on the play Tony Finch got called for a late hit on the QB giving Chester a first down at the Empire 7-yard line and 43 seconds left to play. The idiot Finch was still celebrating the hit on the QB while the referee was making the call. That would be his last play of high school ball as Coach Kelly immediately replaced him with yet another freshman Bobby Parton who was a little bit light for a defensive tackle but would at least be coachable and play for the team and not himself. Chester would score the game-winner two plays later. Aubrey had another good game rushing for 159 yards and 2 TD's on 18 carries. J.R. caught five passes for 68 yards and a TD. Ashley Stacey would have 94 yards on 16 carries and a TD while QB Darcy Williams would run another one in from 24 yards out on a bootleg keeper. Unfortunately, a missed extra point would be the only blemish on Darcy's night and would be the difference in the game when Chester hit their last extra point to provide the winning margin in a 35-34 heartbreaking loss.

In the locker room after the game Tony Finch was still bragging about his hit on the QB; "Man I damn near killed that S.O.B.", he said to no one in particular. "Man, I swear he had a snot bubble coming out of his nose." Stevie Wilbur whose interception had been nullified spoke up, "hey man you cost us the game with that bull crap". Finch immediately got in Stevie's face and dared him to repeat what he had said. To Stevie's credit, he repeated to the big senior that "you cost us the game with that bull crap." Finch shoved Stevie so hard that his head ricocheted off his locker as he fell backwards. Aubrey could not stand for this so he jumped up and got in Finch's face and said," Stevie is too nice to fight you, but I will kick your ass if you ever lay another hand on him or anybody else on this team." Just as it was about to be on, Finch got a big surprise when none other than Jamie Dickinson flew across the room and form tackled him and got on top of him and told him, "Man your stupid shit just cost us a chance to win the region championship—we are seniors and we won't get another chance at it," yelled Jamie with tears in his eyes. "I have always let you call the shots, but I wanted to win a championship; can't you understand that?" Just as the coaches got to the locker room, Jamie told Finch, "I want you gone from this team you stupid bastard and if you ever walk back into this locker room I will kick your ass until your nose bleeds, you hear me, huh, huh?" At this point, the coaches came and pulled Jamie off Finch who got up and proclaimed, "championship my ass—this is Empire not Union Hill. We ain't won a championship since Moby Dick was a minnow and we ain't gonna win one this year either or any other year." The room was deathly quiet but any number of guys would have gladly jumped on Finch if the coaches just gave the okay. Coach Kelly stated the obvious telling Finch to clean out any personal property that he had and do not come back on Monday. To which Finch replied," No problem, dude I never liked playing for you anyway." With order restored, Coach Kelly spoke to the team." Men I take full responsibility for this loss. I stayed with Tony longer than I should have but I want you all to think about this; there were about 120 plays in this game tonight and to put the outcome on one play is not accurate. If we had stopped one of their three TD's in the first half, we would have won or if we had not stalled out on a 4th down and 3 inside their 20-yard line in the third quarter we would have won. What Tony did was wrong, and it is easy to focus on that one play, but honesty compels you to ask is that what the whole game was about? If you think so, then it will be hard for us to get better and that is my goal, and it should be all of yours as well. As for Tony Finch, I will continue to pray for that young man just like I do all of you that something or somebody will get through to him someday soon because his life can still be valuable, and he can still be a blessing to someone less fortunate." With that he led the team in the Lord's prayer and turned to walk to his office but just before going in his office, he yelled "I need to see Stevie Wilbur, Jamie Dickinson, and Aubrey Durrell before you leave tonight". Once he was certain that Stevie was alright Coach Kelly allowed him to go home. He then said to Aubrey and Jamie, "Men, y'all know my policy about fighting in the locker room and using profanity so after practice on Monday we will have a little attitude adjustment period; do either of you have a problem with that?" Both boys answered, "No Sir." When they walked outside, J.R., Darcy, Ashley, and Kenny Dudley were there and asked them what Coach had said. When they told them J.R. said," Aw hell Aubrey, can't be worse than pulling that damn plow." Then he turned to Jamie and said, "Jamie, if you ain't too ashamed to hang with a bunch of freshmen, I will buy you a Dr. Pepper, and by the way, that tackle you put on old Finch was the best tackle I have ever seen you make. You think you might be able to bring that to the next game?" And just like that a friendship was formed and to think just a couple of months earlier, J.R. and Jamie were fighting at camp. Sadly, that friendship would only last for about ten years as Jamie would be killed by drunk driver while on his way home from work in the winter of 1985 leaving behind a wife and two kids. Jamie played some good football the rest of the season making All-Region 1st Team defense and becoming a leader along the way. One of the ministers who preached his funeral was a recently ordained Pentecostal preacher named Tony Finch.

CHAPTER FOUR

Aubrey now had 1,144 yards and 17 TD's and was getting all kinds of attention. Some of it was good like the Macon News and even the Atlanta Daily News were getting in on the story of this amazing unstoppable freshman from Empire, Georgia. Again, Aubrey did not really understand what the big deal was; he simply had to finish plays that the big guys up front started. He honestly wanted them to get the attention and he mentioned them by name in every interview he ever gave. This would endear him to his linemen and all his teammates; it was honestly just Aubrey being Aubrey.

Some of the attention came from the young ladies and, to be quite honest, a few not-so-young ladies. His dad must have known what was going on because he took him for a ride out in the country one Saturday morning and had a talk about temptation and pride coming before the fall. Aubrey assured his dad that he understood and would not let foolish pride, or loose women interfere with his life's mission which was to be a good Christian man just like Wyll Durrell was. They both felt better after this conversation, but the devil comes at a person in many different disguises and Aubrey Durrell was on his radar.

Next up was a trip to Hartford to face the Red Devils who were pre-season favorites to win the region but had already lost to Chester and Union Hill. Empire would pull off a minor upset winning 24-13 with Ashley Stacey leading the way with 132 yards on 19 carries and two TD's. Aubrey added 102 yards on 18 carries and one TD. Aubrey was proud for Ashley and was relieved to not be the one getting all the attention for a change.

Game number eight was a home game win versus Rhine. Empire won handily 38-13 with Aubrey rushing for 144 yards on 19 carries and two TD's and returning the opening kickoff 86 yards for a TD. By now J.R. had begun playing linebacker as well as tight end alongside Jamie Dickinson and he had a monster game with 17 tackles (4 for loss); a QB sack; and a pick-six interception return for a TD in the 4th quarter. Darcy Williams had a solid game at QB passing for 94 yards and a TD to Ashley Stacey from 14 yards out in the 2nd quarter and made a field goal from 42 yards in the 3rd quarter. Their record stood at 6 wins and 2 losses. Next up was homecoming versus Gresston followed by the annual war with Union Hill.

It rained all week leading up to the Gresston game but miraculously cleared up about two hours before kickoff. Gresston was determined to stop Aubrey, so they committed two linebackers to key on him wherever he went. It was rough sledding in the first quarter as Aubrey was limited to 22 yards on 7 carries; however, Darcy Williams made them pay dearly as he gained 43 yards on bootlegs after faking to Aubrey. He ran one in from 18 yards out for an early 7-0 lead. In the second quarter Gresston started to account for Darcy thereby opening opportunities for Aubrey to get going. He would have a total of 87 yards at halftime on 13 carries and two TD's. So much for the strategy of spying on one man when Empire had others that would hurt you. Josh Beasley added a 12-yard TD run and the defense led by J.R. and Jamie was pitching a shutout. The score was 28-0 and the homecoming queen was crowned. The second half was more of the same with Ashley Stacey, Josh Beasley and Darcy Williams proving that Empire was not a one-man team. Aubrey still had a nice game rushing for 146 yards on 21 carries and two TD's. The final score was Empire 49; Gresston 0 This game would keep Union Hill coach Sammy Barnhill up at night trying to figure out how to stop this juggernaut. Chester squeezed out a narrow victory over Union Hill by a score of 10-7 to officially win the region championship. The Empire / Union Hill game would decide the region runner-up and the third-place team. Hartford would finish fourth. This also meant that Empire and Union Hill would face each other to end the regular season and in the first round of the playoffs in a match-up of the #2 and #3 teams. The winner of the first meeting would host the playoff game.

CHAPTER FIVE

After the boys showered, they headed off to the homecoming dance. Aubrey's date was Ella Pipkin, a cute little blonde freshman cheerleader who had been sweet on him since seventh grade. In fact, they had been to a couple of middle school dances together, but this was the first date her parents had allowed her to go on unchaperoned. J.R. was taking Jodi Lynn Rawls a sophomore and Jamie took his long-time girlfriend and future wife Cheryl Patrick. The girls met the guys outside the gymnasium where they went inside together. The gym was already rocking to K.C. and The Sunshine Band's 'Get Down Tonight' and the girls led the boys straight to the dance floor. Aubrey was a good dancer and enjoyed shaking a leg and Ella was proud to be with the most handsome guy in town. After a couple more songs, the boys decided they needed a break and found a table near the refreshments. Aubrey and J.R. mysteriously had to leave for a few minutes but promised to return a.s.a.p. They had a surprise in store for the crowd as they had been asked to perform a song at the dance. So, when principal James Bass stepped to the microphone and introduced them as the singing Durrell's everyone got deathly quiet as the boys sang James Taylor's 'You've Got a Friend'. J.R. was never better and even Aubrey was amazed at how the toughest kid he ever saw could sing like an angel. Aubrey played guitar like a pro and offered backing vocals, but it was J.R. who stole the show and Aubrey was okay with that. When they finished the crowd gave them a standing ovation. J.R. whispered to Aubrey, "I could get used to this man" as they walked off the stage.

Ella Pipkin hugged Aubrey and kissed him on the cheek when he returned to the table and the look on her face showed how smitten she was. There was someone else who was also smitten by Aubrey, and it was a second-year English teacher named Cathy Dehoff. Even though she knew it was wrong, she couldn't help but think of how good he looked and how nice it would be to teach him a thing or two besides conjugating verbs. When the dance was ending, she asked him to help her move a table back to her classroom to which Aubrey gladly agreed to do. When they got to the classroom, she closed the door and hugged him close to her and whispered in his ear that she appreciated his help and if he needed anything at all he could just give her a call. She then slipped a piece of paper into his jeans pocket. Aubrey was caught off-guard and didn't know what to say so he just said the first thing that came into his mind; "Thanks Ms. Dehoff, I could use some help with my book report." How stupid can you be he thought to himself the moment the words left his mouth. Cathy Dehoff smiled and told him, "Just give me a call and we can discuss it." She then kissed him lightly on his cheek and said, "let's keep this to ourselves okay Aubrey?" "Oh no problem Ms. Dehoff my lips are sealed." They went back to the gym with Aubrey feeling a little guilty and a little bit excited. All the guys talked about what they would give to get at Ms. Dehoff and here he was with a chance to live out all those schoolboys' dreams.

The girls all had extended curfews tonight since it was homecoming but still had to be home by 1:00 a.m. so Jamie suggested they all go to Nubby's—a local drive-in burger joint; before it closed. It was about ten minutes till midnight and Nubby's closed at midnight; so, they all piled into Jamie's 1972 Ford Bronco and off they went. Ella held on tightly to Aubrey's arm the whole time and when she laid her head on his shoulder, it would have been easy to fall in love with her, but there was the other issue on his mind.

They got to Nubby' s just in time to order some burgers, fries, and milkshakes. Darcy Williams and his girlfriend Jeannie Hoffs were there, as were some of their Black teammates Ashley Stacey and Kenny Dudley. Aubrey and Kenny had been best friends since first grade when they used to share a grape or orange Nehi depending on who had a dime to buy one at recess each morning. Aubrey and Kenny both hated school; mainly because they did not really know anyone in their class. Aubrey did not like the fact that he and J.R. had been separated and placed in different classes. He and Kenny just hung to themselves on the playground and the other kids just gave them their space. Once a teacher saw them sharing a drink and called Pattie Durrell about the fact that Aubrey was allowing a Black student to share a drink. It is doubtful that she called Kenny's mom. Pattie had a talk with Aubrey about how proud she was that he would share with Kenny but sharing with anyone was dangerous because if they had a cold; Aubrey could get sick or vice versa. She never mentioned race or color. Aubrey's parents were never racist, and they raised their kids to love all God's children. She gave Aubrey some Dixie Cups to take to school from that day forward.

Kenny, Ashley, and Kenny's sister Christina—whom Ashley had taken to the dance came over and said hello. Christina Dudley was a year older than Kenny and was a beautiful girl. She was also smart and outgoing and would go on to become Empire High School's first Black homecoming queen in a couple of years. She had always liked Aubrey as a friend because he was so nice to her brother Kenny, and she knew he was genuinely a nice guy. For a white boy, he was also easy on the eyes. Some of her friends had wondered if Aubrey would ever go with a Black girl, and some of them had vowed to find out.

"What's up my brother from another mother?" asked Kenny as he shook hands and gave Aubrey a big bro hug. Kenny also greeted the other boys in a similar fashion. He gave J.R. props for his performance at the dance saying, "if you had a decent guitar player, you might go somewhere with your voice." Aubrey didn't respond prompting Darcy to ask, "Hey one-five you, okay? Kenny just insulted you and you didn't respond. I just wanted to make sure you didn't take a lick to the head tonight." Aubrey replied, "Huh, yeah I heard him. That comes from a guy that the only musical instrument he can play is the radio." Kenny said "Okay you got me; see you guys later. Y'all be cool my brothers." Ashley said goodbye and Christina complimented the girls on their hair and said her goodbyes as well. They all watched her as she walked away, and Darcy said" If she was a white girl man, oh man." Which prompted Jeannie to punch him on the arm and told him to shut his mouth. "I'm just saying", said Darcy, "she is a pretty girl; but not as pretty as you baby". All the girls agreed that she was very pretty and sweet too.

It was time to go home now they had about twenty minutes to get the girls home, so they took off. Ella was the first to be dropped off and Aubrey walked her to the door. Ella told Aubrey she had a great time and that she thought he played great in the game and on the guitar. "Thanks," said Aubrey; "I had a good time too". After a few seconds of awkward silence, J.R. yelled out the window of the Bronco "Kiss her already and let's go!" At that moment Aubrey leaned in and Ella planted a kiss for the ages on him. She meant it to last a while and it would have except for the kiss he had gotten earlier in the night and the unread note in his left front pocket. He finally read the note when he got home. It said, 'I hope you will call me soon and remember; this is our little secret', and it had her phone number with a heart drawn around it. When he talked to Jesus later that night, he asked for forgiveness and guidance. He was a very confused young man.

CHAPTER SIX

The next morning at church Aubrey told his mother that he did not feel good and could not sing with J.R. The truth was that he did not feel worthy to even be in the Lord's house so singing and playing felt wrong to him this morning. J.R. asked him if he was okay and Aubrey said he had a little bit of a stomach virus which was a lie, but he felt justified lying to J.R. this morning. He didn't even go over to J.R.'s house to watch his favorite team the Dallas Cowboys play the Washington Redskins so J.R. believed him. Aubrey did watch the Cowboys win over their bitter rival all alone in his living room with the note in his hand thinking about making a call.

At school the next morning, Aubrey met Ella at breakfast and walked her to her first period class with a promise to see her at break. Third period was English class with Ms. Dehoff. As Aubrey walked into the classroom, Ms. Dehoff said" Hello Aubrey. How are you doing this morning?" Again, Aubrey lied when he answered "Fine Ms. Dehoff. He then took his seat and waited for the bell to ring. If she only knew the turmoil, she had caused in his brain this weekend she would probably be sorry; or would she? It was hard for him to know anything and hard to concentrate on the lesson today. She was a beautiful woman and Aubrey got lost watching her move around the room knowing that she was his for the taking. At one point, she caught him looking at her and smiled at him knowingly which caused him to look away in embarrassment. When the class ended, she asked him to stay for a moment. She told him to never be ashamed for feeling attracted to her and that she was waiting on his call.

At morning break, he was late to meet Ella and was unusually quiet when he got there. Ella asked, "Are you okay Babe?" Aubrey answered a little perturbed, "Yes; why does everyone think there is something wrong with me? I am okay alright!" Ella was taken aback and almost started crying then said, "I just thought…. well, I …. J am sorry Aubrey." He was immediately ashamed of himself. Ella was every boy's dream girl friend, and she could have any boy in the school, and he was cold to her for no good reason. He told her he was sorry and hugged her which seemed to make her feel a little better. As the bell rang, he told her again he was sorry and that he would see her at lunch. He felt as dirty as ever as he watched her walk off.

Football practice could not come soon enough for Aubrey. It gave him a chance to get away from his problems for a couple of hours and take out some aggression. The coaches unveiled the game plan for Union Hill which involved using Aubrey as a slot receiver and at wing back more than usual to get him more involved as a pass receiver. Aubrey liked the plan and so did Darcy Williams. Aubrey would also be in motion on a lot of plays. The most radical part of the game plan involved the use of the shotgun offense on third and long yardage plays. Everything looked great at practice especially 'twins left motion left square out' which called for Aubrey to align at right wing and motion left pre-snap and run a five-yard out route on the snap. The first time it was called in practice, he took it 65 yards for a TD. Ashley Stacey aligned at the slot receiver on this play cleared the cornerback out of the play by running a deep flag route while the left end Lester Beasley ran a post route and right end J.R. Durrell would run a drag route at 6-10 yards. If the defense allowed those three great athletes to run free in the secondary, Darcy, sprinting left, had the option of throwing to one of them.

Union Hill coach Sammy Barnhill would never know what hit him. When the Knights looked at film on the Barons, one defensive player stood out—Mike Linebacker Zack Winborn—a beast with a mean streak a mile wide. He was a dirty player who made Tony Finch look like a choir boy. Coach Kelly urged his team to not let Winborn lure them into retaliation, and he also said he believed that Coach Barnhill encouraged this behavior. "We have to be focused on the game men. In light of recent events with Tony Finch do I need to remind y'all about what can happen if we lower ourselves to their level?" said Coach Kelly. "Since I have been at Empire High School, this is the only team I have never beaten. Now we are going to have to beat them twice to get to where we said we want to go. Men this is our time and I know you are all ready to change the narrative around these parts. Y'all know we will not be favored to win, but the game is not played on paper, and I believe we are going to shock the high school football world. Are y'all with me? I said are y'all with me?" The team went crazy and to a man wished they could have played the game right then.

As they were leaving the field, Aubrey overheard Coach Jerry Lord ask Coach Trey Jones if he had asked Ms. Dehoff out for this weekend. Coach Jones said he planned to ask her tomorrow. Coach Lord said, "You don't want to let a good-looking woman like that get away man, you had better take care of it tomorrow or Angie (Coach Lord's wife) is going to drive me crazy. She is geeked up about going to Macon Saturday night for Mexican food and a movie. Don't make us have to go by ourselves." "I gotcha" asserted Coach Jones. Aubrey felt sick for himself but more so for Coach Jones. He had to talk to Ms. Dehoff tonight and put an end to anything that may develop.

CHAPTER SEVEN

Aubrey told the guys that he usually walked home with to go on ahead that he had to get something out of the school. When they were well out of sight, he went to the pay phone in front of the school and dialed her number. "Hello" answered a sexy voice on the other end of the line. "Ms. Dehoff" said a nervous Aubrey, "we need to talk. I am still at the high school. Where do you want to meet me?" "I will come up there in about ten minutes. Just come to my classroom window and I will help you in; okay?" said Ms. Dehoff. As Aubrey went around to the back of the school where her classroom window was located, he took extra precaution not to be seen or draw suspicion as to why he was still at school this late.

Sure enough, Ms. Dehoff opened a window and helped Aubrey crawl in. It was after Halloween so the time had changed, and it was dark enough so that no one would see him. When he got through the window Ms. Dehoff asked him what was troubling him. Aubrey told her about the conversation he had overheard between the coaches and about terrible he felt for Coach Jones. Ms. Dehoff laughed and told Aubrey that they had done nothing wrong, so he had no reason to feel badly. "But I thought you…we…. were…. you know about to…" stammered Aubrey. "About to what Aubrey," asked Ms. Dehoff, "have a little fun and make some memories". "We still can if that is what you want to do," she added. "And no one will ever have to know." she said as she moved closer to his face. "What about Coach Jones," asked Aubrey. "Are you still going to go out with him?" "I suppose so," she said, "after all, what's the harm in girl getting a free meal and a movie out of the deal?" at that instant she did not look that pretty to Aubrey anymore. "Ms. Dehoff," he said, "I can't do this. I need for you to let me be from now on. I will never tell a soul about this, but I do not need to be a part of your 'fun'. Not when I know how my coach feels about you. That would be just like going out with a teammates girlfriend behind his back and I could never do that." Even as he said the words, he could not believe he was turning this gorgeous woman down. How many guys in Empire would do that? He may be the only one with enough of a conscience to do it, but he knew it was the right thing to do.

Ms. Dehoff told him she admired his sense of loyalty but also reminded him that if the shoe were on the other foot, none of his teammates would be so loyal to him and, also told him that if he ever changed his mind her offer still stood. "Thanks," he said as he climbed back out the window and headed home. He began to talk to Jesus on his way home and he felt as though the Lord was smiling down on him for not letting himself be taken in by temptation. He had prayed for guidance and the Lord sent him a test by allowing him to hear the coaches' conversation; a test he had passed. He would be playing and singing with J.R. again this Sunday. "Praise Jesus," he said as he walked up the front porch steps to his house. After supper he called Ella and apologized again for being short with her earlier that day telling her that it was just the pressure of a big game and mid-terms and everything coming at him all at one time. She said she forgave him and promised to see him at breakfast the next morning. He almost said he loved her but held up at the last moment.

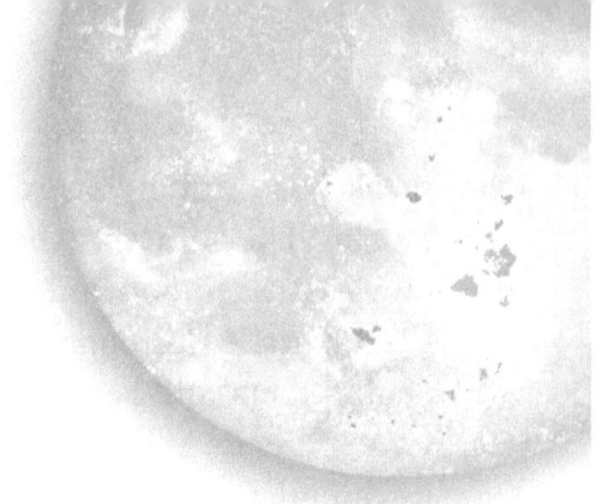

CHAPTER EIGHT

There was a lot of talk coming from Union Hill during the week, some of it coming from Union Hill head coach Sammy Barnhill. In the UNION HILL JOURNAL, he commented that his team had two home games in a row versus that team from Booger Bottom (a slur toward Empire by calling them the name of a local swamp). This was not to be determined until the result of the first game was final so obviously, he was claiming victory in the first game. He also responded to a question about Empire's super freshman class by saying," This will be a case of men versus boys, and I have men on my team." Privately, he had told a couple of his boosters that he had never lost to a Black coach, and he did not intend on starting now. When Coach Kelly read the article in the paper, he nearly laughed out loud but not because of overconfidence, but because Barnhill just made his job a little easier this week as far as motivation was concerned. Later that Thursday afternoon when speaking to his team he told them, "You guys are young, but you are not inexperienced. You have been through the fire this season and you are better for having gone through it. I threw you men to the wolves this season and the wolves high-tailed it out of here. I want each of you to know that I wouldn't trade teams with Barnhill this season or any other for that matter. And when we stand victorious on his field Friday night, I want him to know that this little young team of 'boys' from Booger Bottom just whipped his team of 'grown men' and they can get on their bus and come get some more the next week!"

On Friday the students at Empire High School honored a tradition started years earlier by observing silent day. The only time they could speak was during class with the teacher concerning the lesson being taught. The idea was that they would save their voices for the pep rally that afternoon and then let loose. About 2:15 that afternoon, the band marched through the halls of the school and each class filed in behind them and headed to the gym. They would remain quiet until Coach Prentis Wilson led the school in his favorite cheer. He stepped to the microphone and yelled out "ARE THE BARONS GONNA WIN?" This would be followed by the student body yelling back "WHAT DID YOU SAY?" He would repeat this process three times after which he and the student body would yell "A-B-C-D -E -F-G-H-J-K-LLLLLLLLLLLLLLL NO!" Of course, everyone knew that the students were not saying 'L No' but 'HELL NO!' No one seemed to care about that either so long as the students were fired up, and they were. Empire High School only had around 300 students and with 37 football players, 55 band members, and 12 cheerleaders that did not leave that many in the bleachers, but it sure sounded like a lot more.

The football team entered the gym to the fight song—'SMOKE ON THE WATER' and took their seats on the gym floor. The cheerleaders did a couple of cheers and then a mock funeral was held for the Baron mascot. When it came time for the teacher of the week selection, Ms. Cathy Dehoff was called to the front to be presented her royal blue and silver Knights' coffee mug and a corsage. Naturally, there were whistles and cat calls from the stands. but she didn't seem embarrassed at all. Aubrey was seated between linemen Teddy Robertson and Lamar Pruitt and Lamar whispered "Why is she in Empire? She could make a lot of money elsewhere with her looks." To which Teddy replied, "Yep, she could make a million dollars a dollar bill at a time." Lamar laughed out loud which drew a hard look from Coach Kelly and ended that conversation. Aubrey would have laughed too but he was not too sure that she hadn't stripped at some point in her life. He looked at Coach Trey Jones who was smiling big as you please knowing that he had a date with this gorgeous lady the following night.

CHAPTER NINE

The emotion was at a fever pitch during pre-game drills as the Union Hill crowd was in full throat. Much of their animosity seemed to be aimed at Aubrey. The worst seemed to come from a couple of old men who seemed as if they had enjoyed some alcoholic beverages prior to the game and they were letting Aubrey have it. They were cussing and threatening him with all kinds of physical violence yet the cops who were standing right near them never intervened. If they thought they were intimidating Aubrey Durrell, they were sorely mistaken. His dad has raised him to never start trouble but also never retreat from it. He just told himself to let his pads do his talking for him and God help them it they had a kid or two out there who dared to get in his way tonight.

When the teams took the field the P.A. man introduced the Knights as our neighbors from Booger Bottom and throughout the game, he refused to call the Empire players by name simply referring to them by their jersey numbers. "#15 back deep to return the kickoff" he said as Union Hill lined up for the opening kickoff. They wisely kicked the ball away from Aubrey and the ball went out of bounds giving Empire a first and ten at their own 35-yard line. The first play from scrimmage was 5 Smackover which called for Aubrey to fake a quick pitch around left end while Ashley Stacey would get the handoff off left tackle. Mike linebacker Zack Winborn completely ignored the ball carrier and made his way to Aubrey. Just as Ashley was finishing off an 8-yard gain, Winborn leveled Aubrey with a vicious hit in the back then as he stood over him, he kicked him in the small of his back and proceeded to flip off the Empire coaches, players, and fans with a double handed effort; all of this in front of the head referee Tom "Red" Hogan who did nothing. At that moment Kenny Dudley came running at Winborn and got in his face which prompted Winborn to push the 6'3" 245-pound offensive tackle. That would be a big mistake in the real world as Kenny did what anyone would have done and punched Winborn right in his facemask. At this point penalty flags flew from everywhere. When it was all said and done, Empire was assessed a 15-yard penalty for unsportsmanlike conduct and Kenny Dudley was ejected from the game. Winborn was not penalized at all.

After a heated discussion with Red Hogan, Coach Kelly knew he had to get it together for the sake of the team, so he called them together and told them to play the game no matter what and as for Winborn, get him legally between the whistles. Aubrey would miss the rest of the first series while trying to get over the searing pain in his lower back. Kenny Dudley told him before he was escorted from the field, "Aubrey, you got this brother; kick their ass!" After stopping Union Hill on a three and out Aubrey went back out to return the punt. The Empire crowd went wild when he returned to the field. He fielded the punt at his own 26-yard line and took off down the left sideline and he felt faster than ever. He picked up a key block by Jamie Dickinson at the Union Hill 37-yard line and he was gone. A 74-yard punt return for a TD and miraculously, no penalty flags mainly because it all happened so fast, they didn't have time to make up a penalty. After Darcy William's extra point, it was 7-0 in favor of 'Booger Bottom'. Aubrey was hurting but he owed it to Kenny to suck it up and keep on playing hard.

Early in the second quarter, Union Hill tied the score after a long drive. Empire got the ball with a little over three minutes left in the first half at their own 24-yard line. On first down, the call came in— Power I Right / Blast Right. On this play Aubrey and Josh Beasley were lead blockers for Ashley Stacey on a blast play right at linebacker Zack Winborn. When they broke the huddle, Josh looked at Aubrey and said, "Let's put his ass on roller skates one-five." "I hear you," replied Aubrey. On the snap, they both fired out like rockets and arrived at Winborn as if joined at the hip. The sound that came from his mouth when they hit him was like his soul was leaving his body. He flew backwards but they stayed engaged with him and continued to drive him back about ten more yards finally slamming him to the ground and landing on top of him. As he looked down at Winborn, Aubrey said, "That one was for Kenny; I'll be back for my payback in a few minutes." Ashley Stacey went 76 yards for the TD. Again, no penalty flags so Empire would take the lead 14-7 at halftime.

"Men, we have got to play like we are behind by three scores because you are going to see just how low men will go with these refs being on the take. I am proud of every one of you but mostly I am proud of Kenny Dudley for doing what I wish I could have done," said Coach Kelly. "Let's play for our community, our school, and for Kenny in the second half," he added.

Union hill took the second-half kickoff and drove down to the Empire 14-yard line with the help of two defensive holding calls and seemed as if they were about to tie the game. However, J.R. Durrell and Stevie Wilbur would stop this drive when J.R. blitzed the QB hitting him as he threw the ball into the waiting hands of Stevie at the 5-yard line who proceeded to return it out to the 45-yard line. A clipping call on the return brought it back to the 30-yard line but it could have been worse.

First and ten and it was time for 'The play' that they had worked on so hard this week—'Twins Left Motion Left Square out'. Just like they had practiced; Ashley Stacey took the cornerback out of the play with his flag route and Lester Beasley occupied the middle of the field with a post route. Aubrey knew he would be wide open as he went in motion to the left, all he would have to do was make the catch. The ball was thrown perfectly, and Aubrey caught it in stride. As he turned up field, he was somewhat shocked to see nothing but green grass in front of him. He ran like he had stolen something. He was fast according to all those who knew football, but this was the first time he realized just how fast he could be. Everyone else seemed to be standing still to him as he covered the 70 yards in what seemed like an instant. According to the scoreboard clock it took him less than nine seconds after he secured the catch. He even seemed to win over head referee Red Hogan who told him as he was leaving the field, "Son I have called many a game in my time and you are the fastest and toughest kid I have ever seen." "Thank you, sir and may God forgive and bless you," said Aubrey. Hogan felt a little remorse over letting Zack Winborn get away with assaulting this young man earlier in the game and even though he would catch hell from Sammy Barnhill at their weekly poker games during the off-season he vowed to call the game fairly from this point forward. The icing on the cake was the 'Charlie Brown' extra-point fake whereby the holder, Lester Beasley would place the ball on the kicking tee just long enough for kicker, Darcy Williams to fake a kick then he would get up and sprint out to his left looking to hit J.R. or Josh Beasley who have executed delay routes into the end zone. J.R. was standing wide open in the back of the end zone and caught the ball for two points making the score 22-7.

When the fourth quarter started Empire was twelve minutes away from hosting the first round of the playoffs, but it would not come without a fight. Union Hill would score about five minutes into the quarter making the score 22-14. When Empire got the ball back, they called the square out again but this time Coach Dale James, the offensive coordinator told Darcy to expect Aubrey to be covered by a linebacker and to look for J.R. on the drag route. Just as Coach James had predicted, the will linebacker left the middle and followed Aubrey in motion and Darcy threw to J.R. who took the ball for a 36-yard gain down to the Union Hill 34-yard line. The next play would seal the deal when Aubrey took the ball in on Wing Right Counter with J.R. making a hellacious block on Zack Winborn to spring him for the TD. With the score 29-14 and a little over five minutes left to play, the Empire crowd began celebrating while the Union Hill crowd got an early start on their trips home. When the final horn sounded, Coach Kelly ordered his team to the locker room without shaking hands and when he spoke to Sammy Barnhill, he made sure he knew how to get to 'Booger Bottom' next week. He was brought to tears in the locker room when he told the team, "Fellows I have seen some tough times and some tough men in my time in Viet Nam and over my lifetime as an athlete and a coach, but I have never been prouder of a group of young men as I am right now. I want to thank you all for buying into our philosophy and our program. We have a lot more to play for but tonight I just want to say thank y'all from the bottom of my heart and let's get ready to beat these guys next week at 'Booger Bottom'.

CHAPTER TEN

Union Hill came to Empire the next week with a lot less swagger and a whole lot less talk. Even Sammy Barnhill was reduced to a 'No comment' when asked about the powerful offense of Empire. Aubrey had finished the tegular season 1,631yards rushing and 25 TD's; both school records and possibly state records for a freshman. He was a shoe in for first team All-Region and All Middle Georgia honors but was still humble and a bit embarrassed by all the attention. Even his teammates encouraged him to enjoy it a little bit more and not worry about what anyone thought. When Union Hill got off the bus, they were greeted by signs 'Welcome to Booger Bottom where plenty enter but few get out alive.' They were not ready for the onslaught the Knights would put on them this Friday night and the Empire fans let them hear about it after every score. The final score was Empire 37 Union Hill 6. Aubrey would lead all rushers with 191 yards and two TD's J.R. would get the Nubby's Player of the Week award with five pass receptions for 86 yards and two TD's and would also have 14 tackles on defense with a fumble caused and an interception. Also, just for good measure, he averaged 41 yards per punt even though Empire only punted three times all night long. Incidentally, linebacker Zack Winborn went out of the game early after a particularly crushing block by Kenny Dudley and a taunting by the Empire crowd. He did not flip anyone off on his way to the safety of his sideline. Empire moved on to the second round of the state playoffs versus the Butler Raiders. This would be their last home game this season barring a major upset in this round. The Raiders were tough, but Empire would prevail behind Aubrey's 156 yards and 2 more TD's to go with Ashley Stacey's 98 yards and two

TD's of his own. Darcy Williams added 87 passing yards and a TD pass to Lester Beasley to make the final score Empire 35—Butler 21.

Round three would be tough for the Knights as they ran into the defending state champions the Warm Springs Demons. Aubrey would play okay but had a crucial fumble in the 4th quarter that killed a potential game-tying scoring drive with Warm Springs leading 17—10. Aubrey was inconsolable after the game thinking that he had cost them the game; but Jamie Dickinson told him that he was the greatest football player he had ever seen and how he was honored to have been his teammate this season. He also said that they would not have gotten that far if not for Aubrey; a sentiment echoed by the rest of the team and the coaches. Still Aubrey vowed to work even harder next season to get better and challenged all his teammates to join him. 2,088 yards and 30 TD's would make him first team All-State as a freshman and colleges were already taking notice of his potential at the next level, but all Aubrey could think about was that fumble. He thought about it while lifting weights in P.E. class and he thought about while pulling the plow during the spring and early summer months. He thought about it while loading watermelons during the dog days of July and August. If he needed a humbling experience; and he did not; this was it. The 1976 season could not get here fast enough for him. By the way, Warm Springs would go on to defeat Chester in the state championship game by a score of 23-10.

CHAPTER ELEVEN

Wyll and Pattie gave their son time to get over the season before resuming normal chores and responsibilities but refused to let Aubrey wallow in self-loathing too long. Pattie reminded him that the Lord would not put anything on him that he didn't think he could handle and that there were a lot of people in this world with a lot worse problems than he had. Wyll Durrell told his son he was proud of him not only because of his athletic abilities but that he was a humble servant of God and because the fumble bothered him and would make him better and more focused in the future. He also reminded him that he had other sports coming to help him get over it quicker. His little brother Kelsey was not so subtle. He asked Aubrey whether the ball got knocked from his hands on a hard hit or if he just dropped it. Truth was Aubrey could not really say—everything had happened so fast. Just talking about it to Kelsey seemed to help a little bit too. And when Kelsey said he was proud of being his brother, Aubrey felt ten feet tall. Little sister Paula didn't care much about football yet, but she knew when her big brother needed a hug, so she made sure he got one after supper each night.

Coach Lord's basketball team was set with most of the players coming back from the year before so Aubrey, J.R; and Darcy played J.V. and went undefeated at 10-0. The only two freshman who made the team were Bobby Parton a 6'1" 180 lb. string bean who could leap out of the gym and Kenny Dudley who at 6'3" 245 pounds was an enforcer and a terrific rebounder in the low post. The team won the region championship for the second time in three years over the Chauncey Comets in overtime 76-73. They would fall in the state semi-finals to the Roberta Warhawks who won the state championship over Butler.

When baseball season came around it was a little different story. Coach Prentiss Wilson had graduated most of his starters off a playoff team the season before so there were plenty of roster spots open. These boys had played baseball together since tee ball and had won the Dixie Youth State Title as 12-13-year-olds. When the season started, Empire would start six freshmen—Darcy Williams and Randy Stafford would be the two main starting pitchers. Lester Beasley would bat leadoff and play left field while Ashley Stacey would hit second and play centerfield. Aubrey would hit third and play second base or shortstop when Darcey pitched and J.R. would hit cleanup and play first base. Darcy would bat fifth and Randy would hit sixth and play right field. Sophomore William "Bullfrog" Mullins would handle third base and bat seventh and the catcher was junior Johnny Pickens who batted eighth followed by another junior Dewayne Hollis a utility player who filled in at second base when Darcy pitched and right field when Randy pitched. The bullpen included Johnny "Hondo" Winston and Howell Emerson, and even Aubrey could throw some innings to save arms in a blowout win or loss. Aubrey felt great and he was strong as he was now up to 170 pounds after playing football at around 160 pounds and relying mainly on his great speed. He had put the work in during weightlifting class and had led the team in squats maxing out at 530 pounds on a true parallel rep. He was the 6th best in bench press at 230 pounds. The ball was jumping off his bat and he was the fastest baserunner on the team. J.R. was also working hard and now stood about 6' tall and weighed 185 pounds. He was crushing the ball as well. Darcy Williams was, according to Aubrey, the best baseball player he had ever seen. He never missed a ground ball at shortstop and every throw was true. As a pitcher, he threw a fastball at about 81 mph as a freshman, but his out pitch was his knuckle curve that he called his 'round house pitch'. The first time Coach Prentis Wilson saw it, he gave it a new name commenting, "Son that thing came dancing in there like a 'kicking mule'". So now the pitch was known affectionately as 'the kicking mule'. Randy Stafford was a hard-throwing left-hander with about an 83-mph fastball and a decent curveball. This team was young but loaded with talent. And as J.R. said one day early in the season, "After playing high school football, nothing on the baseball field can ever scare you."

In his personal life, Aubrey and Ella Pipkin were still together and seemingly in love, they made a perfect couple—smart; well-liked; and beautiful. Life was good for Aubrey except during third period English class each day where he had to see Ms. Dehoff.

CHAPTER TWELVE

Cathy Lynn Dehoff was born and raised in Gordon, Georgia in 1953 to parents Margaret and Jerry Dehoff. Margaret was an elementary school teacher and Jerry worked in the kaolin mines. She and her two little brothers were happy and had everything they needed if not everything they wanted. They attended private school and were popular. That is until Jerry Dehoff ran off with a younger woman when Cathy was in the ninth grade. Margaret was shattered but vowed to keep her kids in private school even though Jerry Dehoff never paid child support or alimony on time if ever. This lasted one year and beginning in Cathy's junior year and her brothers in middle school, the Dehoff kids had to enter public schools in Gordon. This meant that Cathy was leaving behind friends, activities, and worst of all, her boyfriend Thomas James Hargrove III. T.J., as he was known, was the most handsome boy in the school and he was the star athlete. He promised to still love and care for Cathy after she had to leave the school; however, with Cathy gone, he began seeing other girls who had patiently waited for their turn to be with him. It was not long before Cathy found out what was going on and went into serious depression. Pretty as she was, she had no shortage of boys vying for her affection, but she was not interested in anyone else at that time. Her grades suffered and her attitude at home changed toward her mother. She should have been homecoming queen and engaged to T.J. but now because her mother couldn't keep her dad happy at home, her life was turned upside down. She managed to keep her grades good enough to get into the University of Georgia where she graduated with a degree in English / Education. Her mother was proud of her and told her that after the graduation ceremony. Her mother was struggling with the two boys with the older boy, Nathan, dropping out of school in the tenth grade, and the younger boy Jonathan constantly getting into trouble at school and delving into drugs and alcohol. Jerry Dehoff was never around to help, and no one really knew where he was. Cathy had come to realize that her dad had to be sorry as hell to not care about his kids regardless of how he felt about Margaret. Cathy had tried to talk to her brothers but to no avail and she didn't know how much more her mother could take. She was worried about her and offered to live at home and get a job to help the situation financially, but her mom insisted that she get on with her own career and life.

Cathy had dated a couple of guys in college and had been intimate with a couple more but nothing serious. She was anxious to move on and find someone she could connect with. Little did she know that that person would be one of her students. God how could she have been so stupid to approach Aubrey Durrell. She could barely look him in the eye now knowing what she had done. She had to hope that his unusual sense of honor would prevent him from talking to anyone about it. She really believed that she could love him, and he reminded her so much of the love she left behind in the tenth grade; yet she knew that was no excuse for what she had done. She was aware that the other boys at Empire High School talked about her in locker room talk but Aubrey was different. She had wanted him so badly and in fact, she still did. But she could not pursue him anymore. She also had been dating Coach Trey Jones who was nice-looking and a good man, but he was not the one either. She had decided to leave Empire at the end of the school year and had been talking to a school in Savannah about a possible job next year.

In January of 1976, she had spoken to her mom on the phone and almost told her what she had done but she did not. One thing she knew for sure was that she needed to talk to someone about her feelings, but her mom did not need anything else to worry about. That would be the last time she talked to her mom. A couple days later she got the call that her mom had died of a heart attack at the age of 47. Her brothers managed to clean up enough for the funeral and at the graveside service she saw a familiar looking man off in the distance. Jerry Dehoff finally showed up but did not stick around to chat. Probably for the best anyway since Cathy had nothing positive to say to him and she never told the boys that she saw him there. That would have gotten ugly!

When she returned to work, all her students offered heartfelt condolences and hugs. She appreciated each of them but especially the one she got from Aubrey Durrell as he hung around at the end of class after all the other kids left. She could have gotten lost in his arms but held strong fighting her urges. She knew she needed counseling and she soon started seeing a psychiatrist.

CHAPTER THIRTEEN

The Saturday before the first baseball game versus Rhine; Aubrey's little brother had a recreation league game at Union Hill. Kelsey was a left-handed pitcher / outfielder with great promise, and he was pitching today. Behind the plate was Union Hill Barons' defensive tackle and first baseman "Big Mouth" Barry Kennedy and he had it in for anyone named Durrell. He blatantly squeezed him on balls and strikes but the worst thing he did occurred in the top of the fourth inning. With the Nubby' s Braves leading 5-2, and Kelsey Durrell on second base, the batter hit a single to right field. Kelsey got the go signal from his third base coach and flew around third and headed home. The throw came in a little up the third base line causing the catcher to get in the path of Kelsey who knocked the catcher to the ground and scored the sixth run. However, "Big Mouth" Barry saw an opportunity to grandstand, so he proceeded to throw Kelsey out of the game and called him a dirty player. "Apparently it runs in your family," shouted Barry and stared at Aubrey as he said those words. Kelsey was heartbroken thinking he had done something wrong, but his coach defended him to no avail. "Big Mouth" Barry had gotten the last word—for now. With Kelsey out of the game Union Hill won a close contest by a score of 8-7. Aubrey vowed to get Kennedy and Union Hill back.

In the first game versus the Rhine Bears. Darcy Williams had the 'kicking mule' working pitching six innings before giving way to Johnny "Hondo" Winston for the last three outs in a 7-0 Empire win. Aubrey went 3 for 5 with a double and 3 RBI and two runs scored. J.R. also went 3 for 5 with a homerun and 3 RBI and 2 runs scored.

Darcy Williams had a solo homerun in the 5th inning to go along with six scoreless innings and 6 strikeouts. Next up was a trip to Chester.

The Chester Tigers were a good team with better than average pitching and timely hitting and a couple of kids who could hit the ball a long way if they got ahold of it, but Empire really had no weaknesses and beat the Tigers by a score of 9-3. Randy Stafford would pitch 5 and a third innings before giving way to "Hondo" Winston to finish the deal. Aubrey would hit his first high school homerun in the 3rd inning—a three-run shot to dead center field. He would finish 4 for 5 with 4 RBI and three runs scored. He would also steal two bases in this game. J.R. would go 2 for 5 with a double and two RBI. Darcy Williams played outstanding defense at shortstop. He also went 2 for 4 at the plate with a walk and an RBI and 2 runs scored. After a road game at Chauncey and a home game versus Roddy, the Knights would travel to Union Hill to face "Big Mouth Barry" and the rest of the Barons.

Empire beat Chauncey in five innings 17-2 and Roddy 10 -3 with Aubrey leading the way at the plate going 5 for 12 with two homeruns and 8 RBI to go with 5 stolen bases and 6 runs scored. To say he was seeing the ball well would be an understatement. J.R. went 4 for 9 during those two games with a homerun and 5 RBI and 3 runs scored while Darcy won his second game pitching a complete game (5 innings). He also had 3 hits in 8 at bats to go with 3 walks and 4 runs scored. Randy Stafford pitched a complete game versus Roddy as well striking out 8 batters and giving up only three hits (one was a three-run homerun in the last inning).

The game versus Union Hill would go a long way toward deciding the region championship as these were the two best teams by far. Aubrey could not help but glare at "Big Mouth Barry" Kennedy as he warmed up in pre-game drills. Kennedy was still running his mouth about overrated Empire and what he was personally planning to do to them today. When he saw his little brother in the bleachers with his parents, he knew he had to perform today. Union Hill was pitching their number one starter Donnie Pack, a big 6'6" 200 pound hard-throwing right hander who already had a couple of scholarship offers from SEC schools in the bag. Darcy Williams was on the hill for the Knights. Lester Beasley would lead off the game and after running the count full he went down swinging for the first out of the game. Ashley Stacey would pop out to the second baseman for out number two. Aubrey came to the plate with two outs and nobody on base and was knocked down with a pitch aimed at his head on the first pitch. The next pitch drilled him in the ribs. Even though it hurt he refused to rub it or whine about it; instead, he ran down to first base where old "Big Mouth Barry" greeted him with a smart aleck response, "Man I'll bet that hurt like hell; it is gonna be a long day for you Durrell. Maybe with a little luck you can get tossed early like your little brother did." Aubrey simply replied, "My little brother throws harder than that. You can bet this won't be the last time I will on first base today Big Mouth; but you had better talk quick because I am planning on stealing second in just a minute." Aubrey took his lead and as he expected Pack threw over to first base to hold him close. When Kennedy applied the tag, he hit Aubrey in the face hard. J.R. saw this and his face turned blood red with anger and Aubrey knew that he was going to try to pull a pitch down the line hard right at Kennedy. After one more pick-off attempt Aubrey was reasonably sure that the next throw would be to home plate, so he prepared to steal second. Sure enough, Pack unleashed a fastball that was down and in and right in J.R.'s wheelhouse. Aubrey had the base stolen, but it would not matter as J.R. hit the ball about 400 feet down the right field line for a two-run homer. As he passed Kennedy at first base, he told him, "Son I hope you got insurance because you are gonna need it today if I get a chance to hit one down your throat." Union Hill had managed to piss off the whole Durrell family in another athletic event and that would not bode well for them again.

Darcy got the Barons out in order in their half of the first inning. The mule was kicking hard today, and Union Hill hitters were baffled all day long, especially Barry Kennedy who would go 0 for 4 with three strikeouts. As promised Aubrey was back on first base in the top of the third inning after drawing a walk. When he got to first base, he told Kennedy, "Boy you have really pissed J.R. off—I have never seen him so mad. If I were you, I would play a deep first base." Obviously, this wore on "Big Mouth's" mind because on the first pick-off attempt, he let the ball get by him on a perfect throw allowing Aubrey to get to second base again. With Kennedy backed up into short right field, J.R. laid down a perfect bunt past the pitcher and Kennedy was in no position to field the ball so he got an easy infield hit and Aubrey was standing on third base laughing so hard he almost fell. He wished he could hear the conversation going on at first base at that moment. Darcy would draw a walk from an obviously rattled Donnie Pack loading the bases with no outs and Randy Stafford at the plate. On a 2-0 pitch, Randy ripped a double into the right centerfield gap clearing the bases and chasing Pack off the mound.

Aubrey came to the plate again in the sixth inning with Empire enjoying a 5-0 lead but even though he had scored a couple of runs and impacted the game, Aubrey was still looking for his first hit of the day. Ashley Stacey was on first base with a leadoff single and Aubrey expected to get the sign for hit and run and indeed he did from Coach Wilson at third base. This was exactly what he wanted—a chance to wake old "Big Mouth" up with a hard-hit ball right at him. Surely enough, Ashley took off on the first pitch which was a little bit outside and perfect for a shot at right field. Aubrey got the barrel of the bat on the pitch and hit a rocket shot directly at the Barons' first baseman. The ball was hit so hard that all "Big Mouth Barry" could do was cover his face with his glove, but the ball hit him a little farther down and right in the groin area. As he was lying on the ground in pain the ball rolled into foul territory, but Barry Kennedy was not going to pick it up. As the Union Hill second baseman ran for the ball Ashley Stacey headed for third base and Aubrey ended up on second base. To everyone's surprise, the Union Hill coach left Kennedy in the game after his pain subsided and no one was happier about this than J.R. Durrell. After fouling off the first two pitches, J.R. stepped confidently back into the batter's box knowing what he intended to do with the first good inside pitch he got to hit. After two more pitches both balls outside, J.R. got what he wanted. His eyes lit up when he saw and inside fastball and he turned on it and got the bat head out in front driving the pitch straight at the first baseman's head at about 130 mph. Old "Big Mouth" just gave up and ducked letting the ball sail into right field for a two-run double and a chorus of boos from the home crowd. It was only fitting that he would also make the last out of the game as Darcy would catch him looking at strike three with the 'kicking mule'. In the handshake line at the end of the game, Aubrey brought Kelsey out to the field with him and as "Big Mouth" walked by Aubrey had his little brother extend his hand instead of himself. As Barry Kennedy refused to shake his brother's hand, Kelsey yelled at him "Why don't you just go home and ice down your little Barrys." Kennedy tried to Charge him but was restrained by his coaches and teammates. Of course, the Empire players thought it was hilarious even Coach Wilson tried hard not to chuckle at it. A 7-0 win had the Knights in first place and feeling good about themselves. Aubrey went 0-1, as the play at first base was ruled an error, with two walks and a hit by pitch; two runs scored and played flawless shortstop. J.R. went 3 for 4 with a homerun; a double; and a beautiful bunt single; 3 RBI; and one run scored. Darcy pitched a complete game shutout with 9 strikeouts and went 1 for 4 at the plate.

Aubrey did not know exactly why the Union Hill players hated him so much, but he soon found out one reason why as a pretty young lady walked up to him as he got on the team bus and handed him a note. It was from a Chelsey Potter a junior at Union Hill who said she was his biggest fan and would love to show him how big a fan she was if he would give her a call. As he learned after reading her letter, she was a former girlfriend of Zack Winborn, the senior linebacker who had assaulted Aubrey and insulted the Empire crowd the previous fall. Apparently, she had made a comment about haw she thought Aubrey looked good prior to that game and when she showed up at Aubrey's church that Sunday it was awkward to say the least.

CHAPTER FOURTEEN

Chelsey Potter was very pretty and seemed sweet and nice enough but what do you say about a girl who openly chases a boy like this. Aubrey did not want to hurt her feelings, but he had to let her know that he already had a girlfriend. She came up to him after church and told him how much she had enjoyed his guitar playing during the service. Aubrey politely thanked her for the compliment and told her he had to be going and that his girlfriend was expecting him over for Sunday dinner. "I am sorry about what happened in the football game last fall," said Chelsey as Aubrey turned to leave. "It may have been my fault." "How so," replied Aubrey. "I told someone that I thought you were good-looking, and it got back to my boyfriend at that time—Zack Winborn #54—and he ain't too sane anyway so…." "It is alright," said Aubrey, "he didn't hurt me too bad." "Well, I just wanted to let you know that I meant what I said about you being good-looking and all that, and if you ever want to go out, I would love that," she said. Aubrey gave her an awkward "thank you" and turned around and left. She started showing up at Empire home games too.

Sunday dinner at Ella's house was nice with all her family there and her dad was eager to talk about his playing days at Empire High School and her little brothers wanted to play catch with Aubrey all day long until her mother made them leave Aubrey alone. Finally, around 4:00 Aubrey said his goodbyes and walked the approximate mile and a half home.

Empire had three games the next week two at home versus Dubois and Chauncey and a road game at Gresston. The first two were blowouts as the Knights easily handle Dubois 12-2 and Chauncey 8-3.

Aubrey would lead the team in hitting in those two games with a 7 for 12 efforts at the plate with three more homeruns and two doubles with 9 RBI and four stolen bases. Ella was there and so was Chelsey and a friend named Susan Dillon who apparently had the hots for J.R. On Friday. the Knights went to Gresston to play the surprising Dodgers who were winning their games handily as well. Randy Stafford was the starter for Empire, and he had an uncharacteristically bad day giving up five runs in four innings and failed to make it out of the fourth inning bringing in Howell Emerson to finish up the game. He would give up two more runs. The offense struggled with Gresston pitching only managing to push across three runs leading to their first loss of the season and firmly placing Gresston in first place. Aubrey would go 1 for 4 with a walk and two more stolen bases and one run scored. J.R. hit a two-run homerun in the third inning in a 2 for 5 efforts with 2 RBI. When Union Hill beat Gresston that next week, it officially became a three-team race for the region title at the halfway point in the season.

Roddy was playing good baseball by this time and had the look of a playoff team as well, so it was not at all surprising when they beat Gresston and Union Hill before they hosted Empire. Roddy had a stud pitcher who would end up playing college ball at Auburn University named Tommy Yoakam and he shut Empire down on a two-hitter and a 4-0 win leaving every contending team with two losses. Empire would finish with Gresston and Union Hill at home while Roddy would only have to beat Hartford and Dubois on the road.

First up for the Knights was a rematch with "Big Mouth Barry" Kennedy and the Union Hill Barons. Kennedy seemed still a little bit nervous about playing first base and played deep all day when the Durrells came up to bat so he didn't talk as much either. Randy Stafford was back to his old dominating self and the Empire bats were hot as they easily defeated Union Hill by a score of 8-2. Aubrey would go 3 for 5 with a 3-run homerun in the fourth inning and 4 RBI and would score two runs while J.R. would collect two more hits and 2 RBI. Darcy Williams would hit a solo shot in the 6th inning and make some dazzling plays at shortstop. Hartford beat Roddy 3-2 helping Empire out as well. It would come down to a rematch versus Gresston for the Knights to win their first region championship in baseball in school history. The only drama that occurred during this game came off the field when Zack Winborn showed up and embarrassed himself and Chelsey Potter with loud accusations concerning her and Aubrey. He was eventually escorted out of the ballpark. Chelsey and her friend Susan left voluntarily not long afterwards. Aubrey knew he would have to answer a ton of questions from Ella and possibly his mom as well, but he knew he had done nothing wrong, so he didn't worry too much about it.

As soon as the game was over Ella dove right in; "who is that girl Aubrey and how do you know her?" Aubrey answered truthfully, "she is a student from Union Hill that wanted to apologize for that cheap shot hit her ex-boyfriend put on me last year in the football game. I told her about you, and she knows I have a girlfriend so please believe me that is all there is to it." "Well, I trust you, but I don't trust her, and I don't like her coming around here stalking my boyfriend. She needs to stay at Union Hill," said Ella angrily. J.R. had a different take on the situation however, and as the boys were walking home, he told Aubrey that he intended to call Susan Dillon and see what she was about. He and Jodi Lynn Rawls had been on and off all year, so he had no reason to hold back. "Suit yourself," said Aubrey. "Just be careful messing around with those Union Hill folks. You know they don't like us over there." "I ain't worried about them jokers. Man, I just want to check her out." J.R. answered.

CHAPTER FIFTEEN

As expected, it was standing room only for the season finale for all the marbles. The Empire Knights versus the Gresston Dodgers for the region title. Darcy Williams was on the mound for Empire and got the Dodgers out in order in the first inning. In their half of the first inning, the Knights would get the leadoff runner on base but could not get him in as Aubrey grounded out to shortstop and J.R. flew out to deep right field to end the inning. The Dodgers would threaten in the second inning getting runners on second and third with one out, but Darcy would strike out the next two hitters to preserve the shutout to that point. In their half of the second inning, the bottom of the order would do some damage as "Bullfrog" Mullins led off with a single followed by Johnny Pickens drawing a walk. Dewayne Hollis, playing second base, would bunt them over into scoring position for the top of the batting order to hopefully bring them in to score. Lester Beasley drew another walk loading the bases for Ashley Stacey who roped a single into left field to score Mullins from third. When Aubrey came to bat, he knew he would see a good pitch to hit and with J.R. on deck, they could not pitch around Aubrey either. So, the first pitch was a called strike on the outside corner meaning the second one would probably be a curve ball; and it was called low for ball one. The pitcher would not want to fall behind in the count, so Aubrey guessed fastball, and did he ever guess correctly? He drove the ball out in right center field probably 400 feet for a grand slam making the score 5-0. J.R. would follow that with a solo shot into right field (the only time all year when the Durrell boys went back-to-back) making it 6-0 in favor of the good guys. The Knights would tack on two more runs while Gresston would manage to push two across but the final score of 8-2 was a dominating performance.

With a region championship in hand, the Knights still had to beat fourth place Roddy to make the state playoffs, or it would be a hollow victory. Gresston and Union Hill would play for the other playoff spot. Roddy would pitch "Big Tommy" Yoakam and Empire would throw Darcy with the entire staff ready to go if needed. Roddy would take an early 2-0 lead when Yoakam hit a fastball about a half a mile in the first inning, but Darcy would settle down and manage to keep him in the park the rest of the game. Empire managed to tie the game in the bottom of the 4th inning when Ashley Stacey hit a two-run homerun off Yoakam. It would remain that way until the bottom of the sixth inning when Aubrey led off with a single then stole second base with J.R. at the plate. Aubrey got a good secondary lead at second base and J.R. hit a single into the gap in right center field. The Roddy center fielder fielded the ball cleanly and made a strong throw to home plate trying to get Aubrey out but with his speed, he barely beat the throw and when the umpire signaled safe, the crowd went wild. J.R. took second base on the throw home. He would be stranded there as Yoakam struck out the next three batters to send the game into the top of the seventh inning with the Knights needing just three outs to make the state playoffs for the first time in school history.

Roddy would not go quietly however, as they proceeded to get the first two runners on base via a single and a walk. Coach Wilson came out and talked to Darcy and almost took him out, but Darcy convinced him to leave him in the game. "I can get them out Coach, I promise you I will," said Darcy. "I know you will," said Coach Wilson, "I just want to make sure that y'all don't hurt each other celebrating after the game," he said with a smirk as he left the mound. "Oh, and by the way don't give Yoakam anything to hit," he added. Darcy got the next hitter to pop out to J.R. bringing Yoakam to the plate with one out. Darcy got a head in the count on the 'kicking mule' and threw strike two on a fastball off the outside of the plate. Yoakam hit the next pitch about 500 feet but thankfully it was a foul ball, but it sure did not miss by much. With the count even at two balls and two strikes, the legend of Aubrey Durrell took a giant leap forward, literally. Darcy hung a knuckle curve that Yoakam took a mighty swing that resulted in a screaming line drive that was headed into left field except for the fact that Aubrey Durrell took two quick steps to his right and dove; or flew rather; and barely stabbed the ball with his glove making a snow cone catch for out number two, but the runner at second base thinking the ball was in for a hit and that he was about to score the tying run had wandered too far off the second base bag and Aubrey came up throwing to double him off thereby ending the game on a stellar defensive play. As the celebration erupted around him, the first thing he thought about was the fumble in the last football game. 'The Lord giveth and the Lord taketh away' he thought as he muttered under his breath, "Thank you God."

Nubby' s offered the guys free meals after winning the region, so the team celebrated their championship and subsequent state playoff trip there. Coach Wilson told them to behave themselves and remember to thank the manager before they left Nubby' s and that he was proud of them and that their journey was not finished yet. He then left the kids there to celebrate on their own. The girls were there as well with Ella hanging on to Aubrey tightly so there would be no doubt who he was with. Kenny Dudley and his sister Christina came over to help celebrate also and Aubrey was glad to see his oldest and best buddy. Christina was nice to talk to as well. Things got a little awkward when Susan Dillon showed up to see J.R. and, of course, Chelsey Potter was with her. Ella didn't have much to say after those two girls showed up even though Aubrey never paid Chelsey any attention.

CHAPTER SIXTEEN

Union Hill beat Gresston to punch their ticket to the state playoffs as well. Empire and Union Hill would both win their first-round matchups—Empire winning their series versus Dahlonega Academy two games to none and Union Hill winning theirs versus Franklin High School two games to one. In round two, Empire beat Gordon High School two games to one while Union Hill defeated Bonaire two games to none. This meant that if the two schools won in the next round, they would meet in the state championship series. Empire would bow out losing two games to none to Ocilla High School while Union Hill lost their series two games to one to Folkston High School. Ocilla would win the state title. For the season, Aubrey would hit for a .430 average with 7 homeruns; 40 RBI; 16 stolen bases; and 28 runs scored. J. R. would bat .329 with 8 homeruns and 36 RBI. Darcy would finish with 9 wins and 3 losses and would strike out 86 batters. Each of these boys were named first-team All-Region and All-State as freshmen.

At the end of the school year Aubrey took stock of his first year of high school and realized how blessed he was. He was a successful athlete with a beautiful girlfriend and lots of great friends. He also realized how tired he was, but he could rest a little bit before he would have to work in the watermelon fields and pull the plow.

On the last day of the school year Ms. Dehoff informed her students that she would not be returning next year, and she thanked them for the love and support they had given her when her mother died. She broke into tears as she told them that they would always be a special group of kids to her and that she wished them all the best.

Aubrey had two thoughts on this—first of all; was it his fault that she was leaving and secondly, how would Coach Jones take the news. After class Aubrey hung around to tell Ms. Dehoff that he wished she would stay for his coach's sake and of course, the students too but before he could say anything, Ms. Dehoff spoke up. "Aubrey, I want to apologize to you for what I did, and I also want to thank you for not telling anyone. I was going through some rough times, and I got counseling and now I think I am going to be okay," she said. "Ms. Dehoff, I understand, and I want you to know that if it had not been for Coach Jones, I would probably have given in to temptation," he replied. "You are a beautiful woman who can have any man on earth, and you chose to like me," continued Aubrey. "How can a guy not consider giving in? I had to pray awful hard, and the Lord answered my prayers when I overheard the conversation between Coach Jones and Coach Lord after practice. And I prayed for you too Ms. Dehoff." She thanked him and told him that she would be following his career and hugged him and wished him luck. Finally, Aubrey reached into his gym bag and pulled out the game ball from the Roddy game and gave it to her to remember him by. She assured him that she would never forget him and that she would cherish the ball forever. They both left feeling better about the situation.

Billy and Ronnie Dobbs had transferred to Empire from Roddy during the school year. Billy was a musician, playing guitar and singing a little bit. He was a better guitarist than Aubrey, but Aubrey sang a little bit better than he did. His little brother Ronnie was a speedy defensive back who would help the football team in the fall. He would be a freshman along with J.R.'s little brother, Donnie Durrell, a defensive end. They would be the two best freshmen on the team next season. Donnie also had discovered a talent for playing the piano by ear and had accompanied J.R. and Aubrey in church lately. Billy had an idea for starting a band and asked the Durrell boys to join him along with a couple of boys from Union Hill—Terry Lampkin (bass guitarist) and Doug Hall (a drummer). Aubrey and J.R. both agreed that they didn't have time for another activity during the school year and Billy said that they could just try it out during the summer months to see if they might enjoy playing together. They told him they would think about it and get back to him. Honestly, neither of them got excited about the prospect of playing with anyone from Union Hill.

Soon the boys were sweating it out in the watermelon fields and Aubrey pulled his plow again. He was trying to save as much money as he could in anticipation of turning sixteen in January and getting his driver's license so he could take Ella out on a real date for a change. J.R. would hit that magic age in August and he already had a 1971 Plymouth Duster (lime green by the way) waiting to be driven. Wyll and Pattie Durrell had purchased a used 1976 cherry red Pontiac Grand Prix that would double as the family car and Aubrey's special dating vehicle, but most of the time he would drive a sweet sky-blue 1967 Chevrolet Impala. But, if he didn't save up money now, he wouldn't be able to do much driving with gas going up to almost a dollar a gallon. Unless they really could get a band going that could work some paying gigs. He would have to talk to J.R. and Donnie to gauge their interest, but after loading 1400+ watermelons for $2.00 per hour, they were more than ready to give it a shot.

Wyll and Pattie Durrell were like most others in Empire in that they were not well off financially, but they managed to provide for their family's needs. Wyll worked for the county roads department and Pattie had worked in the elementary school lunchroom for the last five years. They had the family garden which provided fresh vegetables and Pattie put a lot in their freezer each year as well as canning pickles. Once a year a few of the families got together for the annual chicken killing also. Each year when they got their income tax refund, Wyll always got the kids something even if it was a small gift. When Aubrey was twelve, he got a basketball goal and pole which he had to put up himself. It was on this goal that he honed his basketball skills shooting free throws until dark and working on his Pistol Pete Maravich ball handling skills relentlessly. He shot the game-winning shot many days in the state championship game in his backyard never going inside until he hit the shot while counting down the time in his mind. Of course, J.R. and the neighborhood kids played many intense games as well on this old cheap goal. Wyll had also made it his priority to make sure his kids had a good Christmas each year and when Aubrey started showing musical ability, he got him an electric acoustic guitar starter kit for Christmas when he was ten years old and when he turned thirteen, he got him an electric guitar with an amplifier from a pawn shop in Macon. For about $250 he managed to find a 1971 Fender Telecaster with a Fender amplifier. It would become worth a whole lot more than $250 over the course of time. Aubrey always appreciated the sacrifice his dad and mom made for their kids and wanted to repay them by always making them proud of him. He did not know how they would react to his being in a band, but he had to find out.

When they called Billy Dobbs to inform him about their interest, he was ecstatic and told them to meet at his house after church the next Sunday and bring their instruments. J.R. assured him that he never traveled anywhere without his instrument which was of course his amazing voice. He also informed Billy that he would have to pick them up since none of them could legally drive yet. When they got to Billy's house, Terry Lampkin and Doug Hall were already there. Billy made the introductions and Doug Hall, the drummer, commented "you two boys are talented as hell on the ballfield; if y'all are half as good at making music, this should be a lot of fun." Terry Lampkin was not as friendly toward the Durrells so they figured he had to be a die-hard Union Hill fan. Billy asked the boys what type of music they liked and what they could play. J.R. spoke up and said "Lynyrd Skynyrd; Bob Seger; and The Eagles are my favorites." Aubrey said he could do okay on some Skynyrd and Seger. Billy told them to play something, and Aubrey told J.R. to do 'Night Moves' by Bob Seger. Donnie got on a keyboard that Billy had in his garage and off they went. It was a little rough but not entirely terrible. Halfway through the song, the others tried to join in and after a little while they sounded like there was real potential there. Billy asked Aubrey if he read music and Aubrey said no. He told the group that usually he just listens to a song he likes until he figures out how to play it and that sometimes it takes a while, but he usually gets it pretty close to sounding like the real thing. Donnie echoed that sentiment as well. After attempting a couple more Skynyrd songs, Billy told the group to come back next week with a list of five songs that they would like to play, and they would choose a playlist of about ten or twelve to start working on.

Aubrey's list was easy to come up with as they were songs he had been practicing for a while. The first one was what Aubrey considered to be the greatest rock and roll song of all time—'Honky Tonk Women' by the Rolling Stones. To him it had everything that makes a great song. The opening riff, a great beat, and lyrics that were a little bit risqué. He also loved 'Sister Golden Hair' by America, and The Beatles 'I Feel Fine'. He would finish his list off with 'Long Cool Woman' by The Hollies and 'Folsom Prison Blues' by Johnny Cash. J.R.'s list contained two Lynyrd Skynyrd songs—'Gimme Three Steps' and 'T for Texas' to go along with 'Smoke on the Water' by Deep Purple: 'Drift Away' by Dobie Gray and 'Peaceful Easy Feeling' by The Eagles. Donnie just agreed with the older boys and said he would try to play whatever they wanted to play. The boys felt like this was doable and might just be a lot of fun. Now they had to break the news to their parents.

CHAPTER SEVENTEEN

That night after church Aubrey asked his parents if they knew Billy and Ronnie Dobbs. They said they thought they knew their folks. Aubrey then told his parents that Billy was a good guitar player and Ronnie was a good football player and that they both had transferred to Empire High School from Roddy. After a period of silence, he said, "Billy has invited me and J.R. to play in a band with him and a couple of boys from Union Hill; you know, just for fun." No one said anything for a while until his mom spoke up, "you know you don't have time for a band with all the other things you have going on, and you don't need to get involved with band types anyway." His dad spoke then asking, "well what type of music would y'all play?" "Just a few popular rock and country songs and I think we could be good. Besides, it is just a summer thing; I know I don't have time for it during the school year." Aubrey replied. His dad said, "you reckon you could bring those boys to church so I can meet them; then I will give you my answer." "Yessir, I will try to get them to come next Sunday" answered Aubrey. Later when he called J.R. to see how it went at his house, J.R. told him it wasn't going so well and when Aubrey told him that they had to get the rest of the band to come to church next Sunday, J.R. commented "we better have a great song ready for church so everyone will be in a good mood." "Yep, you pick one for us and I will learn it before Sunday," said Aubrey. "See you tomorrow bright and early in the watermelon field" he added. "Yeah, I can't wait" J.R. answered sarcastically.

The next morning J.R. informed Aubrey and Donnie that he wanted to sing 'My Anchor Holds' at church next Sunday so they agreed to stay after prayer meeting Wednesday night to practice with

Marla Caldwell the church's choir director. She would play the song on the piano and Aubrey would listen and work it out on his acoustic guitar until they had it down. They also informed Billy Dobbs that he and the others would have to come to church on Sunday or the band would not be formed and even if they did come, there would be no guarantees. Billy said he would be there and would try to convince the others to come too.

When Sunday rolled around the boys didn't know whether their potential bandmates would show up or not. When it was time for the boys to sing, Billy, Terry, and Doug walked in and promptly had a seat on the back pew. The boys actually sang two songs that morning 'My Anchor Holds' and their old favorite 'Mansion Over the Hilltop'. It was as if they were auditioning for a job that they already had but they wanted to leave no doubt about what they could bring to the table. When they finished the congregation gave them a hardy round of applause and Billy and the boys were standing and clapping obviously moved by the performance. The preacher thanked the boys for their singing and told the congregation "The Lord has clearly blessed the Durrell family with the athletic ability and musical ability. That comes from serving the Lord and I believe these boys love the Lord; Amen?" The congregation replied "AMEN!"

When church ended, Aubrey and J.R. introduced Billy, Terry, and Doug to their parents who questioned them about their motives in starting a band. J.R.'s mom, Beth Durrell, didn't pull any punches saying "my boys ain't gonna play no devil's music and ain't gonna be around no drinking or anything else that might come with playing in a band. Do y'all understand me?" Billy answered, "Yes ma'am." He added "we just all love music and just want to get together and play with your sons and my parents feel the same way as you Mrs. Durrell." Billy added truthfully, "I have never tasted alcohol in my life, and I don't plan on starting now." The other two did not say a word on that subject.

Aubrey went to Ella's house after church to tell her the good news and that he had to go to Billy's house for band practice at 2:00 that afternoon. She was not too happy to hear that their visit would be cut short, but Aubrey promised her that he would make it up to her. When Billy came to pick up the boys, they started talking about their song selections. Billy agreed with most of their selections and had a couple of additions of his own—Merle Haggard's 'WORKING MAN BLUES' and David Allen Coe's 'YOU NEVER EVEN CALLED ME BY MY NAME'. He also said he liked Waylon Jennings 'LONESOME, ONRY, AND MEAN'. When they met with Terry Lampkin, he said he was a big Elvis Presley and 1950's rock and roll fan and would love to play 'JAILHOUSE ROCK' and 'AIN'T THAT A SHAME' by Fats Domino only rocked up a little bit. Doug Hall just said he didn't care as long as they rocked out. They had a list of about fifteen songs to work on and all summer to get respectable on them. Billy suggested they start out with 'LONG COOL WOMAN' and 'SMOKE ON THE WATER'. The Durrells had to leave at 5:00 so they could make church at 6:00 so after three hours of working on those two songs, they had started sounding okay but not good yet. It would take another couple of practices to get where they wanted to be on the first two songs. They started practicing on Tuesday nights as well as Sunday afternoons. Ella was not happy about it either, but Aubrey asked her to come to practice one night and she cooled down a little bit.

CHAPTER EIGHTEEN

They also started practicing on Thursdays and by mid-July they had gotten respectable on about six or seven songs. Football practice would start the first week of August, so they had to work hard and fast. One Sunday afternoon Billy asked the guys what they should call their band. J.R. suggested the name 'The Billy Dobbs Band' but Billy didn't want to call it that. Finally, Terry Lampkin said "well, we play rock and country hits; so how about 'Rock and Country Gold'?" Doug Hall said 'R.C. Gold'; yeah, I like that." "The R.C. Gold Band" said J.R. "that will look good on a banner don't you think Aubrey?" "I love that name," said Aubrey. So, there it was the birth of the 'R.C. Gold Band'. "I can't wait for people to try and figure out which one of us is R.C. Gold," said Billy. They all laughed at the comment and Billy proposed a toast, with Coca-Cola and Dr. Pepper of course, to the best band in Middle Georgia 'The R.C. Gold Band'.

By the end of July, they had a set list of about ten or twelve songs they could play including 'LONG COOL WOMAN; 'HONKY TONK WOMEN'; 'SMOKE ON THE WATER'; and 'GIMME THREE STEPS'. The band would open with these four songs if they ever had a show to play. That should get the crowd going before they got into the country portion of the show featuring 'PEACEFUL EASY FEELING'; 'WORKING MAN BLUES'; and 'YOU NEVER EVEN CALLED ME BY MY NAME'. they would then go into 'FOLSOM PRISON BLUES'; 'AIN'T THAT A SHAME'; and 'JAILHOUSE ROCK'. That gave them ten songs that they could play well enough to perform in front of people and if they needed or got an encore they could play 'SISTER GOLDEN HAIR'; 'DRIFT AWAY'; and 'I FEEL

FINE'. They still had some work to do on 'T FOR TEXAS' and a couple more songs. Billy and J.R. would trade off lead vocals while Aubrey would sing backup along with Doug Hall and Donnie Durrell. The Three of them harmonized better than expected.

With football practice starting soon they agreed to practice only on Sundays for a while and Billy would actively try to find a gig to play. They also agreed to play for $150 to begin with in hopes that they would take off after playing a couple of small parties or gatherings. They would take $20 per man and put $30 in a band account to pay for incidentals that they may need such as making a banner and brochures. Aubrey and Terry Lampkin had developed a friendship over the course of the summer and at one of their practices Terry had informed Aubrey that his third cousin was Chelsey Potter and that she was a good girl who really liked Aubrey. "Man, you ought to call her up; it would really make her day," said Terry. "She deserves better than that asshole Zack Winborn. The whole family was glad when she broke up with him" he added. "Yeah, he ain't a nice guy" added Aubrey. "Oh yeah, I forgot about the football incident last year," said Terry. "Can you believe our coach gave him the player of the week award at the pep rally the next week? Coach Barnhill is an asshole too," said Terry. "I would never tell anyone at Union Hill this, but I was glad when y'all kicked their asses the next week" he added with a smile. "I have a girlfriend, or I would talk to her. I mean she looks good and seems sweet but I have been with Ella for almost a year now so I don't think it will happen between me and Chelsey," said Aubrey. "Oh well just remember her if something happens with you and Ella," said Terry. J.R. and Susan Dillon were getting hot and heavy so it would make sense to date Chelsey, but Ella was Aubrey's girl and that is all there was to it.

The Empire Knights went off to camp with every position returning from last season except for linebacker Jamie Dickinson and defensive lineman Melvin Hendrix. Josh Beasley would replace Dickinson and Johnny "Hondo" Winston would replace Hendrix at defensive tackle. This could be the championship team all of Empire had been waiting on. Aubrey could not wait to get the season started so he could redeem himself for the fumble in the last game. The offensive line was bigger and stronger than last season and as Teddy Robertson put it "we are going to kick ass and take names this year. I would hate to be a defensive lineman facing us this year." Coach Kelly and his staff would only have to keep the players humble and hungry this year which could be difficult with everyone telling them how great they were. In his first speech to his team, he told them that nobody cared about last season and if they didn't put all the hype aside, they would be another disappointment for the citizens of Empire. To prove his point, he lit a fire in a metal trash can and threw a plaque commemorating the 1975 season into the fire. His point hit home, and he assured the players that he would not let up on them; in fact, they could expect tougher practices. He was not lying about that.

CHAPTER NINETEEN

Billy would come through on getting the band a paying gig when he was contacted by Billy Allen about playing a party at his place out in the country on Labor Day weekend. There would probably be around 200 people there since Billy's parties were legendary around these parts. He agreed to pay the $150 and would also put tip buckets for people to chip in a little extra if they liked what they saw. When they were setting up for the show Terry asked J.R. if he was nervous and J.R. replied "heck no; nervous is when you have to block a beast linebacker knowing he wants to destroy you in front of 3000 people half of them wanting him to succeed." Singing came easy for J.R. and it was his way of releasing the pressures of life. Sensing that Terry was getting cold feet about this performance, J.R. told him to just imagine they were playing in Billy's garage, and everything would be okay. The boys were about to go on stage which was a flat-bed farm trailer made into a makeshift stage when Aubrey saw Chelsey and Susan take their place right in front of the stage and obviously, they had been partaking of the 'hunch punch' Billy Allen had made. They were feeling no pain.

When they took the stage, they noticed all their Empire teammates had showed up to support them even the black players. That was no problem as there were plenty of black folks at the party since Billy Allen had invited everyone he worked with at the local factory where he worked making light fixtures. Billy was a supervisor there and his parties were the talk of the factory each year so naturally most of the people there worked under his leadership. Also, in the crowd were some of the Union Hill Barons and that could be trouble since they were being led by Zack Winborn and "Big Mouth" Barry Kennedy.

Hopefully, they would keep their distance tonight and there would be no trouble.

J.R. announced that they were the R.C. Gold Band and that they were going to play a little music tonight and that he hoped they would enjoy the show. They began with 'LONG COOL WOMAN' and the crowd roared with approval. They knew this would be a good night. Potential for trouble came when the band played 'SMOKE ON THE WATER' which happened to be the fight song of the Empire Knights. When the football players heard this song, they went crazy and started jumping up and down and cheering and singing. The Union Hill Barons started booing and for a moment it looks as if there would be a confrontation, but Kenny Dudley and Teddy Robertson made sure the Empire crowd behaved themselves. It was a basketball player from Empire, Mikey "Pooh Bear" Winston who wanted to fight, or so he said. "Pooh wouldn't let it go and it was probably the 'hunch punch' that made him feel ten feet tall and bullet proof. Most of his anger was directed at Donnie Pack the 6' 6" pitcher / power forward for the Barons who had gotten under "Pooch's" skin in a basketball game last season. Thank goodness for Kenny Dudley who told Pooh that if he did not shut his mouth, he was going to throw in amongst the Barons so he could get all of "Big Pack" that he wanted.

By the time the band got to 'GIMME THREE STEPS', order had been restored. When the band finished playing the crowd gave them a rousing round of applause; even a couple of the Barons players clapped drawing the ire of Winborn and Kennedy. They would have to do an encore, so they came out and played 'Sister Golden Hair' and 'Drift Away'. When they checked the tip buckets, they were shocked to find another $200 along with a few of phone numbers and suggestive notes from various female members of the audience. The boys split the tip money taking $30 apiece and putting $20 in the band account. It had been a good night, but it was about to take an ugly turn.

As Aubrey was heading to a remote part of the property to use the bathroom, he noticed a heated conversation between Chelsey and Zack Winborn. He saw Chelsey trying to get away from him, but he grabbed her arm and snatched her toward him and tried to kiss her and when she refused, he slapped her hard knocking her to the ground. Aubrey instinctively ran toward her to make sure she was okay which prompted Winborn to say "I might have known you would show up and defend your little whore girlfriend. She ain't shit and you ain't either Durrell." Aubrey stood up and got in Winborn's face and told him "I might not be shit to you, but you are less than shit to hit a girl." "What if I hit you punk?" said Winborn and he swung wildly hitting Aubrey in the nose causing his vision to go blurry and causing him to bleed profusely. Aubrey backed up and gathered his wits. The sight of his own blood made him angrier than ever, and he began beating Winborn uncontrollably. By this time, Chelsey had alerted the others and both Empire and Union Hill players showed up ready to rumble. "Big Mouth Barry" Kennedy tried to attack Aubrey but J.R. proceeded to beat the tar out of him while Kenny Dudley pulled Aubrey off Winborn. Pooh Winston finally got his chance to fight Pack and it did not go too well for Pooh. With all hell breaking loose Billy Allen and some of the older men at the party finally restored order. They ordered all the players to go home and attended to Zack Winborn and Aubrey making sure they were alright before letting them go home. Winborn was beaten up badly but insisted on going home and as soon as they got his nose to stop bleeding, Aubrey was fine physically, mentally he was a mess, however. Chelsey had a black eye as well, but she would not leave until she thanked Aubrey for saving her. She told him "I don't know what would have happened if you hadn't come along when you did." "Yeah, lucky me" replied Aubrey. "Well thanks anyway" replied Chelsey. "I know you are a good guy Aubrey, and I don't want to try to come between you and your girlfriend, but you are all I think about, and I can't help it so just know that I am here for you if you ever want me." Aubrey did not know exactly what to say so he just nodded and walked away. As he started to leave, he turned and said, "is your eye okay?" Chelsey smiled and said "yeah, that's not the first time he has hit me, but maybe it will be the last." "Maybe so," said Aubrey. "See you around" he added.

Doug Hall said "man remind me never to screw with either of you Durrell boys. Aubrey, you kicked the ass of the baddest, craziest s.o.b. in Union Hill." To which Terry replied, "yeah but we have got to go to school with that crazy bastard and he can make life rough on us especially in Coach Barnhill's class." "Just don't be scared of him and let him know that you will stand up to him and he will leave you alone, but you may have to fight him once to prove that" said J.R. "Great, I have never been in a fight in my life and now I may have to fight the biggest bad ass in Union Hill?" said Terry. "He bleeds just like everyone else," said Aubrey. "I don't know about that" said J.R. "you seem to be better at bleeding than anybody right this minute." After a pause, Aubrey started laughing which prompted everyone else to laugh as well. Billy Dobbs, who had not said much at all until then said, "welcome to rock and roll boys." What the Durrell's knew that their bandmates did not was if word got back to their parents, this could be the end of the R.C. Gold experience. Before he got home, Aubrey threw his bloody T-shirt in the dumpster at school and prayed that his parents would be in bed when he got there. He snuck in quiet as a mouse and put an icepack on his nose and went to bed. He would have to tell a little white lie about how his nose got busted but he was not going to worry about it right then. Tomorrow would be another day and he would worry about the fallout then. He talked to Jesus then he fell asleep.

CHAPTER TWENTY

Roderick "Hot Rod" Hickey had been a reserve guard on Frazier High School's back-to-back state championship teams and a manager for the championship track teams. He was the last man off the bench, but he wore his championship rings proudly just the same. He was always in awe of Cedric "Sugar Bear" Watson's talent and believed that "Sugar Bear" never got the attention he deserved in Empire. Certainly not the attention that Aubrey Durrell was getting. "That 'white boy' couldn't hold Watson's jock strap" he would say to anyone who brought it up at the barbershop and the locals would bring it up often just to get a reaction from "Hot Rod". On one Saturday morning in August, after getting Rod fired up; one older gentleman said, "All jokes aside that is a bad 'white boy'. I believe he must have some brother in his family tree cause that mother scratcher can go. Wait till you see him on the basketball court. That might be his best sport. He might be better than old "Sugar Bear" all around athletically." Roderick Hickey could not bear to listen to anymore and got up angrily and said, "Man you are full of shit and I ain't gonna listen to any more of this bullshit." To which the old gentleman replied, "I don't care if you listen or not; I am just saying that Durrell kid is a bad ass ball player and you got to recognize game when you see it." "Screw all y'all. I am out of here," said Hickey as he angrily left the barbershop. "Man, that dude trippin" said the older gentleman. "He wants to stay in the past. Man, we are living in the present and I don't give a shit how mad he gets; Aubrey Durrell is the best athlete I have ever seen." "And from what I hear he is a good kid too" added another gentleman.

Roderick Hickey made it personal priority to make sure that the accomplishments of Frazier High School and Cedric Watson were not forgotten, and that Aubrey Durrell never replaced the legendary Watson as the greatest athlete to come from Empire. He didn't know yet how he would accomplish his goal, but he knew he would see to it that it happened.

Rod worked in upper management at the same factory that Billy Allen worked at and even though he had been invited, he did not go to the Labor Day bash, but he heard all about it and the big fight that took place. He knew the details of who started it and who finished it but none of that mattered to him. He now had a way to end the legend of Aubrey Durrell once and for all. He set up a meeting with Coach Sammy Barnhill presumably to discuss a financial contribution to the Union Hill Barons football program so Barnhill took the meeting. He noticed a battered and bruised Zack Winborn sitting out practice until his face healed up a bit. Once inside the coaches' office, he cut to the chase saying, "Coach I have a proposition for you. How would you like to play Empire without Aubrey Durrell on the field?" "That would be nice. Hell, I wish rainwater were beer too but that ain't likely to happen," said the Coach. "But you look like a man with a plan; so, I am all ears" he added. Hickey laid out a plan to have Aubrey arrested at school for assault with charges filed by Zack Winborn's family, but Barnhill balked at the plan saying "any investigation into this matter is going to expose the truth and the truth is that asshole Zack Winborn started the whole thing—he beat that girl's ass for the umpteenth time and Durrell caught him and then he punched Durrell and got his ass royally kicked. Shit man, Durrell deserves a medal, and I would personally like to shake his hand, another issue is this girl has the hots for Durrell so she would never keep quiet about what really happened" he added. "Coach, about two years ago I had to fire Jerry Potter for getting caught selling drugs. He got probation with the understanding that if he ever got caught again, he would serve some hard time. As you may know this is Chelsey Potter's big brother. Perhaps you know someone that could convince her that it would be in Jerry's best interest for her to keep quiet," said Hickey. "I might even be persuaded to give him his job back" he said with an evil smirk that did not go unnoticed by Sammy Barnhill. "Damn Mr. Hickey" said Barnhill, "I don't know who shit in your basket from that family, but they sure as hell screwed the pooch." "Let's just say it goes way back in the past for me and a friend of mine, said Hickey. They both agreed to let the situation rest to see if Aubrey and the others tried to keep it quiet and ride the storm out. Then the week of the Union Hill game, Barnhill would leak a little tease to local press about Empire's star player assaulting his linebacker at a party. He would mention no names, but everyone would know who he was referring to. Coach Jerome Kelly, being an honorable man, would have no choice but to question Aubrey and upon finding out the truth, sit him down for at least one game. And in the meantime, Barnhill would get his friends on the local police force to have a little chat with Chelsey Potter. As he got up to leave, Rod just had to ask why he would keep someone on his team like Winborn to which Barnhill replied, "Birds of a feather flock together Mr. Hickey and if you screw me on this deal, you will find out the hard way what that means. Oh, by the way, I appreciate the $500 donation to our football program. You can just mail the check to me one day next week." "Hot Rod" hickey had just made a deal with the devil. He sure hoped it would be worth it.

Empire would breeze through the first half of the season going 5-0 and winning by an average of twenty points per game. They would reach the toughest part of their schedule in the second half of the 1976 season with games versus Chester, Rhine, Hartford, Gresston, and of course the annual slobber-knocker versus Union Hill. Hartford was strong that year and would beat Gresston and Chester but had lost a close game versus Union Hill. Empire would beat Chester and would be undefeated coming into their seventh game versus the Red Devils. Empire would win a close contest by a score of 17-14 as Darcy Williams would hit a 27-yard field goal with 36 seconds left in the game. Aubrey would rush for 145 yards on 14 carries and two TD's but would have to leave the game late in the third quarter after slightly spraining his right ankle. He wanted to play but Coach Kelly knew that he would need him later in the year, so he told him to sit the rest of this one out. It was a good move because it showed the rest of the team that they could win without their best player. Ronnie Dobbs would fill in for Aubrey and made a crucial run on the game winning drive to keep the drive alive on a third and twelve breaking loose for eighteen yards and getting the first down in Hartford territory. Aubrey was proud of Ronnie and his team but vowed to never leave another game if he could move at all. Next up was a trip to Gresston where the Knights would win a surprisingly easy contest by a score of 35-14. Aubrey would have 134 yards on 13 carries and two more TD's and was able to sit out the fourth quarter because the game was in hand. At 9-0 they would host an 8-1 Union Hill Barons team that was having another good year. The events at Billy Allen's party remarkably had not been spoken about all season and Terry and Doug had said that everything had been calm at Union Hill. But that all changed the week of this game when Coach Sammy Barnhill was quoted in the Union Hill Journal that an Empire star player had assaulted his star linebacker at a party earlier that year. When pressed on who it was, he simply said "their best player—you figure it out." Coach Kelly called Aubrey into his office and asked him if it was true, and Aubrey told him what had happened. He also talked to J.R. and the others who had witnessed it which was pretty much the whole team and they all backed up Aubrey's story. Nevertheless, Coach Kelly informed Aubrey that he would be suspended for the Union Hill game for conduct detrimental to the team. Wyll and Pattie Durrell supported the coach's decision, but Aubrey was angry about it. He prayed for the right way to handle the decision and again for forgiveness for his actions. Ella was upset at him for not telling her about it and, also for him defending Chelsey. She accused him of fooling around behind her back and no matter how much he tried to convince her she was wrong, she wouldn't listen. She informed him that she was breaking up with him. He was at the lowest point in his life. He didn't have football or a girlfriend now and he had lost respect in the community and his church. There was even talk of not allowing him to play at church anymore. Poor little Zack Winborn had been minding his own business trying to patch up his relationship with his girlfriend when this brute had attacked him. At least that was the story being sold by the Union Hill folks. Aubrey wanted his teammates to know that he was pulling hard for them, but he didn't think it wise for him to be on the sideline Friday night and they all understood and vowed to play hard for him and bring home the victory. Where was Chelsey during all of this, Aubrey wondered. She was around all the time except when he really needed her to corroborate his story.

Desperate for redemption, Aubrey called her and explained to her what was going on. She told him how sorry she was and that she wished it had never happened. Aubrey told her that he needed her to tell the truth about what happened, but she said she couldn't, and that she couldn't tell him why. He then asked to meet her for an explanation, but she refused and hung up. What in the world was going on? She had begged him to go out with her for weeks, but now she won't even meet with him. He smelled a rat in this whole situation.

Talking to his parents about it was the toughest part of it all. His mom was convinced that playing in that band was the reason for this whole thing. Aubrey tried to explain that the band performance went great, and they were packing to leave the party when he went to find a place to take a leak, that's when he saws Winborn hit Chelsey knocking her to the ground. "What was I supposed to do?" asked Aubrey, "I couldn't let him hurt a girl" he said. "When I walked over to check on her, he started to insult me and her accusing us of being in a relationship, so I stood up to him and told him that he was a piece of crap for hitting a girl and that's when he hit me and busted my nose" He added. "So, when he punched me in the nose, everything from the football game last fall just came out of me and I beat him up pretty badly." Said Aubrey sadly. "I know I should have told y'all about it, but I was afraid that y'all would make me quit the band and we are good at playing music and the guys are really good guys, and ……" "Calm down son," his dad said. "Yes, you should have told us and Coach Kelly about it so he would not be blindsided by all of this stuff in the most important game week of the season," said Wyll. "He had no choice but to discipline you; you understand this don't you?" he asked Aubrey. He said he understood. "Is there anyone who can verify that Winborn hit you first and for that matter that he hit that girl?" Wyll asked. "Just Chelsey and she ain't talking" answered Aubrey. "Well, there is a lesson to be learned from this…." said Wyll but Aubrey cut him off saying "yeah, don't ever get involved even if a girl is getting the crap slapped out of her," "No" said Wyll, "I am talking about letting your anger get the better of you and trying to hide the truth hoping it will all go away." His mom added "what you do in the dark; comes out in the light. And you will not be playing in that band any time soon!" "Your mom and me still love you and we are proud of the fact that you stood up for someone who could not stand up for themselves, and the Lord brought you to this situation and he will surely bring you through it" said Wyll. He then prayed with Aubrey asking for the Lord to forgive his son for losing his temper; much like the Lord did with the moneychangers in the temple, and he prayed for a good outcome for this situation if it be his will. He prayed for the truth to come out and that he would convict the hearts of the wicked for their salvation.

CHAPTER TWENTY-ONE

Aubrey would spend the week of practice relegated to the scout team giving the defense the best look at the Union Hill offense he could possibly give and that turned out to be a great look. In fact, he got the defense chewed out more this week than ever before. After a play where Aubrey gashed the defense for about a 20-yard gain costing them more grass drills, in the defensive huddle "Bullfrog" Mullins commented "Why is making us look bad? Somebody needs to tell him to slow down—he is trying to kill us." J.R. took offense slapping Mullins helmet and yelling," If we can tackle him, we can tackle anybody in the state much less anybody Union Hill has got, so instead of feeling sorry for yourself it would be better if you just shut your mouth and try to stop him." Then yelling over to Aubrey, "Keep bringing it cuz, I am going to catch you here in a minute and hit so hard your grandkids are gonna be born with a headache." A couple of plays later he did catch him coming through the hole and the sound of the collision would be talked about for years at class reunions. They were both a little slow to get up, but it was nothing that had not been done in the backyard games many times before.

After practice Aubrey, J.R. and Kenny Dudley went to Ross's store for a Dr. Pepper and a good talk. Kenny stated that he didn't understand why Coach Kelly had to be that way when he would have probably done the same thing if he had been in Aubrey's shoes. "Yeah, but I should have come clean about it earlier" said Aubrey "then it would be all over by now" he added. J.R. stated, "we just need to get past Union Hill, and everything will be okay". "Man, y'all's band sounded good. When are y'all gonna be playing again?" asked Kenny. "Who knows?"

said Aubrey. "that's kind of a touchy subject around my house these days." He added. "We just need to take care of football right now" said J.R. "win the state championship first and all will be forgiven."

When Aubrey got home, he saw his dad talking on the phone with a local reporter from the Union Hill Journal and his dad was explaining his side of the story and angrily refusing to let the reporter speak with Aubrey. "He has nothing to hide and that is not why I am not going to let you speak with him" Wyll Durrell said firmly to the reporter. "He is a kid who does not deserve to be hounded by the likes of people like you and I don't want you anywhere near my son this week. Do you understand me?" Wyll said loudly prompting the reporter to hang up. "Danged old root weevils that's all they are" Wyll told Aubrey as he hung up the phone. "Daddy I am really sorry about all of this; I didn't mean to cause you any grief," said Aubrey. To which his dad replied, "well, it is a little late to be sorry son; but I appreciate it just the same". Aubrey felt his dad's disappointment in his actions for the first time in his life and it was not something that he ever wanted to feel again.

Around school most kids were genuinely sorry to hear that Aubrey was not playing in this game, but Ella Pipkin was not one of those kids. She would not even look Aubrey's way in the halls and the lunchroom. He wanted to talk to her so badly, but she was not interested. In fact, the only girl who seemed to even care what he said was Christina Dudley, sister of his best friend Kenny. She told Aubrey at break one morning that she was proud to know someone who stood up against violence against women and girls. Kenny had told her everything that had happened that night and, also told her how good the band was. She said she couldn't wait to hear them if they ever played again. She was nice to talk to and she seemed sincere in everything she said. Aubrey started to look forward to seeing Christina at break each day to get a dose of encouragement and positive energy. When he explained the situation with Ella, Christina told him to get over her and move on and that he would not have to go without female companionship for too long if he did not want to. "Boy you can have any girl in this school, and I do mean any girl black or white" she said. "As fine as you are and smart too; Lord have mercy child". "Thank you" a bashful Aubrey replied. "But I don't want just anyone, and I don't want everyone either—I want someone who trusts me, and I can trust her to love only each other." Christina grabbed his hand and said "I am sure you will find that special someone someday" she said. Aubrey wondered to himself if he had not already found her.

When the Union Hill Journal came out that Thursday, there was an article suggesting there be an investigation into Aubrey and his ordeal at this party. They also recommended that he be dismissed from the Empire football program. Coach Kelly was being bombarded with phone calls from newspapers around the state; all of them wanting to know if he planned on kicking Aubrey off his team. He only gave them the standard 'no comment' answer. He knew that answer would not be good enough if there was an investigation and he had no idea what he would do with Aubrey if the situation worsened.

CHAPTER TWENTY-TWO

It would be a close contest between Union Hill and Empire as the Barons held a slim two-point lead, 15-13, with just over five minutes left to play and Empire driving for the winning score. Aubrey's replacement Ronnie Dobbs had not played terribly but he was struggling to block Zack Winborn on the blast play which made life rough for Ashley Stacey. Ashley had carried the ball twenty-one times and had accumulated 112 yards and one TD. He was the whole rushing game for Empire. Dobbs had run the ball ten times for 49 yards, so Aubrey's presence was missed. On the last drive of the game on a 3rd down and 4 play from Union Hill's 36-yard line, Ronnie Dobbs was hit and fumbled the ball on a wing-right counter and "Big Mouth Barry" Kennedy fell on the ball for Union Hill. The Barons would run out the clock and give Coach Sammy Barnhill a region championship.

The head referee was Red Hogan again and he was sickened by Winborn's trash talking all night long. He continuously taunted the Empire players about their "superstar" being absent. Red had seen the class of Aubrey Durrell firsthand in the infamous game a year earlier and had nothing but respect for Aubrey and Coach Kelly and how he ran his program. Unlike his counterpart, Sammy Barnhill, he had enough dignity and class to sit out his star player. He could not help but feel that the wrong player had been suspended from this game. He determined to do some investigation into this whole messy situation and his job would allow him to do so since he worked as a probation officer in Cochran, Georgia. He would play golf with Sammy tomorrow, and he knew Sammy would talk about the game and would brag about any role he had played in getting Aubrey suspended. Sammy loved to brag when he was on top of his game.

As Red was leaving the referees' locker room, he happened to pass the Union Hill team bus when he saw Barnhill talking to a black gentleman. He conveniently hid behind the front of the bus and overheard "Hot Rod" Hickey tell Barnhill "Coach don't you love it when a plan comes together?" "Yes, I do" replied Barnhill. Hickey asked, "that young lady ain't going to talk, is she?" To which Barnhill replied, "No way. My guys on the police force left no doubt that if she cared about her brother, she had better keep her mouth shut." "With any luck at all, Durrell may be permanently finished if an investigation happens," replied Hickey. Sammy Barnhill finished the conversation by saying, "do what you have to do. I am simply happy we got him kicked out tonight." The two conspirators shook hands and parted ways, and Red Hogan went to his car knowing what he had to do.

The coach was in an especially good mood that next morning at the golf course gladly accepting congratulations from everyone he met on the course. Red Hogan made sure he rode with Barnhill that morning and fed his huge ego every chance he got making sure to tell him what a great game he had called, being sure to mention how he had outcoached Empire's black head coach. About halfway through the round, he set the hook. He said, "Coach, it was also a stroke of good luck that Durrell did not play". Barnhill laughed out loud and said, "Luck ain't got shit to do with it Red. I made that happen." "What do you mean?" asked Red playing dumb. Sammy Barnhill told Red the whole story even down to the fact that Winborn had been abusing Chelsey Potter for months and finally got what he deserved when Durrell kicked his ass. When Red asked him why the girl didn't tell her story, Barnhill beamed with pride as he told the story of Rod Hickey's idea of framing her brother if she did not agree to keep quiet; and how he would get his job back if she kept her mouth shut. "Wow Coach that is why you are the best and why you are a champion today," said Red feigning hero worship, which always motivated Sammy Barnhill to keep running his mouth. "I hate it for Durrell, but a man has got to do what a man has got to do, am I right Red?" asked Barnhill. Red replied, "Truer words have never been spoken my friend." What Red had to do was go home and make sure he got all this conversation on tape. He had worn a wire to the golf course that morning and he knew his name would be mud, but he felt he owed it to Aubrey Durrell since he had allowed Zack Winborn to assault him a year earlier.

When he got to work that Monday, he spoke with Jerry Potter's parole officer and found out that Jerry had never missed a meeting and had never failed a drug test. All evidence showed that he had turned his life around and was clean and sober. He also inquired about his family situation and was told that he lived with his dad and sister in a double-wide on Chester highway about six miles from Union Hill High School. The mom had died of cancer when the girl was ten-years old and Jerry had gotten involved with the wrong crowd for a little while, but he loved his little sister, and they were a tight-knit family who didn't have much in the way of worldly possessions, but they had each other. Jerry had lost his job as a fork- lift operator at the lighting factory when he got busted and was currently doing odd jobs cutting grass and landscaping mainly. "He has learned his lesson and will be okay in the long run," said the officer. "Why so interested in Jerry?" he asked Red. "Oh, a friend of mine asked about him for a possible job offer and I told him I would find out about him," lied Red. Jerry's parole officer told Red to put his friend in touch with him and he would tell him more about Jerry to which Red said he would surely do.

The next call Red made was to the GBI to inform them of two corrupt police officers who had blackmailed a young girl in Union Hill, Georgia. He told them he had all they would need on tape, and they informed Red to lay low until he heard from them.

At the barbershop that same Saturday morning "Hot Rod" Hickey was in rare form telling all the customers how their boy had shown his true colors and that "Sugar Bear" Watson never missed a game because of conduct detrimental to the team. Kenny Dudley was there that morning and he told Hickey that he had his facts wrong, and that Aubrey was his friend, and he would appreciate if he would not talk about something that he knew nothing about. Hickey told Kenny, "Son, I know class when I see it or rather the lack of it." Kenny stood up towering over "Hot Rod" and said, "First of all, I ain't your son. And secondly, you don't know shit about our team. You are just a trouble-maker and everybody in here knows it so how about you just shut your mouth this morning." At this point, a couple of the older gentlemen intervened to keep Kenny from kicking Hickey's ass and Rod was smart enough to know when to shut up. He made a mental note to get Kenny back for embarrassing him in public and left the shop shortly thereafter.

CHAPTER TWENTY-THREE

Empire would have to face Hartford in round one in a #2 versus #3 matchup while Union Hill would get a surprising Rhine team who upset Chester and Gresston to get 4th place. Union Hill would dominate the game and send Rhine home with a 33-10 loss. Empire would be back at full strength with Aubrey back in the lineup provided no more surprises emerged during the week. Other than the usual harassment from the press, there was no reason not to let Aubrey play, so he played, and he played well. He ran for 110 yards and two TD's and Ashley Stacey benefitted from having him back adding another 98 yards and two TD's. J.R. would have a good game on defense with 12 tackles and a pick six interception return for a TD. Empire would win the game 42-14 and would meet Franklin High School in round two.

The only disturbance at the game would be from a group of protestors that Rod Hickey had organized to be at the game holding signs and shouting bad things about Aubrey. Of course, Hickey was in the stands pretending to be cheering for the home team while his minions did his dirty work. Most of them had never even been to an Empire home game and would not know Aubrey Durrell if they saw him; but they had an opportunity to disrupt and that is all they cared about. "Hot Rod" could not help but admire his handiwork, however. It would be the last time he would enjoy himself at Aubrey Durrell's expense though because by Wednesday of the next week, the GBI acting on Red Hogan's tip and recorded conversation with Sammy Barnhill, had filed charges against two police officers who had blackmailed Chelsey Potter and the officers had spilled the beans on Sammy Barnhill and mentioned that the coach had implicated Rod

Hickey. When the agents showed up at the factory to question Hickey about his involvement with this plan, Rod lied and said he only met with the Coach to discuss a financial donation to his program and produced a cancelled check to prove his point. He threw Sammy Barnhill under the bus but when the corporate office heard that he had given unauthorized financial contributions they started their own investigation and found that he had also been contributing to the Hickey Foundation for Racial Equality. He had used the money to travel around the state for meetings with 'civil rights leaders'; but his dirty little secret was that he also met with $500 a night escorts from Atlanta to Augusta paid for with foundation funds. It seemed as if "Hot Rod" thought he could do whatever he wanted but his gravy train was about to end. He may be able to lie his way out of the blackmail scheme, and even though no case was brought against him for lack of evidence; he was fired from his job at the factory. Ironically, he had rehired Jerry Potter the week before. The only evidence against him was Sammy Barnhill's word and that was not worth much at that time. Rod could not believe Barnhill was stupid enough to be recorded bragging about their dirty deal. He even checked with a lawyer friend about the legality of such a recording and was told that in Georgia it was legal if the person recording the conversation was involved in the conversation and if it occurred in a public place. Apparently, this Red Hogan character had the coach nailed and that was that. Red also knew that Rod was involved but he never got a good look at him that night after the game, so he decided to keep quiet about Hickey's conversation with Barnhill. You have to pick your battles carefully and he knew he could not win this one so, Roderick Hickey would skate by on this one. When the Union Hill Journal published that week's edition, the story focused on their football coach's desire to destroy a young man's reputation just to win a game. Barnhill who had been so willing to talk the week before was suddenly unavailable. But Red Hogan was not afraid to tell them what he had done and why he did it. "I have seen Coach Barnhill allow thuggish behavior go unpunished on his team, like last season when one of his players basically assaulted the Durrell kid from Empire and I let it happen for a little extra cash under the table. It sickens me to know that I was a party to this type of activity. I am tired of living like this," Red was quoted as saying in the article. "I realize that I may never get to call another high school game for admitting this, but I don't care. If I go down so, be it but I could not stand by and watch this man hurt an innocent kid like Aubrey Durrell just to further his team's fortunes" he added.

When Sammy Barnhill saw the article, he was livid and swore he would kill Red Hogan if he ever saw him again. He was surrounded by reporters everywhere he went wanting his side of the story, but he refused to talk to them. He was also angry with Rod Hickey for lying about his involvement and he vowed to make good on his threat made to Hickey the day of their meeting. He had a game to prepare for that week versus Dahlonega Academy and he did not have time for this bull crap, or so he thought. Later that night an emergency board meeting was called, and the Coach was ordered to attend. The board voted 4-1 to suspend him until the case was resolved with the only vote for him coming from a former player of his who could not bring himself to vote against his old mentor even though he knew the truth of the matter was his old coach was a ruthless son of a bitch who would stoop to any level to get a win and would put up with thugs and hoodlums on his team if they could play ball. However, they had won a region championship together and that had earned the coach his loyalty. Barnhill was stunned by this decision and tried to plead his case, but their decision was final. Defensive coordinator Tony Rogers would lead the team in the interim. Two weeks later, he was fired outright, and the vote was unanimous.

The two police officers were fired and plead guilty to blackmail and received light sentences in exchange for their statements implicating Barnhill. The officers were sentenced to two months in jail and a fine of $10,000. Barnhill had basically been disgraced and fired for his involvement and fined $25,000 but no jail time for the man who had put Union Hill football back on a championship level. Hickey escaped legal punishment but suffered public humiliation and loss of income. In time he would recover nicely. Sammy Barnhill would re-surface as an assistant coach in Tennessee working for an old buddy of his. He would never be a head coach again. Red Hogan would never call another ball game again, but he was at peace with his decision and until the day he died six years later. He credited Aubrey Durrell with helping him find the Lord Jesus Christ as his savior simply by his actions in the infamous game from 1975 when Zack Winborn had assaulted him in a football game and Red had allowed it to happen. Aubrey had simply said, "may God forgive you and bless you". And he kept playing hard through his pain. This had touched Red more than anything had ever done, and he was thankful that the Lord had allowed him to pay Aubrey back by exposing the plot against him. Aubrey was away in college when he heard that Red had died and even though he could not make the funeral, he sent a letter to his daughter expressing his condolences and his appreciation for Red's honesty and integrity.

CHAPTER TWENTY-FOUR

Aubrey decided to give Chelsey a call to see how she was doing and to let her know that he understood why she couldn't defend him. She was surprised to hear from him and began crying and apologizing to him until he told her it was okay and that he would like to see her and discuss it face to face. They agreed to meet at Nubby's the next afternoon after football practice and Aubrey would buy her a burger and a milkshake. She didn't know what to expect but she was considering it a date with her dream guy, and she went to bed happy for the first time in a long time.

Chelsey was waiting patiently when Aubrey got there around 6:30 p.m. Aubrey thought she looked pretty with her long brown hair put up in a ponytail, and just the right amount of makeup. She also filled out her jeans quite well he noticed. Since he was a free man, he just might go out with her. When she saw him, her eyes lit up like candles and she said "Hey, how was practice?" "It was a good one," he replied. "It was physical, and I am a little sore, but we will be ready for Friday night," he added. "How are things at Union Hill right now?" he asked. Chelsey explained that some of the rowdy fans were upset that Coach Barnhill was suspended but most people knew how he was and really didn't miss him. She said that Coach Tony Rogers is a good man and will run things a little tighter. She mentioned that Zack was really upset and was talking about not playing the next game in protest. "Zack is used to doing whatever he wants and talking to the coaches any way he pleases, but I don't think Coach Rogers likes him too much, so he had better be careful what he says and does now," said Chelsey. "I don't see that happening," said Aubrey. "Maybe they will keep winning and we can see them in the state championship game" Aubrey stated confidently. "That would be awesome" replied Chelsey. "You sound confident that Empire will be in the championship," she said. "I believe we can be if we don't make stupid mistakes. Who will you be pulling for if it happens?" asked Aubrey. To which she replied, "I guess that depends on whether or not I have a reason to pull against my school." "Well, I guess we will see what happens," said Aubrey.

Aubrey asked her how she was approached by the cops, and she said that they pulled her over one day a few weeks back a couple miles from her house told her that they were investigating a fight involving a couple of football players at a party back during the summer and since she was the only eyewitness, they would like to get her version of the story. When she told them what happened, they told her that her story would never need to be told. They also told her that she was to never tell anyone else what she had told them, or her brother might be involved in another drug bust. She told them that her brother had been clean and sober for over two years and was turning his life around. They told her that was even more of a reason to keep quiet; that it would be a shame to see him in prison after working so hard to clean up. She started crying when she said that they told her that she would have to choose which man in her life meant more to her—someone who cared about her or some guy who wouldn't give her the time of day. "Aubrey, I am so sorry for not standing up for you; I was so scared of those men, and I haven't slept much since it happened," she sobbed. "I prayed that the Lord would help you and Jerry and then Mr. Hogan came forward and I knew there was a God," she said. Aubrey slid over near her and hugged her and told her that everything was alright, and he would have done the same thing if he were in her shoes. At that moment, she looked into his eyes, and he could not resist the urge to kiss her. It was a long kiss that was nice Aubrey thought. Chelsey melted right there in his arms, and she was happier than she had ever been. Aubrey told her had to get home but maybe the two of them could go out Saturday night with J.R. and Susan if she wanted to. She said that would be great and they both went home. Aubrey called J.R. when he got home and asked him about a double date on Saturday night and J.R. said it was about time those two got together. They decided to go see a drive-in movie in Dublin. There was a new horror movie out called 'CARRIE'; that should be a good first date movie.

CHAPTER TWENTY-FIVE

Coach Tony Rogers had come to Union Hill High School from Carrollton, Georgia in 1973 as defensive coordinator when he was 30 years old. He had wanted to be a head coach but not like this. He had disagreed with Sammy Barnhill on his lackadaisical attitude toward letting certain players run wild—mainly Zack Winborn— and he had to bite his lip many times when Winborn would do his own thing, like blitzing whenever he felt like it and leaving gaping holes in the run fit on defense. He had tried to explain to the kid that the integrity of the defense depended on each player playing his assignments and carrying out his role, but Winborn would just laugh it off and make comments like "I just do my thing man and I think I am pretty good at it." Coach Rogers would have found out how good his second-string linebacker was if it were up to him. Well, now it was up to him, and he called Winborn into his office and explained to him that his freelancing days were over and so were the days of smart comments to the coaches. The choice would be his to make as to whether he wanted to be a team player or go his own way. Winborn said he understood but Coach Rogers doubted that anything he said would be heeded.

Union Hill would win versus Dahlonega Academy 23-12 and Winborn behaved for the most part. He made a speech after the game giving credit to Coach Barnhill for preparing the team for victory. This was a direct shot at Coach Rogers and the other coaches. the only players who clapped for the speech were the crew he had influenced led by "Big Mouth Barry" Kennedy, his partner in crime. They would have to play undefeated Woodbury in round three.

Empire was on the road in Franklin playing an undefeated region champion and number 3 ranked team. They would pull off the upset by a score of 27-13. Aubrey would have a great game going for 206 yards on 21 carries and three TD's. Darcy Williams would pass for 94 yards on a 11 for 15 effort and a 32-yard TD to Lester Beasley. J.R. would have five receptions for 46 yards and would lead all tacklers on defense with 19 (3 for loss / a QB sack / and a fumble recovery). Ashley Stacey added 85 yards on 15 carries. The coaching staff privately discussed the possibility of winning it all, but they didn't dare let the players know how they felt. Empire would have to travel to Warm Springs for a rematch of last year's semi-finals and the sight of Aubrey's infamous fumble.

After a long bus trip home, Aubrey slept a little later the next morning. In fact, he was awakened by his dad when a visitor showed up. Red Hogan came by the Durrell house to apologize to Aubrey personally for the hit in the 1975 game and thank him for his class, dignity, and his faith. "Mr. Hogan we just want to thank you for what you did recently. You saved my son's reputation and his career, and we can't thank you enough" said Wyll Durrell. "I had to do it because it was the right thing to do but I don't deserve thanks. I need to thank you son for helping me make a change in my life. You see, I was starting to think that Sammy Barnhill's way of doing things was the way of the world and that I may as well join in and not try to fight back. That caused me to lose my way and do things I would never have agreed to a few years ago. The night that Winborn tried to take Aubrey out of the game on that vicious hit, I knew it was going to happen because Barnhill told me before the game that if I looked the other way there would be $50 extra in it for me. Still, I had no idea it would be so vicious or that Winborn would flip off the crowd the way he did. I stuck with my agreement with Barnhill, but I did not like the way it made me feel. When you came back into the game son and played a great game even though I knew you were hurting, it impressed me so much. But what really got to me was when I complimented you after a TD you said 'May God forgive you and bless you'; and that is why I am here today to tell you that I see the error of my ways and have asked the Lord to forgive me and to take over my life. I just wanted you to know that and how you impacted my life," said Red. Aubrey shook Red's hand and told him how the Lord works in mysterious ways and how the events of the last year have brought them together this morning is proof of that. Wyll offered to pray for Red and Aubrey and when Red left, he felt justified in doing what he had to do and prayed for Sammy Barnhill's soul.

J.R. picked Aubrey up at 4:30 that afternoon for their date with Susan and Chelsey. Susan would be at Chelsey's house to save the boys a trip out in the country where Susan lived on a farm. When the boys got there. they were invited inside the double-wide home where Chelsey's dad and brother were waiting to meet Aubrey. Her dad said he was glad to meet the boys and her brother Jerry seemed excited to meet the great Durrell boys and wished them luck in the upcoming playoffs. Chelsey hugged them both and said she would be home before 11:00. J.R. and Susan were a good couple that seemed to get along fine Aubrey noticed and he and Chelsey were off to a good start chatting and holding hands in the back seat of J.R.'s Duster.

The movie was scary, and Chelsey spent most of the night snuggled up close to Aubrey acting scared to death. Occasionally they kissed and cuddled. When they got back to Chelsey's house they sat outside on the porch for a while before it was time for the boys to get home. Chelsey said she had a great time and Aubrey agreed. They kissed good night and the girls went inside as the boys left. On the way home when they reached Sand Hill, they noticed a brown Ford LTD following too close for comfort. In fact, the car was riding J.R.'s bumper then it shot out around them, and they saw that it was Tommy Irwin, a split end for Union Hill with "Big Mouth Barry" Kennedy, Donnie Pack, and Zack Winborn who threw a beer bottle out the window and hit J.R.'s windshield cracking it immediately. J.R. was furious and swore that they would pay for that one way or another. When they got to Empire J.R. didn't go straight home instead he rode around the block until he saw the LTD. He then pulled over in front of the courthouse and reached under his seat for his homemade billy club. When the LTD pulled up J.R. and Aubrey got out and J.R. swung the club knocking the driver's side mirror off the car and telling them to get out of the car and he would whip their asses. He told Winborn that if he thought Aubrey had beat him, he didn't know anything. "I will whip your ass so bad boy you just don't know" said J.R. "Big Mouth Barry started to say something but J.R. reached in the passenger side window and popped him with his billy club. Tommy Irwin immediately put the car in gear and pulled off a few feet. Winborn hollered out his window that the boys better stay away from Union Hill. J.R. told him he would be there tomorrow and if he wanted to fight, he would be easy to find.

J.R. was almost in tears he was so mad. He said, "I understand why you got so angry with him Cuz. That guy is dangerous." "Yep, he is," agreed Aubrey. "I hope we get to play them again. I still have some unfinished business with him" added Aubrey. "We have got to make it happen" said J.R. When Aubrey got home, he called Chelsey and told her what had happened and warned her to watch out for Zack at school his week. She said she would and thanked him for the warning and for the night out. He promised to call her tomorrow. J.R. had to tell his dad about what happened, and he was not happy about it. J.R. inherited his toughness from his dad. His dad wanted to go after Winborn and his crew right then but J.R.'s mom talked him down and they agreed to call the police. When the police got to Winborn's house, his stepdad lied and told them that his stepson had been at home all night long and obviously this was the Empire crowd's attempt to ruin his senior season. As soon as the police left, they drank a few beers together and plotted his next stunt.

CHAPTER TWENTY-SIX

That Monday's practice was noticeably more focused on the part of the Durrell boys. They had dedicated themselves to get to the championship game hoping to face the Union Hill Barons again. Plus, there was the issue of 'the fumble' from a year ago. This was Aubrey's reason for existing for the past twelve months as far as he was concerned—to make amends for the lowest point in his athletic life. The boys had always practiced hard, but they turned it up to another level this week; self-punishing themselves with grass drills if the play didn't go perfectly right and sprinting every play an extra twenty yards. It wasn't long before every member of the team was doing the same. This was the easiest week the coaches had ever seen. They didn't have to yell at anyone for lack of effort or for making too many mistakes. It was so perfect it was scary, and Coach Kelly commented to the coaches after Wednesday's practice "I just hope we didn't peak too early this week."

On Tuesday morning at breakfast, Ella came and sat down next to Aubrey as if nothing had ever happened. She said she wanted to get back together and before Aubrey could tell her he had started dating Chelsey, the bell rang, and they both had to get to first period. It infuriated Aubrey that she would think that she could just pick up where she left off as if he had no say in the matter. Aubrey's cousin on his mom's side, Renee Thomas was a good friend of Ella's and she even asked him if he wanted to get back with Ella. He told her that he was dating someone else, and she asked him who it was. He answered that it was someone she did not know. "Ella feels terrible about how things ended and would like another chance" Renee said. "Well, she should have thought about that before she dumped me and refused to listen to me" replied Aubrey. He had been true and faithful to Ella when they were dating, and he would be the same way with Chelsey and anyone who had a problem with who he was dating could take a hike.

He called Chelsey every night and on Wednesday after church prayer meeting, he called her and found out that she had been in an altercation with some of the rougher girls who Zack had recruited to do his dirty work. Apparently, they had seen her go into the restroom during lunch and four of them followed her in there and began making remarks such as "Booger Bottom slut" and saying that she was the reason 'their Coach Barnhill' had been fired. Chelsey was scared that they were about to attack her physically but before that happened, Susan Dillon came in and told the girls to "get out of here and leave my friend the hell alone." Susan was known as someone you did not want to tangle with. Another reason why she and J.R. were perfect for one another. Chelsey was upset by the actions of these girls and worried that it would get worse, and that Susan would not always be there to save her. She had never been in a fight in her life; not even fighting back when Zack got rough with her. Most of their fights had been over her refusal to have sex with him and he became increasingly rough with her to the point where she was afraid that he might try to force her to have sex. She had broken up with him before it came to attempted rape. She was a virgin and wanted to remain that way for a while. Maybe Aubrey would be the right guy but only time would tell. Susan and J.R. were close but still not there yet according to Susan. Aubrey had invited Chelsey and Susan to ride to Warm Springs with his parents Friday night for the game; unless she wanted to stay home and watch Union Hill, he had said jokingly. She accepted his invitation.

CHAPTER TWENTY-SEVEN

When the team walked the field before the game at Warm Springs Aubrey walked to the spot where he fumbled the ball last year and prayed for a chance to make up for it. He never prayed for a victory because he felt that the Lord did not really care who won or lost a football game and perhaps a player on the other team was praying for the same thing so who would God choose. No, he never prayed for a victory, but he did pray for safety of all participants and for God to allow him to be at his best. He had received a chance for redemption and that was good enough for him. In pre-game warmups the attitude of the team was serious and focused just like during the week of practice. Each player knew that if they could beat this team, they would be favored to win it all.

Coach Kelly did not have to say much in his pre-game speech; he merely told the kids how proud he was of the week of practice they had and if they take that same approach into the game, they would be okay. Warm Springs got the ball first and drove seventy-four yards for a TD to take a 7-0 lead. Empire would answer with a sixty-three-yard drive to tie the score when Josh Beasley took it in from three yards out. Aubrey had four carries for twenty-two yards on that drive. Ashley Stacey was the workhorse carrying the ball seven times for thirty-two yards. J.R. had a big third down reception for seven yards. This would be a theme for the first half—Aubrey would be a decoy faking quick pitches and motioning over from the wing position to block the defensive end like on the pass play to J.R. The plan was working okay because at the half, Empire had a slim 14-10 lead as Ashley Stacey scored on a twenty-five-yard run late in the second quarter. Aubrey was a team player, but he would like to carry the ball a little more. He had only eight carries for thirty-eight yards, but he would never complain. At halftime Coach Kelly told the team that it was time to unleash the full arsenal on the Demons and told Aubrey to get ready to work because he was going to ride him the rest of the night. He explained that during the first half they had only run blasts, leads, sweeps, and dives to the strong side intentionally to set the opponents up for traps, counters away from the strength, and the new shotgun formation in the second half. He told Ashley Stacey to get ready for the windback trap and that the first time he runs it he will bump his head on the goalpost. When it was time to go out for the second half Coach Kelly pulled Aubrey aside and told him it was time to redeem himself. Aubrey told him that he would not let him down and Kelly knew that much was true.

Aubrey took the second-half kickoff back to midfield and the week of practice began to show on the first drive. Power-I right 5 power was the first call which would be Aubrey running the power play off-tackle to the left. The play gained nine yards. On second down the call was power-I left zero quick trap right. The play gained fifteen yards. The next play was power I left zero windback trap and just as Coach Kelly had predicted, Ashley Stacey took it in for a TD and lightly bumped his head on the goalpost in a tribute to Coach Kelly's prophecy. Warm Springs would not go away fighting like the champions they were and drove down to the Empire fifteen-yard line where they faced a 3rd and six and tried to pass the ball for a first down but Stevie Wilbur intercepted the ball on the seven-yard line ending the drive. On first down the call was wing right counter and Aubrey broke loose on a 93-yard TD run making sure to hold the ball high and tight the whole way to the end zone. With a 28-10 lead nearing the end of the third quarter the Knights would have to endure a furious effort by Warm Springs to mount a comeback. The Demons would score on a seventy-eight-yard drive just over a minute into the fourth quarter making the score 28-17. A surprise onside kick gave them the ball back immediately and they scored again to bring the score to 28-24 with 8:36 left in the game. They pooch kicked the ball out of bounds giving Empire the ball at their own thirty-five-yard line. This drive would likely determine the winner of this game. Aubrey would gain seven yards on a quick pitch right then follow that up with a twenty-two-yard gain on power I left 4 powers. On the next play Empire would shift into the shotgun thereby drawing the Demons offsides for an easy five-yard gain. They shifted again on the next play and ran speed option right where Darcy Williams would attack an unblocked defensive end forcing the defender to either take the QB or the pitch man which in this case was Aubrey Durrell. The defensive end took the QB which forced him to pitch the ball to Aubrey who caught it in stride and ran for twenty-three yards ironically getting tackled at the exact same spot on the field where he had fumbled a year ago—the eighteen-yard line. The first thing he did was to double-check to make sure he still had a hold on the ball then he laid there for a couple extra seconds to soak it all in and thank God for this chance for redemption. Of course, they still needed to score so he hurried to the huddle. Ashley Stacey would gain six yards on the next play. Aubrey would score from twelve yards out on a wing left counter to make the score 35-24 for Empire with a little over five minutes left to play.

Defensive coordinator Jerry Lord gathered the defense on the sideline and gave a fiery speech saying, "this is where championships are won" and told them to "turn it loose and play like their heads were on fire and their asses were catching. One stop is all we need," he said. Down by eleven points, Warm Springs would have to throw the ball and they did so effectively, moving to the Empire twenty-eight- yard line where they faced a 2nd down and seven. They tried to sprint out left but J.R. came through and sacked the QB for a seven-yard loss. On 3rd and fourteen they ran a screen pass to the running back for a nine-yard gain bringing up a 4th down and five for the game. The demons QB sprinted out to his right and attempted a throwback screen to his left, but cornerback Darcy Williams intercepted the ball and took it all the way back for a TD unleashing the celebration on the Empire sideline. Aubrey would finish with 219 yards on 22 carries and two TD's. Ashley Stacey would add 117 yards on 17 carries and two TD's. Along with his big interception, Darcy Williams would execute the game plan almost to perfection going 4 for 6 passing for 45 yards. J.R. had two catches for twenty-six yards to go with fourteen tackles and a sack on defense. He also averaged thirty-nine yards punting on four punts.

The first thing the players wanted to know was did Union Hill win. As soon as Coach Kelly was able to call someone to find out he told the players that Union Hill did defeat Woodbury by a score of 25-6. Empire would travel to face Bonaire in round four while Union Hill would travel to Butler. If both teams win then the state championship would be at Union Hill.

Empire had little trouble with Bonaire winning 28-7 with Aubrey rushing for 187 yards and two more TD's. He would enter the state championship game with 1,789 yards rushing and 23 TD's on the season once again he would make first team All-Region and All-State, but he would trade all of it in for a victory over Union Hill in this game. Union Hill would reach the championship game by way of a 20-19 victory over Butler. The stage was set, and Aubrey could not be happier to play this one.

That Saturday night the Durrell boys took their dates out to eat in Macon and followed that up with a trip to the new Macon Mall where the girls bought themselves a pair of jeans and a blouse. When they got back to Chelsey's house, they saw some of Zack's work on Chelsey's 1973 VW Bug where he or someone close to him had spray painted 'Booger Bottom Slut" and 'Durrell's Whore' and 'Union Hill Traitor'. Chelsey was embarrassed and terrified at the same time. She asked her dad if he had heard anything, but he said he had been asleep since around 9 p.m. and hadn't heard anything. Her brother Jerry had been over at a friend's house so he could not help them out either. Even though they all knew who was responsible, they had no proof. Calling the police was simply a futile act so they did not even bother. Chelsey started to cry saying she could not drive to school in that car and her dad assured her that he would get her to school until they could afford to have her car painted. Her dad also told her to stop worrying about Zack Winborn; he was going to take care of him because he had had enough of his mess. Aubrey hoped that he didn't get him suspended from the game next week because he'd had enough of Zack too and he knew he was going to get him back.

CHAPTER TWENTY-EIGHT

Earlier that same morning, "Hot Rod" Hickey, who was now working in an executive position at the kaolin mines near Macon, had found a cool reception awaiting him at the barber shop. All the patrons knew he was guilty of trying to sabotage Aubrey even though no charges were filed against him. He had really come to tell the crowd that he had been informed that the great Cedric "Sugar Bear" Watson was coming home for the funeral of his Uncle James Henderson and would probably be at the game Friday night." He went on to say that Union Hill should recognize his presence at the game to which on older gentleman said, "Man you must be out yo mind if you think they will recognize an Empire boy at their home game." The other men started to laugh which angered Rod and caused him to leave the shop. He may very well be crazy to think that Union Hill would care about "Sugar Bear" Watson, but he had to figure out a way to steal Aubrey Durrell's thunder on Friday night. He thought up a plan to have an autograph stand set up in the parking lot about an hour and a half before kickoff and he had a picture of "Sugar Bear" dunking in his Washington Bullets' uniform that he would get copied with the caption 'EMPIRE'S GREATEST ATHLETE OF ALL-TIME'. He would pay for it through his foundation since he still had a little money left from the factory donations. He knew his old teammate would be glad to cooperate with his scheme. What he did not take into consideration was that the funeral would be Thursday and the Bullets had a game that Friday night so "Sugar Bear" would be gone before the football game would be played. Once again, his desire to get at Aubrey Durrell would lead him to make an unwise decision. He planned to take some food over to James Henderson's house the next day hoping to see Cedric there. Later he received word that Cedric would be at church the next day, so he made plans to attend for the first time in weeks. When he saw Cedric at church, he went up to him and said, "What's up Sugar Bear?" Cedric turned to see his old teammate and gave him a big hug and greeted him with "Hot Rod Hickey. How's it going my man?" Rod was on cloud nine just from the fact that he was recognized by the great Cedric Watson. He told Cedric that they should get together and talk about old times sometime this week and Watson told him that some of the old crew had already planned on getting together and that he should come along on Monday night at the Holland House Restaurant in Cochran. Rod said he would be there but wondered why he had not already been told about this get together.

Aubrey and J.R. did not sing in church that morning because they had not had time to prepare anything with football practice taking up a good portion of their time. Chelsey and Susan came to church with the boys as well and when the preacher declared it Empire Knights Day and recognized the Durrells—Aubrey, J.R. and Donnie the congregation gave them a standing ovation then the preacher prayed for their safety and success versus the enemy from Union Hill. A few weeks ago, many of this same congregation were ready to kick Aubrey out of the church; now they could not praise him enough. He learned about how hypocritical people could be and how to take it all with a grain of salt. Another good aspect of the winning streak and his ultimate vindication was that he could now practice with R.C. Gold again, so the boys were playing and singing one day per week—on Sunday afternoons. They were still improving their repertoire and expanding it. They added a few songs like 'BANG A GONG' by T. Rex and 'SOME KIND OF WONDERFUL' by Grand Funk Railroad, and 'YOUNG BLOOD' and 'GOOD LOVING GONE BAD' by Bad Company. They also added a Conway Twitty country song called 'TIGHT FITTIN JEANS'. They were almost ready to perform 'T FOR TEXAS' by Lynyrd Skynyrd but not quite yet. Maybe in a couple of weeks they would be ready to play it in front of people. They just needed a gig, so Billy Dobbs went to work again searching for places to play. The plan was to get good enough to have two sets at their next gig and they all agreed that they were not there yet, but they were close and above all else; they were glad to be playing again.

Zack Winborn was making plans too, but his ideas were dark and sinister. As a senior this would be his last game at Union Hill and probably his last game ever. More importantly to him was this would be his last chance to get Aubrey Durrell back for stealing his girl and kicking his ass. More important than winning the state championship since Coach Barnhill would not be there to share in the victory and the fake head coach Tony Rogers would get the credit. No, if they win it will be nice, but getting Durrell would be sweeter than that.

CHAPTER TWENTY-NINE

Zackery Paul Winborn was born in Columbus, Georgia in May of 1960 to Joyce and Tommy Winborn and was a good boy until the age of eleven when his parents divorced. Tommy Winborn left for Atlanta and was seldom heard from again. Joyce and little Zack moved to Warner Robins where she got a job on the Air Force base. At first, Tommy took Zack every other weekend but that stopped after Tommy remarried a woman with two kids of her own. After a couple of years Tommy did not call anymore and Joyce met a man from Union Hill, an electrician name Jamie "Quick" Jenkins. He was called "Quick" because he was quick to anger and quick to whip ass. Zack found out the hard way about this when he crossed Jamie early in the relationship. When Joyce and "Quick" decided to get married, they told Zack they were moving to Union Hill to live in "Quick's" house in the country. He didn't like this idea, but he knew better than to say anything. "Quick" was an alcoholic and Joyce had become hooked on prescription drugs and Zack was left to raise himself basically. "Quick" Jenkins' idea of fatherly advice was telling Zack that a real man never had to mix or chase his liquor and he made Zack drink a bottle of Jack Daniels at the age of fourteen to prove his manhood. He also took Zack to a prostitute not long after that incident to make sure he became a man. Both of those acts were illegal but who was Zack going to tell? He just rolled with the punches and developed a 'don't care' attitude.

Zack got involved in football in middle school and his 'don't care' attitude came in handy on the field where he played with reckless abandon and no regard for his personal safety or anyone else's. His play soon caught the eye of the varsity coaching staff and the varsity head coach Sammy Barnhill, who took an interest in him as a football player. Zack also grew to be about 5'9" tall and about 164 pounds as a freshman. He had never thought much about playing ball after high school and no one ever mentioned it to him so he just vowed to have as much fun hitting people for as long as he could and at 5'11" tall and weighing in at just under 200 pounds as a senior, he could do that extremely well. When it was over, would find something else to do. He was known as a party animal as well. He could outdrink and out smoke anyone. Some of his endeavors became legendary around Union Hill. He had been out with plenty of girls and favored the easy girls who gave him what he wanted and there were plenty of them around. The summer before his junior year he met Chelsey Potter who was working as a cashier at a local convenience store. She was a pretty girl and she seemed interested in Zack as a person and not just a football star. In fact, he wasn't so sure she even knew who he was and if he played football. He decided to ask her out and she said yes. He really liked her a lot, but he couldn't control his drinking and when he went to parties with Chelsey, he still had to be 'Crazy Zack' who could outdrink and out party anyone around. He had also tried to have sex with her, but she refused which caused him to get violent with her a couple of times. He had slapped her around a little bit, but he always felt bad about it and apologized profusely promising to never do it again. She would forgive him, and they carried on. but then came the Empire game in 1975 when she had told a group of girls that she had seen a picture of Aubrey Durrell and that he was good-looking and had heard that he was a nice guy. It was a harmless comment but when it got back to Zack, it had been embellished some to include that she would not mind meeting him. Zack confronted her about the comment, and she tried to explain that she meant no harm and had never even met Aubrey, nor did she have any plans to meet him. Still, Zack was furious and told her that he would not be so handsome when he got through with him during the game. The frustrations of his entire life came out when he hit Aubrey and subsequently flipped off the Empire crowd. The fact that he got away with it was because he had mentioned to Coach Barnhill that he was going to take Durrell out of the game early and Barnhill said he would square it with the officials and told Zack to "make it count". Barnhill always let Zack do as he pleased, and Zack very much controlled the defense on the field. He knew that did not sit well with Tony Rogers, the defensive coordinator, but he did not care. Some of the other players knew there was friction between Rogers and Zack most of them were on Zack's side out of fear of Zack and Coach Barnhill.

As for Aubrey Durrell, Zack had to admit that he was the most talented football player he had ever faced, and he was tough. The ass-whipping he had endured at his hands was proof of that. At the party that night, Zack just thought if he could talk to Chelsey, she would take him back, but she would not listen to him. She said he was drunk and disgusting, then he hit her, and Durrell came along at the exact moment she hit the ground. He knew he was wrong, but he did not need Aubrey Durrell to tell him so. He hit Durrell thinking it would be a one-hit and done fight, but he did not know how tough his opponent would be. The other Durrell boy had a reputation as a fighter, but not Aubrey. At least not until that night. Zack did not understand how one individual could seemingly have it all while his life was one big shit-sandwich. He had looks, athletic ability, a tough fighter, and musical ability. Come on man, it was as if Durrell was playing with a stacked deck. No doubt he would go on to have a college scholarship and possibly a professional career while Zack would be stuck in Union Hill probably working as an electrician's apprentice under "Quick" Jenkins. When Coach Barnhill told him about his little plan to get Durrell in trouble, he loved it. It would have worked too if "Red" Hogan hadn't developed a conscience. All of that was irrelevant now. He still had one more shot at payback, and he was not about to let it pass by without a plan of attack. Zack was alone in his bedroom filing his chin strap buckles to a razor-sharp edge and on Friday night, he would wear this chin strap and hit Aubrey Durrell with or without the ball hoping Durrell would contact the razor-sharp edges on his helmet. Anyone else who would encounter Zack would also run the risk of getting cut up as well but that would be okay too. If that did not work, Zack had a plan B—he would have a homemade shank taped under his forearm pad and he would use it to stab Durrell at some point in the game. His hatred for Durrell was real and he would risk going to jail to get him back for being so damned perfect.

Zack had finished his handiwork and was about ready to go to bed when his mom came in and told him he had a phone call from some Coach Sullivan. Zack said he did not know a Coach Sullivan, but he went to the phone anyway. On the other end of the line was Jack Sullivan, recruiting coordinator for Murrayville Junior College near Chattanooga, Tennessee. He told Zack that he had received a call from his old college roommate Tony Rogers who had suggested he look at Zack for a possible scholarship. He mentioned that he had received some film on him and when he played the defense the way it was called instead of freelancing, he looks like someone who could play college football. He also said that Coach Rogers had told him about Zack's issues, but he also explained that this is what junior college football was made for—players who need a break or a second chance because of grade problems or character issues. He finished by saying that he would like to come to the game Friday night If that was okay with Zack. Zack told him that would be great and thanked him for his call. He now had to decide if his hatred for Aubrey Durrell meant more than winning a state championship or getting himself a scholarship. Only time will tell what his decision would be.

CHAPTER THIRTY

By Tuesday of that week Ella had learned of Aubrey and Chelsey's relationship and she was distraught. She came to him during break that morning and told him that she loved him and wanted to get back together and that she was sorry she had ever broken up with him. She begged him to give her a second chance. Aubrey felt badly for her and would never want to see her cry, but he was loyal to whoever he was with at the time and at that time, it was Chelsey. Christina Dudley said "she is torn apart, and I don't know what to tell you Aubrey. She either really loves you and hates the fact that she let you go; or she doesn't like to finish in second place and just wants what she can't have." "I don't think she is that kind of person," said Aubrey. "When you were walking around here all sad over her, did she give you the time of day?" asked Christina. "No, she did not" replied Aubrey. "Well alright; said Christina. "if she really loved you, she would have at least given you a chance to explain" she added. "I know if it had been me, I would have gotten all that mess straight up front and we would still be together right now." Something about the way Christina said that last statement made Aubrey look her directly in her eyes for a long moment—he could not look away for some reason. She was a beautiful girl and smiled d at Aubrey and told him that if he ever needed to talk about it, he knew where she lived. He said "thanks" and gave her a hug and told her that he would see her later. Life was getting more complicated every day for Aubrey but at least there was a football game at the end of the week. Everything seemed to make more sense on a ballfield or court.

On Monday of that week, a group of classmates from old Frazier High School got together at the Holland House Restaurant in Cochran,

Georgia to enjoy a good meal and reminisce about the 'Good ole days' when they ruled the high school basketball world in Georgia at least. The star attendee would of course be "Sugar Bear" Watson who was already there when "Hot Rod" Hickey showed up. When Rod walked in the group went quiet as if they had been talking about him, or so he thought. In fact, they had been talking about the football team and the amazing job that Coach Jerome Kelly had done and of course the exploits of the young phenom Aubrey Durrell. Just before he walked in, "Sugar Bear" had asked them what was going on with Rod and that he had heard something terrible about a dirty deal that had resulted in the kid missing a game and then the head coach getting fired at Union Hill. An old gentleman was about to fill him in when Rod walked in. Throughout the night many stories were shared, and games were replayed all of them ending with the great "Sugar Bear" Watson doing something great to save the day. Finally, Watson himself spoke up and thanked all of them for being there and taking him back to a simpler time. He also mentioned that he wished the Empire Knights all the best versus Union Hill that week and wished he could be there, but he had to catch a plane for Denver after the funeral on Thursday. Rod Hickey could not believe what he had just heard. He had already spent over $100 on photos and assorted items for the autograph session he had planned for pre-game in the parking lot and now he finds out the star attraction will not even be there.

He had to say something so he spoke up saying how he and a few others had planned a surprise autograph signing session for "Sugar Bear" and it would be a shame if he missed it. The line about others being involved was a lie, but Rod was desperate. "Did you coordinate this event with the school Rod?" asked Watson. Taken aback, Rod stammered, "well…umm…I am sure someone did". Cedric Watson replied, "I haven't heard a thing about this until now, so I doubt there was coordination and besides, I have a game to play, and my bosses would not understand if I missed it to sign autographs at a high school football game. Also, how would it look with me stealing the limelight from the boys on the team. No, Rod I won't be here but maybe I can reimburse 'the group' for any expenses if you will give me their names and receipts on what was spent." Humiliated, Rod said he understood and was sorry for any misunderstanding. As the crowd got up and left for home, Cedric Watson asked Rod to hang around for a few minutes. When it was just the two of them, he asked Rod about the rumor he had heard about his involvement in the Aubrey Durrell incident. Rod started to lie again and say that he had nothing to do with it, but Watson stopped him and said "Rod I know how you feel. Sometimes it seems as if no one remembers what we accomplished but that is just the way it goes, and this Durrell kid has nothing to do with it. He doesn't deserve what you did to him." Rod feeling ashamed for the first time replied "I just get tired of hearing how he is the greatest athlete to ever come from Empire when everyone knows it was you. He doesn't deserve the type of accolades he is getting right now in just his second season no less. I am afraid we are losing our identity as a black community and with every great game this kid has, it accelerates that process." That is crazy thinking Rod," said Watson. "Listen, I think your heart is in the right place, but your methods are a little screwed up" he added. "I think I can help you out though if you are interested," said Watson. Rod answered "Sure man. Anything you could do to help would be appreciated." "I want you to organize a committee of white and black citizens who know the history of Empire and Frazier athletics to set up an Empire Hall of Fame. I will financially help y'all and will be glad to endorse this idea if it is done right. This will give you a chance to promote Frazier High School Athletes and, to also rehabilitate your public image—believe me you need it "Hot Rod" and oh, by the way, I will keep this conversation between the two of us provided you get off the Durrell kids back" said "Sugar Bear". "Hey, that sounds great" answered Rod. As they went to their cars to leave, "Sugar Bear" Watson yelled, "Yo Hot Rod, I was damn good, wasn't I?" "You were and still are a bad dude 'Sugar Bear'" Rod yelled back. Rod would sleep good tonight for the first time in months.

CHAPTER THIRTY-ONE

On Tuesday morning Coach Tony Rogers called Zack Winborn into his office for a talk. He told Zack that his old friend Jack Sullivan really liked him as a football player. As a human being however, he told Zack that he still had some work to do. Zack interrupted, "Coach, why did you do this for me when I have been a real jerk to you this year?" After a brief pause, the coach answered, "Because someone did it for me Zack. And yes. it is no secret that we have never liked each other but maybe you need to know something about me. I was raised in three different foster homes from age six to fourteen and I deserved to be kicked out of every one of them. I was a bitter little ass hole because my mom died when I was five years old, and my dad gave my little sister and me up a year later. I fought and cussed like a sailor, and I would not behave or do anything I was told. I blamed the whole world for my situation. "He continued, "at thirteen years old I beat the hell out of a kid who had made fun of me at school and embarrassed me in front of a girl I liked. I damn near killed this kid and left school that day in the back of a squad car. I just knew it was over for me and I really didn't care." Zack asked, "How did you end up coaching if all that is true?" "Because James and Daphne Sullivan took me in as my last chance foster parents. And if that name sounds familiar it is because their son Jack is the college coach that called you last night. He told you he was my college roommate because he doesn't put my business in the street unless he knows I have informed someone first. James Sullivan was a high school football coach in Mobile, Alabama and he told me that on the football field I could hit people legally between the whistles and he placed rules on me with strict punishment when I screwed up. It also got my attention the first time his son Jack whipped my ass. I just thought I was bad—man, Jack Sullivan is a true bad ass, and he was a great football player too— a linebacker." Zack had to ask, "Why did Jack beat you up?" Coach Rogers answered, "Well, we were supposed to dig a ditch for a friend of his dad's so they could lay down a water line and I did not feel like doing it. He told me to grab a shovel and help him do the job, but I told him to go screw himself. I was not going to dig a ditch for someone I didn't even know. He told me to either grab a shovel and start digging or he would make me do it. I told him that I was not going to dig any ditch, so he got in my face. I hit him with a right cross that had taken many others out with one punch, but he just smiled and said it was on, and he was right. I got a couple more shots in, but he just walked right through them and pounded my head.

When he finished whipping on me, he told me I had two choices— either start digging or keep fighting." "So, what happened next," asked an interested Zack. "Well, we dug the best ditch in the history of ditch digging" answered the Coach, drawing a slight chuckle from Zack. "For the next few days, I planned my escape. I even contemplated hurting Jack in his sleep before sneaking out to freedom, but I was afraid he would wake up and beat my ass again. Late one night I snuck quietly downstairs intending to leave, but just as I was about to leave, I heard Mr. Sullivan's voice asking me where I was going. I found out later that he and his wife took turns on watch for me trying to leave. He told me to sit down and listen to him and if I still wanted to leave afterwards, he would help me find a better place to live. He told me about his childhood and how football had saved his life. He talked about learning how to be a part of a team and learning more about yourself in defeat than in victory. He said football would teach a man how to get up after being knocked down," recalled Coach Rogers. "He also told me that he intended to win a couple of championships over the next few years and that he intended for me and Jack to lead his defense. The way he talked about the game of football was inspiring and although I would never admit it at the time, I was completely drawn in by his manner of speaking. He told me his favorite quote was an anonymous one that reads 'Courage is not defined by the man who fought and never fell; but by the man who fought, fell, and rose to fight again.' I had never heard anyone speak so passionately about anything so I thought I would give it a try," added Rogers.

"What happened between you and Jack? Obviously y'all became friends," asked Zack. "Well, we didn't speak to each other too much for the next couple of weeks until one day after school when I got cornered by some thugs behind the gym who took turns holding me and whipping my ass for looking at a girl that they said belonged to one of them. Suddenly, here comes Jack out of nowhere and he took the biggest one out with a perfect form tackle then he grabbed another one a started beating him up. The whole time he is whipping ass, he is telling them that they have messed with the wrong guy's brother and anyone who messes with me is just like messing with him from now on," answered the coach. He went on to explain to Zack that his situation was not unlike Mr. Sullivan's and his own and football saved two lives and could now save a third if Zack wanted to be saved. He also explained that he wanted to the Durrell feud to be over, and that Zack should focus on the game only and let personal issues be settled later if ever. He said that Jack Sullivan would be in town tomorrow, and he would be attending practice. He encouraged Zack to go home and think things over and let him know if he was interested in what he was offering. Zack had one more question, "Coach, you mentioned a sister. Did you ever know what happened to her?" "Yeah, she grew up in a fine family in Birmingham and is currently finishing up her medical degree at UGA in Athens, Georgia.

CHAPTER THIRTY-TWO

On Thursday morning Wyll Durrell took Aubrey and J.R. to James Henderson's funeral. Mr. Henderson had coached the boys in recreation basketball when they were ten years old. They also wanted to meet "Sugar Bear" Watson. Wyll had also taken the boys to watch "Sugar Bear" play for Frazier High School and they were usually the only white people in the gym, but they were always made to feel welcome. The boys had been asked to sing one of James' favorite songs—'WHEN THE ROLL IS CALLED UP YONDER' and they did a good job as usual. After the service, they went up to "Sugar Bear" Watson and introduced themselves. Aubrey told him that he was the reason he wanted to play basketball. J.R. wished him luck for the remainder of the season. Rod Hickey was close enough to hear the conversation and he heard Cedric Watson tell the boys that from what he had been told they had a good chance to surpass anything he had ever done as an athlete, and he wished them luck in Friday night's game. He told them he would love to be there, but he had a game in Denver on Friday night, but he would surely check the score after his game. Wyll then dropped the boys off at school and went to work.

When the boys got to school, they went to visit Coach Kelly who informed them that they along with Kenny Dudley and Ashley Stacey would be captains Friday night if they thought they could handle shaking the hand of Zack Winborn if he showed up as a Union Hill captain. J.R. was still upset over the beer bottle thrown at his windshield but he told Coach Kelly he could behave himself at midfield even if Winborn was standing across from him. J.R. said "Coach, this state championship means more to me that personal payback. I figure I will have a chance to get payback later anyway." Coach Kelly told them he knew they would be okay he just needed to hear them say so and he told them to get to class even though it was already sixth period.

Meanwhile in Union Hill, Zack Winborn was meeting jack Sullivan one on one in Coach Rogers office. Sullivan asked Zack if he ever thought about playing ball after high school. Zack told him when he was younger, he had thought a little bit about it, but not lately. "I know Tony told you about his situation when he was a young boy," said Sullivan. "Yeah, he did," answered Zack. Sullivan immediately corrected him saying, "Yes Sir is what you meant to say, right?" Zack had never given anyone much respect and he thought about cussing this man out and getting up and leaving but he thought about what Coach Rogers had said about Jack being a real bad ass, so he just said, "Yes sir; I apologize I just never—you know—had to …." "Son, I don't care where you start as a human being, but I do care where you end up and I just had to test you a little bit to see how you would respond to being corrected," said Sullivan. "Tell the truth. You almost told me to go to hell and left the room, didn't you?" he added. "Yeah…. I mean Yes Sir, but I didn't," said Zack. "That's right you didn't, and I am glad you stayed with me Zack," said Sullivan. "I think you could be a helluva football player—in fact, that would be the easy part. The hard part will be turning into a dedicated team player and realizing that everyone on your team was a high school superstar and some of them are trying to take your job. You can't make it easy on them to do that either son because if you do, that means I have wasted time and money on you and I don't like to look bad as a recruiter. You understand what that means don't you Zack?" added Sullivan.

Before Zack could try to say anything, Sullivan said "It means that if I invest in you, I will be your mama and daddy for as long as you are there. You will answer to me if you screw up in any way. I will make sure you go to class and pass your classes. Basically, your business will be my business and If this sounds like bullshit that you can't handle, you need to let me Know now and I will take my happy ass back to Tennessee and you can go on with your life. But this opportunity won't come up again Zack." He told Zack that if he goes out and plays up to his capabilities on Friday night with no cheap shots or flipping off the crowd or any other needless crap, that a scholarship would be in the mail in early February. "Oh Zack," added Sullivan, "stay away from this little girl that dumped you. You don't need to get arrested for assault, understood?" Zack nodded in agreement and left the office feeling good about his future for the first time in his life. He just wished he had someone to share the good news with. His mom would not really understand, and "Quick" Jenkins would probably tell him how he would fail. He was not even sure they would be at the game. His mom was late for senior night which was the last home game versus Empire for the region championship. She barely made it to the field in time to escort him on the field and she left before the end of the first quarter. Maybe he should call his dad. He would think about it and decide what to do. He also had to decide what to do about his plan for Aubrey Durrell.

CHAPTER THIRTY-THREE

Gameday was finally here, and the excitement was at an all-time high in both Empire and Union Hill. Barons' Stadium only seated 2500 so extra bleachers were brought in to add 1000 more seats and that would not even be enough. A crowd of 5000+ was expected to pour into the tiny venue among them college coaches from all over the southeast. The Empire student body had their traditional silent day and pep rally while Union Hill had a rousing pep rally planned as well. "Big Mouth Barry" Kennedy was chosen to address the student body and he told Zack that he planned to call out the traitors meaning Chelsey, Susan, Terry Lampkin, and Doug Hall. Zack told him not to do it and Barry argued with him saying "They needed to be called out and identified". If something bad happened to them, so be it, they deserved it. Zack told him to forget about that and focus on the game, but Kennedy was determined to identify the "Empire fans" amongst the faithful Baron supporters. When his turn to speak came he got the crowd fired up and just before he was about to humiliate the girls and the R.C. Gold band members, Zack grabbed the microphone and said, "great job Barry, Y'all come out tonight and help us bring the championship home." And with that the pep rally ended. Barry Kennedy was livid and immediately asked Zack what had gotten into him which prompted Zack to grab Barry by the collar and push him up against the wall telling him to "grow up and quit trying to be a bad ass because you know you are not one. Just try not to get your ass ran over tonight and focus on the job they were there to do." The old Zack would have enjoyed watching the traitors squirm, but now he just wanted to play the game and try to go out a winner. Besides, Chelsey did not deserve to be abused anymore. He had put her through enough hell already.

The crowd arrived early and greeted the Empire buses rather rudely when they arrived at the stadium. As usual, Aubrey was their favorite target, and they were wild with hatred for the young man threatening all kinds of violence toward him. He just laughed it off and prepared himself mentally for the game. During pre-game some of the same old drunks who were there the last time were still there and still drunk and still talking trash but this time the police officers told them to watch their language, or he would throw them out. Aubrey supposed that the increased scrutiny that come with hosting a state championship even made the police do their job a little better.

On the Union Hill end of the field Zack Winborn was in a different state of mind than he had ever been for a high school football game. For starters he was not high and that made him a bit nervous, but he thought he would make it through it even though he felt a bit nauseous. He looked at Durrell at the other end of the field and thought about his plan for getting even, but then he looked in the end zone and saw Jack Sullivan standing there talking to Coach Rogers and he quickly put all thoughts of revenge out of his head.

When the teams went back into the locker rooms it was eerily quiet except for the bands playing and the fans screaming off in the distance. Both coaches gave their final instructions and speeches with Tony Rogers telling his squad that they had endured a strange season with a coaching change at the worst time right as the playoffs started but he thanked them for keeping their focus and their eyes on the prize. He thanked the seniors for their leadership, and he thanked God for bringing him to this point in life. He looked at Zack and said, "Fifteen years ago I would never have thought I would be here now, but God has a plan for each of us if we just let him work in our lives. Men I am so honored to lead y'all into battle tonight and win or lose it has been a pleasure to be your head coach. But since we are here what do say we finish it off as champions?" Union Hill was ready to run through hell with kerosene underwear on when he finished his speech.

On the Empire side, Coach Kelly told his players that he too was proud of the way they had held together through the trying ordeal of the region championship loss and that now they were back to playing Empire football and were at full strength with all their players participating. He said he knew who the better team was and more importantly, Union Hill knew who the best team was and that is why they tried to damage Aubrey and the Knights psyche in the first game. He said, "Well men they didn't count on us being here tonight and I say we make them pay dearly for stealing the region championship and what better way to do that than to whip their tails on their own field and raise that trophy with them having to endure a 'Booger Bottom' celebration and knowing there is not a dadgum thing they can do about it!" The message hit home, and the Knights were ready to hit the field.

When the teams exited the locker rooms the magnitude hit them like a ton of lead. Some of the kids' eyes were as big as saucers especially when they saw all those college coaches on the sidelines. Teddy Robertson was taking stock of the situation calling out the colleges represented; "Alabama Tech, Georgia, Ga Tech, FSU, man will you look at that?" he said to anyone around him. To which Kenny Dudley replied, "man they ain't here to see you and me—they here for Aubrey. If he gets nervous then you can get nervous but until then you just do your job and all that can take care of itself."

Aubrey was not nervous. To him it was just another game and games were meant to be fun. If he did anything to get the college coaches interested in him that would be fine and if not, that would be fine too. The only thing he wanted was to help bring a football championship to Empire. As he walked out for the coin toss, he looked up in the stands and saw his family and Jamie Dickinson was there and even Tony Finch was there to cheer the Knights on. He did not see Chelsey or Susan and he wondered if they might be on the other side of the field. Either way he could not worry about it now, he had business to take care of.

Captains for Union Hill included "Big Mouth Barry" Kennedy and Zack Winborn. J.R. was anxious to hit both of those guys but he kept it strictly about football, but he did glare at Winborn the whole time the referee was talking. He obviously got to Winborn because he kept looking away from J.R. and glancing at Aubrey occasionally. When the referee instructed them to shake hands, Barry Kennedy refused but Winborn and the others did not. Winborn squeezed Aubrey's hand

and Aubrey squeezed back. J.R. said something about payback for his windshield and it was on.

Empire received the opening kickoff and rather than kick it deep to Aubrey or Ashley, they pooch kicked it to the 30-yard line where freshman Ronnie Dobbs, the Roddy transfer, took it and returned it back to the Union Hill 47-yard line. He was one man away from breaking it for a TD, but the kicker tripped him up. No matter, the Knights had great field position to start their first drive. The first play of the game would serve as an indicator of how this night would go. The call was 'Wing Left Zig 38 Tear' which was a toss sweep to Ashley Stacey with Aubrey motioning to lead block along with the fullback Josh Beasley and two pulling guards. However. Center Teddy Robertson swore he heard the QB call for the snap to be on first sound and snapped the ball just as Aubrey was going into full speed motion and full speed for Aubrey was fast. Luckily, Darcy Williams has giant hands and did not fumble the snap but when he turned to pitch the ball, all he saw was Aubrey flying in front of him, so he handed him the football out of desperation. Obviously, Aubrey was not expecting the football, but Darcy made sure to ride it into his belly as much as he could with Aubrey moving so fast. Aubrey took the handoff and did the only thing he knew to do—RUN!!! The offensive line had moved when the ball was snapped so Howell Emerson, the right guard, had pulled to lead Aubrey around the end. Aubrey was so fast that he was around the end before the defensive linemen had gotten out of their stances and when Emerson blocked the cornerback, it was off to the races for Aubrey. A 47-yard TD on a broken play. All the college coaches were talking about this new play Coach Kelly had unveiled and Coach Kelly was busy trying to figure out what he had just witnessed. The extra point made the score 7-0 in favor of Empire. When offensive line Coach Don Rainey got through with poor old Teddy Robertson the boy did not have much ass left that had not been chewed on but nevertheless, Empire had a quick lead. Union Hill Coach Tony Rogers was scrambling trying to find an answer to this newfangled play he had just seen. He knew that if he did not adjust to motion, they would score every time they ran that play. So, he instructed his linebackers and secondary to bump heavily to the motion each time. He knew that would open them up to traps and blasts away from the motion, but he had no choice. Little did he know that Empire would not run that play again. In fact, the whole offense had been chewed out unmercifully because of it, yet it would affect this game and the future of offensive football. Aubrey Durrell did not forget the play and years later as the head coach at his alma mater, he would develop an entire offensive system around this speed sweep concept.

This was the origins of the Jet Sweep that football teams at all levels adopted a version of eventually. A shell-shocked Union Hill squad never mounted much of a challenge offensively, so Empire got the ball back quickly and scored again on a 26-yard TD pass from Darcy Williams to J.R. Durrell. A Charlie Brown fake extra-point made the score 15-0 at the end of the first quarter. On their next possession disaster struck Union Hill again as "Bullfrog" Mullins sacked the Barons' QB causing a fumble that Bobby Parton scooped and scored on from 34-yards out. The extra point made the score 22-0. On Empire's next possession Zack Winborn would make his presence felt as he would disrupt plays in the backfield looking almost unstoppable at times. Aubrey noticed a difference in his play; there was no trash talking and he didn't blitz every pay like he had done in the past. He was playing a good ball game and it was not his fault they were losing. On a blast play where Aubrey and Josh Beasley had pancaked him numerous times before he stood his ground and split the double-team block and helped hold the play to a small gain. Josh told Aubrey after the play, "Something done got into that boy—he's a lot tougher than he used to be." Aubrey had to agree. On a third down and eight to go Darcy Williams rolled right to pass but Zack read the play and stepped in front of Lester Beasley for the interception and returned it all the way for a TD from 43-yards out. The extra point would make the score 22-7 at halftime.

Union Hill would take the second half kickoff and drive to the Empire 12-yard line where on a 4th down and 3 they would be stopped a half-yard shy as Josh Beasley would make a tackle on the fullback giving Empire the ball back with a little over six minutes left in the 3rd quarter. On a 2nd down and 6 to go from their own 42-yard line Aubrey would break loose on a 58- yard TD run but as he crossed the goal line, he heard someone running hard behind him and as he turned around, he saw Zack Winborn still chasing after him. Not knowing what to expect he braced himself for a cheap shot, but none came.

Instead Winborn kept running through the back of the end zone and turned to go to his sideline. Very confusing thought Aubrey. What had gotten into that guy? Unbeknownst to Zack, this was the play that convinced Jack Sullivan that Zack would be a winner. To continue to chase a player that you know you cannot catch showed a desire and a hunger to win that is rare. Zack did not know why he did that, and it had made him look like a fool he thought, but every coach and player on the Union Hill sideline gave him a pat on the back for his effort and the crowd gave him a standing ovation. This caught him completely off guard, but he had to admit it felt good. The extra point made the score 29-7 and all Empire had to do was hold on and finish the drill to bring the first championship since 1958 back home. Union Hill would not quit, and a long drive was paid off with a TD and a 2-point conversion to make the score 29-15 with a little over five minutes left in the game. An onside kick attempt failed, and Empire would ice the game two plays later when Aubrey would score his third TD of the game on a 46-yard run on a trap play. He would finish the game with 263 yards on 16 carries and three TD's and for the season he would tally 1,853 yards and 27 TD's. It was all over but the crying for Union Hill with the score at 36-15 and the Empire crowd started their celebration.

When Stevie Wilbur intercepted a desperation pass on the next possession, it was official. As Darcy Williams knelt to kill the clock Zack Winborn contemplated firing through and taking one last shot at Aubrey, but when he looked over to Jack Sullivan, he decided to let it go. He decided to officially end the feud with the Durrell boys. For once in his life, he felt good about his effort, and he liked the way it felt. Maybe football could save another young man's life.

As the players shook hands after the game, a Union Hill coach was assigned to keep an eye open for trouble; especially between Winborn and the Durrells. Instead, it was "Big Mouth Barry" Kennedy who wanted to act up. He had to be made to shake hands along with Tommy Irwin and then he acted as if he wanted to fight with a couple of the underclassmen on the Knight's team. It was Zack Winborn who went over to restore order for Union Hill and J.R. Durrell for Empire. As calmer heads prevailed, those two found themselves face to face whereupon Zack told J.R. "I'm sorry about the windshield dude. I'll pay to have it fixed." J.R. said "Thanks. You played a good game man."

And then J.R. held out his hand and Zack extended his for a cordial shake. "Where's Aubrey," asked Zack. J.R. called him over and Aubrey came not knowing what to expect. Aubrey spoke first saying, "You played a great game Zack," To which Winborn replied, "Dude, you are the best football player I have ever seen, and you will have a great college career." Aubrey replied, "Thanks and I just want you to know I am sorry about everything that has happened between us. And I also want you to know that I never messed with Chelsey until recently. She was never unfaithful to you at least not with me I promise with God as my witness." "I know," said Zack "but that doesn't matter anymore, you just make sure you treat her right—she deserves it." "I will and Zack, God bless you man." With that the boys shook hands and Zack left the field for the last time feeling conflicted about the conversation he just had but feeling thankful that he did not go through with his crazy plan. As he reached the field house, he heard a familiar voice call his name. it was a voice he had not heard in a long time— he turned to find his dad Tommy Winborn standing there with tears in his eyes. Zack looked at him and thought of all the things he swore he would say to him if he ever saw him again, but what came out of his mouth was" Hey Daddy". "I got your message last night and I took off work this afternoon so I could be here. You played a helluva game son. I know it may not mean much to you to hear this, but I am proud of you, and I want you to know I am sorry about how things turned out between us, but I would like to get to know you better if you want to" said Tommy, "Give me a call sometimes and maybe we can do that," said Zack. "I have to go now but it is good to see you" said Zack and as he turned to leave, he could have sworn he heard Tommy tell him he loved him.

On the field, the trophy presentation was something special. With the entire team coming back for two more seasons, the Empire coaches thought this may not be the last time this would happen.

CHAPTER THIRTY-FOUR

Chelsey and Susan were outside the locker room when the boys came out and when Aubrey and J.R. saw them with their F.F.A. jackets on they knew they had been working the concession stand all night. Chelsey greeted Aubrey with a hug and told him "Great job Babe congratulations. It was tough trying not to cheer for y'all tonight with all eyes on us." "Yeah," said Susan, "but we had a secret code between us and every time y'all scored we would look at each other and say, 'LET'S GO BOYS'. They never knew we were cheering for y'all." The team was planning on going to Nubby' s when they got back, and Aubrey asked Chelsey and Susan if they were coming too. The girls said they would and kissed them goodbye as the bus was ready to leave. It was a rowdy bus ride back to Empire and the coaches did not care so long as they did not destroy the bus and kept the language clean. When they got back to the school, a crowd of about 200 people were there to greet them; most of them students and teachers there to congratulate them and share in the victory. Ella was there and she gave Aubrey a big hug and told him she was proud of him, and she wanted him to call her over the weekend. Aubrey couldn't get away from her fast enough. Christina Dudley also gave him a big hug and it was enjoyable. She whispered in his ear "Great game Aubrey I am so proud of you, Kenny, and the rest of the team." Aubrey noticed how good she smelled and felt and hugged her back for a long time. In fact, it was Billy Dobbs who interrupted the hug with some good news. Aubrey and J.R." he yelled over the crowd, "we have another gig if y'all want it—next Friday night Mr. Bass in hosting a celebration party in the gym and he asked me if we would play. Isn't that awesome?" he asked. J.R. answered, "Heck yeah," we are gonna rock the house." With that he went around telling everyone he could. Aubrey was happy about it too, but he wanted to talk to Christina a little bit more but when he turned around, she was already gone. He must be losing his mind; he had a great girlfriend and here he was thinking about a girl who probably had no interest in him at all. An interracial relationship would be controversial in Empire also and neither he nor Christina needed that type of scrutiny. He decided to put it out of his mind.

Kenny Dudley came up to Aubrey and said," Hey dude, a lot of the boys are going to camp out on the football field tonight, are you in?" "Sure" said Aubrey, "has anybody checked with Coach Kelly about this?" he asked. "I sure did, and he thought it was a great idea. Said he might stay with us," he added. "Make sure to bring your own snacks, drinks, and sleeping bag" yelled Kenny as he went on to the next player. It was a good night to camp out since it was a typically mild December night in Georgia with the low temperature being around 50 degrees. Aubrey wondered how his best friend Kenny would react if he knew how he felt about his big sister.

At Nubby' s the players ate free, and they all took advantage of this deal. Winning sure had its privileges thought Aubrey. Darcy Williams and the Beasley twins; Josh and Lester had the championship trophy and was parading it around with great pride. This had to be the greatest day in each of their young lives and Aubrey took a moment to thank Jesus for this blessing. Ella Pipkin came and sat next to Aubrey at Nubby' s at an outdoor table which prompted him to move to another table without saying a word. It may have been rude to do this, but he did not want to get into it with her tonight of all nights. Besides, if Chelsey saw him sitting with Ella, he would have a lot of unnecessary questions to answer. Thankfully, Ella did not follow him and when Chelsey and Susan showed up there was no reason to worry at first. As Chelsey and Aubrey sat talking, Ella and a couple of other cheerleaders showed up and sat down with the group. One of the girls, a senior cheerleader, started asking questions of Chelsey and Susan such as 'who did y'all cheer for tonight?' and 'How does it feel to be on the losing side?' Finally, Susan had had enough, and she answered back, "not that it is any of your business, but we were cheering for our boyfriends, and I feel great in case y'all are still wondering," Ella was glaring at Chelsey during this whole conversation and Susan could not let it go without questioning her saying, "Blondie you look you want to say something to my friend so let's hear it." Chelsey was embarrassed and a little nervous, but Aubrey put his arm around her, and this sent a signal to the group of cheerleaders to back off. Of course, Susan sent a loud message too with her bravado and they left the table.

As the four of them walked out to their cars, the boys told the girls about camping out at the field and about the performance next Friday night. Aubrey also told Chelsey about his conversation with Zack Winborn after the game. She was surprised to hear this but said she was hopeful that he would straighten up and make something of himself. Aubrey told her he would see her tomorrow night and kissed her goodnight. He and J.R. went to their homes and picked up a couple of sleeping bags, chips and cookies, and a few Dr. Peppers and joined their teammates at the field in a celebration of their accomplishments. The whole team and most of the coaches were there as well. Those that got cold were told to enter the gymnasium but the Durrells, Darcy William, Kenny Dudley, Teddy Robertson, the Beasley twins, and Ashley Stacey stayed outside all night long talking about the game, girls, and anything else that came up. J.R. said "Winborn told me he was going to pay for my windshield, but I don't know if I believe him," "He was different tonight," said Josh Beasley. "He was quiet and played a good game" he added. "Yeah, he was a lot harder to block tonight," said Teddy Robertson. "How about our first TD?" asked Darcy Williams. "Man, I honestly just panicked and gave the ball to Aubrey" he said laughing. "I just screwed up," said Teddy. "It turned out okay" said Ashley Stacey, adding "when you can run like #15 you can cover up a lot of mistakes." "I guess it is better to be lucky than good," said Aubrey. "it is best to be lucky and good," said Ashley. Aubrey overheard a conversation between Kenny Dudley and Lester Beasley concerning Christina and he could not help but listen in. Lester was asking Kenny if he thought she would go out with him. Kenny told him to ask her and find out. Aubrey felt a touch of jealousy at the thought of Lester going out with Christina. Around daybreak the boys started to filter out and head home.

There was going to be a party at the home of Tia and Lee Anne Paisley that Saturday and the Durrell boys were invited along with their girlfriends. Aubrey was concerned about Ella showing up, but Tia told him not to worry about that she had not been invited. At the party Chelsey and Susan were befriended by Aubrey's cousin Renee Thomas and Tia so everything was okay. Renee told Chelsey that she was just starting to date a basketball player from Chauncey, so they were in the same situation. The night was full of dancing and eating and fun was had by all.

Sunday at church was fun when the Durrells were recognized, and the preacher basically preached about the championship. Later that afternoon they went to Billy Dobbs house for band practice. J. R. sang every song perfectly but substituted the words 'danged' and 'darned' every time the word 'damn' was used prompting Billy to question why. J.R. answered "My mama will whip my dang ass if she knows I cussed in public, and she will probably be there so that settles it as far as I am concerned". The playlist was tailored for the crowd with a little more country, which none of the boys minded. The show would be opened with the Empire fight song 'SMOKE ON THE WATER' with the team on stage with the band. Their encore would be 'T FOR TEXAS' which they had finally gotten good enough to play in public.

That week in school was the most fun Aubrey had ever had. All anyone wanted to talk about was the game and the coming celebration at the end of the week. Even the teachers caught the buzz. When Friday came, the Durrells and Billy Dobbs spent the day setting up the gym for the concert. At 7:00 P.M. the R.C. Gold Band was introduced to a packed house by Principal James Bass and when the first riff of the night was played, the football team and coaches came out on stage to a standing ovation. 'SMOKE ON THE WATER' got the crowd going and when Coach Kelly came to the microphone, he thanked the fans, administration, parents, and most of all the players who gave their all for their school, their community, and each other. He encouraged everyone to enjoy the show. As J.R. promised earlier, they rocked the house. When the show was over, the 4 donation buckets contained an extra $250 in addition to the $150 fee for playing paid for by Principal Bass. People get generous when you win. The band members agreed to take $50 each and contribute $50 to the band fund.

Aubrey rode home with Chelsey in her VW Bug that had been repainted to cover up Zack Winborn's handiwork. After an obligatory trip to Nubby' s, Chelsey told Aubrey they needed to go for a ride. They both knew what that meant so they ended up on a little dirt road off Chicken Road for a little privacy. Chelsey had decided that Aubrey would be her first and she would be his. Susan had decided the same for J.R. and herself. They both gave in to temptation that night and for the first time Chelsey told Aubrey she loved him. Aubrey reluctantly told her the same thing. When he got home, he prayed to the Lord for forgiveness and strength to control his urges, but deep down inside he knew that was going to a losing battle.

CHAPTER THIRTY-FIVE

Aubrey was finding it difficult to concentrate in class the last week before Christmas holidays. In Algebra class on Tuesday afternoon, he became lost thinking about Chelsey when the teacher, Mr. Dawson, noticed that he was not paying attention and called on him to go to the board and solve an equation. Aubrey had never been disrespectful to a teacher in his life but there was no way he was going to stand up at that time. He would have to find a way out of this predicament without getting into trouble. He said as politely as he could "Mr. Dawson, I can't do that right now." "What do you mean you can't do it?" asked Mr. Dawson. Aubrey responded sheepishly "I am not feeling well sir." Mr. Dawson asked him if he needed to be dismissed to call home and Aubrey quickly answered, "No Sir." He told him he just needed to put his head down for a few minutes if he didn't mind. Luckily because he had never been a problem student before, the teacher allowed him to put his head down until the bell rang which was about ten minutes. When the bell rang, two female classmates, Joanna Butler and Shelly Sampson came by and asked him if he was alright. These two had a reputation for being somewhat easy but they were both nice looking. Aubrey said he was okay, and Shelly said, "if you need any help with your problem, we will be glad to help you out." They both then started snickering and left the room. How did they know thought Aubrey? Now he has another fantasy to deal with and try to ignore. When he saw J.R. and told him what had happened, J.R. said that he had been dealing with it all day. "Man, that thing was so hard a cat couldn't scratch if and a dog couldn't bite it," said J.R. "Tell me about it," said Aubrey. "I have got to go see Susan tonight or I won't be worth a plug nickel tomorrow in class," added J.R. "I am going to call Chelsey as soon as I get home," said Aubrey. "We need to get some protection before we go see the girls," said J.R. "I'll call you after I speak with Chelsey," said Aubrey.

The football players were given until Wednesday to rest up before attending basketball practice, so the Durrell boys had a perfect opportunity to get with the girls and they took advantage of it. J.R. dropped Aubrey off at Chelsey's house before heading over to Susan's house. They had stopped by a service station and picked up some condoms before heading out. Chelsey was home alone when Aubrey got there, and they didn't take long to satisfy their desires. Aubrey was a slave to his newfound sexual awakening and even though he prayed each night, he still could not fight this feeling. He had been taught that pre-marital sex was wrong but if just felt so right. Would this be his kryptonite? J.R. and Susan had to sneak off to a spot on the backside of the farm but J.R. didn't care where they did it so long as they did it. Even though the boys knew what each other had been up to, they didn't share details out of respect for the girls who had both proclaimed their love for the boys in the throes of passion. The boys also responded in kind that they loved the girls too. Maybe they did love them but neither of them really knew what if meant to be in love at this time. They were however deeply in lust.

When Aubrey got back home, his little brother Kelsey was shooting hoops in the backyard and asked Aubrey to come shoot with him. Aubrey didn't really feel much like shooting basketball at that moment, but Kelsey insisted and like a good big brother, Aubrey gave in. They stayed outside shooting until it was too dark to see anymore. At supper Wyll announced that he had been contacted by Rod Hickey about getting involved in a Hall of Fame for Empire and Frazier High Schools athletes. "After what he tried to do to Aubrey, I hope you told him what he could do with his idea," said Pattie. "No, I told him I would be glad to help out as a committee member," Wyll replied. He explained that there would be plenty of opportunities to tell Mr. Hickey how he felt about him but that a Hall of Fame was a good idea. He also said the Mr. Hickey had denied participation in the scheme. "You don't believe that for a minute," said Pattie. To which Wyll responded, "what I believe and what I can prove are two different things and, in the meantime, maybe a good deed can come from a bad man. I feel it is my duty to try to help." With that the conversation was over and Wyll started talking about the upcoming basketball season.

Billy Dobbs called and said some people in Eastman were having a Christmas party and wanted the R.C. Gold Band to play. Aubrey said it sounded good if it didn't interfere with basketball. J.R. had said the same thing according to Billy. He said he would check the date and get back to him. Aubrey then called Chelsey and talked for about an hour before going to bed.

On Wednesday, the football players came to basketball practice, and they were welcomed back enthusiastically especially by "Pooh Bear" Winston who had been running plays with "scrubs", as he called them for over a week. Empire had delayed their basketball season because of their deep run in the football playoffs so the other region teams had the jump on them. Chauncey, Chester, and Union Hill figured to be the top contenders along with Empire once they got rolling. Chauncey was undefeated at 5-0 and Chester had lost only once, and Union Hill had broken even at 2 wins and 2 losses. Empire's first game would be in an invitational Christmas tournament in Roberta with three other teams—the Roberta Warhawks; Butler Raiders; and the Barnesville Spartans—so they would get broken in early versus a double-A team in Barnesville and two class B powerhouse programs that would probably make a run for a state championship in Roberta and Butler. In early January, the Knights would make up the postponed games, but it would me a crowded schedule, but Coach Jerry Lord knew his guys could handle it.

A total of ten football players would make the varsity roster led by Aubrey; Ashley Stacey; "Big" Randy Stafford, an offensive tackle and pitcher on the baseball team; Kenny Dudley; Bobby Parton; Lester Beasley; J.R. Durrell; Darcy Williams; Johnny Pickens; and in somewhat of a surprise, Johnny "Hondo" Winston who made it on his ability to frustrate opposing players with his man-to-man defensive skills. When "Hondo" locked you down he played you so tight he could tell what flavor of chewing gum you were chewing. So, this would be the team along with "Hondo's" cousin "Pooh" Winston and a couple of kids to round out the fifteen-man squad. It did not take long to see that Aubrey was the point guard. He had amazing ball-handling skills. He put his "Pistol Pete" Maravich ball handling drills to good use and dribbled through his legs and behind his back as well as most people could dribble regularly. And he loved passing the ball more than scoring as he could penetrate the defense breaking it down and dish the ball off to the open man with a fancy behind-the-back pass of a no-look pass. Of course, if the defense gave him an open path to the basket, he could finish it off with an easy two points. Kenny Dudley would start at center; while Ashley Stacey would be a hybrid guard / forward; and Bobby Parton would be a forward; and Mikey "Pooh" Winston would be the shooting guard. First off, the bench was J.R. Durrell and Darcy Williams at forward and point guard and Randy Stafford at center with Lester backing up "Pooh". The thing about "Pooh" was his indifference to playing defense. It wasn't that he couldn't play tough; he just focused on his offense too much. He was a great guy and a good teammate however who kept things light when it got intense. He had a habit of doing play-by-play on his own game. For instance, when he shot the ball, he could be heard saying "Pooh from the corner…. he hits another one." Or "Pooh on the drive for a layup, count it". As he left the huddle on the sideline, he would always tell Aubrey "Get the ball to Pooh and watch what he does." Of course, if he was open, he did get the ball and he usually hit his jump shot from the corner.

The first game of the tournament had the Knights versus Butler and Butler prevailed by five points which meant that Empire would face the loser of the Roberta versus Barnesville game for third place. It would be Barnesville as they fell to a good Roberta team by twelve points. Empire would win the game by three points as Kenny Dudley would lead the way with seventeen points / fifteen rebounds / and four blocked shots. "Pooh" would also contribute thirteen points and Bobby Parton would add ten points of his own to go with nine rebounds and two blocked shots. Aubrey would have eight points / seven rebounds / and fourteen assists. The rest of the team would contribute twenty-two points including five from J.R. It was a good win and just what the doctor ordered for this team to come together.

Luckily, the party in Eastman was on a Saturday night when there was no basketball game, so R.C. Gold rocked another group of people and made about $50 each again. In early January Aubrey got his driver's license and was now able to take Chelsey out on dates if he ever had time for dating. During the month of January, the Knights played every Tuesday, Friday, and Saturday to make up lost non-region games. Region play would begin the third week of January so the first two weeks would be huge in preparing for the tough region schedule. They would win four and lose two games to make their record 5-3 heading into region play with a game at Roddy. Meanwhile, absence from Chelsey and Susan was starting to get to the Durrell boys. They still loved sports and competition, but there was something competing with their love of competition now for the first time in their lives. This is where many would-be great athletes choose another path and leave their potential in the dust. Only time would tell if the Durrell's would fall victim of this same thinking.

CHAPTER THIRTY-SIX

Another benefit of playing basketball was that Christina Dudley was a starting guard and leading scorer on the Lady Knights basketball team which meant that Aubrey got to see her every day, and that was always nice. Since the boys and girls rode the same bus to the games, he also had many conversations with her even though the girls rode up front while the boys rode in the back. Aubrey strategically took a seat in the middle of the bus along with Lester Beasley who liked Christina a lot and was trying to work up enough nerve to ask her out. Lester was a great guy and Aubrey liked him a lot, but he certainly did not want Christina to like him too much, but he did not want to interfere, so he was cool with Lester's efforts to woo Christina.

On a trip home from Rhine one Saturday night Christina asked Aubrey if he thought she should go out with Lester. Little did he know that this was a test she was using to gauge Aubrey's reaction to the situation. She had like Aubrey for a while now but had no idea that he felt the same about her. She was not sure he would go for an interracial relationship, and she was also not sure how her family and friends would feel about it. When she asked him the question about Lester he hesitated before saying, "Lester is a great guy and I think he would treat you the way you deserve to be treated," said Aubrey. "Oh yeah," said Christina. "And how should I be treated?" she continued. Aubrey's answer told her what she needed to know. "Like the beautiful and intelligent young lady that you are," he said. "Is that how you would treat me?" she asked before thinking about what she was saying. Aubrey looked her in the eye and said, "No doubt about it!" She wanted to kiss him so badly at that moment and he wished he could do the same. But he had a girlfriend. Chelsey loved him dearly and he was very fond of her too, but a heart wants what a heart wants, and his heart wanted Christina Dudley.

The first test of the season would come when Chauncey came to town for a big region game. Both teams were undefeated in region play at 4-0 so first place would be at stake. Aubrey's cousin Renee Thomas' boyfriend Earl Rabun was a star guard for the Comets, so Aubrey really wanted to play well and win this one. The game would go to overtime where Chauncey would take a one-point lead with twelve seconds left to play when Rabun would hit a running bank shot for his eighteenth point of the game and the lead. On the inbounds play Aubrey got the ball and dribbled through an attempted half-court trap and flew through the lane for an attempt at a game-winning layup but he was fouled rather roughly and was sent to the free throw line for two shots for the win. As Aubrey stepped to the line to shoot his free throws, Earl Rabun walked by him and said, "Don't choke Durrell." Aubrey smiled and thought if this guy only knew I have made this shot in my back yard thousands of times he would not have said anything. He drilled the first shot and took the ball with complete confidence that he would make the game-winner and the thought went through his mind—what would "Sugar Bear" Watson do? When he let the ball go, he turned and walked away with his hand in the air as the ball hit nothing but net. With two seconds left on the clock Empire simply had to play defense against the homerun pass and not commit a foul that would result in free throws on the other end. "Hondo" Winston was brought in the game to shadow Earl Rabun so he would not see the ball for sure. With their number one option taken away, they panicked somewhat and threw the ball up for grabs. When Ashley Stacey intercepted the inbounds pass the Empire crowd went wild.

Aubrey would finish with fourteen points / twelve assists / and six steals. Kenny Dudley would pour in nineteen points / eleven rebounds / and six blocked shots. Bobby Parton added ten points / twelve rebounds / and four blocked shots while "Pooh" Winston poured in nine points and even played enough defense to amass three steals. When the game ended, Earl Rabun came and shook Aubrey's hand and told him great game and that he would probably be in Empire this weekend to visit Renee. He seemed like a nice guy and Aubrey was happy for Renee.

At the barber shop that weekend the patrons could not stop talking about the tribute to "Sugar Bear" Watson. Even "Hot Rod" Hickey had to admit that it was cool on behalf of the kid. He also told the crowd that he was starting a Hall of Fame for Empire and Frazier High Schools. He told them that he was taking nominations for the inaugural class until May 1st and left some nomination forms with the proprietor. They were all supportive of this idea and it made Rod feel better than the last few times he had been in the shop. He still had one more committee seat to fill and he wanted Daniel Dudley to fill the role. He was the father of Kenny Dudley and Christina Dudley, whom Rod did not know. He did however know Kenny and he knew he was not well-liked be at least one member of the family. When he left the barber shop. He went by the Dudley house. When he got there, he saw the most beautiful young lady he had ever laid eyes on as Christina was outside. He thought he recognized her from the basketball team, but he had never seen her dressed up and looking fabulous as she was at this moment. When he got out of his car he said "Hello young lady. Who might you be?" "Christina Dudley is my name," she answered, "who are you?"

"Roderick Hickey and I was wondering if Mr. Daniel Dudley might be available to speak with me about something important," asked Rod. Kenny walked out about this time and saw Rod talking to his sister and said, "what are you doing here?" I just wanted to see your farther for a few minutes," said Rod. Kenny asked Christina to go get their Daddy. As they waited for Daniel to come outside Kenny told Rod that he didn't like him being there and if he was starting more trouble, he could take his sorry ass away from there. Rod said he understood why Kenny was angry at him, but he assured him that he had only the best of intentions for visiting this morning. He made a mental note to teach that boy a lesson someday about respect. Also, to find a way to get his sister for himself as soon as she graduated high school of course.

Chelsey had missed the Chauncey game because she had to work that Friday night, but she planned on going to Chester for the Saturday night contest. Back-to-back tough games was the norm in this region, but Chester was undefeated in region play and had only one loss on the season. The Tigers were a little too tough for the Knights on this night beating then 75-67. Chester was the best team in the region and one of the best teams in the state.

CHAPTER THIRTY-SEVEN

February was a busy month for basketball and for football recruiting. At union Hill High School, Zack Winborn received his promised scholarship for Murrayville Community College and from three other junior colleges from Mississippi and Kansas, but he felt loyalty to Jack Sullivan and decided to sign with Murrayville. At his signing ceremony his mother and "Quick" Jenkins were not present, but his dad was, and this gave them a little bit of time to work through their issues to a certain degree. Tommy Winborn apologized for being a terrible father but blamed it on his mother who he said told him to leave Zack alone because every time he was with his dad, he came home upset and belligerent. Zack knew this was true to certain extent because he had come home once and smarted off to "Quick" which resulted in a terrible beating at the hands of his mom's boyfriend at that time. He also explained why he left them behind saying Joyce had become depressed and turned to anti-depressants and had started accusing him of being unfaithful, which he swore he had not been. When if all got to be too much he decided to leave and he said he had worried about Zack for years and had wanted to reach out to him but wan not sure how it would be received. He then told Zack that he understood if he hated him but he wanted him to know that he loved him and would support him financially from that point on if he wanted him too, Zack sat and listened to his dad and finally said, "I hated you for a long time and I still don't know how to feel about you, but I would like to try to have a normal relationship if that is what you really want." He also told his dad about the busted windshield he owed J.R. for and asked his dad for help in paying for it. His dad agreed to give him $150 and told him to keep whatever was left over. Zack didn't know how to feel about the situation, yet it felt good to finally sort of make amends with his father. When he got home, he asked his mother why she missed the ceremony and she said she thought it was next week. He didn't even bother to ask "Quick" about it. He also got J.R.'s phone number from Susan Dillon who was skeptical about giving it to Zack until he convinced her that he had only good intentions and that the last thing he wanted to do was fight J.R. Durrell. When he spoke to J.R. later that night, J.R. was taken aback about this new Zack Winborn but agreed to let him come over and pay him what he owed him. When Zack arrived J.R.'s dad Eli Durrell told him he would be just inside the door if he needed him, but J.R. assured him that he would be alright. Zack paid him $100 and told him he was sorry for acting like an asshole. J.R. told him not to worry about the past and just to concentrate on the future and wished him luck in college. The two boys shook hands and went their separate ways.

In their region the schedules of all sports were in the same order meaning that Empire and Union Hill always finished against one another. In basketball each team played versus each other twice in a home and home format. So, about the second week in February the Knights would make a trip to Union Hill for the first meeting of the season. Ordinarily this was not a problem but this year however the boys and their R.C. Gold bandmates had agreed to play the Union Hill F.F.A.'s Valentine dance the Thursday after the game on Tuesday of the same week. So, win or lose, the Durrell boys would probably be the targets of much scorn and ridicule. They would have to keep things professional and not let the hostile crowd get to them. Besides, maybe they would play so well it wouldn't matter.

Empire would win a close game by a score of 57-53 and Aubrey would figure prominently in the victory with fifteen points / thirteen assists / and five steals. J.R. would ice the victory with two free throws in the closing minute to go along with nine points / six rebounds / and two blocked shots off the bench. So, into the lion's den they went not knowing what to expect.

Chelsey and Susan had the honor of introducing the band and beamed with pride as the boys took the stage. For obvious reasons they decided not to play 'SMOKE ON THE WATER' and decided to replace it with Union Hill's run through song 'CAT SCRATCH FEVER'. Aubrey thought it was crazy for the Barons to use this song but hey, it was their choice. When Aubrey hit the opening riff, it set the night off on a great start. J.R. sand his tail off and the band played excellently. They had two encores to perform in which they played 'T FOR TEXAS' again for their last song of the night. The donation bucket didn't have much in it since the crowd was high school student who did not have much money, yet they still managed to collect an extra $65.00 to go with their usual $150 fee. The boys took $30 each and place $35 in the band account. Thy also got a couple of letters from girls asking them to give them a call and a couple more encouraging to do something to themselves that was physically impossible. One such note was signed by "Big Mouth Barry" Kennedy who apparently had not got the memo that the war with Zack was over. Zack did not attend the dance.

When the night was over, Chelsey and Susan told the boys they had something for them and off they went to their favorite parking spots. Aubrey told Chelsey that he had to be home by midnight, so they took care of things rather quickly and said goodnight. Chelsey told him she loved him again and he told her that he loved her too, knowing in his heart that was not entirely true. On his way home he prayed for forgiveness for what he had just done and asked for guidance on what to do about the situation. He believed he was falling for Christina; someone he did not even know for sure felt the same about him, yet he wanted to do right by Chelsey. After all, she had been his first lover and she really loved him. How could he turn his back on her love for an interracial relationship in Empire, Georgia? He must be losing his mind. He would be run out the church for sure and probably run out of town. It was not even sexual desire he felt for Christina, although he knew that would be wonderful too; it was how he felt whenever she was around him. He felt like they had a connection that he and Chelsey would never have. He would let his feelings remain hidden and hope they went away but seeing her every day at basketball practice would make that rather difficult.

CHAPTER THIRTY-EIGHT

The Knights would continue their winning ways until they made a road trip to Chauncey where Earl Rabun would put on a shooting clinic dropping 36 points on Empire leading the Comets to a ten-point win. Aubrey would have fifteen points and twelve assists of his own. They would bounce back nicely defeating Chester behind Mike "Pooh: Winston's 22 points as he was on fire from the corner with his jump shot and his play-by-play assessment of his game. It would come down to the wire as to who would win the region championship between Empire, Chester, and Chauncey since each of them had only one region loss. Union Hill would finish in fourth place. Empire got a break when Rhine upset Chauncey and Union Hill upset Chester. All they would have to do was win out and they would go into the region tournament as the number one seed. The last game of the season versus Union Hill was played in Empire and the old gym was packed. The Lady Knights would get things started by winning in a blowout behind Christina Dudley's 28 points thereby securing their number one seed. The boys' game would be a lot closer with the Barons Billy Pack going off for 32 points but thanks to Kenny Dudley's 24 points and "Pooh" Winston's sharp shooting from the outside the game was a back-and-forth contest until the end. With three minutes left to play and Union Hill up by four points the legend of Aubrey Durrell added another chapter. Aubrey jumped in front of a pass intended for Pack and raced to the other end of the court for what everyone assumed would be a layup but as he went up for the shot, Aubrey felt a burst of energy and kept rising until he two-hand dunked the ball. He had dunked before a couple of times in practice but never in a game. The crowd went wild and so did the bench. Union Hill had to call a timeout to compose themselves, but it did not work. Using that momentum, Empire players turned up the defensive intensity and the Barons only scored one more basket while the Knights would score eight more points to pull out a hard-fought four-point victory—75-71 thereby securing the number one seed. All anyone wanted to talk about was Aubrey's dunk but honestly, he couldn't explain where it came from; it just happened. Aubrey only scored thirteen points, but that play was the play of the game. He would also have sixteen assists and five steals. Bobby Parton would contribute 11 points and six blocks while grabbing twelve rebounds. "Pooh" Winston added another 17 points. Ashley Stacey would contribute five points and four steals and J.R. had four points off the bench to go with five rebounds. After the game, with everyone hugging and patting him on the back it was Christina who gave him a big bear hug and Aubrey hugged her back for what seemed like forever. It seemed as if neither of them wanted to let go. Aubrey knew he could go on forever in that moment, but he had to get to the locker room. Chelsey also noticed the hug and wondered if she had anything to worry about.

When he came outside, Chelsey was waiting for him, but she was apprehensive about asking him about the hug with Christina. She was unusually quiet and just kept telling herself that she was overreacting, but she couldn't get over what she had seen. Later when they were alone, she worked up the nerve to ask him about Christina and Aubrey knew he had been exposed. At first, he told her that she was just a close friend and the sister of his best friend, which was not a lie, but she was no fool and Aubrey finally admitted that he had strong feelings for Christina, and he thought she had feelings for him too. He tried to explain that he had never cheated on her, and he did not want to hurt her, but the damage was done. She told him that she did not want to see him for a while and that he had to figure out what he wanted out of a relationship. She said she had never loved anyone like she loved him but if he did not love her back then he was free to go. She left crying and Aubrey felt badly for what he had done. She would surely tell Susan and then J.R. would know. The cat was certainly out of the bag now and the only one who knew nothing about it was Christina. He had to tell her before the street committee did.

When he pulled up to the Dudley house Kenny came outside to greet him and said, "What brings you out here this time of night?" Aubrey asked him if Christina was home, and Kenny said she was but why did he want to see her. When suddenly it dawned on Kenny he said," it is about damn time. I wondered when the two of you were going to quit beating around the bush." He told Aubrey he would let her know he was here. When she came out Aubrey asked her if she could take a ride with him. She said she could if her daddy didn't mind. When she came back outside and got in the car with Aubrey, he started to speak, but she wouldn't let him. Instead, she pulled him close to her and kissed him passionately. She told him she had been waiting to do that for the longest time. "Christina, I think I may be in love with you," Aubrey said. He told her about Chelsey and what had happened. Christina said she felt badly for her and thought she was a good person who didn't deserve such bad fortune. But she also said she had been trying to find a way to tell him for a long time how she felt about him but that she always chickened out. Aubrey cranked the car and drove to Nubby' s just before it closed. "How are we going to handle this?" asked Aubrey, "I mean this is Empire, Georgia and some people won't understand. It could be stressful and some of our friends might treat us differently." "I don't know," answered Christina, "some black folks won't like it either." Aubrey replied, "They say love conquers all—I guess we are about to find out." "Do your parents know?" asked Christina. "Not yet," said Aubrey, "I guess that is a good place to start." He had no idea how his folks would react to this news, but he thought they would be okay with it; after all, they had always been tolerant of all races of people and had raised him to be the same way. He would have to tell them this weekend. "Can I see you tomorrow night?" asked Aubrey. "I think that will be okay," she said and gave him one more kiss to hold him until tomorrow.

By the time he got home, J.R. had already found out about it when Chelsey showed up at Susan's house crying and told them all about it. J.R. was not shocked since he had noticed their flirtations for some time now. He told Susan that he would see her tomorrow and left the girls to talk it over. He drove straight to Aubrey's house, but he was not there yet. He went to Nubby' s and had a milkshake and talked to a couple of students who worked there. Just as he was leaving, Aubrey was pulling in with Christina sitting by his side. J.R. just missed them. When Aubrey pulled up to his house, J.R. was waiting on him and said, "What's up Cuz?" as Aubrey walked over to his car. "Hop in man; we need to talk," said J.R. "I guess you already know what happened," said Aubrey. "Yeah, Chelsey came to Susan's house crying and real upset" replied J.R. Aubrey started to explain, "I never wanted to hurt her but…." J.R. interrupted saying "Cuz, I understand. Ray Charles could see this coming. I mean the way y'all have been looking at each other at school and sitting near each other on every bus trip; it was just a matter of time before y'all got together." "It was that obvious?" asked Aubrey. "Man, some of the guys have been talking about laying bets on how soon it would happen" said J.R. "Well, what do you think?" Aubrey inquired. "I think Christina is the finest girl in Empire and she is sweet and smart. She is a perfect catch except for one thing" said J.R. "Most of the guys on the team will be envious of you but they won't ever admit it," he added. "Why does it have to be like this? Asked Aubrey. "Would you go out with her if you were me?" he added. "Oh, hell yeah, like I said Christina is fine as hell, but you need to be prepared for certain people to treat you different; and it will start in the church. All those good Christians will forget brotherly love and all that bullshit, but you know what I say, screw all of them. The first time you break a long run or hit a game-winning homerun they will be right back with you," said J.R. Aubrey just wanted to know that J.R. would not think badly of him and once he was assured of that, he felt better, "Well I guess I have to go in and talk to Daddy. I will see you later," said Aubrey. "Good luck Cuz. See you tomorrow," answered J.R.

His dad always waited up for him to talk about the game but tonight he could tell something else was on his son's mind. When he told Aubrey to spill the beans, he was not quite ready for what came up. "Daddy, I need to tell you something that you may not like to hear," started Aubrey, "Chelsey broke up with me tonight because I told her I was interested in somebody else." "Well, that happens, and she will eventually get over it; sure, it will hurt for a……" Wyll started to respond. "Daddy, it's Christina Dudley," interrupted Aubrey. Silence filled the room for what seemed like an eternity. Wyll eventually broke the silence by saying, "Are you sure son?" "Yessir, I have known for a long time, and she feels the same way about me," said Aubrey. "I know there will be some people who don't like it, but we really like each other, and she is a beautiful person inside and out Daddy and she comes from a good family." "You are correct about the fact that some people won't like it probably most of them good church folks, but I know enough dirt on most of them to keep them quiet" said Wyll, "I just hope you know what you are getting into. People can be ruthless and cruel; so be careful son." Are you okay with it though?" asked Aubrey. "Well," said Wyll "It is not what I would choose for you because I know how the world operates but I do know that the Dudleys are fine people and Christina is a beautiful young lady so I suppose what will be; will be." "Thanks Daddy. I want you to know that I have prayed about this many times," said Aubrey. "And we are going to pray one more time tonight" said Wyll as he hugged his oldest son and began to pray for God's blessings on his son and Christina. "You know you still have to tell Mama, don't you?" asked Wyll. "Yeah, unless you want to do it for me," said Aubrey. "I think it will be better coming from you, but I will help with her after you break the news. You know she really liked Chelsey," replied Wyll. "Yessir, I know" replied Aubrey. He slept better that night than he had in a long time.

Christina was also in the process of telling her parents and her dad did not take to the idea at first; not because he disliked Aubrey, but because he was afraid of how his daughter would be treated by other folks both in the white and black communities. He personally like the Durrells and thought Aubrey was a nice kid but he told Christina he would have to think it over before giving his blessings. Her mother Priscilla was more understanding and told Christina that her daddy would come around. Christina had never had a serious boyfriend before mainly because most guys were too intimidated by her beauty to even talk to her. She had spent many lonely nights waiting for someone to come along. She had dated Ashley Stacey, but he only wanted one thing and he couldn't get that from Christina, so he moved on to the next girl. Lester Beasley was a nice guy, but she knew who she wanted, and it was Aubrey Durrell. The only problem was that every other girl in Empire wanted him too but when they started having daily conversations at school, she fell for him 100%. She never dreamed that he would feel the same way toward her but now he said he thought he was in love with her. Thank God was all she could say as she lay her head on her pillow that night.

Chelsey Potter was praying also but it was for her lover to take her back she did not sleep at all for the next few weeks.

Chauncey was playing at Chester the following night and Christina said she would not mind going to the game, so Aubrey, Christina, and Renee Thomas went together. Renee went to watch her boyfriend Earl Rabun play for Chauncey. At first it was a little bit awkward with Christina and Renee, but they soon warmed up to one another and the conversation was flowing. When they walked into the Chester gymnasium, they received a couple of strange looks especially when Christina sat up close to Aubrey, but mostly they were unnoticed and unbothered. After the game, which was won by Chauncey behind Earl Rabun's 19 points, meaning that Chauncey would finish the season as the number two seed and Chester would be the number three; they talked to Earl for a few minutes and congratulated him on his great game. Aubrey noticed that Earl could barely take his eyes off Christina, so he knew at least one other white boy who obviously approved of his date and probably wanted to take his place. After taking Renee home, Aubrey and Christina went to visit his little parking spot off Chicken Road for some privacy. He had no intention of making a move and she had no intention of letting things go too far so they mostly sat and talked about things in general and kissed a few times and it was a nice time for them both. Aubrey had never felt this close to any girl before. It was like she understood him and he her as well. Christina had promised her dad that she would be home before midnight and the last thing Aubrey wanted to do was upset Mr. Daniel Dudley especially on the first date. Kenny had just returned from his date and he and Aubrey talked for a little while after Christina went inside. "Kenny, you really okay with me dating your sister?" asked Aubrey. Kenny thought about his answer for a few seconds then said," I just want her to have somebody to respect her and love her and somebody that I can trust to take care of her in any situation and I believe you are that fellow." "But understand this one fact," continued Kenny, "I will beat any man's ass who mistreats my sister even my best friend. You got that Aubrey Durrell?" Aubrey almost looked for a smile coming from his best friend but there was a serious look on his face, and he knew Kenny meant what he said. "You know I hear you loud and clear. Christina is a special person and I like her an awful lot. I just hope she likes me as much as I like her," said Aubrey. Finally, the smile returned to Kenny's face when he told Aubrey "Man, you could not wash that smile off her face all day today. I think see really likes you, my brother." They spent a few minutes reminiscing about their days in elementary school sharing a drink together and liking no one else in the whole school but each other. Aubrey gave Kenny a big bro hug and told him goodbye and left for home. He thought about the last twenty-four hours and how good things felt at that moment, but that was the calm before the storm.

CHAPTER THIRTY-NINE

Chelsey was not handling things well at all and her cousin Terry Lampkin felt sorry for her. She told him how Aubrey had told her he loved her, and she believed him. All Terry could do was tell her she deserved better and that this too shall pass, but he didn't know for sure if she would recover any time soon. He would see Aubrey Sunday at band practice, and he didn't know what he would say to him if anything at all.

The preacher told the boys that he would not need them to sing that Sunday since they were in a rush to get out and do a local radio show, but Aubrey and J.R. sensed there might be another reason. So be it thought Aubrey. If this was true Christianity, then he wasn't sure he wanted to be a part of it. After the service some of the other kids acted like they had been told not to associate with Aubrey. Maybe he was just being paranoid, but he couldn't let them get to him.

At Billy Dobbs house the band members showed up and Terry was cold as ice to Aubrey barely speaking when Aubrey told him hello. They had played through their repertoire when Billy told the group that he thought they needed a few more songs to play and asked for suggestions. Terry couldn't help himself when he said, "How about 'BROWN SUGAR'? I'll bet Aubrey could play the hell out of that." It got deathly quiet as everyone waited for Aubrey's reaction. Finally, Aubrey said "well, I have got to hand it to you Terry, that was a good one but if you have something you want to say come on out with it." J.R. suggested the rest of the band take a break and they all went inside Billy's house to give the two boys a chance to vent. Aubrey started the conversation by saying "I don't expect you to understand but I didn't plan to hurt Chelsey, it just happened." "Did you plan to tell her you loved her, or did that just happen too? The fact pf the matter is you got what you wanted from her and lied when you said you loved her then you found a better deal, or so you think. But a black girl Aubrey? How do think she feels right now?" said Terry. Aubrey was at a loss for words and for the first time he felt like he had done Chelsey wrong, but he could not help falling for someone else. The fact that she was black didn't matter to Aubrey, but he understood how it might look to others. He didn't feel like he owed Terry an explanation or an apology, but he offered one anyway. "Look, I am sorry it seems that way, but I didn't intentionally mislead or lie to her, and I really did like her a lot, but when she confronted me about Christina, I had to tell her the truth," said Aubrey. "She confronted you?" asked Terry. "Yes, after the basketball game she noticed Christina giving me a hug and she asked me if there was anything going on that she needed to know about. I told her that I thought I had developed feelings for Christina, and she told me to take a hike," said Aubrey. "But I want you to know that Christina and I never had been together before Chelsey broke up with me. In fact, I had never even told Christina how I felt about her until that night, and I had no idea that she felt the same about me until I went to see her" he added. "You can tell me anything Aubrey and I wouldn't know if you are lying or not, but I won't ever look at you the same way again," said Terry. "I am sorry to hear that Terry and I guess one of us has to leave the band and that will be me," said Aubrey. Then he went to his car and left riding around wondering how much worse it was going to get. When the rest of the boys came back out, Terry told them what was said, and Doug Hall told Terry that what he had said was funny as hell, but he wished he hadn't said it because good guitarists are hard to find. Billy asked J.R. what he thought they should do and J.R. said "I think all of us should mind our own business and not let our cousins talk us into saying things we shouldn't say. Terry that is between Aubrey and Chelsey and you should have stayed out of it." Terry snapped at J.R. "I am defending my cousin just the same as you are now. I fail to see the difference in you and me right now." J.R. told Terry "Aubrey doesn't need me to defend him; I am trying to keep this band together and you are trying to tear us apart. I am out of here boys. I hope to see y'all again sometime soon."

Christina was having an awakening to the ways of the world as well. She was on the prom committee—the black prom committee that is (Empire High School still had separate proms for blacks and whites; a holdover from segregation days and sponsored by private citizens). When she asked if she could bring Aubrey to the prom, she was told no; not until she was free to go to the white prom. Even though he was friends with 99% of all the black students at Empire High School, adults decided that rules were in place preventing her from bringing the boy she loved to the prom. All they were doing is promoting segregation and racism. She would not be going to her first prom if this were the case. Later that night she called Aubrey to inform him of this news and when he got through telling her about his ordeal, she felt badly for him and apologized for his problem. He corrected her immediately saying "Baby you don't need to apologize for anything, and I love you so much. I don't need anybody's approval as long as I have you by my side," she told him that she loved him more than anything in the world and couldn't wait to see him tomorrow at school. Aubrey hung up the phone and began his nightly talk with Jesus.

CHAPTER FORTY

The region basketball tournament started that Monday at Roddy High School. Empire and Chauncey earned byes until Friday night based on their regular season records, but everyone else had to play on Tuesday and Wednesday nights. As expected, Chester and Union Hill came out of the fray in third and fourth place, respectively. Empire would face Union Hill in the semi-finals while Chauncey would take on Chester. Chauncey defeated Chester 65-58 to punch their ticket to the championship game on Saturday night. The Knights would have to defeat the Union Hill Barons for a third time this season which is always hard to do. The Barons' players started on Aubrey early with Big Billy Pack making a racial comment toward Aubrey trying to get under his skin. During an early timeout, Pack told one of his teammates that the reason Aubrey had dunked in the last game was because he had been getting some black stuff. Aubrey simply told him to have a little class and kept on playing. Apparently, Pack did not know that he was talking about the sister of the man who would be covering him most of the night, so when Kenny Dudley overheard one of the more particularly raunchy comments, he whispered to Pack during a dead ball situation that he didn't appreciate his comments about his sister and his best friend, and he would be sorry if he didn't apologize immediately. Pack told Kenny to do something to himself that is biologically impossible, and Kenny told him "Don't say I didn't warn you." At halftime, the score was Empire 39 and Union Hill 32. The second half was more of the same with Empire dominating and Union Hill more content to talk trash than to try to win the game. "Pooh" Winston was on fire with 29 points and Ashley Stacey poured in 15 more. Kenny Dudley scored 19 points over Billy Pack in the paint and held Pack to 12 points—about ten points under his season average. Aubrey chipped in with 12 points / 13 assists / and 4 steals as Empire won rather easily by a score of 81-59. Finally, in the last two minutes of the game with the outcome no longer in doubt, Kenny told Aubrey "It is time brother" and Aubrey knew exactly what that meant. On their next trip down the floor, Empire had to break a tough full-court press. Normally Kenny would be in the middle of the press to assist in getting the ball down court; however, on this possession, he and Aubrey worked a play that if executed perfectly would put a nice bow on this victory. When the ball came inbounds to Aubrey, Kenny would turn and run on a fast break. If open, Aubrey would throw a long pass to him thereby drawing coverage from Billy Pack. Instead of shooting the ball, Kenny would bounce the ball off the backboard where Aubrey who followed Kenny would catch the rebound and go up and dunk the basketball or at least lay the ball in for an easy two points. As the ball came inbounds to Aubrey, Kenny broke for the basket. Aubrey lobbed a perfect pass that hit Kenny in stride then streaked quickly as he could behind the pass. As Pack came to defend Kenny, he went up for an apparent layup but flipped the ball off the backboard nonchalantly. Aubrey leapt and grabbed the perfect rebound and threw down a perfect two-handed dunk, and as luck would have it, Billy Pack was underneath the basket as the ball and Aubrey came down on top of him. Aubrey told him that one was for Christina which infuriated Pack who went after Aubrey and tried to throw a punch at him, but Aubrey was too quick and ducked the awkward punch. Pack was ejected from the game with a little over a minute left, but he would have to sit out the next game for Union Hill. As he went by him, Kenny told him "I told you that you were going to be sorry-bye bye now."

After the game, they could not wait to tell Christina what they had done. The girls' team had won their game versus the Chauncey girls also putting themselves in the championship game as well. Christina had 23 points to lead the way. They would face Rhine for the tournament championship while the boys would face Chauncey, in what would prove to be a tough game. Earl Rabun was fired up and ready to do battle with his girlfriend's cousin and he would score 23 points to keep it close for a little over three quarters, but in the end, Empire had a couple more playmakers than the Comets had and pulled away to win by twelve points by a score of 77-65. Aubrey would have 9 points / 9 rebounds and / 6 steals but made a great contribution on defense taking away the second leading scorer for Chauncey, a quick and tough point guard named Will Hatton. This would force Rabun to have to win the game by himself which the Knights did not think he could do. They would enter the first round of the state tournament with a home game versus Gordon High School. Empire and Chauncey would win their first-round games while Chester and Union Hill would lose.

Empire would win their next two games putting them in the final four at the Macon Coliseum while Chauncey would lose in round three. Meanwhile, things were going well with Christina and the girls' team was in the final four also. To say that Empire was having a banner year athletically would be an understatement. The boys would face the Roberta War Hawks in the semi-final game and Coach Lord told the team in practice that he had noticed that no one had pressed Roberta much this season probably because they were afraid of their athleticism, but he felt that Empire could test them with a full court press from the opening tip to the final buzzer. "I want to make them have to work hard to get the ball over half court and see if they can handle it. It may lead to a couple of dunks along the way, but over the course of four quarters I believe they will crack," said the coach. On the game's first play "Pooh" Winston would hit a 15-foot jump shot and the Knights immediately went into their full court trap defense. When the Roberta player got himself trapped with the ball he panicked and threw a pass that Aubrey would intercept and drive to the basket executing a fancy behind-the-back pass to Bobby Parton who threw down a monster dunk for a 4-point lead, but it may as well have been 40 points because Empire's trapping defense was brutal and involved every man on the team so the starters would remain fresh and out of foul trouble. It was almost as if Roberta had never seen a full court press before and Empire scored 36 points off steals or turnovers in route to a rather easy 85-57 win. Aubrey had 11 steals and 14 points to go with 13 assists—a triple double. Kenny and Bobby put on a dunking display with each of them getting three big dunks. Another sport and another state championship to play for. Aubrey told the team that God had been good to them and wanted to lead the team in a prayer of thanks. When he finished, all the knights yelled an enthusiastic "AMEN!" The state championship game would be a re-match of the early-season Christmas Tournament game versus the Butler Raiders who were undefeated and had a talented team. The Lady Knights would defeat Hiawassee for their first state championship in school history. Christina would be the leader again with 24 points and she looked good while scoring those points too. She was the talk of all the young boys in the bleachers and developed a little fan club. When someone said she had a white boyfriend, and he was the starting point guard for the boys' team they could not believe it until someone said his name was Aubrey Durrell then they understood. Aubrey had already developed a name for himself among serious sports fans in the state of Georgia. To these guys race did not matter—they recognized game skills if you had them, and Aubrey definitely had skills. Oddly enough, Christina's fan club became Aubrey's also probably out of envy more than anything else.

In the first meeting back in December Butler had won by five points but that had been Empire's first game of the season and things were a lot different now. Coach Lord told them that they would employ a half-court press every time Butler had the ball luring them into a false sense of security bringing the ball up the court early in the game. They would pounce on the ball the second it came across the half-court line and hopefully catch some poor unsuspecting kid by surprise and get a couple of easy baskets early. When Butler least expected it, Empire would jump back into their full-court trap press. "Boys, we have got to make them uncomfortable every time they bring the ball inbounds. If they are looking around wondering where we are; then they will take their eyes off the ball and maybe make a mistake or two that can change the game." Coach Lord said. Butler won the opening tip and thought they were getting into their offense, but they were mistaken. As the point guard dribbled across the line, Aubrey and Ashley Stacey trapped him and caused him to make an errant pass which "Pooh" Winston intercepted and took off for a layup, however, he was fouled and had to make two free throws.

He calmly hit both shots while doing his play-by-play "Pooh steps up to the line and drains his first shot" he said. "Pooh hits his second shot and it looks like he could be ready for a good night" he added for the second one. The Butler players thought he was crazy, and they were not far from right. The half-court trap effectively disrupted Butler's offensive strategy and when they did not throw the ball away or get called for travelling or an offensive foul, they were forcing bad shots that resulted in long rebounds and fast breaks for the Knights. Ashley Stacey got two quick fouls on him, so Darcy Williams played more than usual in the first half, and he responded with great defense and six points off steals. J.R. also played extensive minutes when Bobby Parton got poked in the eye about midway through the first half. He contributed 10 points and four steals in the first half. Aubrey also had six steals and eight assists to go with four points. Empire had a lead at halftime of 41-28 and they knew that the Raiders would press them hard in the second half attempting to get back in the game. Sure enough, the press was on, but Aubrey proved to be too quick and too adept at ball-handling to get trapped as he weaved his way through the defense and drove the lane time and time again for an easy layup or dishing off on a beautiful no-look pass for another assist. He noticed that some of the young fans had moved to sit around Christina and were cheering loudly for him every time he touched the ball. They were probably doing it to try and impress Christina, but it still felt good to have fans cheering for him that did not even know him, so he decided to try to give them something to really get excited about. If he got a chance to dunk one, he would throw one down hard and watch then go crazy. As fate would have it, he got an opportunity with about three minutes left in the game when J.R. intercepted a pass and looked up to see Aubrey streaking down the court on the left side. After taking four or five dribbles, he threw a perfect bounce pass to Aubrey who took off and jammed the ball through the hoop sealing the deal for Empire and setting off a wild celebration in the stands especially among Christina's new friends who were jumping around like crazy, and they were not even from Empire. After the game he would ask them where they were from.

Aubrey would have another triple double going for 14 points / 11 steals / and 15 assists. J.R. got hot off the bench and scored 21 points with 9 rebounds and 5 steals. Darcy Williams would add 8 points and 7 assists and Kenny Dudley would lead all scorers with 26 points and 14 rebounds. When the dust cleared Empire had won its' second state championship in boys' sports during this school year by a score of 88-

64. Before the trophy presentation he went over to get a hug from his family and Christina, and he got pats on the back from the seven boys who had cheered for him and Christina. There was three white boys and four black boys all claiming tb from Roberta and proclaiming Aubrey as the best athlete they had ever seen. Aubrey was embarrassed by such talk, but he found these guys to be funny and nice. He told Christina he loved her and would see her back at the school and she told him she loved him too. Aubrey couldn't help but notice when he turned around that Susan Dillon, who had come to watch J.R. play, was staring a hole in him as if she wanted to say somethin

CHAPTER FORTY-ONE

"Can I ask y'all a question?" asked Susan Dillon to J.R.'s parents on the way home from the game. "How do y'all feel about Aubrey dating that black girl?" she said before getting permission to ask her question. "Well," said Eli Durrell, "Aubrey is a good kid and Christina is a good girl from a good family, so I guess I am okay with it," added Eli. He went on to say that he was glad he did not have to deal with this problem. Not exactly the answer she was hoping to get but about what she had expected.

The players decided to honor the tradition started after the football championship and spend the night in the gym to celebrate together and reminisce about the season. So, when the bus returned to the high school, there was the crowd of students, teachers, parents, and community leaders there to welcome their conquering heroes for the second night in a row as they had been there for the girls the previous night. Aubrey rushed to Christina as soon as he got off the bus and hugged her tightly. "Baby it doesn't get much better than this" he told her. "I know" she answered, "I can't believe how God has blessed me this year with a championship for both of us and a boyfriend that I love more than anything in this world." "I love you too more than you will ever know" Aubrey told her as he stared into her beautiful hazel eyes. Not more than twenty feet away Susan Dillon was watching them and getting sick to her stomach. She was not really paying attention to J.R. when he told her that he was spending the night in the gym and that he would see her tomorrow night. J.R. sensing what was bothering her told her "Hey babe, don't let that bother you. There ain't nothing you can do about it. I love you and I will see you tomorrow night okay" he said and gave her a little good-bye kiss. Susan left thinking she might be able to do something about it. A phone call would take care of a little bit of payback for Chelsey.

Aubrey saw a group of friends standing with Teddy Robertson, so he went over to say hello. When he got there a couple of them walked away and Aubrey told Teddy he was sorry they left to which Teddy replied "Screw them. They would do the same thing if they had the chance. I don't blame you, my friend; Christina is sweet and has always treated me nice. And that ass doesn't look too bad either" he said with a big smile. Darcy Williams had come up and added "Yeah, all I want to know is details brother. I want to know everything dude. You know I have always thought she was hot." Aubrey told them they were crazy and thanked them for their support. Darcy told him that he had gotten two championship rings because of him so he could do no wrong. They all had a good laugh and Aubrey went back to Christina. "Some guys have it all don't they?" asked Darcy when he left. "Yeah, if he weren't such a good person, it would be easy to be jealous" answered Teddy. Aubrey and J.R. went to get some snacks and Dr. Peppers and came straight back to the gym. "Man, that was a nasty dunk at the end of the game" said J.R. "where does that come from man?" "I don't know" answered Aubrey, "I guess it comes as a blessing from God." "My goal is to dunk one before I graduate" replied J.R. "I am sure you will" said Aubrey, "I know you good enough to know that if you set your mind to do something, it will be done," said Aubrey. Years later as a coach, Aubrey would make the connection between leaping ability and speed. The faster players without a doubt are the better leapers and he found this correlation by testing vertical leap and standing long jump of his players. But for this night, it was just something that happened by the grace of God.

The next day was Sunday and of course the basketball championship was the topic in church. The preacher congratulated the Durrells but not quite as enthusiastically as he had done in the fall. The Durrells did not sing that Sunday either and after church the preacher shook J.R.'s hand and gave him a big pat on the back but only gave Aubrey a quick handshake. It seemed like a cold fish greeting to Aubrey, but maybe he was imagining things. He was not imagining things at all. A called deacon's meeting to deal with Aubrey's interracial relationship was being held that afternoon before the evening service. Wyll Durrell was a deacon.

Aubrey had not been to band practice since his dust up with Terry Lampkin, but J.R. had convinced him to return so he went back and played guitar without saying much at all. He and Terry did not speak to one another for the entire two-hour practice session. Afterwards, he went to Christina's house for a while. He tried carrying on a conversation with her dad Daniel Dudley, but the big man had little to say to Aubrey. Later as he was about to leave, he told Christina that he didn't think her dad liked him very much. She told him not to worry about that. She told him that her dad did not like anyone she ever dated and that it was not personal.

Meanwhile at the deacons' meeting, Wyll Durrell was being told that the church did not approve of his son's relationship and that they were expecting him to 'do the right thing' and put an end to the relationship. Then and only then could Aubrey be brought before the church where he would contritely ask for forgiveness. Wyll thought long and hard before answering the deacons. Finally, he said "the good book says judge not lest ye be judged'. I really don't think most of you are good judges of my son's character or his chances of getting to heaven. Buddy Camp you still taking a stiff belt of moonshine before bed each night? And Bill Carswell are you still giving free months' rent to the widows in your rental properties in exchange for certain favors? And preacher how is the young lady receptionist at the radio station doing. You did see her last weekend in Atlanta didn't you." He continued by saying "I have known how some of you live for quite some time now, but I have kept quiet because I know no one is perfect and I don't judge anyone—that's God's job. Now y'all want to criticize my son for falling in love with a beautiful young lady who comes from a great family and basically tell me that y'all don't approve of my parenting. Well, I want y'all to hear me loud and clear on this one thing—I am proud of all my children and the fact that they are good god-fearing young people. But y'all do not have to worry about me and my family embarrassing this church anymore, because we won't back. And I will keep y'all's secrets safe; like I said God will judge each of us in the end." He turned and walked out leaving them shocked and feeling embarrassed about what Wyll had revealed.

When J.R. got to Susan's house after band practice, he noticed a big, muddy four-wheel drive and recognized it as her cousin's truck— Harley Dillon. He was a tobacco chewing; cussing; beer drinking 'Good ole boy'. J.R, did not personally like him because he disrespected him when he first met him by cussing at him and trying to be a bad ass in front of Susan. J.R. had really wanted to kick his country ass but he kept the peace out of respect for Susan's family. He had gotten drunk at a family cookout and told J.R. "boy if you ever mistreat Susan, I will personally kick your ass; you hear me boy?" Any other time J.R. would have given him the opportunity to keep his promise but love makes a man do crazy things. As J.R. was entering the house Harley was leaving. Harley stared J.R. down as he walked out the door and gave him a short greeting saying, "how's it going?" J.R. replied "All right." "I'll take care of that for you Darling" said Harley to Susan and she replied "Okay, thanks. I'll talk to you later." When Harley was gone, J.R. asked her what that was about, and Susan said he was checking on something for her concerning the F.F.A. J.R. did not give it any more thought. Later they made it to the backside of the farm for some private time then he left to make it to church just in time for the 6:30 service. He noticed that Aubrey and his family were not there and thought it strange and hoped they were okay. After church, he called Aubrey and was told about the deacons' meeting. He was furious at the bunch of hypocrites and told his dad that he didn't want to go to church there anymore. Hid dad told him to calm down and everything would work itself out. J.R. was not sure of that but he was sure that he would never sing in that church again.

CHAPTER FORTY-TWO

When Aubrey got home from school the next day, he found two letters from colleges letting him know that they would be following him over the course of his high school career and would like to talk to him about playing football at their school. They were from Southern California and Michigan. He filed them in a bedroom drawer where eventually he would have over 300 letters from all over the country. His dad thought it was great that his son would have all these options, but he wanted him close to home so he could go watch him play and they could help him if he needed anything. J.R. also got a couple of letters from smaller schools in the south. Aubrey did not want to think about life after high school right now and life without J.R. They had been together since they were knee-high to a grasshopper, and they were close as brothers even though they were cousins. Life without his 'brother' was something he had never even considered.

Christina was still upset by the prom news and talked to Aubrey about not even wanting to go without him. Aubrey felt badly about the situation and thought he might have a solution. "What if we have a school dance instead of the proms?" he asked Christina, "I think R.C. Gold would be able to play and we could call it the 'Spring Formal'. What do you think?" She thought it was a good idea, but they would need a sponsor. Aubrey told her they should speak to Principal Bass about it and see if he would support their idea. After school they went to his office and told him what they wanted to do. He told them he supported their idea, but he did not want to get involved in a racial situation. He told them that some of the parents who sponsored the proms would not take to kindly to him trying to undermine the regular proms, but that he would love to see it happen and that it was long overdue for Empire to stop the segregated proms. He told them that if they could convince one of the school clubs and some teachers to sponsor it, that he would let them use the gym. He wished them good luck and sent them on their way. Aubrey decided he would talk to Coach Kelly about sponsoring and chaperoning the dance. The next day he talked to Coach Kelly and Coach Lord and they both said they would be glad to chaperone it Aubrey could pull it off. Next was a conversation with the F.F.A. sponsor Mr. Curtis who said he would be interested in it if it made money for his program. Aubrey said he would get back to him on the finances of the situation. The dates for the proms were May 15 for the black prom and May 8 for the white prom. Christina had told him that they should not try to compete with those two events this year, so they chose May 22 for the Empire High School Soring Formal. They would charge $20 per couple and serve light refreshments. They told Mr. Curtis that if they could get fifty couples at $20 per couple, his club would clear $650. When he heard this, he was sold. Aubrey then told Billy Dobbs that they had a gig if they wanted it and Billy liked the idea and so did J.R. The rest of the week Christina and Aubrey got the word out that there was going to be a formal dance that was a lot cheaper than the prom. Most kids said they would probably attend.

On Saturday night Aubrey took Christina to a movie and dinner in Macon at Westgate theatre and the Quail's Nest Buffet. They went to see a movie called 'ROCKY' and it was great. On the way home Aubrey asked Christina if she wanted to be alone for a little while out in the country and she said that would be nice. They got to the parking spot off Chicken Road at about 10:00 and sat talking for a while. At about 8:45 p.m. "Quick" Jenkins got a phone call and seemed excited by the call. He told Zack to come go with him. When Zack asked why he told him that he and some friends were going on a little "coon" hunt. When Zack asked what that had to do with him, "Quick" said, "That Durrell boy that whipped your ass is dating a little "coon" and we are going to put the fear of God into them and let them know that some people don't approve of mixing the races. I figured you might enjoy a little payback and might want to rough him up a little bit. You sure as hell owe him a good ass whipping." "What are y'all planning on doing—I mean how and where are y'all planning on catching him" asked Zack. "Quick" Jenkins answered, "One of the guys found out where his parking spot is, and we are going to pay him a little visit. Lord help that boy if we catch him in the act of fornicating with a black girl. So, let's go; get in the truck." Zack did not want any part of this, but he knew that if he didn't go, they may hurt his old nemesis, or they might get hurt if Aubrey gets ahold of them. He knew he had to find a way to warn Aubrey but how could he prevent this when the plan was already in action. He told "Quick" he had to use the bathroom and he would be right out. He still had J.R. Durrell's phone number, so he made a quick call and Eli Durrell answered the phone. Zack told Eli, "Mr. Durrell, I need to speak with J.R. if you don't mind sir." "He ain't here son, is something wrong? You seem a little upset," said Eli. Zack told Eli what was going on and told him he had to go that he would be there to protect Aubrey and his girlfriend as much as he could, but he sure could use some help. Eli told him he would be there if he could find out where Aubrey liked to take his dates. He immediately grabbed his gun and went to get Wyll Durrell. At Wyll's house they called Susan Dillon's house to see if J.R. was there. It was now about 9:45 and J.R. and Susan had just got home from their date and had stopped by the house before heading to the far end of the farm for a little privacy. It was a stroke of luck that the call came before they left the house, or maybe it was divine intervention. When J.R. got on the phone with his dad he told them what they wanted to know—that Aubrey liked to park off Chicken Road at the little dirt road near the crossroads and Eli told him to meet him there as soon as he could. J.R. told him that he was on his way. He told Susan he had to go and that he would see her and explain it all later. There were five guys besides Zack ready to deal with Aubrey's interracial relationship. They decided to park their trucks on either entrance to the dirt road so they would see Aubrey come in no matter which direction he chose. Zack saw Aubrey's 1967 Chevy Impala pull slowly into the beanfield and shut off his lights. "Quick" Jenkins gave him about five minutes to settle in and get comfortable before making his move. He pulled in behind Aubrey and flashed his headlights to let the others know they had him in their sights. Aubrey cranked his car and was about to leave when the other truck came over the hill and blocked him in. Christina said, "What is going on Babe?"

"I don't know" said Aubrey, "but you stay in the car okay." Aubrey got out to see what was happening and was greeted by three grown men who told him that it was time to pay a price for mixing with blacks. Aubrey asked, "Who are y'all and what do y'all want with me?" "You can consider us the committee on white purity" said the biggest of the bunch. "I think you might know these guys" said the leader of the group. Aubrey turned around to find Zack and "Quick" walking up behind them. "Quick" looked in Aubrey's car and said "Look what we have here. Dang boys, she is dang near white and ain't a bad looking little coon girl." Aubrey told him to leave her alone and tried to move that way, but three guys grabbed him and held him back and it took all three of them to hold him. "Quick" Jenkins and the fifth guy forced Christina out of the car and told her to watch what happens to a white guy who forgets he is white. It took all three of them to subdue Aubrey who was more worried about Christina than himself. "Quick" stepped over to where Aubrey was being held and pulled a club from under his coat. He called Zack over and handed him the club and said, "I want you to do the honors boy since you owe him some payback." Zack took the club and thought about all the hatred he once had for Aubrey Durrell and how he would have relished this opportunity just three months ago. But now he knew the problem had been with him and not Aubrey and that this was a good kid who didn't deserve this. So, he drew back the club and took a mighty swing which landed in the chest of Curtis Chatfield who was holding Aubrey by the right arm. Curtis went down immediately, and Aubrey broke free and went straight for "Quick" who braced himself for the fight. The other two men had grabbed Zack and were punching him and cursing him out the other man who had been watching Christina started helping "Quick" with Aubrey. At about this time, J.R. came running over the hill and saw what was going on and immediately jumped into the fray to help Aubrey. He was followed by Wyll and Eli Durrell and Daniel Dudley who they had stopped to pick up on the way. When Wyll saw two grown men trying to hurt his son, he lost his religion for a few minutes and attacked "Quick" Jenkins with a fury few had ever seen from him. He was beating him senseless to the point where Aubrey had to pull him off for fear that he was going to kill him. Daniel Dudley grabbed the other man who had been harassing Christina and was beating him badly. Eli and J.R. went to help Zack and when J.R, saw who one of the ringleaders was he knew immediately what the deal was. "Harley Dillon," said J.R. as he pulled him away from Zack, "what are you doing here?" "Don't you worry about it boy" answered Harley. When he said that J.R. told him, "That's the last time I am gonna hear you call me boy. You are about to find out how much of a boy I am." The two of them were about to square off when the blue lights came over the hill. Eli had told his wife to call the police and tell them where to go and they got there just in the nick of time before someone got seriously hurt or worse. J.R. managed to get a good punch in on Harley before the cops came and cuffed him and took them away, as he was being led away, "Quick' Jenkins made threatening remarks to Zack about what happens to traitors who turn on their family members and how he would get him good when he got home from jail. Zack just stood and endured the threats knowing full well that he could not stay at home after tonight. Once his mom found out, she would be on "Quick's" side, he was sure. Aubrey thanked Zack for his help telling him, "You saved my life tonight and Christina's." When things had settled down and it was just Aubrey, Wyll, Christina, and Daniel there, Daniel said to Aubrey, "Son I don't mind saying this in front of your daddy—you had my daughter in a bean field for what purposes? She could have been killed tonight by those racist rednecks because you brought her out here to do whatever you intended to do. I don't think she will be allowed to see you anymore." Christina started to cry and beg her dad to reconsider saying, "All we were doing was talking Daddy. Please don't blame Aubrey for what happened." Daniel Dudley replied, "My mind is made up Christina, and someday you will understand this part of the world ain't ready for whites and blacks to be together. So, no I have spoken and that is that." When they left the field, Daniel would not even let Aubrey take her home instead he made her ride with him and Wyll. She cried all the way home and so did Aubrey. He was heartbroken and didn't know what else to do but pray.

When he got home, his mother Pattie was waiting at the door and hugged him and asked what in world had happened. Aubrey explained the situation to her, and she told him that she was sorry, and she wished she could take his hurt away, but they prayed together, and Aubrey tried to get some sleep. He wondered for the first time how they knew where he would be and the only answer he could come up with was Chelsey. He decided to call her tomorrow and find out once and for all.

J.R. knew who was responsible and he could not wait until tomorrow. He told his dad he had to see someone and would be home before midnight and got in his car and left headed back to Susan's house. When he got there, she had already heard what had happened and she knew that there was no use in lying to J.R. She just hoped he could forgive her because she loved him very much. But forgiveness was not in the cards for Susan as J.R. met her outside her house and told her that they were through. She started to cry and beg him to understand her position. She told him she had done it for Chelsey and that she only meant to scare Aubrey a little bit. J.R. told her that their idea of scaring someone was to gang up on them and beat the hell out of them for what—being in love with the wrong person according to her and them. He told her that he never wanted to see or hear from her again and that she should probably be in jail herself. Her dad came out and said "What is going on out here. J.R. why are you yelling at my daughter?" J.R. responded, "I will let her tell you Mr. Dillon. I won't be around here anymore. Susan, have a nice life." He cried all the way home and prayed also. Why did life have to be so evil and complicated? Why couldn't people love whomever they chose to love without anyone interfering with them? Then he thought what if I hadn't been at Susan's house when his dad called? The Lord works in mysterious ways. He needed to tell Aubrey how this whole thing went down so he stopped by his house before going home. Aubrey got out of bed and went outside to see J.R. When he was told about Susan, he told J.R. that he was sorry this involved him and Susan and he didn't expect him to break up with her just because of this, but J.R. told him it was over between the two of them and that he would always choose family and especially his brother over some girl. Aubrey told him he loved him and J.R. said he loved Aubrey too and they parted ways.

Christina was having a hard time explaining why she was out in the bean field with any boy, but her mom tried to explain to her that her dad loved her so much and didn't want to accept the fact that his little girl was growing up. She said she had never seen fear in Daniel's eyes like she had tonight when Wyll Durrell showed up at their door. She promised her that her dad would eventually calm down and things would get better. As her mother hugged her, Christina cried and said, "Mama I love Aubrey and I don't care who likes it and he loves me too. I swear to you with God as my witness, we were just talking out there, Mama. Aubrey likes to go there because it is so peaceful. You do trust me don't you Mama?" "Yes, baby I do trust you, but you have to understand how it looks to other people and especially to a dad' said Priscilla Dudley to her only daughter. She told her to pray over it and God would work it all out. Christina would cry herself to sleep.

CHAPTER FORTY-THREE

When Zack got home his mom was passed out on the couch, so he decided to wait until the morning to break the news to her. He didn't know yet how the gang had found out about Aubrey's parking spot, but he hoped it was not Chelsey who had told them. He decided to call her to find out and to see how she was doing. Her brother answered the phone and Zack told him who he was, Jerry Potter told him he did not want him calling anymore. Before he could hang up, Zack said, "I just want to say I am sorry for being a jerk." Jerry did not say anything for a minute but at least he did not hang up the phone, "I was screwed up, but I am okay now and I just wanted to see how she is doing," said Zack. Jerry told him that if he let him speak to Chelsey, he had better not upset her, or he would have to deal with him. Zack was not really worried about Jerry Potter doing any harm to him, but he respectfully said "Yessir, I understand." When Zack heard Chelsey's sweet voice on the line, he couldn't help but feel sad for what he had lost because of being the town bad ass. Zack asked how she had been, and she said it had been rough, but she thought she would make it. Zack told her what had happened, and she was upset when she heard the news. She said that she did not wish any harm to Aubrey or the girl, and she asked him how he got involved and how he knew where they would be. Zack told her about "Quick" and how he came to be involved and how he had tipped the Durrells off. He also told her how he was going to have to find somewhere else to live once "Quick" Jenkins got out of jail. Chelsey told him that he had changed and congratulated him on his football scholarship. Finally, Zack had to ask, "Do you think we could try again with our relationship?" To which Chelsey responded, "I think maybe we can but Zack you have to promise never to hit me again. I can't put up with that." Zack promised that it would never happen again and that he was not drinking anymore and had a goal in life to be a college football player and graduate with a degree in teaching and coaching. She agreed to meet him the next afternoon at the Crossroads store as she didn't think it was a good idea for him to come to her house with her dad and brother feeling the way they did about him. He agreed and told her it was nice talking to her again. He hung up and for the first time in years he said a prayer thanking God for a second chance. The next call Chelsy got was from Susan.

Aubrey woke up sore Sunday morning and with no church to go to, he was lost and sad. His dad came into his room to see how he was doing. Aubrey told his dad that he did not know he had that in him to fight like he had last night. Wyll told him that he was not always the nice guy he had become. He told Aubrey that the Lord had changed his life about twenty years ago and had probably saved him from a terrible ending. He said that he and Eli were a rough pair when they were young and would fight anyone at any time. They had been heavy drinkers and never did anything good for anyone. "if it were not for the prayers of your grandma Nellie, I don't think I would be here now" said Wyll. "Then I met your mother and thank God for that. She was a good Christian lady and I fell for her at first site" he added. "When Eli met Beth, she changed his life as well. Then when you and J.R. were born we had a whole new purpose in life; to raise you two up in the way of the Lord," said Wyll. "I guess I have been a bit of a disappointment lately," said Aubrey. "I have gotten us thrown out of our church and caused you to fight. Daddy I am sorry if I have ruined your life," said Aubrey. "No son, you are never a disappointment to me, and you need to know that. What happened in the church was a result of hypocrites who would have done the same thing you did if they had the chance. Christina is a beautiful person and I see what you like about her and as for last night, I do not feel badly about defending my son against a group of racist thugs. I just hope you are responsible enough to not do anything with Christina that might lead to a baby" answered Wyll. "No sir, we were just talking I promise," said Aubrey. "Well, if it comes to that with her or any girl, please be careful son" said Wyll. "I don't think you have anything to worry about since I won't be seeing her anymore," said Aubrey. "if it is meant to be it will be. And in the meantime, prayer will help the situation" said Wyll. He then prayed for God's will to be done and for the Lord to deal with the gang of hoodlums they had encountered last night.

Aubrey reluctantly went to band practice that afternoon but was not in the mood for any smart comments from Terry Lampkin. To his credit, Terry recognized the situation and kept his thoughts to himself. After practice he thought about riding by to check on Christina but thought he might not be welcome, so he resisted the temptation. When he got home, he played catch with Kelsey and got his stuff ready for baseball practice tomorrow. Later that night he called Christina and her mother answered the phone and told him she was glad he called and put Christina on the phone. He asked her if she was alright, and she told him yes but that she missed him already. He told her he loved her so much and could not wait to see her at school and she said she felt the same and that she loved him too. As he hung up the phone, he knew he would see her again because God was merciful, and he could not bear to live without her in his life.

The next morning at school he saw Kenny first thing and found out that Kenny had been at Ashley Stacey's house, or he would have been there to help" whip racist ass." Aubrey said he understood and knew he could count on Kenny for anything he ever needed. In fact, he asked Kenny to help him out with his dad. Kenny said that would be tougher than dealing with the racists since his little girl had been put in harm's way, but he would try. Christina had been in a Beta Club meeting and when she came out, she immediately came over and gave Aubrey a big hug and took hold of his hand and they headed to the cafeteria for breakfast.

The baseball team knew they were in position to do something that had not been done before or at least since integration and that was to win a state championship in three team sports in one school year. They had everyone back from last season, so they felt good about their chances. Their first game was in three days, and they had to get ready quickly. Hitting was always behind pitching so their pitchers would have to carry them for a while until the bats heated up. During the school day, Aubrey and Christina kept promoting the Spring Formal and by the end of the week, they had signed up twelve paid couples, so things were looking good for the dance. It was being billed as a cheaper alternative to the prom and the kids seemed to be interested in saving money. The only people who seemed to have a problem with it were the kids of the parents who were sponsoring the traditional proms. Ella Pipkin was one of those kids and she was working hard to undermine their efforts. But the Spring Formal had a live band and a good one, so it was hard to compete with that.

The following Monday was the first baseball game versus Eastman in a non-region contest. Empire won a close game with Darcy Williams pitching five innings giving up four hits and two runs and "Hondo" Winston finished the game with two scoreless innings. Empire scored three runs with J.R. leading the attack with a two-run homerun int the fourth inning to provide the winning runs. Aubrey went 1 for 3 with two walks and was on second base when J.R. blasted his shot to dead right field. The Knights would go on to win the Dublin Invitational Tournament and would be undefeated when region play started. They would also breeze through the region schedule losing only once to Gresston so they would enter the state playoffs as the number one seed again. They would win the first three rounds of the state tournament sweeping all three opponents, but in the semi-finals versus Ocilla, they would find themselves down one game to none and losing the second game by a score of 7-2 in the seventh inning. Coach Prentiss Wilson called the team up before their last at bat and told them "If this is their last at bat of the season, be sure to make it one to remember. Men, there is no such thing as a 5-run homer so don't go up there trying to swing for the fences just try to save the next man in the order an at bat and I will be proud of you either way it turns out." This seemed to relax the Knights as there was no pressure to try to win the game and each player just trying to have a quality at bat. Randy Stafford would start things off with a single up the middle and would go first to third on another single to right field by "Bullfrog" Mullins. The number nine hitter was the catcher Ronnie Dobs who hit deep fly ball to left center field to score Randy Stafford from third base. Mullins remained at first base with the top of the order coming up. Lester Beasley would draw a walk bringing up Ashley Stacey who launched a three-run homer making the score 7-6 with one out. Darcy Williams would hit a double to right center field and J.R. was intentionally walked to set up the double play. Aubrey Durrell, hitting 5th in this game, walked to the plate with a chance to win the game with a homerun as Empire was the home team in game two even though the game was played in Ocilla. He took an inside fastball for ball one and dug in expecting to see another fastball. He did get the fastball inside and he took a mighty swing and missed for strike one. The next pitch was a curve ball for strike two and Aubrey was in a protective mode at the plate. He fouled off two straight curve balls, then the pitcher hung a third straight curve ball which Aubrey launched onto the back porch of a housing project unit in deep left field for the win. The greatest comeback victory in Empire Knights history and Aubrey Durrell was the hero again. The win gave them the confidence they needed to win game three by a score of 6-4 and propelled them to the state championship series versus Dahlonega Academy.

It was May 16th when the series started—just six days before the spring formal and things were looking good with 43 couples sign up and paid so the dance was a go. Aubrey was getting more mail each day and life was good with one exception—the girl he loved was still forbidden from seeing him outside of school. He could still talk to her on the phone each night and he anxiously awaited hearing her voice every night. She still said she loved him too, but he was starting to wonder how much longer they could expect to be apart and still in love. He was worried about that. Empire would host the series and Dahlonega came in riding a 15-game winning streak and they were loaded with pitching. In game one, Darcy Williams and Randy Stafford teamed up for a three hitter and gave up only two runs in a 3-2 Knights victory. Ashley Stacey was the hero at the plate in this game hitting a two-run homerun in the fifth inning to break the tie. Aubrey went 1 for 4 with a walk in this game. The Knights were one win away from making history, but Dahlonega would not go quietly winning game two by a score of 6-3. It came down to one game for all the marbles and J.R. and Aubrey would be more than ready. Darcy Williams would start and pitch five innings holding Dahlonega to 4 runs, and he scattered nine hits never letting Dahlonega string more than two hits back-to-back. Howell Emerson closed the game for Empire getting the opponents out in order in the 6th and 7th innings. Empire would explode for ten runs with J.R. going 4 for 5 with two doubles and a homerun and four

RBI. Aubrey would go 3 for 4 with two walks and three stolen bases and would score three runs and have five RBI. The history-making year was complete, and Empire had won three state championships in team sports. No one could think of that ever happening since before integration so as far as the community was concerned, this was a first. With all the starters being sophomores, the future looked bright so long as everyone stayed humble and hungry. Empire would have a target on their back as well. Major league scouts were at this series, and they all wanted to talk with Darcy, Aubrey, and J.R. but Aubrey just wanted to see Christina, so he did not speak with the scouts for very long. When he saw her, he hugged her tightly and did not want to let go until he saw her dad looking at them. He wished he could talk to Mr. Dudley, but the time was not right. For now, he would take what he could get.

CHAPTER FORTY-FOUR

The celebration was becoming routine with a free meal at Nubby' s followed by spending the night at the ballfield, but it never grew old. Aubrey asked Christina to come to Nubby' s and she said she had to ask her dad. To her surprise he said she could go with Aubrey, but she had to come straight home afterwards. She hugged her dad and told him she loved him, and he told her he loved her too and off she went. Aubrey was happier than he had been in a long time, and he even danced around with the championship trophy with Darcy and Ashley for the first time. When he took Christina home, he wanted to go somewhere where they could be alone, but he knew better than to push the issue. Christina however told him she had about thirty minutes to spare if he wanted to ride out in the country. So, off the went to Chicken Road for the first time since that terrible night. They both were somewhat shaken when they rode up the dirt road where it all went down, but Christina grabbed Aubrey and kissed him passionately and everything about that night was soon forgotten. Christina stopped Aubrey at a certain point telling him she did not want to go any further at that time and he respected her wishes even though he wanted her so badly. She wanted him too, but she knew it was not the time or place for it and she was a virgin and did not want to lose her virginity in the back seat of an Impala on a dirt road, but she wanted Aubrey Durrell to be the one when the time came. She loved him even more for respecting her boundaries. He took her home and told her again that he loved her more than he had ever loved anything or anyone including sports. She told him she did not believe that and kissed him goodbye. When she went inside her dad told her to have a seat that he wanted to talk to her.

Daniel Dudley said, "Baby girl, you are my special blessing from God, and I want to make sure nobody ever hurts you. That includes me. So, I have decided that if you and that boy really do love each other, then I guess I should not stand in the way. But you have got to promise me that you will get a college degree and still chase your career dreams. Do I have your word?" "Christina started to cry and told her dad, "I love you more than anyone Daddy and I will always be your little girl. I have never lost sight of my dreams and I promise you that I will graduate from college with a law degree. I am in love with Aubrey, and he loves me too and he is the nicest guy in the world Daddy—just ask Kenny; he will tell you. But he will never replace you Daddy and I love you so much." Christina immediately called Aubrey to give him the good news and just in time for the spring formal too. Priscilla Dudley came in and hugged and kissed Daniel and told him she was proud of him. Daniel told her he could not stand to see his little girl unhappy but if someone ever hurt her, he would go straight to jail for killing them. Priscilla told him that she prayed that it would never come down to that.

The F.F.A. had signed up 67 paid customers for the Spring Formal and attendance at the other proms was only down slightly as some kids chose to attend both dances but Aubrey and Christina were ecstatic over the results for the first year. Christina had to officially ask Aubrey to the dance since he was only a sophomore, so she jokingly made a big deal out of it at break one morning. He told her he would have to think about it and get back to her. She told him he had better hurry up and decide because she had a few more guys to ask if he said no. They both laughed at that, and he said he thought he could fit it into his schedule. It would be a busy day for Aubrey and J.R. who would have to set up for the performance and get dressed and pick up their dates before the dance, then take down everything and take their dates home after the dance so they would not get much rest on that day. J.R. was asked to the dance by Jamie Simpson a senior who was cute and sweet but had never really dated anyone before. The other band members all had dates except Donnie Durrell, a freshman, whose girlfriend was also a freshman. Terry Lampkin and Doug Hall were told they could bring dates from another school, and they chose to do so, bringing girls from Union Hill. Incidentally, the Union Hill prom had been held a week earlier and one of the most handsome couples there had been Chelsey Potter and her date Zack Winborn who was now living at Coach Tony Rogers' house to keep "Quick" Jenkins away from him.

Christina had been getting bothered lately by a troublemaker named Victor Spivey. He was one of those students who only came to school to start trouble and harass teachers. He was never interested in graduating or doing anything productive for Empire High School and lately he had taken aim at Christina's relationship with a white boy. He would see her in the halls and say things like "Hey baby why don't you come let me show what a real man can do? That little 'Cracker' boyfriend can't satisfy a beautiful black queen like you." When he was closer to her, he said worse things with more colorful language. She had not said anything to Aubrey or Kenny for that matter because she knew they would confront Victor and may get in trouble. The night of the dance as Aubrey, Christina, J.R. and Jamie were leaving the gym, Victor and his gang of hoodlums were parked beside Aubrey's car looking for trouble. They had not been to the dance but now here they were ready to ruin a good night. As Aubrey went to open the door for Christina, Victor said," Look at those boys, the white boy opens the door for his girl. Baby I will open doors for you too—the door to my bedroom." When he said this his gang started to laugh and fall over each other. Aubrey said, "what did you say?" "You heard me Honky" replied Victor. "You ain't man enough to handle a fine black woman like this" he added. "I know you Victor Spivey and you ain't never been nothing but a troublemaker," said Aubrey. J.R. walked over and asked if there was a problem here and Victor told him to move along if he didn't want trouble. Well, telling J.R. something like that meant that trouble was just around the corner. J.R. said "Buddy if you get out of that car, I will show your smart ass what trouble looks like." Victor told Aubrey that it must be nice to have a cousin fight his battles for him to which Aubrey said, "pal I don't need any help to whip your butt so get out and we can get it on." Christina was crying by this time and begging Aubrey to go but he was standing his ground now and would never back down. Victor got out of his car along with three other guys each ready for action. Soon Aubrey and J.R. were surrounded and things were looking bad but about that time the rest of the band came out and saw what was going on and rushed over to help. Billy Dobbs, who was a big strong boy, came over and announced that he was ready for action for whoever wanted some and immediately got rushed by two of the hoodlums. Billy threw one of them across the hood of Aubrey's car and the other one backed up. J.R. attacked one of the other guys who immediately found out what J.R. Durrell was about and that left Aubrey and Victor Spivey face to face. Aubrey told Victor that he remembered him from recreation football, and he has been a wimp then and it looked as if things had not changed much since then. Victor drew back to throw a punch, but Aubrey was much quicker and caught Victor with a left jab and them a right cross that stunned the big kid. Aubrey then took him to the ground and was about to pound him but the guy that Billy Dobbs had thrown over the car now came back and blindsided Aubrey and was about to attack him when out of nowhere came Terry Lampkin and dove onto the hoodlum and started wailing away on him. Doug Hall had to come pull Terry off the guy to keep him from killing him. Meanwhile, Aubrey Durrell was pummeling Victor, but he stopped when he realized that Victor was not fighting back but was crying like a little baby. Finally, Coaches Kelly and Lord and Principal Bass came out and broke up the fight. "Victor Spivey" said Mr. Bass, "you were banned from all school activities three months ago so what in God's name are you doing here?" "I will tell you what he is doing here" said Aubrey, "he is trying to get his butt whipped messing with my girlfriend, and I am about to make his wish come true." Coach Kelly said "I think he understands this, Aubrey. I think you have made your point painfully obvious. If he can clean his drawers out and wipe the tears from his eyes, he might be able to make it home tonight." This comment made everyone laugh except Victor who tried to get up and come after Aubrey again, but Coach Lord grabbed him and told him he better be glad he grabbed him, or Aubrey would finish him off. Principal Bass told Victor that he was suspended along with all his hoodlum buddies who were still in school and the two who were not in school would be getting a visit from the local police. As he got in his car to leave, Victor told Aubrey that this was not over to which Aubrey replied, "I hope not you wimp. I got some more of this butt whipping for you punk."

When they drove off, Principal Bass asked Aubrey what had happened and when he told him he said he would have to write it up and he was glad it did not happen before everyone left or else it could be the end of the Spring Formal with what would be perceived as a racial fight. Aubrey told him it was not about race but about Victor insulting his girlfriend. Mr. Bass told him he understood that, but the community would see it as something different if they heard about it. Afterwards, Aubrey looked at Terry Lampkin and said "Thanks Terry. I don't know where that came from, but it was good to see it." "I don't know where it came from either" said Terry, "I just couldn't stand by and watch my friend get double-teamed and you and Christina did not deserve to be talked to like that. Christina, I am sorry for being a jerk to you for the last few weeks. I think you are a very classy person." "Thank you, Terry" said Christina and she gave him a big hug. Aubrey could not help but think that she had won another person over with her charm and personality.

When Christina got into the car with Aubrey, she said that she did not think this kind of thing would ever end. Aubrey told her that it was just a few stupid racists in Empire and Union Hill and that it would all be alright in the end. "Yes, but I have had to watch you fight for your life twice and it scares me because there may not always be someone to come help you out and that scares me baby," said Christina. "I know, but I will always fight for you, and I won't care how many guys I have to fight," said Aubrey. Christina threw her arms around him and hugged and kissed him and told him she had a little time before she had to be home if he wanted to be alone for a while. Aubrey said that would be nice and he headed for Chicken Road. That night she decided to go all the way with the boy she loved.

CHAPTER FORTY-FIVE

When Aubrey got home, he thanked God for bringing Christina into his life and asked for protection for her over all racists white and black. The next day at band practice they played better than they ever had, and everyone enjoy being around each other for the first time in a while. J.R. summed it up by saying "Well, fellows we have a story to tell when we get older—the night Terry turned into a bad ass." "That sounds like the title of a good country song" said Billy as he started to sing it and play a tune on his guitar. They all laughed, and Billy said, "Any band that fights together, stays together." They even added a couple more songs by Bob Seger and the Eagles.

Aubrey took stock of his sophomore year just as he did the previous year and he felt considerably better this time around. He had a lot to be thankful for with three state championship rings and the most beautiful girl in the school as his girlfriend, and the recruitment letters were coming in by the bushel. He was still reasonably healthy considering he had played three sports that could take a toll on anyone's body. He would get some much-needed rest now for a few days then he would pull the plow; load watermelons; and go to band practice. Before too long it would be time to start up again and try to defend their titles. Aubrey was one of only six athletes to win rings in three state championships in one school year. The others were J.R., Darcy Williams, Ashley Stacey, Lester Beasley, and Johnny "Hondo" Winston. To Aubrey they were just as big a part of these championships as he was, but most people would tell you that without Aubrey Durrell, Empire would not have won in football or baseball at least. Whether he liked it or not, he was bringing much attention to his small little town.

He never felt comfortable being the center of attention so he would not be comfortable doing interviews with newspapers across the state and certainly not when a TV station from Macon wanted to do a story on 'The Great Aubrey Durrell'. Channel 15 WMSB called and wanted to feature Aubrey for a story on how he prepared for each school year. They had heard about him pulling a plow and thought it would make a great human-interest story. Aubrey told his dad that he did not want to do this because it made it look like the team was not important without him and he did not want that to happen. His dad told him to talk to Coach Kelly about it and see what he said. The next week he went to see Coach Kelly who told him that he would call a team meeting and let the team vote on whether he should do it or not and that if Aubrey wanted to do so he could address the team. The last week of school a meeting was called for all male athletes in the school and Coach Kelly told them what was going on then, he asked Aubrey to speak to them. Aubrey said, "Fellows we have known each other since we were pups and y'all know me and what I am about—BIG TEAM / little me. I don't want anything to ever change the relationship I have enjoyed with y'all since day one so it won't hurt my feelings at all if y'all vote no on this, I will only do it under a couple of conditions; 1) the vote has to be unanimous and 2) the TV station has to agree to mention the other five guys who won three rings this year." Coach Kelly then told them that when a college coach comes to look at one player, he will see them all and any attention that could be brought to Empire High School would eventually benefit then all. The team then voted unanimously for Aubrey to do the interview. Aubrey also wanted Christina to be in the story with him and the station agreed with all Aubrey's demands. It was to be done in early June when the garden would be in full glory and the plow would need to be pulled.

The reporter started at the city limits sign coming into Empire from Cochran and proceeded to give a brief history of Empire and their past athletic glory including Frazier High School and the great "Sugar Bear" Watson. He then proceeded to show highlights from Empire's three championships from the past year and pointed out the common denominator in all these championships was Aubrey Durrell. He then switched to an interview with Coach Kelly who sang Aubrey's praises on leadership as well as talent. From there the interview switched to shots of Aubrey pulling a plow and commenting on how it was responsible for his attitude of never give up and working past the point of pain. He also talked about how he and his cousins J.R. and Donnie Durrell and Stevie Wilbur loaded watermelons all summer every summer and how J.R. was a big part of winning those championships along with the other guys who had three rings. Aubrey tried to bring the names of the other guys into the story, but the reporter did not seem too interested in doing that. When Aubrey introduced Christina to the reporter however, he seemed to perk up. The reporter was a black man and he seemed thrilled by the fact that the most well-known athlete in Middle Georgia had a black girlfriend. And a beauty queen at that. In fact, he was convinced that the two of them made up the most beautiful couple he had ever seen. He was not gay, but he had been awestruck by Aubrey's handsome features and knew that he probably enjoyed great success with the girls, but he never suspected that this beautiful young black girl would show up before his camera. He had his story, and it was not so much about athletics as it was this beautiful interracial couple sitting before him. He also interviewed Christina individually about Aubrey and got the quotes he needed about her being in love with him. The reporter decided to interview some of Aubrey's teammates about Aubrey's athletic skills and he was especially interested in what they thought about his relationship with Christina. He spoke with J.R. first who said that Aubrey had always been the fastest player on the field or court and that was because he worked so hard to be great. When asked about Christina, he said he liked her a lot and that he thought they made a perfect couple. He then interviewed Kenny Dudley who told him that Aubrey had been his best friend since first grade and that he was an awesome athlete and a great teammate. He also said he was happy when his sister started dating his best friend. Darcy Williams echoed the same saying that he admired Aubrey for his athletic ability, and he had always thought Christina was a nice girl. Lester Beasley was a little less glowing in his assessment of the relationship saying he did not care to comment on it since it had nothing to do with the team and how they played the games. Ashley Stacey said it was no big deal and that he liked them both. It was obvious to those who knew the situation that Lester was a little bit perturbed over the fact that he had liked Christina and maybe felt that Aubrey had stolen her from him. He interviewed the last of the six three-time champions Johnny "Hondo" Winston and was told that Aubrey was a cool dude and Christina was cool too and that they planned on winning three more championships next year.

The interview aired at the end of June and was billed as "LOVE CONQUERS ALL". The reporter stated in the lead in that "despite some who exhibited racial hatred toward an athletic superstar, Aubrey Durrell did not let it deter him from professing his love for the girl of his dreams, a young African American beauty named Christina Dudley, herself a great athlete and an "A" student. The story focused almost entirely on their relationship and not much about the team or athletics. When Aubrey saw it, he knew it would not be good for him or Christina. Now all racists from Middle Georgia would be up in arms. He just hoped his teammates would not blame him for this terrible job of reporting.

One of those who saw the story was "Hot Rod" Hickey who had been so busy with the Hall of Fame that he had not heard any talk of these kids dating. He really was jealous of this kid who had it all including the most beautiful black girl he had ever seen. He wished Aubrey Durrell had never been born and he made up his mind to get to Christina Dudley somehow if it was the last thing, he did. At the barber shop one Saturday morning, the patrons were discussing the story with varying opinions about the relationship with some saying they did not support interracial dating and other saying it did not really matter to them and they saw it as changing times in America. One old man said that he hoped it did not cause a reaction from racists around Empire. Rod Hickey overheard the conversation and commented that their 'Golden Boy' wasn't quite as popular now that he was dating the best-looking black girl in the state. They told him that his comments were worthless since he hated Aubrey Durrell from the start. "I am just saying that we will see if a few TD runs, or dunks, or homeruns will make up for all this recent information with the black and white communities," said "Hot Rod".

There were editorials written in the Macon newspaper; the Union Hill Journal; and the Eastman Times among a few others that supported the story yet more who criticized the relationship and the TV reporter who reported it. Aubrey's dad had gotten a few phone calls spewing racist thoughts and one or two that threatened violence. Christina had told Aubrey that her dad had seen strange men riding slowly by their house and a couple of suspicious looking pickup trucks had stopped in front of the house. She said her dad had not slept much since all this had broken and that he kept his gun by his side. Christina was scared and Aubrey was a little worried about it too. He also noticed that some of the southern colleges stopped writing him letters. He did not know if it had anything to do with the story or not, but it sure seemed like a strange coincidence. Some of the local adults who had not previously known about the two kids dating, started making comments around town and telling their kids not to associate with Aubrey anymore. Meanwhile, he also had to worry about the fallout with his teammates. He went to see Coach Kelly who told him that this too will pass and that he thought the team would be okay since they had voted for the story to be done. Aubrey asked him if he thought the colleges had heard about the story and were holding it against him. Coach Kelly said he wanted to be completely honest with him and that while he had not heard anything official, a couple of his college contacts did tell him they were having second thoughts about dealing with the trouble it would cause them. Aubrey said they were gutless racists and Coach Kelly agreed but that it was all about boosters and their money at that level and just give it time and it will pass. Aubrey left Coach Kelly's office not too sure that it would pass without trouble for his family and the Dudleys. He did not understand why two kids in love had to endure such terrible things just because certain people did not approve of their choice of who they dated. He did not really choose Christina; you can't really choose who you fall in love with—it just happens. He felt that God had brought them together and race never was an issue with either of them. All he knew to do was pray about it and he did enough of that in the coming days and weeks.

R. C. Gold was scheduled to play a big 4th of July celebration in Warner Robins at the International City Stadium and sponsored by the U.S. Air Force Base. The organizers had told Billy Dobbs that they could still play but they should not introduce the band members or have printed materials listing the band members' names so hopefully they could prevent any reaction from the concert goers who might not approve of the relationship. They were told that was the only way they could play, and it was a take-it-or-leave it deal. They would also be rescheduled to play at 3 P.M. instead of the 7 P.M. time slot they had originally been promised. That way the rowdies might not be in the crowd yet. Billy presented this deal to the band and Aubrey apologized to them for causing the trouble. Billy said he did not blame Aubrey because there are racists out there. Terry Lampkin said "I don't care when we play, we are going to rock out and the people who are there will see a great show. And as far as getting my name called out, hell y'all know that don't matter to me." J.R. said "I don't know how we can play for people who think like that, so I say we tell them to shove it up their asses if they want to change our time slot. As for introducing the band, I will introduce myself as Buck Naked if they screw with me." Doug Hall said that "after the shit we have gone through in less than a year together, I don't mind a little trouble, so I say we play at 3 P.M. but introduce the band at the end of the show. What are they gonna do to us after we rock the house, tell us we can't play there anymore?" J.R. said "Hell yeah Doug, I like the way you think." So, Billy accepted the deal verbally but never signed any contract since the band was planning a 'screw you moment' at the end of the show. Aubrey could not help but think they would be better off without him in the band but he thanked them for their friendship and loyalty at which point Doug said, "damn son we ain't doing this for you, this is for sweet little Christina." The others laughed at that and so did Aubrey and then they started playing a killer set of music. They were getting better each time and they knew it.

The day of the concert in Warner Robins the boys went up early and started setting up their equipment and doing a sound check. They had never played through speakers as huge as these were, so it took some getting used to, but they soon worked out all the kinks and were ready to go. When 3 o'clock arrived, they took the stage and proceeded to get the crowd fired up with some good old-fashioned rock and roll and country gold. There were probably around 500 folks already there so it was a good crowd, but it would get bigger as the night went on. Finally, right before the last song, J.R. stepped to the microphone and said "folks we are the R.C. Gold Band from Empire, Georgia and I would like to introduce our members for y'all. On rhythm and lead guitar and singing background vocals is Billy Dobbs; and on bass guitar is Terry

Lampkin; on drums and background vocals is the wild man, Doug Hall; on piano and backing vocals is my little brother Donnie Durrell, on rhythm and lead guitar and backing vocals in my cousin and the fastest running back in Georgia Aubrey Durrell." There did not seem to be any boos or trouble in the stands when Aubrey was introduced. J.R. continued, "and my name is J.R. Durrell, and we are going to leave y'all with one of our favorites—'T FOR TEXAS' by the great Lynyrd Skynyrd. When they finished playing, the concert organizer came up to Billy and said, "You gave me your word you liar." Billy stepped up and was about to say something but J.R. intervened and told the man, "Sir with all due respect, I decided to introduce the band not Billy so if you are mad at anyone it needs to be me." The concert organizer told J.R. that he hoped he enjoyed his moment because they would not be paid for their performance (they had been promised $300). "Well, that being the case," said J.R., "I would like to tell you that it has been a pleasure playing for these good people and we will be mingling with them for a while and expressing our disappointment at having to play for free. And you see that TV camera over there? it has been here since we took the stage, and I am sure they would like a story on how you screwed the subject of their recent top story because you were a racist S.O.B." "Kid, I don't know who you think you are trying to strong arm, but you are barking up the wrong tree and I don't scare easily" answered the man. J.R. said, "Sir, as I said before, with all due respect, I am not attempting to threaten you but if you screw us out of our money, we will do what we have to do to let the people know what a first class jerk you are. Now, if you do not care about that, then we will end this conversation and go our separate ways". They had not gotten thirty feet away when he said "alright, alright, you can get your money, but don't ever think about playing this concert again" yelled the man. "Man, you would be lucky to get us next year anyway," said Terry Lampkin. They received a check for $300 which they voted to split six ways giving each man $50, but Aubrey told J.R. that he could have part of his for his leadership in standing up to that jerk. The other guys told Aubrey that they all wanted to chip in and give some of their money to J.R., so they all gave $5 of their share to him for his bravery and calmness in the thick of things. They went home shortly afterwards and went to see their girlfriends. Aubrey knew J.R. would stand up for him because he always had. Even though Aubrey could fight his own battles, it was almost as if J.R. protected him from having to do it sort of like a guardian angel. That is why recruiting from colleges had made Aubrey a little sad because he knew there was a good possibility that he and his cousin would be split up for the first time since first grade and Aubrey did not like it then and he would not like it now.

CHAPTER FORTY-SIX

When August rolled around, it was back to football practice and as usual Aubrey had been working hard in the watermelon fields and pulling his plow, so he was in great physical condition. So was J.R. and the rest of the team looked good too as they prepared for their third campaign but their first as defending state champions. Nothing was said about the TV story, so Aubrey felt that he was in the clear. That would change when they went to Rock Eagle for camp. On the second day there during a scrimmage Lester Beasley was having a bad day and the coaches were on him hard about his blocking. On one play Coach Kelly got on him bad and Aubrey tried to encourage him by patting him on the back and saying, "Come on 82 you are the best blocking end in Georgia. Let's pick it up man." To which Lester responded by saying, "Get your hands off me Mr. TV star. I don't need your bullshit to make me play better." Aubrey was shocked to hear his old friend talk like that, but he just chalked it up to something bothering him outside of the team and ignored it. Josh Beasley immediately went to his twin brother and told him to calm down, but Lester was not hearing it. He went into a tirade over how Aubrey was the perfect player and never did anything wrong. Even when he got suspended last year the coaches and everyone took up for the 'Golden Boy'. "You know there are others on this team who are just as important you Aubrey, and your little TV special forgot to mention any of the rest of us who got three rings last year" yelled Lester as Josh was trying to pull him off the field. Coach Kelly blew his whistle and called the team up and said, "I suspected that we would have to cross this bridge eventually so let's get it out in the open. Aubrey, do you want to address this situation?" Aubrey stood up and started to speak but he could not get the words out before he started to cry. Finally, he summoned the strength to say, "Fellows, I am sorry about the TV story and if I had known it would be like that, I never would have agreed to it. It has caused problems that y'all do not even know about. I can't undo it, but I can promise each of you that it will not ever happen again with my approval. I just want us to be close like we always have been and win another championship together. Empire means everything to me and if I don't have the friendships that I grew up with then I don't want to be here." Darcy Williams spoke next and said, "I was a little hurt by the story, but I just chalked it up to being the way the world works. And Coach Kelly told us that when the scouts come watch one of us, they will see us all, so I just put it out of my mind and went about my business." Stevie Wilbur said, "if I didn't know my cousin Aubrey so well it would have bothered me too, but I do know him well and he is a good person, and I don't ever want to have to play without him on my side." Kenny Dudley spoke next and said, "Y'all know that me and Aubrey been boys since first grade and we always will be, also my sister Christina dates him so that makes it even better. Lester, I know what some of this is about. You liked Christina first and maybe you feel like Aubrey slipped in and beat your time, but I can tell you for fact that Christina has liked Aubrey for a while now and there is no telling about love and who will end up with who, so brother all I can say about that is get over it dude." At that Lester got up and walked away and Josh told everyone to let him have his space. Finally, J.R. stood up and said, "As for that crappy little TV story, we all voted for Aubrey to do it so let's don't' forget that important piece of information. And as for Lester and Aubrey, well that is just something they will have to work out in due time. But as for this football team, we cannot ever let anything get in the way of our commitment and desire to succeed. Winning was fun last year, wasn't it? So, what would be more fun than winning it all two years in a row or for that matter, three in a row. I and all of you know that Aubrey is a team player and if you doubt that, you need to leave right now. And on top of that, he is the best athlete to ever come along these parts, so I don't care what anyone outside this team says, I will not play without you 15. Just don't do anymore TV news stories, okay?" Coach Kelly ordered the team to hit the showers and asked Aubrey if he thought he was okay with Lester and Aubrey said that it was up to Lester, but he thought everything would be okay.

After supper they had a team meeting and then it was lights out at 10 p.m. Aubrey lay in his bunk thinking about last season and how he had been motivated by the fumble the previous year and wondering what his motivation for this season could be other than loving to win. Then it hit him; he hated losing at anything and he always had; so, he decided that his hatred for losing was greater than his desire for winning. He had seen that somewhere before but could not remember where, but that became his adopted slogan—'HATE TO LOSE MORE THAN YOU LOVE TO WIN'. He wrote this on everything he had including his locker at school and in the field house. Before he fell asleep, he prayed for Lester to ease up and be his friend again.

The coaches sent a subtle message the next day when they split playing time between Lester and freshman Daryl Winston, brother of "Hondo" Winston. Daryl would never be able to take Lester's job unless Lester gave it away. Lester did a little bit better blocking, but it was still not up to his usual standards. Something had to be done. It was the last scrimmage before heading home when they had a breakthrough. On a quick-pitch left, Daryl Winston missed his block and Bobby Parton flew into the backfield and hit Aubrey for a 5-yard loss. When the coaches got onto Daryl for missing the block, he hung his head which pissed Aubrey off and he let Daryl know about it telling him," Man, you got to grow up and quit hanging your head or you ain't never gonna play much around here. They lined up to run the same play again with the same result. Aubrey looked over at Lester who seemed bothered by what he was seeing. But Aubrey did not say anything, and they ran the same play again with the same results. The coaches were going crazy, and the freshman seemed to be getting worse on every play. When they entered the huddle next time to call the same play again, Lester Beasley checked himself in and told Daryl Winston to take a break and watch how this play is supposed to be blocked. This time when Aubrey caught the pitch, he could easily hit the corner because Bobby Parton was laying on the ground with Lester Beasley on top of him. Aubrey took it all the way for a TD, and everyone was congratulating Lester on his pancake block of Bobby Parton; even Bobby told him "Good job". When Aubrey got back to the huddle, he told Lester "Thanks man I was about to get killed on that dang play." Kenny Dudley slapped Lester on his backside and said, "Welcome back my brother." Josh Beasley looked at his brother and asked, "you okay now Les?" To which Lester replied, "Yeah bro, let's do this." Left tackle Randy Stafford who never did say much spoke up saying, "it's about damn time, hell all this over a girl who is gonna end up looking like Kenny before it is over with." Everyone in the huddle cracked up laughing and a timeout had to be taken but Coach Kelly did not mind. He had his team back and ready to play.

CHAPTER FORTY-SEVEN

They returned home on Friday late so Aubrey could not see Christina until the next day and they had planned a double date with Kenny and Deidre Randall to go to Macon to see a movie and get something to eat. They would pick Aubrey up at his house at 5 p.m. They ate at THE QUAIL'S NEST BUFFET, which was a favorite of Aubrey's. As they were sitting down to enjoy their meal an elderly white couple sat near them and started a conversation asking them where they were from and how old they were. Finally, the elder lady said to them, "I think it is great that black kids and white kids get along and enjoy one another's company. Y'all are a good-looking group of kids." "Thank you maam," said Kenny. Around that time the unofficial fan club of Aubrey and Christina came in the restaurant—the group of guys from Roberta who had flirted with Christina at the basketball game last year. When they saw Aubrey and Christina, the came running over to say hello. They also wanted to know if Empire was going to win another championship this season. Aubrey told them he thought they had a better team this season than last year. They also could not take their eyes off Christina and asked her if she was going to win another championship and if she was going to play basketball in college. As she told them what she thought, Aubrey could not help but think about Christina going off to college next year. She was a senior and certainly would have her choice of schools to go to just off academics alone. When the group left the elder lady commented that she thought they looked familiar, but she could not place them until those boys started talking about sports. "Y'all are that couple that was on the news aren't y'all?" "Yes maam," said Christina. "Well, I just want to tell y'all that y'all make a beautiful couple regardless of race," said the lady. "Thank you very much," said a blushing Aubrey. "And y'all are a beautiful couple too," the lady said to Deidra and Kenny. "Thank you maam," said Kenny. The elderly couple got up to leave and said goodbye to the kids. When the kids went to pay their bill, the cashier told them it had already been paid by the elderly lady who had befriended them. "Oh, how sweet," said Deidre. They started talking about why everyone could not be that open-minded. They then went to see 'THE SPY WHO LOVED ME'. When they got to Westgate Theater, they got some strange looks from white and black folks, but no one said anything. A couple of folks pointed at them as if they recognized them from the TV story. When they took their seats in the theater, a white couple got up and moved away mumbling something about folks need to know what race they were. But that was the only incident of the night, and they went home feeling good about things. When they got home, Kenny and Deidre left Christina at Aubrey's house where they visited with Wyll, Pattie, Kelsey, and Paula. Paula really took to Christina telling her how pretty she was. Kelsey also seemed mesmerized by Christina's beauty. Wyll and Pattie were very cordial as well. After about thirty minutes of visiting, Aubrey announced that it was time to get Christina home, but there would be a stop off Chicken Road for a little while first.

The next day at band practice Billy Dobbs announced that Billy Allen wanted them to come play his Labor Day bash again but this time he told Billy that it would be $300, and he had agreed to it. He said the people were asking for them to return and play. They all said they would look forward to playing and that it could not possibly be as bad as it turned out last year.

The first game of the season was the Friday before the gig and since they were defending state class B champions, it was hard to find teams willing to play them, so they had to play a couple of larger schools for non-region competition. The first game was versus Fort Valley a Triple A playoff team the previous season. It was a tough contest, but Empire got a two-point victory by a score of 14-12 as Aubrey scored the game-winning TD with 45 seconds left in the game on a 32-yard quick pitch left behind a great block by Lester Beasley. J.R. had three receptions for 59 yards including a big third down and 10 catch on the final drive to give Aubrey a chance to score on the next play. He also punted 5 times for a 44-yard average and keeping Fort Valley pinned deep in their own territory all night long. So, they prepared for a gig coming off what most considered an upset victory feeling good about their chances for the season. Union Hill won their opener also beating Jeffersonville 34-14. Some of the Union Hill players would surely be at Billy's party but the Empire boys determined to leave without incident this year. The crowd was bigger this year no doubt because of R.C. Gold's appearance at the party. They were achieving a reputation as one of the best bands in Middle Georgia and were becoming in demand more every day. The women were wilder as well with most of them drunk and flirting with the band members at the front of the stage. J.R. loved this fact and he played it up with the women and girls who tried to get his attention and Aubrey found it funny that he toyed with their affections just to get them to donate more money in the bucket. They were a bunch of good-looking country boys who could play their tails off so why not play it up. As the show started off, J.R. said, "what's up folks? Y'all ready to rock and roll?" The crowd went wild, so the band launched into their performance with 'BANG A GONG'. They tore up the makeshift stage and the women were hot to trot. When they left the stage, a couple of drunk older ladies came after Aubrey and J.R. and told them what they wanted to do with them. Billy and Doug had a couple of the groupies wrapped up tight and even Terry Lampkin was talking to one of them. J.R. said to Aubrey, "man it sure is tempting to get with a couple of these women ain't it?" Aubrey replied, "I guess so, but this is too close to home, and I would not want to get involved with anyone who is going to tell everyone she knows about it." "You are probably right but it sure would be nice" said J.R. As they were getting something non-alcoholic to drink, Susan Dillon came up to J.R. and said hello. Aubrey would not even look her way as she said hello to him also. "J.R., I wanted to tell you how sorry I am for what I did." J.R. shot back at her, "you need to apologize to Aubrey and Christina. They are the ones who were put in danger. I don't think you have any idea what that bunch of ass holes were planning on doing to them that night. I was really afraid of what almost happened and all because of you." "I know now how dangerous it was but at the time, I was just trying to take up for my best friend and I wasn't thinking straight. I didn't know what kind of stuff Harley was capable of; I just thought he was going to scare them a little bit, that's all," said Susan. "Susan, I can forgive you for what you did, but I can never forget it. I am not scared of too much in this world, but that night haunts me to this day and probably always will. It also almost cost me a chance to be with the girl I love more than anything else in this world so while I will forgive you and pray for you, don't expect me to be cordial to you," said Aubrey. Susan started to cry and told Aubrey she did not blame him, and that Chelsey won't have much to do with her either. She sobbed, "but J.R. I love you dearly and I don't know if I can live without knowing that you don't hate my guts." J.R. answered, "I don't hate you Susan, but I can't respect you after what you did. Maybe in time I will see things differently but not right now." Aubrey told them he was going to give them a little privacy so they could talk, and he went to hang with the Empire boys who had come out to support the band. Kenny was there but her dad had decided that Christina would not be allowed to go based on events that had occurred last year. Aubrey had promised her that he would behave himself and that he would see her tomorrow. Aubrey saw J.R. and Susan holding hands and walking out to the car, and he was happy to see that. He lost track of Billy, Doug, and Terry but assumed they were somewhere with the groupies. He and Donnie would have to hang out with the team and wait for the boys to finish handling whatever business they were handling. As Aubrey was talking to Darcy Williams and Teddy Robertson a couple of young women came up to him and told him how much they enjoyed the show. Aubrey told them thanks and they started flirting with him and hugging him. Suddenly, an older white lady came up and told the girls that they were wasting their time saying, "y'all ain't got a prayer with this one, he likes his women a little bit darker don't you honey?" One of the young ladies asked her what she was talking about, and she said, "he likes black girls—tell them baby, so they won't make fools out of themselves." Aubrey did not know what to say except that he had a girlfriend, and he was not interested in cheating on her. "Is she black?" asked one of the girls. Aubrey answered, "Does it matter?" "Not to me baby as fine as you are," said the other young lady. "I will do both of you if she looks good as you do" she continued. Aubrey told her "Thanks, but no thanks." The young women left disappointed, and Darcy said, "Dang son, I wish I could be you just one night. Dude, you don't know how good you got it." "I gotta get out of here," said Aubrey. As he turned to walk away, he saw some of the Union Hill players coming over. He expected trouble but just the opposite took place. The quarterback, a sophomore named Robert Morrison came up to him and said he enjoyed the show and congratulated him and the other Empire players on their victory over Fort Valley. He told them that he did not get to play varsity last year, but he looked forward to competing against them this season and that maybe they could get a rematch in the state championship game. Aubrey said that would be nice and wished the Union Hill players good luck on their season. They shook hands and parted ways. When they left, Teddy Robertson said, "well that was different. I guess their new coach has had a positive influence on those guys." Darcy added, "There ain't no "Big Mouth Barry" Kennedy or Zack Winborn around either." Kennedy had graduated and started vocational school training to be a diesel mechanic while Zack Winborn was playing football at Murrayville Junior College.

About twenty minutes later the rest of the boys came out of the house smiling big old country smiles and buttoning their shirts. Aubrey went over to them and asked them if they had a good time. Terry Lampkin said he had met someone nice and thought he might take her out on a date. Doug Hall said his two had been nice too, but he was not interested in dating them. Billy Dobbs seconded that thought saying, "Yeah I had a wonderful, giving young lady too, but dating was never discussed. In fact, I don't remember talking much at all." When J.R. came back alone Aubrey asked him what happened with Susan. J.R. said that he may call her later, but he was not sure but at least she had tried to apologize and has seen the error of her ways. Aubrey said he was proud she had showed up and had talked to J.R. The boys gathered up their equipment and headed home. When they counted the money, they had $400 more in the buckets to go with the $300 Billy Allen had paid them. They agreed to take $100 apiece and put $100 in the band account. "What a night," said Billy. "We made $100 each and got laid. It doesn't get much better than that." Aubrey saw a change and he hoped it was still about the music and not what the music could get you.

CHAPTER FORTY-EIGHT

Wyll Durrell wanted to try a new church that next day, so the family packed up and headed to Hawkinsville to a Church of God. They were welcomed with open arms and the preacher talked about Aubrey and how God had blessed him with amazing talent, and he hoped to get out to some games this season. The band did not practice on this day since they had played the night before. Coach Kelly called Aubrey and asked him to come in for a meeting so before he went to see Christina, he stopped by the school to see what the Coach wanted. Coach Kelly simply wanted to know if there had been any incidences at the gig last night that he needed to know about. Aubrey assured him that everything was fine and there had been nothing out of the ordinary taking place. He told Coach Kelly that last year had taught him a valuable lesson and he would never repeat that again. Coach told him that he was glad to hear that and said he had film to watch, and he would see him tomorrow.

He then went to see Christina and spent the afternoon with her and her family except for Kenny who was at Deidra's house. Aubrey watched the Cowboys versus the Giants with Daniel Dudley who was pulling for the Giants while Aubrey was a diehard Cowboys fan. When the Cowboys won, Aubrey had a little fun picking at Daniel, but he did not push it too far.

Since their new church did not have Sunday night services, he was able to spend a little more time with Christina and he asked her if she wanted to go to Nubby' s for supper and she said she thought that would be nice. After Nubby' s there was a trip to Chicken Road for a little private time. Aubrey was so in love with her that he could not stand to be away from her for too long and he cherished every moment they had together, especially since she would be leaving at the end of this school year for college. It made him sad to think about that, so he wanted to make every minute count now.

The next game was a trip to International City Stadium to play Southside Warner Robins, the defending Quad-A state champions from last season. This would be no contest on paper with Southside dressing out over a hundred players and Empire dressing out only forty-one and with most of the starters playing both ways and on special teams. Surely the numbers would catch up to the Knights in this one. Coach Kelly reminded them that games are not played on paper and no matter how many players they had on the sideline they could only play eleven of them at a time. All the pressure would be on Southside. "Imagine having to explain how you got beat by little old Empire," said the coach. "Go out there and have some fun men. You are playing with house money tonight," he added. As they took the field the Knights were loose and ready, and it showed when they took the opening kickoff and Aubrey broke free for an 83-yard TD. Darcy's extra point put Empire up 7-0 early in the game and sent a message to the Quad-A champs that Aubrey Durrell was for real. When Southside got the ball, they drove down to the Empire 7-yard line and had a first and goal when Bobby Parton hit the running back in the backfield causing a fumble that was recovered by "Bullfrog" Mullins at the twelve-yard line. On first down Ashley Stacey would break loose on a 35-yard run and Josh Beasley would run for eight more yards setting up a second and two from the Southside 45-yardline. Darcy Williams would hit Lester Beasley for 26 more yards taking the ball to the 19-yard line. Aubrey would run it in on an inside trap play on the next play and the extra point made the score 14-0 near the end of the 1st quarter. Coach Kelly was coaching in a loose mood as well and called for a surprise onside kick which Donnie Durrell recovered for Empire. The first play was a favorite of Aubrey and Darcy, 'Twins Left / Motion Left Square out'—the same play they had used to beat Union Hill in Sammy Barnhill's last season at the helm of the Barons. Aubrey went in motion feeling that he would be open on the route and he was right. Darcy delivered another perfect pass and Aubrey caught the ball and flew down the sideline for a 47-yard TD reception. The extra point was blocked leaving the score at 20-0 in favor of Empire. Southside would finally score on their last drive of the first half to make the score 20-7 at halftime and causing them to get a cussing out at halftime so loud that the Knights heard it through the wall of the locker room. Empire kids had never heard a team talked to like that before and they hoped they never did. "Men" said Coach Kelly, "I am proud of the way you guys showed up to play this game. I will be proud of you no matter what the outcome is. But I want y'all to understand, that I expect to win this game and if you think the halftime speech was rough, wait till you hear the post-game speech when we beat their tails tonight."

Apparently, the cussing out worked on Southside as they took the second half kickoff and scored on a 7-play drive that covered 85 yards. The extra point cut the Empire advantage to six points at 20-14. Aubrey would have a great game and would score his fourth TD of the game on their next drive on a power play right behind J.R. and Kenny. A two-point conversion attempt would fail leaving the score at 26-14 with a quarter and a half left to play. Southside would unleash a furious attack and would score early in the fourth quarter to bring the score to 26-21. On the ensuing kickoff, Lester Beasley would break free and looked like he was gone for a TD. However, he was run down by a fast Southside player who not only tackled Lester but stripped the ball from him as he was going down. Southside got the ball back and scored the go-ahead TD two minutes later, on a long pass when a speedy division one recruit named Jamie Hiller, got past Stevie Wilbur. With the score at 28-26 and six minutes left to play, the Empire offense went to work. Ashley Stacey would score an apparent game-winning TD, but a holding call brought the play back and cost the Knights ten yards. Two plays later Aubrey would break loose on a 53-yard TD but another phantom holding call would bring that one back. Facing a 3rd and seventeen from their own 37-yard line and time running out, Darcy would have to throw the ball with the defense knowing it. He would try to hit Lester Beasley on a flag route and Lester had his man beat but the defensive back grabbed Lester's jersey hindering him from going for the ball, but no flag was thrown. On 4th down Darcy threw a desperation pass that was intercepted by Southside to kill any chance of a last-second comeback by the Knights. After the game, the Southside players and coaches all told Aubrey that he was a bad dude, and they did not envy the class B teams that would have to deal with him. As they were leaving the field, Aubrey saw the man who had been the concert organizer earlier that summer shaking hands with the referees as they were leaving the field. When the man saw Aubrey looking at him, he smiled a big crap-eating grin and waved at Aubrey. He decided not to inform J.R. about this while they were still in Warner Robins or there would be trouble. Lester was inconsolable in the locker room and Aubrey knew full well how he was feeling. He went over to Lester and told him everything was going to be okay and that he would win a game or two for the Knights before the season was over. He also told him that he knew how he felt and that he could not let that feeling eat him alive, but he could use it as motivation. Lester told him he would be alright eventually but not right now. As Aubrey walked away, Lester said, "Aubrey, thanks man." Aubrey said, "Love you brother and if you need to talk, you know where to find me."

Coach Kelly told the team that he was never prouder to be associated with a group of young men than he was at that time. He also said that Southside knows who really won that game tonight and if they take the same approach into the region schedule, they will earn another ring.

Empire would breeze through first part of their schedule winning by an average of 28 points per game. The fifth game of the season was homecoming versus Roddy and Empire would win easily, more significantly however was that Christina Dudley would become the first black homecoming queen in the history of the school. She would win in a landslide proving how well-liked she was by almost everyone. After the game, at the homecoming dance Aubrey told her how proud he was to be dating the most beautiful and popular girl in the school. She told Aubrey that she was happier than she had ever been in her life, and he was a big part of that. They would dance the night away and fall deeper in love than either of them ever imagined.

Game number six was at Union Hill for first place in the region. Union Hill came into the game undefeated and ranked in the top ten two spots below Empire at number three in the state. You could tell a difference in the attitude of their team since Coach Rogers had taken over. They played good fundamental football and talked a lot less. This game would be a battle with Empire pulling out a six-point win scoring the go-ahead TD halfway through the fourth quarter when Darcy

Williams hit Lester Beasley on a 43-yard TD pass and the defense held on and beat back a furious comeback attempt by the Barons stopping them on the 8-yard line when Stevie Wilbur intercepted a pass in the end zone to kill the comeback attempt. The final score was 26-20 and Aubrey had 145 yards rushing and scored two TD's, but he was happier for Lester who redeemed himself and proved Aubrey correct when he told him he would win a couple of games for them along the way. Ashley Stacey would rush for 90 yards and a TD and J.R. would lead the defense with 12 tackles / 3 sacks /and a fumble recovery. He also punted four times for an average of 47 yards.

All the Knights had to do was win their final four games versus Gresston, Dubois, Chauncey, and Rhine and they would return to the state playoffs as the number one team in the state.

Game number seven would see the inaugural class of inductees to the newly created Empire Athletic Hall of Fame and "Sugar Bear" Watson was back as one of the twenty-six inductees as was "Dixie Dan" McGee the last football coach who had won state championships at Empire, legendary Frazier coach Albert Chambers, and Daniel Dudley, who had been a star defensive end for Frazier High School in the late 1950's and was headed toward a college scholarship until a knee injury his senior year had derailed his plans of going to law school. Instead, he became a correctional officer and now a security guard at Middle Georgia College. He was proud of Christina for wanting to be a lawyer and he was so protective of her because she represented all his hopes and dreams. "Hot Rod" Hickey was on top of the world that night as he had redeemed himself in the eyes of many and had proven once and for all that he had nothing to do with the attempted takedown of Aubrey Durrell as far as anyone could prove. He also came up with a plan to get to Christina Dudley. He asked "Sugar Bear" for financial backing to award a $5000 scholarship to a deserving black student to be awarded by the Hickey Foundation for Racial Equality. Christina would be the recipient and maybe she would be so appreciative she would do anything to show her appreciation.

Empire would win all four games handily and would face the fourth place Chauncey Comets in Round one. Empire had beaten Chauncey by a score of 33-13 earlier in the season but the playoffs are a different animal so all the Knights players and coaches knew this would be a challenge. Aubrey had put together another fine season with over 1400 yards and 26 TD's. during the regular season and he would have a great run in the playoffs. The Knights would handle Chauncey by a score of 34-21 and move on to a second-round matchup with their old nemesis the Warm Springs Demons who had managed to get back to the state playoffs after graduating 12 starters from the year before. Empire would win this one 29-10 as Aubrey would tally 156 yards rushing and 53 yards receiving with a rushing TD and a receiving TD. J.R. would catch two TD passes as Darcy Williams was on that night hitting 13 for 15 for 178 yards passing. Ashley Stacey would gain 95 yards and score one TD. Union Hill was winning as well so a rematch was becoming more possible each week.

Round three was versus Franklin who again was highly ranked at number two right behind Empire. The Knights would win in overtime by a score of 18-12 as Aubrey would score from seven yards out in the second five-minute overtime period to secure the win. Union Hill would defeat Butler to move into the semi-finals versus Ocilla. Empire would face Folkston.

Empire would take care of their opponent by a score of 32-13 with Aubrey going for 198 yards and three TD's. Ashley Stacey would add another 124 yards and a TD. Union Hill would lose to Ocilla but would be back in the hunt for the next few years.

Even though Empire was the number one ranked team in the state, they still had to travel to Ocilla for the title game. The atmosphere was electric when they took the field and Aubrey lived for these types of games. He would respond with a monster game rushing for 214 yards and four TD's one on an 89-yard kickoff return to start the second half. Stevie Wilbur would be the defensive star of the game intercepting three passes and recovering a fumble. Empire completely dominated the game winning 48-10 and bringing home the second championship in football since integration. For the season, Aubrey would have 2,262 yards rushing and score 37 TD's making him the #1 recruit in Georgia as a junior. Still very few letters came from southern schools, but Aubrey was not focusing on that, he just wanted to enjoy high school and his last year with Christina there. It was a long ride home, and they did not get back until close to 3 a.m. but the players still honored their tradition of spending the night at the football stadium and honestly, it never got old.

CHAPTER FORTY-NINE

14-1 was a good record but it was not perfection, so each player made a commitment to try to go 15-0 next season to cap off the seniors' careers the right way. Now it was on to basketball season. Aubrey had only about six months with Christina before she left for college, so he wanted to enjoy every minute of that time. He took her out to nice places to eat in Macon and Warner Robins and bought her things that he knew she wanted but would never ask for. He did not know how he was going to survive without her around. Aubrey had hoped that Florida State University would try to recruit him, but it never materialized, and he was told they were prioritizing defense this year with their scholarships and that they were set pretty well at running back at the time. He was offered a chance to walk on but that seemed almost insulting to Aubrey. He never considered Florida since he was a dedicated "Gator Hater" from an early age since he was raised a Georgia Bulldog fan. The feeling was obviously mutual since they never showed much interest in him anyway. So, unless something changed, he and Christina would be miles apart when he went off to college. He chose not to think about that at that moment.

The R.C. Gold Band was getting well known and were asked to play a spring formal at Mercer University for a fraternity—Lambda Chi Alpha. it had to be on a night when there was no basketball game and that would be difficult to pull off in February, but they eventually agreed on a Thursday night at the Family Inn in Macon. They charged $700 and the fraternity agreed to pay it without even flinching. So, on the night of the dance all the boys except Aubrey and J.R. went to set up for the gig. The Durrells would come up after basketball practice.

They would get there around 8:30 and play for a couple of hours, pocket $100 apiece and get back in time to get a decent night's sleep before school the next day. Around 10:30 the show ended and Aubrey, J.R., and Donnie had to get back home, but the other boys decided to hang around and party with the college kids for a while.

The basketball season was going predictably well with Empire winning their first ten games easily. Next up was Chauncey on Friday night and their star player Earl Rabun was having a great year averaging 22 points per game. The only starter who graduated from Empire's state championship team was Mikey "Pooh" Winston who was playing and probably still doing his own play-by-play at Middle Georgia College. He was replaced by J.R. who had developed a great outside shot from either corner and played better defense than "Pooh" had ever dreamed of playing. The game would come down to the wire just as most of these games had in the last few years but ultimately, Chauncey would win the game 76-75 behind Rabun's 28 points including the game-winner with three seconds left. Chauncey would not lose a game until the rematch the last week of the regular season in Chauncey when the Knights would play "Hondo" Winston man-to-man on Rabun and held him to 14 points and frustrated him all night long leading to an altercation which resulted in Rabun getting a technical foul and Aubrey hitting two important free throws to extend the lead to ten points with four minutes remaining. The Comets would not quit and cut the lead to two with 45 seconds remaining. Aubrey received the inbounds pass and was fouled immediately. He would hit the first free throw, but his second shot rimmed out and Chauncey would score as Earl Rabun got free for a layup to cut the lead to one point. Aubrey was denied the ball on the inbounds pass and "Hondo" Winston, who was not a good ball handler, would get the ball and proceed to dribble it off his foot and out of bounds. Chauncey would try to get the ball to Rabun but "Hondo" would not allow it so Will Hatton took a shot with 12 seconds remaining and hit nothing but net. The Chauncey fans went crazy thinking they had the game in hand but Aubrey and J.R. had other ideas. Darcy Williams would replace "Hondo" for offensive purposes, and he received the inbounds pass and immediately gave it up to Aubrey who proceeded to drive the lane and draw the defense to him while J.R. set up in the left corner. Aubrey would go behind the back on a perfect pass to J.R. who calmly knocked down the game-winner. After the game. Earl Rabun apologized to "Hondo" and to the coaches and congratulated Aubrey and J.R. on their great game. He told them he would see them on Sunday when he came to Empire to visit Renee. Another victory on Saturday night and Empire would be in no worse than a tie for first place with Chauncey. They would get that victory over Rhine while Chauncey would travel to Chester for a tough finale. Empire needed the Tigers to defeat the Comets to secure sole possession of first place bye in the region tournament. Sometimes it pays to be more lucky than good and as luck would have it, Chester would come through in a minor upset winning 64-59. Chauncey was obviously still feeling the effects from their loss to the Knights. The Empire girls' team was in first place again this season as well with Christina leading the team in scoring with 25 points per game. 'A HOMECOMING QUEEN WITH A KILLER JUMPSHOT' is what the headline in the Macon News sports section said about her in an article that came out the following Sunday. They also made mention of the fact that her boyfriend was the #1 recruited football player in Georgia and a pivotal player in Empire's unprecedented title run in three sports last school year. Christina told them that the relationship has been challenged at times, but it was well worth the hassles that some wanted to give them because Aubrey Durrell was a wonderful person who she loved very much.

On Sunday Earl and Renee came to watch the band practice and so did Christina and Kenny. The boys played as if they were doing a show and it helped them hone their skills. For a couple of hours, they rocked the garage and their small audience appreciated it very much especially Earl Rabun. He could not speak glowingly enough about the band and the Durrells in particular. After the practice session, he and Renee invited Aubrey and Christina to go to a drive-in movie in Dublin. After getting permission from her dad, they agreed to go watch 'SATURDAY NIGHT FEVER'. Aubrey was a little embarrassed by the sexual nature in the movie, but he still enjoyed it. The Bee Gees immediately became one of the kids' favorite bands. At the end of the night Aubrey and Earl shook hands and wished each other good luck in the playoffs. Aubrey took Christina home and went home and talked to Jesus and thanked him for all the good fortune in his life. He then slept like a baby.

The following week was a big week for Aubrey as he received a phone call from a coach at Alabama Tech, the defending national champions of college football and winners of five of the last eight championships. They were interested in him as a football player and wanted him to visit their campus in Selma, Alabama as soon as basketball season was over. He was also told that legendary Coach Pete "The Bull' Ripley would be in touch as soon as possible and wished him good luck in basketball. Aubrey was in awe of this situation. Recruiting just became real to him. He could not wait to tell Coach Kelly tomorrow and he called Christina and J.R. and told them immediately. His parents were proud of him as well telling him that the Lord takes care of his faithful servants. Apparently, Alabama Tech did not care who he dated and that said a lot about them as far as Aubrey was concerned. Lost in all his euphoria was the fact that Alabama Tech had a plethora of running backs collecting them like some collect baseball cards. Aubrey was just so excited that they liked him. The reality was that they thought he could play but not right away for them, but they would rather give him a scholarship and stow him away than play against him at Georgia, Florida, or LSU. That's why they got involved before others in the south.

Empire would win the region tournament in boys' and girls' basketball and enter the state tournament ranked #1 and #3 respectively. The girls' team would make it back to the championship game but would come up short falling to Bonaire by a score of 54-50. Christina would average 23 points per game during the tournament and would be first team All-State. She would also be a finalist for the Hickey Scholarship. Other than the loss in the championship game, she was enjoying a good week. The boys' team would cruise back into the championship game to face Gordon High School who was undefeated and ranked #2 behind the Knights. Kenny Dudley would have a monster game scoring 29 points / 14 rebounds / and 6 blocked shots in leading Empire to a second straight championship by a score of 84-74. Aubrey would add 13 points and 14 assists and J.R. added 13 points / 8 rebounds / 2 steals. Ashley Stacey would have 10 points while Darcy Williams would add 8 points. It was a great team effort said Coach Lord and he was proud to be a Knight. You know the routine—a free meal at Nubby' s followed by a night spent at the gym and so the beat goes on.

Aubrey and Christina began making plans for the second Empire High School Spring Formal and Aubrey suggested maybe DJ instead of the band this year since Saturday Night Fever was so popular and R.C. Gold would never play disco music. Christina thought this was a good idea but wanted to gauge what the student body thought first. She also was informed that she was indeed the recipient of the $5000 scholarship from the Hickey Foundation. She was supposed to meet Roderick Hickey for lunch in Eastman at the Carriage House inn Restaurant on Friday to discuss the details. She was asked to come alone, and they would discuss a public announcement later. Meanwhile Aubrey was scheduled to visit Alabama Tech the next weekend before baseball season started.

CHAPTER FIFTY

On Monday before he was to go for his visit to Alabama Tech at the end of the week, Aubrey received a call from Coach Pete "The Bull" Ripley telling him how they wanted him at Alabama Tech and were anxious to meet him this weekend. He told Aubrey to be ready at noon on Friday and a coach would be over to pick him up along with a few other athletes to bring them over and would bring them home on Sunday. When he hung up the phone, "The Bull" told a small group of coaches and boosters that Durrell was coming this weekend and he hoped they all had their ducks in a row to guarantee his commitment to the War Hawks Football Program. They told him that everything was in order including the girls who would seal the deal and the coach smiled when he saw the pictures of three young ladies who 'worked' for the program. He said, "Damn, I would not mind being recruited by these three. He's a lucky bastard, and don't even know it yet."

When Friday came Christina told Aubrey goodbye and set off for her meeting with Rod Hickey while Aubrey got into the van marked Alabama Tech Warhawks and headed off to Selma. Rod Hickey was ready for Christina as he was decked out in his finest suit and when she walked into the Carriage House, she was breathtakingly beautiful and drew the attention of everyone in the room." Hot Rod" was almost speechless, but he managed to compliment her saying, "you look stunning Miss Dudley." Christina didn't know what to say to that, so she said, "Thank you Mr. Hickey." He told her to call him Rod and that they did not need to be so formal. He congratulated her on the award, and they ordered their meal. He told her to order anything she wanted from the menu, so she ordered a ribeye steak with a baked potato and a salad. He had the same. As the meeting progressed, he talked to her about her future and where she hoped to attend college. She told him that she hoped to attend Bethune-Cookman in Daytona Beach, Florida and major in pre-law. He said that was a good choice for a fine young black lady and he would support her decision in every way possible and that he would be glad to check in on her from time to time and see if she needed anything. He also told her that if she ever needed anything at all she simply had to call him, and he would see that she gets it. Christina started feeling a little uncomfortable and it must have showed because Rod told her, "Look, I know you are going to be successful, and I just want to help you along on your journey. It can be a cruel world out there and it does not hurt to have a successful black man in your corner." Christina began to wonder what the cost would be for his services, and she thought she knew the answer. When the conversation began to lull, "Hot Rod" Hickey told Christina that she could expect a check by July 1st, and it would be made out to her to do with as she pleased. When they got up to leave, he asked a nearby diner if she would take a picture of the two of them and a lady obliged. Rod hugged Christina uncomfortably close to his side and ran his hand across her backside as the picture was being taken. She could not get away from him soon enough. She left the restaurant feeling a little bit dismayed and disgusted but $5000 would come in handy. On her way back to school she started thinking about Aubrey and hoped he would have a good visit to Alabama Tech.

When Aubrey got in the Warhawks van he was the second player picked up so far. He introduced himself to a defensive lineman from Vidalia named Nick Worley and they hit it off quickly. Next, they stopped in Warner Robins to pick up a receiver from Southside Warner Robins; the same one who had the game-winning TD versus Empire earlier that year. They also hit it off well since they had a game in common to discuss. The receiver's name was Jamie Hiller, and he gave Aubrey the ultimate compliment when he told him he was the best player his team faced all season. Aubrey humbly thanked him for the compliment, and they talked about things teenaged boys liked such as music, cars, and of course girls. They had two more stops to make on the way to Selma. A defensive back from Carrollton and an offensive lineman from Lagrange. Aubrey could not believe he was in this elite group of athletes; obviously, he knew he was a good athlete but in Empire he was just one of the guys now he was going to meet "The Bull" Ripley and possibly play football for the five-time national champions. It all seemed surreal to him. They got to Selma around 8:30 Alabama time (9:30 Georgia time) and checked into their hotel rooms. Strangely enough they all got private rooms, but Aubrey reckoned that is the way they do it at the big schools. Money certainly was not an issue. Aubrey called home and checked in with his parents then he called Christina and talked to her for about 45 minutes. The phone bill would be paid by the school, so he did not worry about it.

At 9:30 p.m. they got to meet "The Bull" when they had a meeting with about fifteen other recruits from around the country and watched a highlight film from the previous season's national championship campaign. Pete "The Bull" Ripley spoke to the group and told them they were here because they were the best football players around and Alabama Tech only recruits the absolute best. He told them that he hoped they would all choose to be Warhawks after next season, but he understood if they wanted to keep their options open for now but just remember that if he sees you on the opposing sideline, that he would take no mercy on them for making a bad career decision. He smiled when he said that, so Aubrey guessed he was joking but he was not entirely sure. He laid out the itinerary for the next day, which had them eating breakfast at 7 a.m. followed by some athletic testing; then back to their rooms to get ready for lunch and the spring scrimmage at 2 p.m. After that there was a team social off campus at around 8 p.m. held at the ballroom of the hotel where the boys were staying. Aubrey went back to his room; talked to Jesus and went to bed.

Pete Ripley held a meeting around 10:30 p.m. to discuss strategy on a couple of the boys. He knew that Hiller was being recruited heavily by Georgia, Florida, LSU, and practically everyone else in the country but was leaning heavily toward Georgia and Alabama Tech. The offensive lineman from Lagrange was leaning toward Tennessee and Aubrey Durrell was getting attention from everyone in the country except most southern schools because of his dating preference Alabama folks were not crazy about interracial relationships either but they trusted "The Bull" to handle these types of issues and if he decided to sign Aubrey Durrell, they trusted his judgement. He knew that

Aubrey had been recommended for the Naval Academy and that he was strongly considering taking the appointment. He also knew that it was important to Durrell that he be allowed to play baseball as well but playing baseball meant missing spring football practice and that was not allowed. So, Ripley knew that as soon as Aubrey found out that there would be no baseball, he would lose a football player, so he put him in the category of 'one who needed a little insurance policy to guarantee his commitment to the Warhawks'. All totaled there were six players in that category. The plan was for three beautiful girls to convince these players to take them to their room for some extracurricular fun. Pictures would be taken and would mysteriously show up in Pete Ripley's possession. He would tell the player that if they signed with Alabama Tech, he could make sure the pictures disappeared but if not, the player was on his own. Of course, the boys would not want these pictures publicized, and would be more than happy to sign with Alabama Tech. The three girls who were assigned to Aubrey Durrell were two brunettes and a blonde each of whom was amply endowed and could fill out a pair of jeans and a t-shirt. One of the brunettes was Maria Oliver, a psychology major from Mobile, Alabama. The second brunette was Jenny Barkley, a biology major from Atlanta, Georgia, and the third girl was a beautiful blonde from Barnesville, Georgia named Gwen Parker who was a secondary education major and was new to this game. She had been told by a friend of hers that she could make $1000 for a weekend of hosting football recruits, and she decided to take advantage of the opportunity. She was a sophomore and had helped in the recruitment of a quarterback last spring. She had taken the pictures and was shocked at the actions of the two girls who were with her. Sex had taken place last year, but she was working with two new girls this time so maybe they would be a little more modest. She had felt remorse at first over what she had done but the young man seemed to be doing fine and enjoying his time at Alabama Tech and when she received $1000 in cash for her efforts, she soon got over it. When she was approached this year, she needed the money and she said she would help this year as well. She quickly volunteered to take the pictures and grabbed the camera. Something about Aubrey Durrell seemed familiar to her but she could not place him in her brain. It was a job to her, and as far as she knew, this type of thing was probably going on at big-time football factories across the country.

After a good nights' sleep, Aubrey was ready for a good day. Around 9 a.m. the recruits reported to the practice field for a brief workout and test period so the coaches could get some information on them. First was a bench press test where each player would have to lift 225 pounds as many times as he could. Anything over 15 reps they were told was exceptional. Aubrey did 19 reps—the fourth best and the best by a non-lineman. Next was vertical leap where Aubrey leaped an impressive 38 inches. Finally, the 40-yard dash saw Aubrey slip and almost fall on his first attempt and still he posted a 4.39 time, but he promised to do better next time when he would make sure not to slip on his takeoff. Sure enough, his second run was clean and came in at 4.35. At 5' 10" tall and weighing in at 188 pounds, the coaches were sure he could contribute to the program quickly. Aubrey had never been clocked in the 40-yard before; he just knew that since he had never been run down from behind, he was fast enough. Although some considered him to be a bit undersized, the coaches discussed the fact that he was approximately the same size as Tony Dorsett and was a little bit faster so there was some potential for greatness there if they could get him signed. "Bull" Ripley was certain that after tonight that should not be a problem.

After lunch and a shower, the recruits were shuttled over to Angus T. Spearman Memorial Stadium for a scrimmage game in front of 80,000+ screaming fans. Aubrey had never seen that many people in one place at one time. It was like a mid-season game; and he was amazed. The gold team defeated the black team in a close contest and Coach Ripley said they made enough mistakes to last a lifetime, but he assured them that those mistakes would be corrected before the fall came. Aubrey wanted to meet the star tailback Jacquez Saunders who would go on to win the Heisman Trophy at end of that next season. He was big and fast and when he shook Aubrey's hand, it was as if Aubrey's hand was swallowed up. Saunders told Aubrey to take care of himself and be careful tonight. Aubrey thought that was a little bit of a strange comment, but he said he would be careful and that was the end of the conversation.

Around 8 o'clock p.m. Aubrey went downstairs to the banquet room for the party. There was sandwiches and cookies and drinks everywhere and beautiful girls dressed in Alabama Tech miniskirts were acting as hostesses. Every girl in the room was a beauty queen and Aubrey could look even if he could not touch. Not long after he arrived three of the girls came over to Aubrey and introduced themselves. Maria, Jenny, and Gwen were their names and they seemed nice and asked Aubrey where he was from. When he told them Empire, Georgia, two of them said they had never heard of such a place; but the third girl, a blonde named Gwen told them she sort of knew where it was and then it hit her. This was the guy from the news story last summer with the black girlfriend. She had thought it was a sweet story about true love and she was envious of them both for having someone devoted entirely to one another. Now here she was about to lay a trap for this nice boy from rural Georgia who had no idea about the dirty business of big-time college football. Gwen started asking him about his girlfriend and she saw Aubrey's eyes light up when he mentioned Christina. "She's a lucky girl" said Jenny Barkley obviously struck by this handsome young man. Aubrey told them he had to use the men's room and excused himself. "This should be a fun one to do," said Maria. "Yeah, I think we may enjoy this one don't you think Gwen?" asked Jenny. Gwen wanted to protect him from what was about to happen, but Aubrey needed no protection. When Aubrey returned from the men's room, he found the three girls waiting where he had left them eagerly awaiting his return. "Can I get you something to drink?" asked Maria. Aubrey replied that a Dr. Pepper would be nice, and Maria said she would be right back. When he returned, Maria suggested that they go up to his room for a little more privacy, but Aubrey knew better than to fall for that. He told them that he did not think it was o good idea. Instead, he told them about his girlfriend and how he loved her so much. Jenny told him that she would never know unless he told her, but Aubrey said that he and Jesus would know and that was all he could say about it. He thanked the girls and excused himself. Gwen was impressed and relieved. As he was leaving, he ran into Jamie Hiller leaving as well but the lineman from LaGrange was leaving with three beautiful girls. Jamie said to Aubrey, "Man, we must be crazy. I mean these girls are amazing." Aubrey replied, "Just think about your girl back home man and it is easy to walk away." Jamie agreed and the two of them went outside to talk a little more about their futures. Gwen Parker saw Aubrey and came over to speak to him. "I just want to tell you that you made a wise decision tonight. And your girlfriend is a lucky girl." "Thanks," said Aubrey. "This is my friend Jamie Hiller, and he did the same thing I did. Why did you say it was a wise decision?" Gwen explained the whole thing and told them they might not get paid now but that was okay; she was just proud to know that someone decent was still around. She also gave him her phone number in case he chose to attend Alabama Tech next year and needed someone to show him around. The two boys decided to try to warn the lineman, so they went to his room just in the nick of time. When they told him about the plan, he asked the girls about it and when they did not deny it, he asked them to leave his room. They were angry with Aubrey and Jamie but neither of them cared. They felt that they had saved a buddy from an embarrassing scenario. They all three decided to look for somewhere else to go to school perhaps together.

CHAPTER FIFTY-ONE

On the way home the boys never mentioned the girls or what they had been told because the coach driving the van might have been in on it or maybe he wasn't. Either way they saw no good outcome from mentioning it in his company. They all agreed to stay in touch concerning recruiting and other things.

Aubrey got home around nine p.m. and he was never happier to see Empire. J.R. was there when he got home with a lot of questions about what "The Bull" was like and if he met any of the players. Aubrey told him everything went okay and how awesome the scrimmage game had been; but he did not mention the strange occurrence at the party. Kelsey also was fired up about his big brother being recruited by the defending national champions. Wyll and Pattie were asking some questions about what they had done while there and he told them about his 40-yard dash time and the rest of the workout. After J.R. left he called Christina to tell her about how he did and to find out about how her meeting went. She told him it had went fine and neglected to tell him about Rod Hickey's flirtations. She told Aubrey she could not wait to see him tomorrow at school and she said she loved him, and he told her the same. He then talked to Jesus and went to bed.

The first baseball game was a week away and Empire was expected to make another run at the championship. They would start the season ranked number one and would not relinquish that ranking all season on their record setting sixth straight state championship in team sports. They would breeze through the regular season undefeated and would lose only two games in the state playoffs—once in the second round to Ocilla, and the opening game of the state championship series to

Hogansville. They would come back to sweep Hogansville in the final two games with Aubrey going 6 for 9 in those two games with two homeruns; six RBI; four stolen bases; and four runs scored. J.R. would put up big numbers as well with two homeruns; going 5 for 10 at the plate; with five RBI; and three runs scored. Darcy Williams was a year stronger and had gotten his fastball up to 88 mph and the mule was still kicking. He only lost once during the season and that was to Ocilla—a 3-2 loss. Hs was drawing attention from major league scouts who showed up at every game Empire played that season. The scouts were also talking to Aubrey, J.R.; Randy Stafford; and Ashley Stacey as well. This was an unprecedented run of success, and it would never be equaled again. And the great thing about it was this group still had another year to add to this incredible run.

The R.C. Gold Band had been kept busy with high school proms and college fraternity parties and were getting a reputation as the best party band in Middle Georgia. They were now charging $1000 per gig. Life Was going well for Aubrey but he was still a little bit sad that with each passing day he got closer to seeing the love of his life go away to college and leave him behind. He also knew that he would be going off to college in another year and that would separate them even more. He only knew that he loved her so much and the thought of being without her made him sad. Christina felt the same way and she even had doubts about going away, but she had promised her dad to carry out her dreams and desires and she would do that. It would be a lot easier if Aubrey were to get a scholarship close to her, but she did not think that would happen. He had to go where he could make a life for himself and hopefully her someday.

As Aubrey took stock of his life at the end of another year, he realized that this little town that he loved so much and that had made him the person he was would soon be in his rearview mirror. He started thinking about his childhood and how he used to walk the railroad tracks with Stevie Wilbur barefoot during the hottest summer days to see who could last longer. Or he and J.R. picking up coke bottles off the side of the road and taking them to Ross' store or to Mattie Ella's store and cashing them in for 3 cents apiece then turning around and buying a bag of candy or pinwheel cookies with the money they earned. He thought about the time that Tia and Lee Anne Paisley's dad brought home a parachute from the air force base where he worked and hung it up between three pine trees in their back yard. All the neighborhood kids would show up every day and climb up in a tree and jump into the parachute. Man, that had been fun until one kid landed wrong and fell to the ground and broke his arm; that ended the parachute jumping. There had been Sunday school parties and spin the bottle. Vacation Bible School and backyard ball games, and swimming at the Bar Pit. Aubrey had ridden his bike over every square inch of Empire, Georgia most of the time with Kelsey sitting on his handlebars. He wished he could go back and do it all over again. To pick plums and blackberries beside the railroad tracks without a care in the world; but life goes on and nothing lasts forever. His motivation for his senior year would be 'one more time with his friends'. He wanted to go out on top like no one before had ever done with his Empire boys,

That summer would be his last chance to pull the plow and load melons and now he had to share that duty with his little brother who was getting old enough to take over when Aubrey left for college. As hard as that work was, the finality of that even made Aubrey sad. J.R. was thinking the same way and he and Aubrey vowed to make every moment count over the next year so they could leave Empire as winners that no one would ever forget.

CHAPTER FIFTY-TWO

It was bound to happen sooner or later but with all their recent success, other schools had been inquiring about hiring some of the Empire staff to run their programs. Even Coach Kelly was getting offers from larger schools for a lot more money, but he decided to ride it out with the kids who had turned the program around. Maybe they had another championship run in them, and if so, the opportunities for advancement would still be there.

Coach Dale James, offensive coordinator for Empire during this incredible run would take a job as head coach at he and Coach Kelly's alma mater in DeKalb County while Trey Jones would head back to his hometown in South Carolina to be the head coach at his alma mater too. He had never quite gotten over Cathy Dehoff leaving the way she did, so he was leaving behind some bittersweet memories as well as some great times coaching. These two would be missed and as each year passed, someone else would leave or retire. That's the thing about winning big—change is inevitable and you only hope to get good people to replace the ones you lost. Coach Don Rainey would be promoted to offensive coordinator, and he would remain as offensive line coach, so there would not be a new hire there; but Coach Jones would be replaced by Eldridge Cooks who had recently finished his playing career at Tennessee as an all-conference fullback. He would inherit a great group of running backs lead of course by Aubrey Durrell, but also included Ashley Stacey and Josh Beasley.

The Empire High School spring formal would be another success and Aubrey and Christina felt good about leaving a legacy of racial harmony at the school with the formation of this event. Another thing that would have to end soon would be the R.C. Gold Band. With everyone making plans for life after high school, it would be impossible to keep the band going so the guys started making plans for their last official performance. It would have to be an epic event, and they had a year to plan where and when it would happen. J.R. was still seeing Susan Dillon who had satisfactorily apologized for her role in the attack of Aubrey and Christina. Chelsey Potter had moved on and was planning to become a nurse. Recruiting was in full swing for the Empire stars as Ashley Stacey was being recruited heavily by Florida State as a defensive back and Kenny Dudley was being recruited by a few small schools for basketball. Darcy Williams was counting on the Major League draft since college was not something he was interested in anyway. The Beasley twins were headed for the military and Randy Stafford was planning to play baseball at Middle Georgia College. Teddy Robertson was going to play division III football and J.R. was getting recruited be several mid-major schools as a punter and linebacker. Aubrey was seeing more interest from southern schools since Alabama Tech had broken the ice, but he was still upset at their racist philosophy in the beginning.

CHAPTER FIFTY-THREE

Bull Ripley instructed his recruiting coordinator for Georgia to call Aubrey and see what he was thinking, so on a Sunday night in May Aubrey got a call asking him if he is ready to be a Warhawk and Aubrey told him that he was leaning toward going somewhere else. The coach told him that he was sorry to hear that and was there any way to change his mind. Aubrey told him that it just didn't feel right at Alabama Tech but did not go into detail about why. When the coach called Jamie Hiller and the lineman from LaGrange and got the same answer, he knew something had happened, but he did not know what. He was not a member of "The Bull's" inner circle, so he knew nothing about the plan with the girls.

When Bull Ripley was told about it, he fumed," What the hell happened? I mean losing one is bad enough; but three five- star athletes suddenly turning against us is ridiculous." He added, "I know the lineman and the receiver are really good, but I am not sure about the running back. Is he really that good coach?" he asked his running backs coach. "He put up numbers at the workout that I have not seen since Jessie Ferguson was here, and his game film is amazing, so yes I think he is worth having" answered the coach. Jessie Ferguson was a three-time All-American and Heisman Trophy winner at tailback on Bull Ripley's first national championship team at Alabama Tech and was currently a star with the Baltimore Colts in the NFL.

Aubrey was unaware of such comparisons. He was just trying to make the most of his time left with Christina and preparing for his senior seasons at Empire High School. In the meantime, Alabama Tech's offensive coordinator, Jerry Cook was hired to be the head coach at Kentucky A&M. He had been the one who had timed Aubrey's 40-yard dash, so he knew what type of talent he was dealing with. The Eagles had become one of the worst teams in division-I football recently and the powers that be there thought Coach Cook would be the man who could turn things around. He knew that Aubrey Durrell wanted to play two sports and he had no issues with it. He also liked J.R. Durrell so he felt like Aubrey would be open to a scholarship offer if he knew J.R. would get one also. He did not know about Bull Ripley's scheme to trap certain recruits since he was not in his inner circle. He was also engaged to be married to a black woman, so the issue of interracial dating was a non-issue.

During the last week of school, Coach Cook and the Kentucky A&M baseball coach, an ex-major league pitcher named Max Ellison came to Empire to visit with Aubrey and J.R. They stopped in to visit with Coach Kelly first and get his take on the Durrell kids. After Coach Kelly spoke glowingly about their character as well as their athletic ability, they knew they had to have these two boys. When Aubrey and J.R. came into the coaches' office and Coach Kelly dismissed himself so they could speak freely, Coach Cook told them he had been at Alabama Tech for the previous five seasons and had taken a big chance on his career by taking the job at Kentucky A&M, but he had always felt that the best bet to make was on yourself since you control the effort and enthusiasm you put into a job. He told the boys that he was prepared to offer them both full scholarships and that baseball would not be a problem. Aubrey told him that he was waiting to see if he were getting an appointment to the Naval Academy, but he would definitely consider Kentucky A&M. He offered Aubrey an iron-clad guarantee that he could play both sports, but he understood if he wanted some time to think it over. When the baseball coach spoke, he told them that he still had friends at the major league level, and he knew that both the boys would probably get drafted, but he hoped they would consider playing for him at Kentucky A&M. They had qualified for the NCAA regionals last year and he thought they could put them at another level. When the coaches left, Aubrey told J.R. that this was great and J.R. agreed.

Aubrey had to admit that this offer took a lot of pressure off both himself and J.R. to know that they had a division-I scholarship in the bag and, more importantly, they could remain teammates for four more years. But he wondered if Coach Cook had been involved in the dirty plans at Alabama Tech.

CHAPTER FIFTY-FOUR

Christina's birthday was in early June and Aubrey had managed to save up enough money to buy her a gold necklace with a heart-shaped locket in which he had placed a picture of the two of them at the first spring formal. He had it engraved with the words 'AUBREY AND CHRISTINA 4-EVER'. He took her out to Steak and Ale in Macon for her birthday and gave her the necklace. She cried happy tears and swore to never take it off. Suddenly, an older white man came over to the table and asked if the two of them were on a date. Aubrey said "Yessir". The man turned around disgusted and said, "I bet your folks are really proud of you boy." Aubrey started to get up and follow him to his table, but Christina stopped him and said, "Aubrey we have heard and been through a lot worse. Please let this pass."

After they finished their meal, they returned to Empire and spent some time alone. When he took Christina home, he rode around Empire for a while just to think about life and what the Lord had in store for him. He always thought clearer riding around his community and waiting for the 11:00 train to come through. He parked at the courthouse and got out of his car and waited for the train. Surely as the sun rises each morning, at 11:00 the train came through Empire and Aubrey counted the cars. 67 cars and a caboose. He wondered as he usually did where it was going and what it was hauling. It seemed like a little thing, but he would always long for the sound of that train wherever he might be in life. He prayed to God and went home and went to bed.

After church the next morning, he went to band practice. Amazingly, the boys had been asked back to the Warner Robins 4th of July celebration. It seems there had been a change in command

and the new boss wanted them back and he wanted them to play at night when more people could see them. When Billy informed him that they were getting $1000 per show, he laughed and told Billy that he did not understand; he wanted them to be the lead in act for the headliners—the Atlanta Rhythm Section and that paid $2000. The boys were excited about the prospect of playing on the same stage as one of their favorite bands in front of a couple thousand people and of course the money was nice too. Billy Allen had also asked them to play his labor-day bash for the third year in a row and agreed to pay the $1000 fee. They had added a couple more Lynyrd Skynyrd songs—'SWEET HOME ALABAMA' and 'ON THE HUNT'. They could play for an hour and a half if need be. They knew they would have to practice hard to be perfect for this show, so they got to work.

Meanwhile, Aubrey had received a call from the recruiting coach from Alabama Tech and was told that Coach Ripley, for the first time ever had agreed to allow Aubrey to play baseball so long as he made the SEC All Freshman team his first year there. Of course, that all depended on Aubrey cracking the rotation at tailback and returning punts and kickoffs. This did not seem to be a great deal for Aubrey, and he started thinking more about the Naval Academy and Kentucky A&M. Aubrey told the coach that he would think about it even though he knew he would not attend that school. The audacity of Bull Ripley saying that he would 'allow' him to play baseball did not sit well with Aubrey either.

Aubrey continued to pull the plow and load watermelons just to stay in shape mainly since he did not really need the money as bad as he once did. He also agreed to help J.R. make good on his promise to dunk a basketball before he graduated. He and J.R. worked out at night at the high school weight room. They did more squats than J.R. ever thought possible, and they worked on a new machine called a 'Leaper' and it was brutal. J.R. was getting his vertical leap and standing long jump to increase and he was improving his foot speed as well. By the time school started, J.R. would be running a 4.65 x 40 yards, and he stood 6'3" and weighed 225 pounds while Aubrey would be clocked at 4.32 x 40 yards, and he stood 5'10" tall and weighed 190 pounds. Both the boys were determined to be better than they had ever been this season and that meant trouble for their opponents.

One night after a tough workout, they sat by the railroad tracks waiting for the train with a cold Dr. Pepper and talking about life in general and their futures. J.R. remembered when the boys were about 12-years old, and they followed Stevie Wilbur on a supposed bicycle trail through Booger Bottom only to find out there was no trail. They got lost in the woods for over two hours and only managed to get out just before dark when they happened to come out at the Empire High School baseball field. Aubrey said, "Yeah, and I had Kelsey on my handlebars that day and he was scared to death, but at least he never told Daddy about it. He would have killed me if he had known." "I seem to remember you threatened him if he did tell your Daddy, "Said J.R. Aubrey replied, "Yeah I guess I did, but not nearly as bad as you threatened Stevie." J.R. started to laugh and said, "man we have had a great time in Empire over the years—it is hard to believe we are going to have to leave it behind soon." "Yeah, but we can always come back, and I intend to do just that as often as I am able" declared Aubrey. Just as they heard the train coming, J.R. added, "You know I love this place and I will always try to represent Empire in the right way no matter where I am and what I am doing." They both watched the train come by and then went home and got some sleep.

CHAPTER FIFTY-FIVE

Jn early July, Kelsey and J.R. and Donnie's younger brother Gerald "Gerry" Durrell, who was already 6' 2" tall and 195 pounds in the eighth grade, were playing in an All-Star baseball game in Dublin. Eli and Wyll Durrell were sitting in their usual seats along the first base line talking about the futures of their firstborn sons when Aubrey and Christina showed up and said hello to the men then went to sit in the bleachers. Eli, who was three years older than his brother Wyll said, "she is a pretty girl." "Yeah, she is, and she is nice and sweet too" said Wyll. "Does she remind you of anyone you know?" asked Wyll. Eli looked hard at Wyll before saying, "You had to bring that up, did you?" "I didn't mean anything about it I just wondered if you ever think about her" said Wyll. He was referring to Darlene Kittle the beautiful daughter of Zachariah Kittle, the black man that Eli and Wyll had worked with sharecropping when they were young boys. Darlene had brought water to the boys and had flirted with Eli during breaks. Eli had given in to temptation and Darlene Kittle was his first lover. They had gotten caught behind a barn one night by Darlene's cousin, Willamena. Shortly thereafter, Eli was taken by their dad Walter to join the Navy. He spent two years stationed mainly in Okinawa. 'I was young, and my hormones were raging, and I made a mistake," said Eli. "I am not judging you Eli, I just wondered if you ever thought about her, that's all" said Wyll. Eli replied, "not so much anymore, but every day I was in Okinawa I thought about her all the time. I thought I was in love, but I knew there was no future for us, so I gave up on it. She used to write me letters and send me pictures of herself and at first, I wrote her back, but eventually, I stopped answering her. When I got home, I met Beth and fell head over heels for her, and I still love her more than life itself. But, in case you are wondering, I don't blame Aubrey for falling in love with Christina. Maybe they can make it in this crazy world." "I know that, and I never blamed you either, just so you know" said Wyll, "you know I have always looked up to you and I love you brother." Eli replied, "same to you, now let's watch the game." The younger Durrells won the game and the tournament.

The following Saturday was the 4th of July and the day of the big show in Warner Robins, so the boys were excited about playing at night, but even more excited about meeting some of their musical heroes, The Atlanta Rhythm Section. Even J.R. was a little nervous about playing in front of ARS. A bunch of people from Empire would be there and even Christina was going to be backstage along with Renee and Earl Rabun. When 7 p.m. rolled around, the concert organizer introduced them by saying, "next up is the most talented group of high school boys you will ever see. They rocked the house last year and they are back to rock Warner Robins once again. Ladies and gentlemen welcome to the stage from Empire, Georgia the R.C. Gold Band." The boys started the show with 'SWEET HOME ALABAMA' and the crowd went wild. They played for about an hour and got a standing ovation as they left the stage. Even ARS was impressed and when they cane on stage and played their first couple of songs, the lead singer said "how about the R.C. Gold Band? They have a lot of talent, don't they?" That meant more to the boys than the money, but the $2000 was nice too.

The guys watched the headliners show from backstage and enjoyed it immensely. Christina was happy to be there with Aubrey and when they went home, she suggested they go off to Chicken Road for a while since she had an extra couple of hours and did not have to be home until 1:00 a.m.

Billy Dobbs was receiving many calls for gigs, but he had to turn a lot of them down since football season was coming soon. He did accept a date for another fraternity party at Mercer for Lambda Chi Alpha again early August before the Durrells went off for football camp. That along with Billy Allen's party would end their performances for a while but it had been a great summer and they had made money.

The fraternity party gig went well, and football practice was starting back; yet Aubrey knew he only had a couple of weeks left with Christina before she went off to college. He was happy for her but would miss her badly. As the Knights went off to football camp at Rock Eagle, he could not get it off his mind. Would their relationship survive being away from each other for the better part of the next four or five years? He told himself that if it is meant to be and it was the Lord's will; then it would work out okay. Meanwhile, he would pray for Christina and himself to be together as often as possible and to marry someday and live happily ever after.

The team was looking good with all the boys being seniors and vowing to go undefeated this season. That was the only thing they had not accomplished in their amazing run over the last two seasons. The new running backs coach, Eldridge Cooks was tough. Aubrey never thought that they could be in any better shape, but he was wrong. Coach Cooks kept them after every practice and made them run a mile telling them, "You boys get your names in the paper and on the tv sports shows while the linemen get nothing but a pat on the back. So, this extra mile is to let them know that you are paying in advance for all this special treatment." He also told them that they would be responsible for shining the linemen's cleats before every game and that on Monday after a game when the team rushed for 300+ yards, the linemen would eat pizza in the locker room instead of eating a school lunch. He told them that if they had a problem with any of that; that they were free to transfer to Union Hill or Roddy where things were a little bit easier and winning was not as important. None of the boys were leaving Empire and none of them had a problem with the new rules; but that mile at the end of practice was rough. He was a big believer in a running back being aggressive and physical. He explained to them, "men show me in the rulebook where it says that just because I have the ball in my hands that I can't punish a tackler. It ain't in there. I want you guys to understand that anyone who has the nerve to step in front of you in the first quarter to try to take you down will be a helluva man if he does it in the third and fourth quarters. We are going to punish people who think they want to tackle us, and we will find out if he still has the heart to do it late in the game." His practice drills were designed to get that point across and he absolutely went berserk if one his backs did not fall forward after a run. He called it 'finishing off a run the right way'. And don't even think about going out of bounds and foregoing the chance to get that extra yard. He told them that he learned in college that the difference in players at that level is not in the level of talent because they were all high school superstars. No, it came down to mental toughness and the desire to be the best and the ability to block out any pain or doubt that you may be experiencing. That, he said, was what made an undersized walk-on from Adairsville, Georgia who was too slow to play in the SEC according to most experts, into an All-SEC fullback at the University of Tennessee and that is what is going to make them all successful in life in whatever they decide to do. Aubrey liked his approach even if he did not like the mandatory mile at the end of practice, but after a couple of practices, the receivers and defensive backs were running with the backs to show unity and that made it a little easier. Overall, Coach Cooks was a great addition to the staff. He lived for competition and on Fridays he went to another place mentally. Aubrey talked to him about choosing the right college and recruiting matters and the coach told him to choose a college where he felt that the coaches cared for him personally and not just as a football player. Aubrey asked him how he felt about Alabama Tech and the coach said it was a good football school, but he had heard some things about "The Bull" that cast some doubt on whether he could have ever played for him or not. Things about always blaming the players for a loss, although they did not lose that often. And sitting a player down for perceived disloyalty to him; not necessarily the program. "But that's just what I have heard through players I have known who played there. It could be all b.s. for all I know" said Coach Cooks. "Like a lot of coaches at that level, they will just use you up and if you get hurt, you are no longer any use to them, so they throw you away like garbage" he added. "But keep in mind that I was not recruited by any big schools, so I am probably not the best person to ask about the process" he told Aubrey. Aubrey thanked him for his honesty and his advice.

CHAPTER FIFTY-SIX

It was the weekend before the first game versus Fort Valley and Christina had to leave for college. Her dad was moving her to Daytona Beach, Florida and into a residence hall at Bethune-Cookman University. Aubrey would have loved to go with him to help her move in, but this was a time for a dad and his daughter to be alone, so Aubrey said his goodbyes and left her house before he broke down and cried like a baby. He would have the memory of the night before to get him through the times when he missed her the most.

R.C. Gold practiced for a couple of hours that Sunday afternoon in preparation for Billy Allen's party. Afterwards J.R. asked Aubrey if he wanted to go fishing at the Walton Creek bridge and Aubrey agreed. The boys grabbed a couple of cane poles and dug up some worms from the ditch in front of Aubrey's house and took off. They grabbed a couple of Dr. Peppers and sat on the bank under the bridge and fished and talked just as they had done so many times in the past. They caught seven or eight bream and had a good time just being country boys. J.R. did not ask many questions—he just planned on listening if Aubrey wanted to talk. Aubrey finally said it was going to be tough without Christina around and he did not know if he could stand it. J.R. told him that he would make it and she would stay in touch with him he was certain of it. He also said that she would be home for holidays, and it would make it sweeter when he did get to see her. The boys went home and cleaned the fish and put them in the freezer and reminded each other about their hard work that had been put in over the summer and how they had to go out in style this year.

School would not start for another week so all they had to do was practice football. Fort Valley would come to Empire this year and would have revenge on their minds for last year's 14-12 loss in the last minute. They had lost in the Triple-A state championship last season and were looking to go all the way this season. The Knight's coaching staff knew they had to be prepared for a war on Friday night and they were fired up at practice each day. They were relentless about perfect execution on every play, and they coached maximum effort the entire time practice lasted. By Thursday afternoon the Knights were ready to play after the toughest week of practice any of the boys could ever remember.

This years' game was in Empire and the crowd was ready for another championship run and, on this night, they would see one of the finest football teams ever put together in the Empire Knights. The Knights would win by a score of 35-19 behind Aubrey's 158 yards rushing and three TD's including a 3rd quarter punt return of 64 yards to break the game open. The running backs emphasis on physicality became painfully obvious to the Fort Valley free safety early in the 2nd quarter when Aubrey broke loose for a 43 yard score—his first of the game—and all that stood between him and the goal line was the 6' 1" 178 pound all-state free safety who broke down and prepared to tackle Aubrey, however, Aubrey lowered his pad level and ran through the free safety and never broke stride on the way to the end zone. This was like a dunk in a basketball game and the crowd reacted accordingly. This sent a message to Fort Valley that they had better buckle up their chin straps because it was going to be a physical night. Ashley Stacey got in on the act by running hard through attempted tackles on his way to 101 yards and two TD's. The most impressive thing was J.R. and his improved speed thanks to he and Aubrey's workouts all summer long. He was a one-man wrecking crew on defense finishing with 18 tackles and a fumble caused; an interception; and three sacks of the Fort Valley QB. As usual he played both offense and defense as well as punting for the Knights and barely broke a sweat. In fact, all the skilled players were in the best shape ever because of the one mile runs at the end of practice and they knew who to thank for that. Coach Eldridge Cooks was pumped up and slapping kids on the head for being physical with ball in their hands. He was especially impressed by Aubrey, and he told him that he was as good or better than the running backs he had played with in Tennessee and that he thought Aubrey could play for anyone in the country. This made Aubrey feel good about his future. When the guys asked Aubrey If he was going to Nubby' s to celebrate, he told them he might be there a little later, but as for now, he had to go home and wait on a phone call from Christina. She would have to use the hall phone since she had not gotten one in her room yet and she had promised him she would call sometime around 11:00. Aubrey rushed home just in time to hear the phone ring and on the other end of the line was the sweetest voice he had ever heard. "Hey babe, did y'all win?" asked Christina. "Heck yeah, we blew them out," answered Aubrey. "I miss you so much," he added "I can't wait until Thanksgiving break when you can come home," he added. "Aww, I miss you too Aubrey and I will be counting the days until I see you again. Just don't let some other girls replace me while I am away," said Christina. To which Aubrey replied, "No one will ever replace you. You have my heart 100 percent." They talked for a few more minutes until someone else needed to use the phone and Christina said her goodbyes. Aubrey found out that her classes were going well and that she was being recruited by all the sororities who wanted her to pledge them. She had left out the part about a couple of the boys asking her out on a date. She had said no so there was no reason to mention it. Aubrey headed out to Nubby' s to be with his teammates for a little while, but when he got there and saw them all paired up with their girls, he felt like a third wheel and just went home. He prayed that night that Christina would be safe from all ill will and harm and that she would return home safely to him as soon as possible.

The next game was a rematch of last year's barn burner with Southside Warner Robins. It would be played in Warner Robins again this season because of a deal that the coaches had worked out between them that allowed Empire to receive half the gate receipts. This would be a good deal for Empire since International City Stadium held about 12,000 people and it would be packed for this game featuring the two-time defending class B champions and the two-time defending AAAA Champions. The Knights knew that if they could pull off the upset that had eluded them last year, that they stood a great chance of going undefeated and winning their third straight football championship.

The practices were crisp that week with every man wanting to be perfect, especially Lester Beasley whose fumble had cast Empire a chance at winning last season. Lester was focused hard on redemption just as Aubrey had been after the Warm Springs fumble his freshman year. Aubrey received a call from Alabama Tech on Wednesday night informing him that Bull Ripley would be landing by helicopter near the stadium right before kickoff and wished him good luck. Coach Jerry Cook from Kentucky A&M also called the Durrell boys to inform them that he and his baseball coach would be attending the game. Kentucky A&M was in the process of adjustment to Coach Cook's system and way of doing things and in his first year they had won their first game versus a mid-level opponent and had lost versus a non-conference division-I team. They would finish the season with a 4-7 record. He did not mention arriving in a helicopter so the boys surmised that he would probably be driving. They were correct.

As the teams were finishing their pre-game warmups, a helicopter was landing across the street on a practice field. Everyone in the stadium, including the players stopped to notice the chopper emblazoned with the Alabama Tech Warhawks logo on the side come to a safe landing and the famous "Bull" Ripley escorted by six Alabama state troopers emerge from inside the chopper. The players were instructed to get focused by their respective coaching staffs, but the crowd in the stands continued to be in awe of the most famous coach in America arriving in Warner Robins, Georgia. Bull Ripley was very aware of the excitement he had caused, and he enjoyed every minute of it. Also in attendance was a beautiful young blonde named Gwen Parker who just wanted to see what all the fuss was about with Aubrey Durrell as a football player. Gwen watched as "The Bull" made his way through the adoring crowd on the home side and eventually down to field level. He spoke briefly with the head coaches from both teams and settled in in an end zone to watch his recruits Jamie Hillman and Aubrey Durrell do battle against one another. He spoke with the Kentucky A&M coaches for a while also.

The game started with Southside Warner Robins taking the opening kickoff and driving 69 yards for a TD. On the ensuing possession, Darcy Williams was sacked and fumbled the football which was scooped up and returned 32 yards for a Southside TD and a 14-0 lead in the first ten minutes of the game. Naturally, Southside felt good about their start and decided to kick the ball to Empire's number 15—Aubrey Durrell. This would prove to be a bad decision as Aubrey fielded the kickoff at the 3-yard line and turned on the speed going basically untouched for Empire's first score of the game. Empire decided wisely to kick the ball away from Jamie Hillman, so Southside took possession of the ball at their own 32-yard line where they went to work on another scoring drive to take a 21-7 lead with nine minutes left in the first half. Jamie Hillman was exceptional on the drive catching four balls for 46 yards and finishing the drive off with a 13-yard TD catch. Southside executed a surprise onside kick to get the ball back and Hillman caught a 33-yard TD pass two plays later to give his team a huge lead of 28-7 with just over four minutes left in the first half. Southside kicked away from Aubrey so Empire got the ball on their own 36-yard line and the coaches just wanted to get to halftime so they could regroup, but Aubrey and J.R. had other ideas. Aubrey would bust a trap play for 24 yards to start the drive. With time running out in the first half Empire would need to throw the ball so Darcy Williams would have to get rid of the ball quickly to avoid the Southside pass rush. Play action passes would work best so after a play fake to Ashley Stacey; Darcy booted out to his left and hit Lester Beasley on a 31-yard corner route. On first and goal from the Southside 9-yard line Aubrey would score his second TD on a quick pitch left behind a ferocious block by Lester Beasley. The score at halftime was Southside 28 and Empire 14. Bull Ripley left at halftime to fly somewhere else and watch another recruit. A he left he told his state troopers that Empire was in over their head and this game was going to get ugly before it was over. That was the feeling of everyone in the stadium except the Empire coaches and players.

Coach Kelly's halftime speech was simple and to the point. He said, "Men over the last two seasons we have not been in this situation where we have had the opportunity to play in the most memorable game in school history. That's right, I said this is an opportunity because I believe we are going to make a game of this before this night is through. I know you guys will respond to the challenge before you tonight and please understand that Southside wants to embarrass us; to set the pecking order and show their dominance and if we lay down in the second half, they will succeed in that goal. So, the choice is yours—you can either lay down for them and take your butt whipping, or you get up off the deck and make this the most memorable night of your athletic lives. I won't quit on you so don't you quit on me." Every player understood what they had to do so they were ready to play when they took the field in the third quarter. Lester Beasley took the second half kickoff at his own 14-yard line and ran it back to the Southside 45-yard line before being pushed out of bounds. From there Aubrey and Ashley Stacey took turns gashing the Southside defense with Aubrey gaining 23 yards and Ashley gaining 17 yards bringing the ball to the Southside 5-yard line where on first and goal, Darcy Williams faked a power play to Aubrey and booted to his left where he had a run / pass option. When the cornerback came up to stop Darcy, he left Lester Beasley wide open in the corner of the end zone. Darcy tossed him the ball for Empire's third TD of the night making the score 28-21 in favor of Southside.

Defensively Empire would have to play better versus an extremely talented bunch of athletes including Jamie Hiller who was having a career night catching the ball. Defensive coordinator Jerry Lord devised a way to contain Hiller by lining up in a cover two shell pre-snap and moving to a cover 3 zone at the snap by having J.R. drop from his mike linebacker position to deep middle coverage on all passing downs or when Hiller lined up in the left slot receiver position. Coach Lord had noticed in the first half that the only time Hiller ran a dig route over the middle was from the left slot position. This was a crucial tell for what they may be running, and it was a hunch that paid off. He also knew that Southside would throw the ball at least 50-60 % of the time even when they had a great running game. Their coaches would want to show their superiority and would not have patience to go on long time-consuming drives. On their ensuing possession, Southside would run the ball on first and second down gaining 21 yards but decided to throw the ball on the next play. Jamie Hiller lined up at left slot receiver and predictably ran his dig route. The ball was delivered perfectly, and Hiller caught it in stride and took three more steps before J.R. almost took his head off with a brutal hit that caught the entire Southside team completely by surprise. Hiller went one way, and the ball went another. Stevie Wilbur scooped the ball up and returned it back inside the Southside 15-yard line. On first down Josh Beasley snuck threw the Southside defense for eight yards making it second down and 2 from the 7-yard line. Aubrey would score his third TD of the game on power left. The extra point was blocked leaving the score 28-27 with three minutes left in the third quarter.

Southside would drive down and kick a 35-yard field goal making the score 31-27 early in the 4th quarter. Ashley Stacey would break on a long run to start the Empire possession going for 35 yards on a blast right behind Josh Beasley and Aubrey's lead block on the Southside linebacker. Ashley would pick up 11 more yards on the next play off tackle with Aubrey faking a quick pitch left and taking the Southside defense with him allowing Ashley to gain good yardage. On first and ten from the Southside 47-yard line, Darcy Williams would boot to his left again after faking power right to Aubrey but this time he would lob a perfect screen pass to Ashley Stacey on the right side and Ashley would take it all the way for the score behind a crushing block by Aubrey on the Southside free safety. A failed two-point conversion would leave the score at 33-31 in favor of Empire with just under six minutes left to play. Jamie Hiller was not on the field for the kickoff because of J.R.'s hit he was on the sideline with a concussion, so Empire kicked the ball deep and this proved to be unwise as Hiller's backup almost took it all the way back. If Lester Beasley had not run him down at the Empire 12-yard line he would have scored. All Southside had to do was run a couple of plays and then line up for the go-ahead field goal. After two incomplete passes which stopped the clock saving Empire's timeouts, the Empire defense sacked the QB on third down forcing a 36-yard field goal attempt with 3:37 second left to play. The field goal was good giving Southside a 34-33 lead. Empire would get the ball on their own 35-yard line after the kickoff went out of bounds and the greatest comeback win in Empire history began. On first down, the call was Twins Right Motion Right Square out with Aubrey in motion and running a 5-yard out route. He was covered on the play, but Lester Beasley was wide open on a drag route and Darcy hit him in stride for a 16-yard gain. Aubrey gained another 14 yards on a quick pitch right. Ashley Stacey would gain 12 more yards on 4 Smackover with Aubrey faking another quick pitch right. The clock was running, and Southside had to call a timeout with 2:10 remaining in the game. On a power play to the right Aubrey gained 7 more yards and Southside burned their second timeout. On second and three Aubrey gained another 5 yards on power left. With 53 seconds left Southside called their last timeout. On first and ten from the Southside 21-yard line, Coach Kelly called a play that they had been working on for a few weeks. It was a power pass by Aubrey who would take the handoff from the QB and fake a power run for three or four steps before pulling up and throwing to either J.R. on a flag route, or Lester Beasley on a deep post route. Surely enough the Southside defense came up hard to try to stop Aubrey allowing J.R. to run by them and get wide open at the goal line. All Aubrey had to do was deliver the ball which he did. J. R. caught the ball and scored the easiest TD he would ever score. Josh Beasley would drive across the goal line for a two-point conversion making the score 41-34 in favor of Empire with 41 seconds remaining in the game. A pooch kick gave Southside the ball on their own 29-yard line. Two completions gave them a first down at midfield with 32 seconds left and no timeouts. After killing the clock, it was second down and ten from the Empire 49-yard line. Bobby Parton sacked the QB on second down and the clock kept running with 23 seconds left. Panic took over on Southside's behalf, and the QB spiked the ball to stop the clock but in doing so, he made it fourth down and 16 to go for a first down. One play for the game. The Southside QB scrambled around for what seemed like forever before throwing the ball over the middle of the field where J.R. stepped in front of the receiver and intercepted the ball and unleashing a wild celebration on the Empire side of the field.

CHAPTER FIFTY-SEVEN

After the game. Aubrey noticed that the Kentucky A&M coaches were still at the game while Bull Ripley was long gone. Maybe this was a small thing but to Aubrey took it to mean that maybe he and J.R. were the top priority for A&M whereas Alabama Tech had others they valued more than the Durrells. Either way, it meant a lot to Aubrey to see them there at the end of the game.

Gwen Parker was impressed with Aubrey's football skills, and she now understood why coaches from across the county wanted him so badly. She wanted him too, but she knew that was not possible. She and her sister went home, and she tried to put it out of her mind. Her sister Judy told her he was the best-looking boy she had ever seen to which Gwen added that he was genuinely nice too. Judy had always understood Gwen ever since their mother and father had divorced when Gwen was four years old. Judy was three years older and had been a guardian angel for Gwen and she had needed her quite often. When her mother remarried a man, who had molested the girls when Gwen was twelve years old, it was Judy who told her mother about it and had gotten the man arrested. When Judy moved out on her own at age eighteen, she got a good job selling real estate, and told Gwen that she would help her out financially if she wanted to go to college. Gwen decided to attend Alabama Tech and study to become a teacher. She had taken the job as a football escort to ease the financial burden on Judy, but now she felt cheap and dirty. At least she had done the right thing regarding Aubrey and Jamie Hiller by telling them about the setup at Alabama Tech. However, she was now starting to notice some strange looks on campus by some of the girls who also participated as escorts and one of them had sort of threatened her with physical violence one night at a local club. She had decided to transfer to another school but was taking the spring semester off to figure out what to do next.

Christina called at 1:00 a.m. to get the news about the game. She told Aubrey that she was pledging Alpha Kappa Alpha Sorority and she wanted him to come visit her as soon as football season was over. He promised that he would, and they expressed their love for one another before hanging up.

Aubrey got a surprise during homecoming week when Christina surprised him by coming home to crown the next queen. She did not inform Aubrey that she would be there on Thursday; instead, she showed up at the high school around 2:00 in the afternoon and met him after his sixth period class in the hallway. He was so glad to see her that he almost skipped seventh period, but she made him go to class promising him to meet him after school before football practice. Empire would blow Dubois out 48-0 for their eighth victory of the season and the homecoming dance was just like old times with Aubrey and Christina. They also spent some alone time together off Chicken Road. The next night Aubrey told her that they would go to Macon to see a movie, but he had another idea. He had rented a room at the Hilton Hotel in Macon and when he took Christina there instead, she was shocked. Aubrey explained that he wanted his last night with her for a long while to be more than just the back seat of his impala. They enjoyed room service and a couple of hours of passion and then went home. It was expensive but he did not mind. Nothing was too good for the love of his life. The next day he left for college again this time more in love than ever before.

When Aubrey got home from football practice the following Monday, he had a package waiting on him that had no return address. He opened it and found $5000 in cash with a note which read 'THERE IS PLENTY MORE WHERE THIS CAME FROM IF YOU MAKE THE RIGHT CHOICE ON WHERE YOU PLAY FOOTBALL'. He immediately told his daddy about it and Wyll was at a loss for words. Neither of them wanted to keep the money, but they had no idea who to return it to. It could have been from any school since they were all recruiting him heavily. It could be from Coach Cook from Kentucky A&M or possibly from Alabama Tech. Aubrey called J.R. to see if he got anything from Kentucky A&M today but he said he had not and when he asked Aubrey why he wanted to know; Aubrey told him to come to his house and he would show him. He trusted J.R. to keep a secret and showed him the money. J.R. told him to spend the money since no one would ever admit to giving it to him anyway so why worry about it? Aubrey saw his point but still felt like it would be wrong to spend this dirty money.

In Selma, Alabama Bull Ripley wanted to know if the package was delivered, and the Birmingham businessman assured him that it had been. They would give it a while before letting him know it had come from Alabama Tech boosters in Atlanta. Of course, Bull Ripley would not be associated with this in any way as far as Aubrey knew. If it had not been for Gwen Parker, they would not have to spend the extra cash, but he was worth it according to his assistant coaches.

Empire would breeze through the regular season undefeated, and Aubrey would total another 1760 yards rushing and score 27 TD's earning him another first team All-Region selection along with J.R.; Ashley Stacey; and Darcy Williams. The toughest game of the regular season was against Union Hill whose QB—junior Robert Morrison— was a terrific athlete who single-handedly kept Union Hill in this game. However, Empire would eventually prevail by a score of 35-21. Morrison, Coach Tony Rogers, and the Union Hill Barons would win their state title the next season after the super class of Empire graduated.

The Knights played well in the first three rounds of the state playoffs winning by an average of fourteen points per game defeating Hogansville, Dahlonega Academy, and Sandersville. In the semi-finals they would meet Folkston in Empire and it would be a great game. Empire would hang on to win 16-12 on a goal line stand when J.R. stopped the running back on the two-yard line on fourth and goal as time ran out. Folkston would lose to Union Hill the following season in the state championship game.

Empire would host Wrens in the state championship game the following week. With a chance to go undefeated and win their third state football championship in a row, the Empire Knights would not be denied. In mid-December with the temperature at 43 degrees and the stands at full capacity and with Christina home for the Christmas break, Aubrey would have another great game. He would rush for 209 yards and 3 TD's. in 49-14 victory. J.R. would go out in style too with two TD pass receptions and 5 catches for the game for 85 yards while collecting 14 tackles on defense with 3 QB sacks and an interception. Ashley Stacey would rush for 134 yards and two TD's. Darcy Williams would throw for 137 yards on 9 for 12 passing and two TD's. The third state championship in football but the seventh straight team championship made it official—Empire has been the best athletic program in the state for the last three school years and quite possibly in the history of the state of Georgia. Incidentally, Southside Warner Robins and Fort Valley would also win their respective classifications state titles as well. There was joy for sure, but also a bit of sadness knowing that this was the last time these boys would ever take the football field together. There were plenty of tears on the field and in the locker room. Coach Kelly barely kept it together long enough to tell the seniors how much they meant to him personally and professionally. "When I came here in 1970, I did not know how long I would be here or if I would succeed, but I had a couple of things going for me—first of all, I had the greatest coaching staff a man could ever hope for. Secondly, I had a group of kids coming up that I knew if I could hold on to this job long enough to get them in our program, I might be able to finally beat Union Hill." he said to mild laughter from coaches and players. "Little did I know that we would win three in a row and multiple championships in other sports. I just want to say to all you seniors that you are the greatest winners I have ever seen; and not just on the field, but winners in life as well and I know that each of you will be successful in whatever you do after you leave Empire High School. And men, I love each of you and if you ever need me for anything, all you have to do is ask." Coach Kelly would win his third consecutive Coach of the Year Award and his eighth overall and would stay at Empire for four more seasons and win one more state championship in Kelcey and Gerry Durrell's senior season. His son Quay Kelly would be the feature running back on that championship team. He would end up back in Atlanta coaching in AAAA and winning two more state titles before retiring in 1996. He would be inducted in the Empire Athletic Hall of Fame in 1997. He would leave Empire with a 103-39 record and four state titles to go along with 5 region titles. Aubrey would finish his high school football career with 8,713 yards rushing and 126 TD's. Both those numbers would be state records until broken in 1997 and 2009, respectively. Despite the cold temperature, the tradition of spending the night on the field after another championship was continued. This time it was special for all the seniors who spent all night talking about games from the past four years.

CHAPTER FIFTY-EIGHT

Aubrey and Christina spent as much time together as they could over the Christmas break and basketball practice started so Aubrey was busy as ever. He also knew that signing day was coming in early February and he was leaning toward Kentucky A&M, he was also probably going to receive an appointment to the U.S. Naval Academy; as soon as the Georgia state senator got around to it; and of course, there was still Alabama Tech. He had also gotten a few more offers from schools from Southern California to Pennsylvania. J.R. had received a handful of offers too but he was leaning toward Kentucky A&M. By mid-January, the Knights basketball team was winning games, and everything was going fine. On a Sunday night Aubrey received a call from an anonymous caller who asked him if he had gotten the package a few weeks earlier and told him to expect another one this week. He also told Aubrey that he hoped he would do the right thing and sign with Alabama Tech. Aubrey started to tell the man that he did not want any money and that he had not spent a penny of the other money, but the man hung up before he could tell him.

Meanwhile, Jamie Hiller at Southside Warner Robins was also getting money from an Alabama Tech booster. He wondered if Aubrey and the offensive lineman were getting money too. On Wednesday of that week, he took a day off school and drove to Empire High School to speak to Aubrey in person.

On Tuesday of that same week, another package arrived at the Durrell home containing another $5000 and this time it had an Alabama Tech bumper sticker in the package. When school let out the next day, Jamie Hiller saw Aubrey and flagged him down. Aubrey was shocked to see him but was glad he came to Empire to talk to him. They had a couple of hours before basketball practice, so Aubrey suggested they go to Nubby' s and enjoy a milk shake and Jamie agreed. When they got there and sat down with their shakes, Jamie told Aubrey what had happened saying, "I need to ask you something Aubrey, I wanted to find out if you had received a package from an anonymous booster" Aubrey answered that he had, but that he had, but he had not spent any of it, "What are you going to do?" asked Aubrey. "I am probably signing with Alabama Tech," said Jamie. "Is this what you want to do?" asked Aubrey. "Maybe, but this money can come in handy. What are you going to do about the money?" asked Jamie. "I think I am going to send it to bull Ripley along with a letter informing him that I appreciate his interest in me, but I have decided to go elsewhere." answered Aubrey. He told Jamie that he did not blame him for his decision, and he wished him luck. They wondered if their lineman buddy in LaGrange was receiving money as well. While Aubrey was somewhat disappointed in Jamie's decision, he knew that kind of money was hard to turn down and he also knew that if not for the R.C. Gold Band he would not have any money and would be tempted to take the money and never look back. He would not be attending Alabama Tech however, because he knew how Bull Ripley felt about baseball. He told Jamie to stay in touch and went to basketball practice. He prayed for Jamie that night.

Aubrey had sent the $10,000 back to Bull Ripley along with a letter explaining that he would not be attending Alabama Tech and that he wanted no more money from boosters. This put "The Bull" in a sticky predicament. If he took the money back from Aubrey, it would be an admission of guilt if it ever came out; so, he begrudgingly sent it back to Aubrey denying any knowledge of how it got sent to him and expressing his disappointment that he would not be playing for him. Deep down inside, he despised this self-righteous kid who thought he knew best. And even though he said the right thing, he hoped to play against this punk and teach him a lesson about messing with "The Bull". After all, everyone knows if you mess with the Bull; you get the horns!

Aubrey liked the idea of going to the U.S. Naval Academy just like his hero Roger Staubach had done. He could go to school for free; play football and baseball and even if he got drafted in the major leagues, he would still serve his country for five years and perhaps play baseball after his commitment was up. If not, he would still be able to retire after 20 years in the military and that seemed liked a great deal to Aubrey. J.R. was signing with Kentucky A&M and, they had signed a junior college transfer name Zack Winborn to play at Kentucky A&M, so that would be a good option too.

The basketball team was winning and that was good, but Aubrey was a bit distracted by recruiting. As the region tournament was approaching, there were two super teams—Empire and Chauncey. Earl Rabun was having a super season averaging 23 points per game and was getting interest from schools all around the southeast. He was a handful and in the first game versus Empire had scored 32 points in leading the Comets to an 88-78 victory, Empire had managed to win the second game by a slim margin 76-71 with Rabun scoring 21 points but Kenny Dudley had a great game for Empire scoring 19 points and blocking 5 shots. Chauncey would win the region tournament over Empire by a score of 78-73 with Rabun scoring 34 points. Empire would lose in the second round of the state tournament to Bonaire, but J.R. would get his dunk early in the second half. They would watch Rabun lead the Chauncey Comets to a state championship victory over Butler. Aubrey wanted to win the championship but if he could not win; he was happy that Earl Rabun did. He liked Earl and his cousin Renee would probably marry him someday.

In early February, Jamie Hiller had called Aubrey and told him that he could not accept the money with a clear conscience and was sending it back so was the lineman from LaGrange. Aubrey told him that he had sent his back and that Ripley had sent it back to him claiming to know nothing about it; but he still had not spent a dime of it. He also told Jamie that God would bless him for his decision. They also agreed to consider going to the same college and Aubrey told him about Kentucky A&M. He also said that he would call the head coach and tell him about him and the lineman. Aubrey knew right then where he would be attending school. When Aubrey called Coach Cook to tell him that he would love to come play for him at Kentucky A&M he also told him about his two friends who might accept an offer as well and the Coach thanked him for his commitment and his information about the other two players.

CHAPTER FIFTY-NINE

Baseball was starting up in less than a week and the Knights were determined not to lose a chance at another state title. After all, they were the defending state champions and number one ranked team in the state. They did not like the way basketball had ended but they still had one more chance to redeem themselves. Everyone had already made their plans for after high school except Darcy Williams who was depending on the major league draft. Ashley Stacey had signed with Florida State University to play defensive back in football. Lester Beasley and his twin brother Josh had signed to attend the Northrup Grumman Apprentice School where they would learn a trade; get paid; and play division III college football. Randy Stafford would play college baseball at Middle Georgia College. Kenny Dudley was going to play basketball at Albany State College. Teddy Robertson was going to play division II football at small school in North Carolina, and of course, J.R. and Aubrey had their plans worked out, so there should be no distractions on the team. On signing day in February, Kentucky A&M had a great day inking the Durrell's; Jamie Hiller; Zach Winborn; and a big lineman from Lagrange, Georgia. Coach Jerry Cook was ecstatic and could not wait for the season to start. The school's baseball coach, Max Ellison was also present at the signing ceremony, and he was happy about his two new players as well. A young lady in Barnesville, Georgia also made her mind up about where she would transfer to for the spring semester of 1980— Kentucky A&M.

Baseball season started the next week and Aubrey was glad since this would be the last time that he and his mates would represent Empire on a ball field. Aubrey wanted to take in every second of this season. He took a few more timeouts when at the plate so he could notice his family in the stands or smell the popcorn and hamburgers cooking in the concession stand; or just to look out over the left field fence where he, J.R., Stevie Wilbur, and Kelcey had finally emerged from their two-hour trek through Booger Bottom a few years ago. He knew that he had been blessed and that life would never be any better than it was now. He thanked God and then stepped back in the batter's box and usually destroyed the opposing pitcher. They were 5-0 to start the season and were rarely challenged during this stretch.

Two more games and two more victories and Aubrey played well going 4 for 9 with two doubles and a homerun. He was hitting .450 so far this season with 3 homeruns and his defense was flawless. J.R. was crushing the ball too to the tune of a .435 average with 5 homeruns and 13 RBI. There began to be some talk about how high they both may go in the upcoming major league draft, but unless it was the first or second round, they would be at Kentucky A&M in the fall. Darcy Williams on the other hand would sign for meal money if he had to; but at 6' 1" and 175 pounds and with his fastball now reaching the low 90's and the kicking mule still kicking; he would not have to worry about it. He would end up as a second-round pick by Texas and get a $40,000 signing bonus. Darcy had never been more than a hundred miles away from Empire so when he was told to report to rookie camp in Arizona, he was excited but also scared. He asked his long-time girlfriend Jeannie Hoffs to marry him later that year and she said yes, and she went to Arizona to live with him, which did not sit well with her parents, but she did not seem to care. Darcy would finish his last season in Empire a perfect 12-0 with an E.R.A. of .083 to go along with 126 strikeouts.

Empire would finish the season undefeated and would breeze through the state playoffs with only one loss and that was to Hogansville in game two of the semi-finals when Hogansville would hit a walk-off homerun off "Hondo" Winston for a 4-3 victory, but Empire was undaunted and crushed them, in game three by a score of 9-3 to make the state championship series versus Ocilla. Empire would take care of business in two games with Darcy Williams winning the deciding game and Aubrey and J.R. both hitting homeruns to win the game by a score of 12-1 in five innings. A fitting end to their careers at Empire High School.

It really hit the boys that it was finally over after the game when the crowd gave them all a standing ovation that seemed to last forever and indeed, they wished that it could last forever. Tradition continued with a free meal at Nubby's and spending the night at the baseball field. They would all graduate in two weeks and move on with their lives, but for now they did not want this day to end.

That Sunday at band practice, they decided that their last gig would be the 4th of July celebration in Warner Robins and all they had to do now was decide what their last song would be. Billy Dobbs plan was to move to Nashville and try to break into the music businesses. Terry Lampkin was joining the Navy. Doug Hall was going to work for his father in the auto parts business and would eventually take over the business. They would all remain lifelong friends and hoped to reunite someday to play again. After graduation, which was attended by a record number of people, they had a party at the farm of Teddy Robertson's grandpa and R.C. Gold played and brought down the house. It was b.y.o.b. so there were some drunks there, but nothing got out of hand. Aubrey had invited Jamie Hiller and some of his buddies from Southside Warner Robins to come and they had a great time as well. They had been working on Queen's 'WE WILL ROCK YOU / WE ARE THE CHAMPIONS', and they unveiled their efforts at the graduation party. It was met with such enthusiasm that they decided to make it their last song on the 4th of July.

In early June, the major league draft took place and as mentioned earlier Darcy Williams was taken in the second round by Texas. Since it was well-known that both the Durrell boys wanted to play college football major league teams shied away from them; nevertheless, Aubrey was drafted in round seven by Detroit and J.R. in the ninth round by Boston so they both were heading to Florence, Kentucky to start their college careers.

CHAPTER SIXTY

Christina came home for graduation and for the summer and she and Aubrey spent as much time together as possible. She had gotten a job at a lawyer's office in Eastman, so she was busy a lot of the time and Aubrey kept pulling the plow for his daddy and loading melons one last time. Some of the guys thought it would be cool to have one more party at the Bar Pit for old times' sake, so it was planned for the last Saturday in June. All the players were there, and all their girlfriends and it was a great time for all. Aubrey and Christina went for a little while but soon left for some private time that had been lacking. Aubrey had no protection on him, but they threw caution to the wind and carried on anyway.

The next weekend was the concert in Warner Robins and this time the headliners were .38 Special and again R.C. Gold would lead into the main act. When they were introduced, the announcer told the crowd that this would be there last performance so give a big round of applause for the "best little party band in Middle Georgia—from Empire, Georgia—the R.C. Gold Band!" Most of the crowd had heard them the year before and responded loudly; and the rest would be on their feet before the show had ended. When they played their last song "WE WILL ROCK YOU / WE ARE THE CHAMPIONS' the crowd showed its appreciation by standing with their lighters lit and swaying to the music. It was something special and something that none of the boys would ever forget. As they left the stage, they hugged each other like brothers and told each other they loved them and would always cherish their time together. They also thanked Billy Dobbs for bringing them together in the first place. They then watched as the headliners tore up the stage. Aubrey and Christina rode home talking about how things move fast when you grow up. They spent some time alone and then Aubrey rode around Empire for a while thinking and praying before going home to get some rest.

About three weeks later Christina noticed that she was feeling sick early in the mornings, and she was late. She knew why but she did not want to face facts. Her whole life would be ruined by a moment of indiscretion and so would Aubrey's life. She had to tell him, so she went to see him early on Saturday and asked him to take a ride with her in her daddy's car. He knew something was up, but he was not ready for the bombshell she dropped on him that morning. When she uttered the words 'I'm pregnant', Aubrey felt like he was going to throw up. He was speechless at first but eventually he told her that he loved her and would do whatever she wanted to do even if it meant marriage and foregoing college. He loved her that much. She told him she loved him too but that she did not want to have a baby right now and he didn't need one either at this stage of life. She thought about what her parents would say if they found out and what about Rod Hickey and the scholarship she had earned? Aubrey hugged her close and told her not to worry but he had no idea what to do in this situation. Christina said she did not have the money for an abortion and did not know what to do about it. Aubrey was caught off-guard by the mention of the word abortion. He was always against what he considered murder. He wanted to tell Christina that, but he decided now was not the proper time. How could he justify an abortion but also how could he ask the love of his life to have a baby and give up her dreams. He still had the $10,000 from the Alabama Tech Booster and he told her not to worry about the money. She could have every penny of it as far as he was concerned. She asked him if he would go with her to Atlanta to see a doctor who performed abortions and he said of course he would. He told her she was never going to have to face anything alone and he pulled her close to his side and kissed her gently. They went to eat at Nubby' s then went home. Aubrey prayed for forgiveness and guidance and accepted this as the Lord's way of teaching him a lesson about pre-marital sex—a lesson he had managed to forget or ignore many times. He prayed for Christina also and hoped that God would bless her and not punish her for his sins. He was so conflicted about what was about to happen.

Two weeks later they concocted story about going to the Cyclorama and the Atlanta Zoo and headed up I-75 North to Atlanta. They left early one Monday morning and made it in time for a 1:00 appointment. After consulting with the doctor, he told her that he would perform the procedure for $500. Aubrey said that would be no problem and an appointment was set for the next week. Aubrey was set to leave for football camp at the end of that week, so timing was critical. The next week they concocted another excuse for going to Atlanta. This time it was a Braves' game, so they had to make sure they knew the score and certain game particulars before they returned home. Wyll Durrell thought it a little strange that they would go to a Braves' game by themselves and leave so early to make a 7:30 start time, but he wanted to trust his son, so he did not ask any questions until Aubrey returned. The procedure went fine, but on the way home, Aubrey could not help wondering what their child would look like; would have been a boy or a girl? He could not shake the feeling that what they had done was wrong, and yet it had to be done for their future. When Aubrey got home, his dad started quizzing him about the game asking him where his seats were located and how he liked the great catch Barry Bonnell had made in the 6th inning. When Aubrey said it was awesome his dad knew he was lying because Bonnell had not played in this game, instead Eddie Miller had played centerfield. He knew his son watched every game intensely and would not miss a detail like this, so he confronted Aubrey with this fact. "Son why don't you tell me where you really went?" asked Wyll. Aubrey hung his head and his daddy told him he could tell him anything and he would understand. "I don't know about this one Daddy," said Aubrey. Wyll already had an idea, so he asked, "Is Christina in trouble?" Aubrey said, "Not anymore, but Daddy you have to keep this a secret, please." To which Wyll responded, "don't worry about it. Anything you tell me in confidence is between you and me." "I don't know what to say Daddy, we just slipped up and now I have to live with the consequences of my actions. Christina had an abortion and I paid for it with the dirty money from the Alabama Tech boosters," said Aubrey. He started to cry and said he knew abortion was wrong, but they didn't know what else to do. His daddy went to him and hugged his neck and said "Son, you are not the first to have to deal with this and you won't be the last. Right now, you just need to be there for Christina because she will need you and continue praying for the Lord's guidance," "You mean forgiveness don't you Daddy?" he asked. His Daddy told him, "We all need forgiveness on a daily basis, but the God is good Aubrey, and you know that." Aubrey told his Daddy how sorry he was to disappoint him again; but Wyll stopped him and said, "Son, I can never be disappointed in you as long as you pray to the Lord above and live a good life. And I want you to know that watching you play ball the last four years has been the highlight of my life and I know the sky is the limit for you so long as you keep God first in your life. We have all sinned and come short of the glory of God. That's part of being human but don't ever think for one minute that I am not proud of you." Aubrey hugged his Daddy like he had not done since he was a little boy and he felt like a little boy again and he and Wyll had a good cry together. Aubrey thanked God for his parents and begged for forgiveness and guidance and he prayed for Christina then he tried to sleep, but sleep would not come that night or any other for the next few weeks.

He would be leaving in five days to start life as a college athlete, so he naturally wanted to spend as much time with Christina as possible, but she was not in a mood for seeing him or anyone for a while. He understood but it hurt him a little bit just the same. When he finally did get to see her, he told her that he wanted her to know that he would always love her, and he would miss her so much when he was gone but that he would not leave until he knew she was going to be okay. She assured him that she would be fine eventually, but for now, she had to deal with her feelings in her own way. He told her that he understood but wanted one more date before he had to leave. She agreed and on Friday night they went to see a movie in Macon and ate at the Quail's Nest Buffet. On the way home Aubrey asked if they could go to Chicken Road one last time. He told her not for sex but just to talk and be alone before they would have to leave and go their separate ways. She said yes but she did not want to get anything started. When they got there, they remembered good times and bad and especially the night that the rednecks tried to hurt them before their dads showed up. "I thought I would never be able to see you again after that night," said Aubrey. "Over this last month you probably wished that I never did see you again," he added. "Don't you ever say that again Aubrey

Durrell, "said Christina. I loved you a long time before you ever knew it and I will always love you. You are the most decent person I have ever known, and I want us to be together forever someday," she added. "I cannot imagine going through this recent ordeal with anyone other than you," she stated as tears began to roll down her cheeks. Aubrey grabbed her and kissed her as he felt himself starting to get emotional.

"Christina, I want you to have something," said Aubrey as he reached across her into the glove compartment. He pulled out an envelope with the remaining money from the Alabama Tech booster. He told her there was $9500 in there and he wanted her to have it so she could concentrate on her studies and not have to worry about money. She protested at first, but he would not hear of it insisting that she take the cash. She reluctantly agreed to do so insisting that someday she would pay him back. Aubrey told her that it was not a loan and she never had to worry about paying it back. They sat and enjoyed one another's company for as long as they could before she had to be home. When Aubrey said goodbye, he barely made it to the car before she came running after him and hugged him tightly telling him she loved him more than life itself and she would be the biggest Kentucky A&M fan in the world. He told her he would play every game for her and that he would be counting the days until he could see her again. It was only when Kenny arrived home from his date that they let go of each other. Kenny told Aubrey that he was proud to have been his best friend since first grade and hoped to someday call him brother-in-law. They hugged each other and Aubrey got in his Impala and left for home; but first he wanted to ride around Empire one more time.

Aubrey and J.R. would be leaving early the next morning and Wyll and Eli would take them to school since freshmen were not allowed to have cars. Aubrey had already packed his bags so the only thing left to do was say goodbye to his mama and his siblings and off he would go. Of course, there was tears from Pattie and even Kelcey and Paula shed a few as did Aubrey. The boys got a surprise visit from Jimmy Wardell, the farmer they had worked for loading melons since they were old enough to work, and he gave them both a going away gift of $500 each and told them it was because they had always been dependable when others were not. He wished them luck and carried on with his day's work. It was about 575 miles to Florence, Kentucky from Empire,

Georgia up I-75, so the boys had a lot of time to think on the trip up there. Aubrey thought about Christina and how she would have to deal with their actions alone. She would have a follow up appointment with her doctor on Monday that she would have to handle alone, and this broke his heart.

CHAPTER SIXTY-ONE

Wyll saw it first as it was his turn to drive. A huge red and white-water tower with "FLORENCE Y'ALL" written in big letters. He woke the boys and Eli up to see this monstrosity, and of course to let them know that they were almost there. Florence was not a huge city, but to a couple of country boys from Empire, Georgia; it looked huge and may as well have been New York City. About four miles north of town was the campus of Kentucky A&M University. Coach Cook was there to meet them at the football office and got them assigned to their rooms and introduced them to their roommates. Aubrey was assigned to a quarterback recruit from Oberlin, Ohio while J. R. was assigned to live with a defensive lineman from Louisville, Kentucky. Aubrey was hoping Jamie Hiller and his lineman friend from Lagrange had showed up. After settling in, Wyll suggested they all go on an unofficial campus tour. They found the cafeteria, the student center, and the football stadium. It was an older stadium—the Ernest W. Riley Stadium. It only held 49,000 people and it had not been sold out in years. Perhaps this recruiting class would change all that. That was what Coach Cook hoped would happen anyway,

When Aubrey and J.R. went down to walk the field—the first time either of them had ever been on Astro-turf—they had only gotten to the 30-yard line when the heard a familiar voice call out from the bleachers. "Hey Empire, are y'all lost?" the voice boomed. Looking up to see who it was they both were glad to see the familiar face of Zach Winborn. He came out on the field and told them how good it was to see them and how he looked forward to playing with them instead of against them. Aubrey noticed a difference in the way he looked; it was as if he was at peace with life instead of the tortured soul that he used to be. If so, then glory be to God for providing a way for Zack to realize his potential through football. "So how long have you been on campus?" asked J.R. Zack told them that he had enrolled in summer school to try and get ahead so it would not be so difficult during football season. He asked them if they had any plans for supper and when they told him no, he recommended a little pizza place near campus. He then went up to say hello to Wyll and Eli. Over supper Zack explained how he had been saved by football and the influence of Coach Jack Sullivan who had showed him what a real man was supposed to do and how football could save lives and make people change their coursed for the better. He said he owed a lot to Coach Tony Rogers at Union Hill also. And he also thanked Aubrey for the butt whipping he had put on him which brought him down a notch or two and made him realize that he was not the biggest bad ass on the planet. 'I just want to win here at Kentucky A&M, and I want to get my degree and coach high school football so maybe I can influence some kid to do something good with his life when the odds are stacked against him. And I believe with the two of you here we can make winning a regular occurrence around here and fill that stadium up every Saturday in the fall. Heck maybe we can force them to spend some money to add some seats," said Zack. J.R. had to ask what had happened to Quick Jenkins after the night they tried to hurt Aubrey. "Well," said Zack, "he swore to get me back for turning on him and he tried coming to Coach Rogers house one night to kick my butt. But Coach Rogers stood up to him and had his wife call the cops and they placed a restraining order on him for me and locked him up for drunk and disorderly conduct. When they started investigating him, they found out about his drug dealing and that he had been stealing copper wire from the base and others in the county. He is serving five years in Reidsville mainly for stealing from the U.S. government." "How about your mom?" asked Aubrey. "She would not have anything to do with me after the incident and she blamed me for ruining her marriage, but she has since gone to rehab, and we are talking a little more these days" answered Zack. "I hope she can get straight and move on with her life" he added. Wyll said, "we will keep her in our prayers Zack." Zack thanked them and changed the subject back to football. Aubrey wanted to ask him if he was still seeing Chelsey, but he thought better of it for now.

They talked about the first team meeting scheduled for the next afternoon at 2 PM in the team meeting room and the first practice Monday morning at 6 AM in the weight room. After about an hour at the pizza parlor, the boys went to unpack their things and get settled into their rooms. Eli and Wyll went to a hotel room for the night. They would head back home tomorrow afternoon. Aubrey scraped up enough change to call Christina and let her know they had made it and to find out how she was doing. She was glad to hear from him and told him that her doctor's appointment had gone fine and that she was getting ready to return to college. She wished him the best at practice and told him she loved him. and he told her the same thing. He agreed to call her tomorrow night the first chance he got.

Aubrey's roommate came in about this time and they introduced themselves to one another. Chad Walker seemed like a nice guy so Aubrey thought this would work out okay for him. It was Aubrey's first-time rooming with anyone so he was sure that he would have to adjust and not only that; Chad was a black player and although Aubrey did not have a problem with it, he did not know how his roommate felt about it. J.R. also had a black roommate named Cedric Gooch and they were hitting it off fine so far. It was obvious that Coach Cook had a plan for bringing the team together by rooming black and white players together, and that was fine with the Durrells.

The next morning Eli and Wyll said their goodbyes and headed back home to Empire. Aubrey wanted to go back with them but knew his future was right here in "FLORENCE Y'ALL", Kentucky so he set his mind on getting to work tomorrow morning.

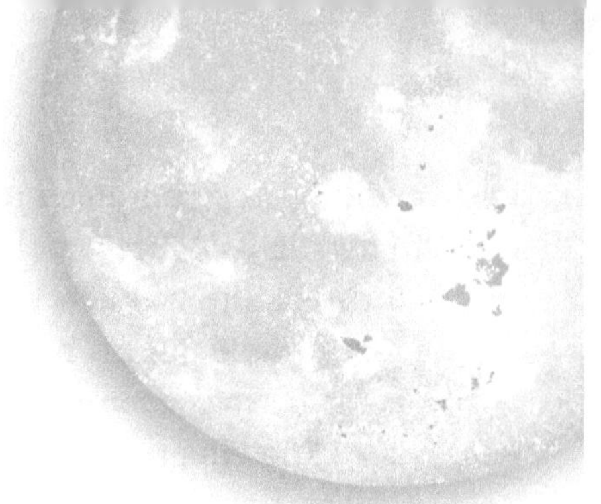

CHAPTER SIXTY-TWO

When the alarm went off the next morning at 5 AM, Aubrey got up quickly and got a shower and got ready to head down to the weight room. His roommate, however, was slow to get up so Aubrey nudged him slightly and told him he was going to be late. Chad responded with "Okay mom I am getting up." Aubrey was not sure if he was dreaming or just being a smart aleck, but he left him there just the same. When he got to the weight room, he saw J.R. and Gooch there and he also saw Jamie Hiller and the lineman from Lagrange; so, he felt at home a little more than before. Chad Walker came in about 30 minutes late and took a tongue lashing from his position coach. He walked up to Aubrey and said, "thanks for looking out for your roommate dude." Aubrey told him he had tried to wake him, but Chad just brushed him off and kept walking.

The schedule was brutal. They would be in the weight room every morning from 6 until 7:30, then breakfast at 8 AM. This was followed by meetings with their position coach at 9 AM then practice from 10 until 11:30. Lunch was from 12 till 1 PM. They were back with their position coaches from 1:30 and on the field for afternoon practice from 2 until 4 PM. Supper at 5 PM then a team meeting from 7 till 9 PM. It would be this way until school started in another month, then study hall would be from 7 till 9 PM and it was mandatory for all freshmen players. The coaches would handle scheduling for the freshman since they were all taking core courses anyway and they would be assigned a tutor whether they needed it or not. It soon became obvious to Aubrey that big-time college football was more like a job than a game and only the very dedicated athlete would make it. This would prove to be a problem for Chad Walker who could not seem to be on time for anything and continued to blame Aubrey for not looking out for him. Many nights Aubrey got home so tired that he fell asleep before calling Christina, but he knew he had to toughen up and make it for the next month, so he put his nose to the grindstone and kept plugging ahead just as he had done many times pulling the plow. J.R. also trudged ahead knowing that it was all a test to weed out the pretenders.

The first game was a home game versus Eastern Kentucky who would win the inaugural I-AA national championship later that year, so they had to prepare for a smaller school but a powerful opponent, nonetheless. Kentucky A&M played as an independent so they could schedule anyone they wanted to and there were some big games on this season's schedule. They had Georgia Tech in Atlanta in October and the Naval Academy in Florence in November. The season finale was at Louisville for bragging rights in the state of Kentucky. Louisville had beaten them eight years in a row, so it had lost much of its luster as a rivalry. Any hopes for a bowl game were just that—a hope and a dream for this season—but the future might be different. Right now, they just needed to make some progress in this program.

In his first meeting with his position coach, a burly man named Frank Whitton, they were given a good lesson on what college football was all about. The coach told them, "I don't give a damn about who you think you are or what you accomplished in high school, nor do I give a damn about what your mama and daddy think about you or what your hometown newspaper thinks about you. The only thing I give a damn about is whether you can get the job done up here in division I football. Until you prove to me that you can handle it at this level, you ae all just shitheads to me. I hope I make myself clear to each of you." He rode them hard at practice as well. They never got too many compliments even when they mad good runs. "Y'all are supposed to make those runs, that is what got you here," he would say. Aubrey struggled with pass protection. He had never had to do that much at Empire, so Coach Whitton stayed on him calling him every derogatory name in the book but coaching him up just the same. As it got closer to the first game, Aubrey did not feel good about his chances of making the rotation at tailback, so it came as a surprise to him when it was announced that he was the number two man behind senior tailback Montez Robinson. Robinson was a big back who blocked well and knew the playbook backwards and forward, but he did not possess great speed and Aubrey did. Aubrey would also return punts and kickoffs for the Eagles. On picture day Aubrey was given number 5 and he proudly wore his maroon and silver home uniform with "EAGLES" on the front and A. Durrell on the back. Chad Walker had been sent home for insubordination when he got into it with his position coach during a 7 on 7 drill one day. He had been given many opportunities to amend his ways and had run many miles for punishment for being late, yet all he ever wanted to do was blame someone else for his own misgivings. It had come to a head one day when Aubrey came back to his dorm room and Chad started cussing at Aubrey for ben a suck up punk. Aubrey had heard enough, and he told Chad that he would not tolerate him cussing at him. To which Chad replied, "What are you going to do about it, run tell the coaches?" Aubrey said no but I will kick your butt if you cuss me again. When Chad told Aubrey to do something to himself that was physically impossible, it was on. Before Chad knew what hit him Aubrey had him by the throat up against the wall and told him "Enough is enough. I don't know what your problem is, but I have worked for everything I have ever gotten so I don't want to hear your sorry butt accusing me of sucking up. Just because I am on time to meetings and practice hard and take coaching to make myself better and you want to complain and argue with the coaches does not make me a suck up. Maybe you need to look inside your own self and try to fix your situation instead of blaming me. But regardless of what choices you make, I will not be cussed by the likes of someone as sorry as you are. You got that?" Chad, to his credit, knew that he had better let this country boy alone. So, when Aubrey let him go, he stormed out of the room and called his cousin to come get him. Aubrey was without a roommate now and as fate would have it, so was Jamie Hiller so the coaches put them together. The sad thing was that Chad could have been at least the backup and perhaps could have beaten out last year's starter. He had that much talent, but he had been coddled in high school to the point where he was allowed to talk to the coaches any way he wanted to and that does not fly in college football. That would not have been tolerated by Coach Kelly at Empire either. Aubrey prayed for Chad and for his own forgiveness for losing his temper, and he called Christina for the first time in 3 days. Then he went off to sleep.

CHAPTER SIXTY-THREE

The first game of their college careers got off to a shaky start. Eastern Kentucky would take the opening kickoff and drive down the field covering 80 yards in 6:29 to take a 7-0 lead. Enter Aubrey Durrell. Taking the ensuing kickoff at his own 3-yard line and turning on the jets he would take it all the way back exciting the sparse home crowd and tying the score at 7. The first time he touched the ball in college, and he scored a TD; Aubrey felt truly blessed and he thanked God as he crossed the goal line. He would add 63 yards on 13 carries for the game and would set the Eagles up for the game-winning score with a fine run of 23 yards with just over 2 minutes left to play. Setting the offense up with a first and goal at the Eastern Kentucky six-yard line. Montez Robinson would pound it in from there in three plays to make the score 23-21 with 47 seconds left to play. On the ensuing kickoff, J.R. would make a bone-crushing hit on the return man knocking the ball loose and Zack Winborn would recover the fumble to secure the win. There was a Middle Georgia vibe on the field this day. The three boys along with Jamie Hiller celebrated by going out for pizza and discussing the game. Aubrey could not wait to call Christina and his folks to tell them the news. His dad said they already knew because they had seen the highlights on a college football scoreboard show. Christina was ecstatic about the news as well and promised she would watch sports later that night to see if they would show it again. Although she was incredibly happy for Aubrey, she neglected to tell him that she had been seeing a counselor for issues concerning her abortion and the guilt she was feeling over the whole thing. Next up would be a trip to Missouri and the Eagles would pull off a minor upset winning 19-14 with J.R.

punting for a 41-yard average and pinning the Tigers inside their own 10-yard line three times in this game. Zack Winborn would have twelve tackles and another fumble recovery while Aubrey would tally 54 yards on nine carries and would be on the field on the go-ahead scoring drive to make a block on a blitzing all-conference linebacker as the Eagles quarterback Paul Kersey hit Jamie Hiller on a 24-yard TD pass in the 4th quarter. He also had 63 yards in punt returns for the Eagles. The Eagles were now 2-0 with a game versus Indiana at home next week. Indiana would break the Eagles' hearts winning on a field goal as time expired by a score of 27-24. They would lose their next two games to Purdue and Kansas State leaving them with a record of 2 wins and three losses heading to Atlanta to face Georgia Tech. This would be a must-win game for Kentucky A&M if they had any hopes of posting a winning record this season. Wyll and Eli had purchased their tickets early and the whole Durrell family would be in attendance as would the Empire coaching staff, and the Union Hill staff. Gwen Parker bought a ticket also. Even Rod Hickey would be there. The Eagles would get off to a fast start and Montez Robinson was having a great game in the first half rushing for 67 yards on 14 carries and two TD's. Paul Kersey would throw for 183 yards in the first half with a TD pass of 33 yards to Jamie Hiller and Kentucky A&M would take a commanding 24-10 lead into the locker room. Aubrey was limited to 24 yards on 8 carries and would only be able to return two punts for 14 yards but the team was winning and that was all that mattered. J.R. had punted three times for a 47-yard average and on coffin corner kick that pinned the Yellow Jackets at their own 2-yard line in the second quarter. He was seeing less time on defense because the coaches had decided that he was too valuable as a punter to risk injury. This did not sit well with J.R. but he would never complain if it were best for the team.

The second half saw Georgia Tech rally and get within four points in the fourth quarter. Clinging to a 37-33 lead with the ball and 5:30 seconds left to play Aubrey was in the game at tailback when the call came in counter-tray left from the A&M 38-yard line. Aubrey took two steps to his right as if running the sweep right then planted and came back behind QB Paul Kersey who handed him the ball. When Aubrey saw the gaping, hole open he immediately accelerated and got behind the big pulling right tackle from Lagrange, Georgia and it was off to the races for a 62-yard TD to put the Eagles ahead for good. It was an impressive run so much so that even Frank Whitton felt compelled to tell Aubrey "Good job." Aubrey would finish the game with 93 yards on 17 carries, but that TD run was the biggest play of the game. Montez Robinson would be the game's leading rusher with 113 yards rushing and two TD's, but he knew the freshman was the future and he told him so after the game. Robinson's leadership meant a lot to this team and to Aubrey personally. After the game, the boys got to spend about 30 minutes with their families before the bus left for the airport; so, they kissed their moms and hugged their siblings and headed back to Kentucky. When Aubrey tried calling Christina the next day, he could not get her to the phone because she was in the library according to her hall mates who answered the phone. He asked them to give her a message to call him when she got back but she never did. Perhaps she never got the message.

They would win the following week versus the Naval Academy but would lose convincingly to Clemson and Ole Miss leaving them at 5-5 with the last game of the season at Louisville. The Cardinals had a complete lack of respect for A&M, and it was obvious from the start. Aubrey had never heard such trash talking; not even from "Big Mouth Barry" Kennedy. Louisville brought it to another level, and they were the biggest and nastiest bunch he had ever played against. It was honestly a little intimidating for a freshman, but Aubrey would raise his level of play since he was never scared of anyone for long and football was supposed to be a game and these guys were making it personal. One of the Louisville defenders made the mistake of saying that he would like to do it with his girlfriend Christina. How did he know her name? It did not matter; Aubrey was determined he would make him pay before this game was over. Louisville would get out to an early lead 14-0 and the trash talking intensified. On a possession late in the second quarter, Aubrey got his chance for payback when the Louisville defensive back who had the big mouth got between Aubrey and the goal line. He heard the words of Coach Eldridge Cooks saying 'show me where it says in the rulebook that you can't punish someone just because you have the ball in your hands; it ain't in there' as he lowered his pad level and destroyed the defensive back on his way to a 14-yard TD making the score 14-7 in favor of Louisville at the half. It turned out that the defensive back was from Macon, so he knew about

Christina and Aubrey from local news coverage. He also now knew that Aubrey Durrell was a bad dude on a football field.

Aubrey and J.R. were reminded of Coach Kelly's halftime speech at Southside Warner Robins their senior year when he told the Empire Knights that this game would be an opportunity of a lifetime and that they had no choice but to get up off the deck and play hard or lay down and take this butt whipping. Just before the team left the locker room for the second half J.R. spoke up and said "Men, we have 30 minutes left to play and a lifetime to live with the results." It seemed to have worked because the Eagles took the opening kickoff and drove 68 yards for the game tying TD on a 21-yard pass to Jamie Hiller with Aubrey in to block in pass protection. This was a lot of trust to put in a freshman who had struggled in pass protection this season, but Aubrey came through like Coach Cook knew he would. Montez Robinson was the first to congratulate him when he came off the field. Louisville would score once more in the 3rd quarter while A&M would score two more TD's—one by Montez Robinson and another on a defensive interception return by Zack Winborn in the 4th quarter. Kentucky A&M would finish this season with a 6-5 record. This was a major improvement for the program, and they had most everyone coming back next season except for Montez Robinson and a couple of defensive starters. Robinson would wrap up his career with 1103 yards on 256 carries and 12 TD's and would be named second team All-American. Paul Kersey was returning at QB for his senior season and Aubrey Durrell would be the number one tailback. For the season, Aubrey would rush for 602 yards on 118 carries and scored 5 TD's. He also had 339 return yards. Not bad for a freshman. J.R. would make honorable mention All-American as a punter and had settled into his role on the team; but make no mistake, he was the toughest darn punter in America. Zack Winborn also made honorable mention All-American at linebacker as did Jamie Hiller and two offensive linemen including the one from Lagrange, Georgia. All that was left for the boys was to pass all their classes with flying colors which they did. Aubrey would have three A's and a B while J.R. would have all A's. Both would make the dean's list. Aubrey had spoken to Christina a few times, but she always had to go quickly to do something with her sorority or to study. Aubrey tried to understand, but he had a bad feeling about things, and he could not wait to see her over Christmas break to sort things out.

CHAPTER SIXTY-FOUR

Christina had been seeing a counselor for about six weeks to help her sort through her emotions and she was making progress. The counselor seemed to suggest that talking to Aubrey always set her back, but she loved him she tried to explain. The counselor told her that for her own good that maybe she should take a break from the relationship and see other people just to see how it made her feel. She also implied that Aubrey was probably seeing other girls at Kentucky A&M, but Christina knew that was not the case. She had never met someone more dedicated and loyal than Aubrey Durrell. Yet she had tried to avoid his phone calls to see if she could break free from their relationship and she had managed to forget the abortion for a while. She had even gone on a date with a boy form one of the fraternities, but nothing happened, not even a goodbye kiss. She felt so guilty for doing this, but the reality was that she and Aubrey were hundreds of miles away and missing out on a lot of socializing by staying together. It was not fair for him either, so she made the decision to break up with him over Christmas break. She could not believe she was even considering this option since she knew she still loved him dearly, but the counselor had convinced her it was in both of their best interests.

One day in October, Rod Hickey showed up to check on her to see if she needed anything and she assured him that everything was okay, but she acted different, so he pressed her, and she had told him that the pressure of studying and trying to make all A's had led her to see a counselor but that she was feeling much better now and she thanked him for his concern. He had asked for the counselor's name, and she had foolishly told him thinking it would do no harm, but she did not know the depths that Rod Hickey would stoop to get rid of Aubrey Durrell. Before he left Daytona Beach, "Hot Rod" did two things—first he had a rendezvous with a $500 a night hooker; then he went to see the counselor. Under the pretense that he was looking out for his scholarship winner he proceeded to explain how dating Aubrey Durrell had caused Christina Dudley all sorts of problems from racist attacks to a loss of respect in the black community. He characterized Aubrey as a controlling and dangerous young man who was prone to violence. He told her about the fight that had gotten Aubrey suspended for one game when in fact, he should have been kicked off the team. He left no doubt that Aubrey Durrell was no good for a young black woman with a bright future in front of her. When he left, he gave the counselor $200 for her time even though the lady had agreed to see him for free and told her that she had to convince Christina that Aubrey Durrell was no good for her and that if she succeeded in doing this, that he would see her again with more money for her. Also, he did not want Christina to know that he was looking out for her best interest, so confidentiality was important. So once again Rod Hickey was trying to manipulate a situation involving Aubrey Durrrell and this time, he would hurt him more than missing a football game ever could. After two more visits to Daytona Beach and a little bit of wining and dining the counselor, "Hot Rod" had even gotten her to divulge the conversations with Christina and he found out about the abortion. He now had all the ammunition he would need to make his move on Christina.

CHAPTER SIXTY-FIVE

As soon as Aubrey got back to Empire and said hello to his family, he was out the door and headed to see Christina but when he got to her house, his whole world came crashing down. They rode off together but when Aubrey tried to kiss her, she pulled away. He asked her what was wrong, and she told him, "Aubrey I have been seeing a counselor for the past three months concerning what we did about our situation. The counselor thinks we should take a break from each other and that maybe we should see other people. I think maybe she is right. I cannot move forward with my life until I let go of everything that reminds me of what I did." Aubrey asked her if she had met someone else and she assured him that she had not. She also told him that she still had most of the money he had given her and that she would give it back to him, but Aubrey told her that he did not want the money back; that all he wanted was to be with her forever. He told her, "Christina, I love you so much that I would give up my life for you if that was required and I know you still love me too, don't you?" Christina said, "Yes I do love you, but I can't function with you in my life Aubrey, and the counselor says…." "Screw this counselor, this makes no sense at all to me. Can we just think this thing out for a couple of weeks and see how we get along?" asked Aubrey. "No, I just want to be able to move on with my life and I want you to do the same. And maybe sometime in the future we can get back together and pick up where we left off," said Christina immediately realizing her poor choice of words. She handed Aubrey the necklace he had given her with their pictures in it. He broke down at that point and she could not handle seeing him like this. She only knew that she had to trust the professional counselor and her gut instincts and that meant letting go of her past and starting anew no matter how bad it hurt at the time. Aubrey started his car and took her home from Chicken Road one last time. When she got there, he told her that he would always love her no matter what and she told him she would always love him too, but he would see that this was the best decision for them both and then she got out and walked out of his life. Both would shed many more tears over the next two weeks, but life goes on and soon it was time to get back to Florence and get ready for baseball season.

Before Aubrey left, Kenny Dudley came by to see him and to let him know that Christina was taking it hard, but she had made up her mind that moving on was the best thing for them both. He said, "I tried to talk to her about it, but she just kept telling me that I would not understand. Well, she finally told me about y'all's situation, and I just want you to know that I do not hold any animosity toward you, my brother. Hell, it could have happened to any of us boys the way we were acting, you know what I mean. But I think she is really confused and conflicted about it at the present time and this being my sister and all, I must support her decision. I think she will always love you Aubrey, but she is struggling with this decision to have the abortion and being with you only reminds her of it, so I want to encourage you to move on as well and if it is meant to be, then it will be." Aubrey said, "Kenny the last thing I want to do is be the reason Christina is hurting and if being free of me is what she needs, then that is what I will do, You know how much I love her and being with her has been the best time of my life and I do hope someday that we can get back together, but in the meantime, please take care of her and let her know that if she ever needs me all she has to do is call." "Consider it done my man," said Kenny. Then he left Aubrey standing in his front yard.

Wyll came out to check on his son and asked if he wanted to take a ride. They rode around Empire together for about 30 minutes when finally, Wyll said, "You know son women are hard to understand, but they are definitely worth the trouble. I know you love Christina but like the old saying goes: 'if you love something, set it free; if it returns to you then it was meant to be. It not, it was never really yours to begin with.' From what you have told me, it seems that Christina is having problems dealing with the abortion. I think that is to be expected.

Apparently, she believes that severing ties with her past will cure her from any remorseful feelings, and who knows, maybe it will. I know you want what is best for her and you think being with you is what is best. That may be true, but that is something she will have to figure out on her own. And if she ever decides that she needs you back in her life, then it was meant to be. I know that is tough to do but son, it is what is required right now." He added, "You have a responsibility to yourself and to Kentucky A&M to give 100% of your effort to make them better than they were when you got there. no matter what life throws your way. If you cannot do that, we need to let them know now before they wasted any more scholarship money on you. So, I need to know are you up to it or not?" Aubrey was taken aback by this 'tough love' approach, but it was what he needed to snap him back into reality. Was he a man or a mouse was basically what his daddy was asking him, and he was determined to be a man. So rather than feeling sorry for himself, he would pick himself up; dust himself off and get back to living his life. Christina would always be special to him, and he would pray for her daily but if she moved on successfully without him, then that was God's plan all along. One-week later Wyll received a check in the mail for $7500 with a note from Christina explaining how she did not feel right taking Aubrey's money and she wanted to do the right thing and get it back to him, but he would not accept it. Wyll tore the check up and wrote Christina back telling her that if Aubrey did not want it back then he did not either and that he wanted her to keep it and use it wisely. He also told her that she would always be welcome in their house, and she would continue to be in his prayers.

CHAPTER SIXTY-SIX

The boys were scheduled to return to Florence on January 5th. They had gotten Greyhound bus tickets to save their daddies from having to make the trip. When they returned to town, there was fear and panic in the streets of Florence from a double homicide attempt at the local Western Auto Store, so they were locked down on campus until further notice. This gave Aubrey time to think about his situation and how much he loved Christina. This was not what he needed to be doing but it was all he could think about. All football players were still required to work out three days a week at 6 AM and in February they were required to participate in a team building activity known as the 'EAGLE MAT DRILLS'. It was about an hour of intense cardiovascular workouts that required teammates to pull each other through each activity. Failure in any activity was considered a failure for the whole team. They worked to build a team chemistry and it seemed as if they had gotten better because of the activities. Aubrey needed this activity as a means of distraction to get him over his problems. He slowly began to come back around and back to life again.

There was a young lady on campus named Gwen Parker who accidentally, on purpose managed to run into Aubrey in the cafeteria one day and when he saw her, he was shocked. He asked her what she was doing here and if she remembered him from Alabama Tech. She said of course she remembered him and sat down with him to eat her lunch. She explained that she had to leave Alabama Tech because of feeling threatened because of telling Aubrey and Jamie about the plot to trap them. She did not tell Aubrey that she had followed him to Florence; it was just a coincidence that they ended up at the same college. The two of them began eating lunch together almost every day and eventually, Aubrey asked her out. They were dating seriously in about a month and a half. She was not Christina, but she was beautiful and nice, and Aubrey had found someone who understood him and cared for him.

Baseball season started in early February, and they would play over 50 games mostly on the weekends. Coach Max Ellison ran a tight ship, and he was a strict disciplinarian. When an outfielder missed a cutoff man or failed to back up a play, he was given 10 poles to run for each incident. When an infielder failed to line up correctly on relay throws or made a mental mistake, he was assigned 10 poles to run. If a hitter missed a sign or swung at a 'pitcher's pitch' he had to run poles. Coach Ellison was a big proponent of teaching the mental approach to hitting which involved clearing a hitter's mind of fundamentals when at the plate during a game and replacing those types of thoughts with predicting the next pitch based on the ball and strike count. He told them, "Men in the major leagues, a good hitter can accurately predict what pitch he will see next about 65% of the time and that is versus pitchers with three or four great pitches if he pays attention to the men on base, the number of outs and the inning and score of the game. He should not be at the plate going over hitting fundamentals. That is for practice. So, if I can be done 65% of the time at that level, then we should be able to predict at a 75-80% rate at our level." He also told them that, "All hitting is simply playing pepper with a stride." He taught them to hit the ball to the opposite field to raise their batting average by about 50 points or more. He showed them pictures of some of the all-time greats such as Babe Ruth, Ted Williams, and Hank Aaron to prove his point that all great hitters look the same at the point of contact, but all choose different way to stand at the plate. Some have high leg kicks, and some do not. Some wiggle their bat before swinging while some are quieter at the plate. He did not want to try to take a cookie-cutter approach to hitting a baseball. Instead, he focused on the point of contact and left the hitter to decide how best to get to that perfect swing position with palm-up / palm-down contact with the bent arm 'push stroke' and 'L-shape' in his back leg and a firm front side. And all hitters, 1-9, would know how to bunt the baseball.

Aubrey liked what he heard and would respond by hitting .342 with 7 homeruns / 34 RBI / 19 stolen bases and 29 runs scored. J.R. would explode hitting .314 with 14 homeruns / 39 RBI. More importantly, the team advanced to the super regional where they were eliminated by Mississippi State. The Durrells only had to run poles once for misunderstanding a sign. The Eagles record was 41-17 for the season and they finished ranked number 9 in the country.

The boys hitched a ride home for the summer from Gwen. Aubrey wanted her to meet his parents. They were cordial to her, but something was not right. His mom acted as if she did not like Gwen, but she never said anything at least not to Aubrey. Gwen was the perfect girlfriend—she was beautiful, and sweet, and completely devoted to Aubrey. But honestly, Aubrey was not in love with her yet. He still missed Christina and being back in Empire brought back memories of all the good times he had with her. Gwen went back to Barnesville after a couple of hours, and Aubrey promised her he would see her that weekend. He had some time to hang around with his old buddies and visit his old familiar stomping grounds. One of the people he wanted to see was his old friend Kenny Dudley, but he did not want to risk seeing Christina, so he called ahead to see if she was home. She was not there at the time, so Aubrey went to see Kenny. When he got to the Dudley house, Kenny came out to greet him and so did Priscilla who gave him a big hug and told him that she missed him around their house. The two boys talked about their seasons in college. Kenny had played in 18 games at Albany State and had averaged 9 points per game and 3 blocked shots. He stated that he should be a full-time starter next season and that college ball took some getting used to. Aubrey agreed and added that they should all be thankful that they had played for demanding high school coaches who prepared them for the grind of college athletics. Finally, Aubrey had to ask how Christina was doing. Kenny told him that she was doing fine. That was not entirely true. She seemed different somehow. She did not seem to be happy and was not as outgoing as she once was. Kenny did not know if she had regrets over ending it with Aubrey or something else was bothering her, but he was worried about her. Aubrey said, "Let her know I asked about her if you don't mind. And if she needs anything from me, you know I am here for her." He never stopped to consider how Gwen would feel about this. Aubrey went to hang out at Nubby's where he ran into Teddy Robertson, and they rode around together for a couple of hours. Finally, at 11:00, Aubrey sat and waited for the train which did not disappoint and arrived on time. J.R. had gone to visit Susan so Aubrey went home alone and went to bed.

CHAPTER SIXTY-SEVEN

Christina had been shopping in Macon all alone. She had to get out of Empire for a while. She thought she might need to stay away from there altogether. Too many memories depressed her for some reason. But that was not what was bothering her the most. She had been seeing her counselor until mid-March when the lady told her that she would not be seeing her anymore. When she asked why, she was told that she was doing well enough to stop the meetings. Christina had told her about an encounter she had with Rod Hickey where he had tried to make a move on her, and she had rebuffed him. Rod had come to Daytona to discuss renewal of Christina's scholarship, which she never knew was an option, and he had asked her to meet him at his hotel room between meetings he had to attend. Of course, there were no meetings, but Rod had to appear to be on official business. When Christina arrived at his hotel room Rod told her that her scholarship could be renewed if she gave him what he wanted. He told her that he had wanted her for a long time and that she was the most beautiful creature he had ever seen, and then he pinned her against the wall and tried to kiss her while running his hands all over her body. She immediately told him that she was not interested in him and that she would be leaving and that she never wanted to see him again. He told her that since Aubrey was no longer in her life, he thought she might want a strong black man and he could do her a lot of good. He did not mention that he knew about the abortion just yet. She had left shaken and upset and called her counselor to set up a meeting to vent and see what her course of action should be against Rod Hickey. If she wanted to get him seriously hurt, she could just tell Kenny or her daddy and that would be it for "Hot Rod", but she did not tell anyone except her counselor, and that had gotten her dismissed rather abruptly from the sessions. So, being back in Empire meant having to deal with the possibility of seeing Rod Hickey. She had wondered if Aubrey would be at home, so she rode slowly by his house after leaving work at the lawyers' offices in Eastman. She had purchased a used 1976 Chevrolet Monza and would not be recognized by anyone in the family. She had almost convinced herself to stop if she saw him outside the house, but she was not prepared for what she saw. She saw a beautiful blonde hugging and kissing Aubrey when she passed by, so she quickly left and headed home, but before she went home, she had stopped at Chicken Road where she and Aubrey had spent so many nights and she cried for what seemed like an eternity to her. What had she done? The love of her life was now gone forever into the arms of another girl. And Christina had no one to blame for this but herself.

Dorothy Simmons had been a counselor for nine years, first at a local high school, but when an opportunity came available at her alma mater—Bethune-Cookman—she took it. She was born and raised in Apopka, Florida by a week, frail, and sickly mother and an alcoholic dad. She was the third youngest of four children and the only girl. She idolized her dad, and she was a daddy's girl, but she recognized he had a drinking problem, and when he got drunk, he became abusive to her mom and brothers. When she was nine-years old she had made her dad promise that he would never drink again one morning after he had come home and beaten the boys and slapped her mom around a little bit. But he could not keep his promise and it was not long before he came home drunk again, but this time her mother stood up to him telling him that it he touched her children she would shoot him and pulled a pistol on him. Dorothy had run next door to ask the neighbors for help, and they had called the cops. By the time the officers got to the scene, her dad had taken the gun away from her mom and had knocked her down and was standing over her with the gun pointed at her head and telling her that he was going to kill her. The officers had no choice but to use deadly force when he refused to put down the gun. Dorothy witnessed the whole thing. Obviously, this was too much for a nine-year old daddy's girl to take, so it took a team of child psychologists to help put her back on the right path. When the time came for her to make a career choice, it was a no-brainer; she wanted to help others who had been through traumatic experiences, counseling was an obvious choice. She felt as though she had done others a lot of good over the years but had never been able to find time for herself. She had rarely dated and the prospect of finding a life-partner looked bleak until Rod Hickey had come into her office that day in October. She felt a connection to him, and she thought he had felt it too. Little did she know that he was using her to get to Christina. She had believed every word he had said about Aubrey Durrell and had thought that she was giving Christina some sound advice when she told her that she should break all ties with him and her past. Now she had to wonder if anything Rod had said was the truth. Worse still was that she had trusted him enough to break privacy laws in telling him about the abortion. Would he stoop low enough to use this information to blackmail Christina into getting what he wanted. If this ever came out, she would be ruined professionally. She had to stop Rod somehow. She called him to see when he was coming back to Daytona to see her, and he told her he did not know. For two months she tried to get him to come see her, but to no avail. He was always busy at work. In early June, she called him and when he said he could not get away she told him, "No matter," said Dorothy, "I am coming to Georgia to see you." Rod tried to protest, but she told him she would see him later that week. He had told her on a couple of occasions that he loved her, but that was his way of gaining her trust and using her to get what he wanted. She was determined that he would pay for misleading her and outright lying and trying to get with this young, innocent girl who was going through a lot on her own.

CHAPTER SIXTY-EIGHT

Aubrey had been to see Mr. Jimmy Wardell to see if he had any work for him over the summer and Mr. Wardell told him he wanted him and J.R. to oversee the watermelon production that summer and take them to market in Cordele and Atlanta. He said he could pay them each $7.00 per hour to run the farm for a couple of months. Aubrey accepted the job on the spot and told him that he was sure that J.R. would too. The boys would start the following Monday. Aubrey then went to watch the Empire Knights workout. Led by a terrific group of sophomores— QB Kelcey Durrell; Gerry Durrell; Quay Kelly; Ronald Paisley—the Knights had gone 7-5 the year before but were expecting improvement this season. They had to watch Union Hill win the state championship last season and that was not sitting too well with any of the players or coaches. Aubrey was joined by J.R.; Ashley Stacey and Kenny Dudley and it seemed a lot like old times; especially hearing Coach Eldridge Cooks harping on being tough with the ball in your hands. As the days went by, more ex-players joined them at the weight room each night. Aubrey felt good in Empire. He was home again for a little while and that would help him recharge his batteries for another year away.

He had a date on Saturday night with Gwen. They were going to see a movie in Macon. They chose to see 'Friday the 13th' which caused Gwen to spend the whole date grabbing Aubrey's arm and hiding her face on his shoulder. Aubrey did not mind and when they got back to her sister Judy's house in Barnesville, he realized that Judy was gone for the weekend, so they had the house to themselves. Gwen did not waste this opportunity and she gave herself to Aubrey that night. This was the first time for Aubrey since his breakup with Christina. He went home thinking about Christina and wondered whether she had been with anyone else since their breakup. She had not been intimately involved with anyone, but Aubrey had no way of knowing this. It suddenly dawned on him that it was officially over with her, and he now had Gwen to focus on.

Dorothy Simmons had taken a couple of days off to come to Empire, Georgia to see Rod Hickey and find out what his story was about assaulting Christina Dudley. That is what it was—a sexual assault—she was not sure what she would say to him, but she had to see him face to face. She got there at about 3:30 p.m. on Sunday afternoon and realized that she was in the most country place she had ever seen and that included her hometown of Apopka, Florida. As luck would have it, she had a flat tire about a mile from Ross' Store and she had no idea how to change it. She pulled over at the store, which was closed on Sunday, so she really was at a loss for what to do next. As panic was about to set in, a young man pulled up and helped her out. He was extremely nice, and she could not help but notice that he was a very handsome young man as well. After he finished fixing her tire, she asked him for directions to Rod Hickey's house and he told her how to get there and even offered to lead her there in his car. She thanked him and asked his name. When he told her 'Aubrey Durrell', she could not believe this was the monster that Rod had made him out to be. She had destroyed this boy's love life for a chance to have one of her own.

When Rod saw Dorothy get out of her car and wave to Aubrey acknowledging his help in finding the house, he could not believe how fate had allowed that to happen. He did not want her here, but he had to be cordial, so he welcomed her in with a hug and a kiss on the cheek. If he only knew why she was there he probably would have run out the back door. Dorothy, for her part, would play it cool until the time was right, then she would confront him about Christina. She did not know where the conversation would go from there. Rod asked her if she wanted to go somewhere for supper or just fix something at the house. She told him either way would be fine with her though she did ask where there was to go on a Sunday night in Empire. He explained that it was either Nubby' s or his cooking, So, she chose to eat in. Rod started to flirt with her a little bit after supper anticipating a night of passion. Dorothy was not bad-looking, and he enjoyed being with her, but he was not in love with her. But she had proven to be a good lover and he could handle another couple of nights with her. He was in love with Christina Dudley, and he would stop at nothing until he got her. Dorothy had fallen in love with him however, and she thought he loved her. He had told her that he did a couple of times in the throes of passion, but now it seemed that he was just using her. Still, she found it hard to resist his advances, so she gave in. When she told him she loved him, he hesitated before answering, "I know, and I like you a lot too." "Rod," said Dorothy, "Christina Dudley came to see me a few weeks ago and told me that you made a pass at her. is this true?" Rod was caught somewhat off guard by her question. Finally, he answered, "No, it was the other way around," he lied. She came to my hotel room and offered me sex in exchange for more scholarship money." "And you turned her down?" asked Dorothy. "A beautiful young woman like that, and you turned her down?" she repeated. "I find that hard to believe Rod," said Dorothy. "Well believe what you want, I know what really happened," said Rod angrily. "It is just that she was so upset when she came to see me, and I believe her story Rod. I believe you sexually assaulted that girl, didn't you?" Dorothy asked as she started to cry. "And the worst part of the whole thing is that you used me to convince her to get rid of her boyfriend; who by the way, I met earlier today; and he seems to be the opposite of what you said he was. So, I need to inform you that I am encouraging Christina Dudley to file sexual assault charges against you," she added as she was getting dressed to leave. Rod Hickey was impressed by her boldness, but he had an ace in the hole. He informed her that he would file an ethics complaint against her for violating privacy laws by telling him about Christina's abortion, and that she would never work again as a counselor. The truth was that Dorothy Simmons had already decided that she would never work anywhere again. She surprised Rod when she pulled out a pistol and told him that she had never violated any privacy laws until she had met him, and she did not deserve to be a counselor. Rod Hickey was scared for the first time in years, and he tried to talk her down from shooting him he begged her not to shoot him and that he was sorry for lying to her about Aubrey and Christina and that he was in love with her. He would have promised her anything at that moment to spare his life. But it was not his life she would take. She put the gun to her head and pulled the trigger. The police took his statement about how he had met her in Daytona and how they had dated a couple of times. She had become infatuated with him and when he told her that he did not feel the same way towards her, she had killed herself. He was shaken up and he had to leave his house for a few days. He got a hotel room in Cochran and went to assess his situation.

Obviously, this was big news in Empire. When the word got around that she had been a counselor at Bethune-Cookman, Aubrey knew this had to be the counselor that had advised Christina to break up with him. If he could speak with Christina, he could get to the bottom of what she was doing in Empire and what she had to do with Rod Hickey. He knew he would eventually run into her since Empire was so small, but he could not wait for a chance encounter. He wanted to go see her as soon as he got off work.

Christina could not believe it when she heard what had happened. She also wondered what Rod Hickey had to do with any of this. On Tuesday of that week, a letter arrived addressed to her from Dorothy Simmons. As Christina read it, she began crying. Dorothy had confessed all to Christina in the letter about being in a relation with Rod Hickey; and taking orders from him on what too advise Christina to do about her relationship with Aubrey; and finally, about telling Rod about her abortion. She apologized for violating the privacy laws and betraying Christina's trust and told her that she too had been involved in counseling concerning her past and her lack of intimacy. She said that she felt worthless and when Christina told her about Rod making a pass at her, it crushed her and sent her over the edge. She expressed her love for Rod and how betrayed she felt when she found out that he had used her to try and get at Christina. That was why she had stopped seeing Christina. She also told Christina that she had a case of sexual assault against Rod if she wanted to pursue it, but she had to be prepared for the news of her abortion becoming public. She ended the letter with 'Goodbye' Christina wished she had never told Dorothy about Rod, but if she had not, he would have done something else to hurt her. She wished it had been Rod who had been killed.

Aubrey had tried to contact her the night before, but she had not felt like talking to anyone. But she knew she would have to face him eventually, so this time when he called, she took the call. Aubrey asked her if he could come over to see her and she said yes. When he got there, he almost grabbed her and hugged her tightly, but he resisted the urge. She also wanted to hug him, but she knew better than to trust herself to let him go. Aubrey asked, "Is this the woman who was your counselor?" "Yes," she answered. He also wanted to know what Rod Hickey had to do with the situation. Christina lied and said she did not know. She saw no point in telling Aubrey about the letter because she knew what he would do, and she did not want him to get into legal trouble by going after Rod. She explained that Dorothy and Rod had been dating and she thought Dorothy caught him cheating with another woman and could not tolerate it. Aubrey told her that he had changed her tire for her and had led her to Rod's house. "If I had not came by when I did…" he said before Christina cut him off saying, "It was not your fault. She would have found him eventually." "yeah, I know but I can't help but feel a little bit responsible," said Aubrey. He also felt that it was a bit ironic that he had been the one who had helped her when it was her that had caused him to lose the love of his life. He still felt weak in the knees around Christina, and he could not help but ask her if they could go out sometime this summer. Christina asked him, "What about the blonde girl?" Aubrey had almost forgotten Gwen when he was around Christina. "Oh, she is someone I met at college, but she is not you Christina," answered Aubrey. "But she is your girlfriend, right?" "Christina, I would break up with her tomorrow if I knew you would have me back," he said. Christina wanted to tell him to do just that, but she knew that would not be right and she had to be strong. She just hoped this new girl knew what she had in Aubrey Durrell. She told him that they both needed to move on from each other, and that she was sure this new girl was a good girl who did not deserve to be stabbed in the back. She told Aubrey that she would always love him and wished him the best. She gave him a big hug and told him goodbye. Aubrey left her house feeling badly about what he had tried to do to Gwen. Afterall, Gwen was a good girl, and she was beautiful, and she loved Aubrey dearly. He had to move on from Christina no matter how hard it would be to do so.

CHAPTER SIXTY-NINE

Aubrey and J.R. spent the rest of the summer working for Mr. Wardell and working out at night at the Knights weight room. He was seeing Gwen every weekend as well. Kelcey was becoming a good high school QB, and the team was looking good for the upcoming season. Aubrey and J.R. were getting into tip-top shape in preparation for the upcoming season and soon enough the summer came to an end, and it was time to report back to Florence, Kentucky.

Aubrey was the number one tailback, and he still could not catch a break from his position coach who told him that he had recruited his replacement in a phenom from Illinois named Nate Jolly. Aubrey welcomed the challenge and knew that if he lost his job, the new guy would have to be a terrific player. He tried to be an example to Jolly the way Montez Robinson had been for him. On their schedule this season was a trip to Nebraska as well as a road game at Ohio State. This was done to get more national exposure and a nice payday to boot. They would host Louisville in the end of the season showdown as well as early season games versus Arkansas and Ole Miss. So, the schedule would provide an opportunity to show improvement and possibly bowl bid if things went right for the Eagles.

The Eagles would get off to a good start going 3-0 versus lesser competition and then defeated Ole Miss by a score of 24-21 on a last-second field goal. Aubrey would amass 94 yards on 16 carries and a TD on a 59-yard punt return in the third quarter. After four games he had 356 yards on 87 carries and 4 TD's. Nate Jolly would accumulate 234 yards on 69 carries and 2 TD's. He struggled a bit in pass protection, but Aubrey worked with him after practice on this skill. They became good friends.

If Kentucky A&M could defeat the Naval Academy and the University of Arkansas, they would almost assuredly crack the top 25 for the first time in forever. They would defeat Navy 32-10 to go to 5-0 and Aubrey would rush for 121 yards on 23 carries and catch 4 passes for another 45 yards and a TD reception in the second quarter. J.R. would punt Navy inside their own 10-yard line three times in this win, once at their own 2-yard line where the defense caused a fumble and a defensive TD. Next was Coach Lou Holtz and the Arkansas Razorbacks.

The Eagles would lose a close ball game by a score of 38-32. Aubrey would play well garnering praise from Coach Holtz after the game. He would rush for 143 yards on 24 carries and score two TD's. Nate Jolly would play well too with 84 yards on 12 carries but had two crucial fumbles—the second one coming in the fourth quarter on a potential game-winning drive. Aubrey consoled him the best that he could telling him he had been there, and he must use the fumbles to motivate him to get better. Coach Whitton noticed this from Aubrey and made a mental note to lighten up on him just a bit in practice.

A victory against Tulsa the next week took Kentucky A&M into their bye week with a 6-1 record and a number 25 national ranking. They would have two weeks to prepare for a trip to Ohio State. They would need to control the ball versus the Buckeyes and keep the powerful Ohio State offense off the field. They would take the opening kickoff with Aubrey fielding the ball at the four-yard line and would return it back to the OSU 43-yard line. Paul Kersey would hit Jamie Hiller on a 24-yard TD pass to take an early 7-0 lead. OSU would go 84 yards to tie the game on the ensuing possession. On the Eagles third possession of the game, they would go three and out and OSU would take the punt and return it back almost the whole way, but J.R. would unleash a brutal hit on the return man causing a fumble which he recovered at the A&M 12-yard line. Aubrey would rush for 43 yards on this possession on 8 carries and would score from 4 yards out to take a 14-7 lead. It would stay this way until the second half. On the 6th play of the second half, Zack Winborn would intercept a pass and set the offense up with a first and ten at the OSU 36-yard line. After two running plays netted 4 yards, a halfback pass was sent in from the sideline. Aubrey took the pitch to the right side and tucked the ball away for 4 steps before pulling up and heaving a long pass over the middle to Jamie Hiller running a post route. Hiller caught the ball for the third score of the game giving A&M a 21-7 lead early in the second half. OSU would score a field goal to cut the lead to 21-10 as the third quarter ended. On the ensuing kickoff, OSU would kick away from Aubrey and that meant Nate Jolly would take the kickoff at his goal line and would return it all the way for another TD giving A&M a 28-10 lead with 12 and a half minutes left in the game. Aubrey made the key block that sprung him at the OSU 34-yard line. OSU would have to throw the ball to get back in the game and that was just what the Eagles wanted them to do. They would score once more while A&M would score again making the final score 35-17 in favor of Kentucky A&M. This game would lead all the sports highlights shows and all of Empire watched the highlights and was extremely proud of the boys. Even Rod Hickey was a little bit proud of his hometown getting represented so well, but he would never admit it.

At 7-1 and with a quality win over a big ten program, the Eagles moved up to number 19 in the AP rankings and had an outside chance at a bowl bid. A home win over Memphis State before a trip to Nebraska had them at 8-1 and they were the darlings of the college football world.

Nebraska was bigger and stronger and faster than anyone the Durrells had ever competed against. The Cornhuskers won easily by score of 37-17. Aubrey would rush for 67 yards on 15 carries and score a TD from 8 yards out in the fourth quarter. This left the Eagles at 8-2 with their rivalry game versus Louisville left on the schedule. With representatives from the Sun Bowl, Astro-Bluebonnet Bowl, and Liberty Bowl at the game the Eagles would win by a score of 42-15 and would accept a bid to the Liberty Bowl in Memphis, Tennessee where they would face the Purdue Boilermakers on December 27th. The Boilermakers had gone 7-3 on the season and they had faced stiff competition in the Big 10 Conference. They had a balanced offense running and passing the ball equally well. This would be a challenge, but the Eagles were up to it.

The boys would spend Christmas away from Empire for the first time in their lives, but it was for a good reason, and they would be home soon enough after the game. Purdue would take the opening kickoff and proceed to drive 75 yards for the game's first score. Aubrey would take the ensuing kickoff and return it back to midfield where Paul Kersey would go to work hitting Jamie Hiller for 16 yards on first down. On the next play, he would fake a blast to Aubrey and look for Hiller on a flag route. Jamie would catch the ball for another first down at the Purdue 12-yard line. On a first down toss sweep Aubrey would score to tie the game at 7 after the extra point. A surprise onside kick gave the Eagles the ball back at the Purdue 48-yard line and a draw play to Aubrey worked to perfection with him taking it all the way for a 14-7 lead Aubrey felt faster than anyone on the Boilermaker defense and they knew it too. They had not seen speed like he possessed all year, and they were worried about stopping him. As it turned out, they should have been worried as Aubrey would have his best game as a college athlete so far rushing for 188 yards on 24 carries and two TD's and capturing the Liberty Bowl MVP trophy in leading his team to a convincing 33-21 victory. He was humbled by this recognition and quickly praised the offensive line, the coaches for a great gameplan and the defense for slowing Purdue down. Kentucky A&M would finish the season with a 10-2 record and a number 15 ranking in the final AP poll. This was quite a turnaround for the school and Coach Cook was named the Sporting News Coach of the Year. Aubrey would finish this season with 1,331 yards on 317 carries and 17 TD's and would be named second team All-American. J.R. would unofficially lead the nation in punting with a 43.6-yard average and would pin opponents inside their own ten-yard line 12 times during the season. He would be named first-team All-American.

In Barnesville, Georgia a young lady watched with pride as her man-made national sports news. She could not be any prouder to be the girlfriend of Aubrey Durrell. Meanwhile, in Empire, Christina Dudley was depressed thinking she should be the one sharing in this moment of athletic triumph the way they had in high school. She still could not get over Aubrey Durrell even though she had a new man in her life, Jaquez "Quez" Bailey was a nice guy and a pre-law major as well from Jacksonville, Florida and he had come up to be with her on Christmas and meet her family. He was there when the Dudleys watched the game on TV and had heard her brother Kenny go on about representing Empire and how the Durrells were his boys, and they were doing it up right. To his credit, he never mentioned that Christina had dated Aubrey, but Quez could tell by Christina's demeanor that something was not quite right. He asked her after the game what was wrong, and she decided to tell him about Aubrey. He told her that he had a prior life too and that all disappeared when he met her and that he knew she had been extremely popular in high school and had her choice of suitors but that was all in her past now and he was all she would ever need. She told him she knew he was right, but deep down inside, she knew better.

CHAPTER SEVENTY

A hero's welcome awaited the team back in Florence when they arrived at the Cincinnati airport and followed the team bus back to campus. The players would leave for home following a 9 am team meeting the next morning. When the team gathered in the field house meeting room, they never expected to hear the news they heard. Coach Cook told them that he was leaving Kentucky A&M to take a job at the University of California at Berkeley. He thanked them all for giving 100% to him and his staff and to the university. He also told them that they would always have a special place in his heart. Most of the staff would be leaving with him, including Coach Whitton, Aubrey's position coach whose gruff manner had grown on Aubrey. When Aubrey went to say goodbye to his coach, he thought he saw a glint of a tear in Coach Whitton's eyes, but he would never dare to say anything about it. He simply wanted to tell his coach how much he appreciated his pushing him to constantly be better. When he finished telling the coach what he had to say, he was surprised that Coach Whitton grabbed him and hugged him and told him that he was one of the best he had ever coached, and that he would never forget him as long as he would live. Aubrey was taken aback by these kind words from this man who had just referred to him as a worthless tick-turd just a week ago at practice. He said, "Thank you Coach. I will never forget you either." Then he turned and left before it got too emotional. He also wanted to thank Coach Cook for believing in him, but there were too many reporters around him, so Aubrey decided to just write a letter later.

J R. and Aubrey followed each other home in separate cars and Aubrey gave Jamie Hiller a ride home and Zack Winborn rode home with J.R. They discussed who the next coach would be and how things might change. By the time they reached the Georgia line, it was official. The next head football coach at Kentucky A&M was Roy Burns an up-and-coming young coach who had been an assistant at BYU for the past six seasons and who had a reputation as a passing guru. Jamie was happy with the news, but Aubrey was not sure what role an I-formation tailback would have in a pass-happy offense. He would try to keep an open mind and wait and see how it would play out.

When Aubrey got home, his family was excited about the bowl game and wanted to know how it felt to be a bonafide star. He just laughed it off and wanted to talk about the Empire Knights season where they returned to the upper echelon of class B teams with a trip to the state quarterfinals before bowing out to eventual state champions the Montezuma River Dogs. Kelcey had become an All-Region and All-Middle Georgia QB, and Gerry Durrell was a big-time recruit at defensive end and had led the Knights to a 10 and 3 record. More importantly perhaps, was the fact that they had beaten Union Hill for the region championship. The world was set right again!

Aubrey called Gwen and agreed to come see her the next day. She told him she loved him, and he reluctantly told her the same thing before hanging up the phone. The next call was from Darcy Williams who was home and wanted to get together with the old gang that night at Nubby' s. Aubrey agreed and called J.R. who was ready to go. Darcy looked good. He was bigger than he had been in high school standing at about 6' 2" and weighing around 195 pounds. He said he was throwing his fastball at around 93-94 mph and the mule was still kicking. He had a good season in single-A ball as a member of the Asheville Tourists going 8-3 with an E.R.A. of 3.32 and 72 strikeouts with 4 complete games. He expected to start the season in AA with the Tulsa Drillers, but that depended on what kind of spring training he had. He and Jeannie Hoffs had gotten married in October, so life was good for him at that time. He told the boys that he had watched the Liberty Bowl and was so happy to see them playing well. He did give J.R. a little grief about just being a punter saying, "Those coaches don't know what they have got with you big man." J.R. agreed but told Darcy that life is much easier when all you worry about is punting the ball. Teddy Robertson and Hondo Winston cane up about that time and the boys were together again and enjoying themselves immensely. When Stevie Wilbur, Ashley Stacey, and Kenny Dudley came up it became a party. Darcy suggested that they all get together on Saturday night at his folk's new house he had bought them and have a good time for old times' sake. They all agreed to be there and for about another hour they talked and laughed about old times and rehashed old games. Afterwards, Aubrey went to wait on the 11:00 train. As always, it didn't disappoint.

Coach Prentis Wilson had talked to the Durrell's parents about the boys helping him run a baseball camp when they got home. He charged $100 per kid and expected about boys and girls from age 6 to 16. He had agreed to split the fees with the boys, so they could pocket approximately $1800-$2000 each for 3 days work. They both needed the money, so they gladly accepted the job. The camp started on Tuesday of that week.

On Monday night Aubrey went to see Gwen and she was awfully glad to see him. She was all over him when he came in the door. He had never seen a girl so giddy to see her man, but he had to admit, it was not a bad feeling. He told her about the party at Darcy William's house in Saturday night and she said it should be fun. They spent most of the night in her bedroom and then Aubrey went home. He thought about how Gwen was a good girl and how much she loved him, and he had to admit that he was starting to have feelings for her too. Maybe there was life after Christina.

CHAPTER SEVENTY-ONE

The baseball camp was a smashing success mainly because it was advertised widely that the Durrells would be there, and they were celebrities around Middle Georgia. The attendance at the camp was about 110 kids from 6-16 and included girls' softball players as well as boys' baseball players. Moat of the girls had crushes on Aubrey and J.R. by the end of the camp and the boys hinged on every word they had to say about hitting and fielding. As promised, Coach Wilson split the money with the boys allowing them to pocket $2,750 each for three days.

Aubrey went to a new years' eve party that Thursday night in Barnesville with Gwen's sister Judy at the home of her boss. It was a nice event and Aubrey was the center of attention for most of the night. One loud and obnoxious Georgia fan kept giving him grief about not playing for the home team and what would happen if Kentucky A&M played his beloved Bulldogs, who were playing Notre Dame in the Sugar Bowl the following day for the national championship. Aubrey was pulling for Georgia and tried to explain that to this fellow, but he was not in the proper frame of mind to hear anything positive. He got progressively drunker and more obnoxious as the night wore on. Aubrey did not think he would make it till midnight without punching this guy's lights out, but he told himself to ignore him if he did not put his hands on him. The other party guests tried to calm the guy down but were not having much success. "GO DAWGS!!!!," he yelled every time he got near Aubrey. At one point he got in Aubrey's face and told him that he could not hold Herschel Walker's jock strap. Aubrey told him that he might be correct since Herschel was the greatest player to ever play college football in Aubrey's opinion, but he was sure he could outdo his drunk butt. The drunk fellow just smiled and said, "Yep, I think you could. But the Dawgs are still number one!" Aubrey figured the guy just wanted to see how far he could push it before he got angry enough to fight back. He found out by the look on Aubrey's face that he had had enough. He spent the rest of the night telling Aubrey how much he admired him as a football player and how much he thought Gwen was fine as hell. Aubrey laughed it off and thought this man is going to feel awful in the morning with a hangover and embarrassment over how he has been acting. His wife apologized profusely, but Aubrey told her not to worry about it; he had been through worse. When the clock struck midnight, the man was passed out in the corner and his wife was left with no one to kiss to ring in the new year. Gwen however did not have that problem and she planted a big wet kiss on Aubrey and told him she loved him and was proud of the way he handled himself with the drunk fool. Aubrey told her that he was used to people trying him and that it would take more than that to get a violent reaction from him. Still, Aubrey could not resist when someone pulled out a red magic marker and suggested that he right 'KENTUCKY A&M' on the man's forehead before he left. Everyone got a kick out of it, including the wife.

That Saturday night was Darcy's party, and it was basically a reunion of Empire Knights and their dates. Aubrey was introducing Gwen to everyone, and she seemed to be having a great time. Around 9 pm Christina and Quez Bailey showed up and things got awkward to say the least. Gwen noticed the beautiful girl and asked Aubrey if this was his ex. He told her it was and that she should just enjoy herself and not let anything bother her. if only he could take his own advice. At some point, Quez Bailey came over and introduced himself to Aubrey and told him he thought he had played a great game versus Purdue. Aubrey thanked him and then asked him how long he and Christina had been dating. Quez told him for about two months and Aubrey told him that Christina was a special girl and that he wished them the best. Of course, this was a lie, but it seemed like the right thing to say now. Christina introduced herself to Gwen as well and lied to her also telling her basically the same thing about Aubrey. Gwen thanked her and told her that she could see why Aubrey had been in love with her—she was beautiful and sweet. Christina told her that she was pretty as well and that they made a lovely couple. With the awkwardness over, they proceeded to have a good time, yet Aubrey could not help but watch Christina throughout the night and a couple of times he thought he saw her looking at him too.

Around 10 pm Kelcey came to the party to tell Aubrey and J.R. that they needed to come home. They asked him why and he said he could not tell them there, so they left the party and followed Kelcey back to Aubrey's house. Not knowing what to expect was a terrible feeling, but not as terrible as the news they got when they got in the house. It seems that a plane crashed in the Rocky Mountains and killed all passengers aboard including two ex-football coaches at Kentucky A&M—Jerry Cook and Frank Whitton. They had been speakers at a coaching clinic in Minnesota and were on their way back to Berkeley to start their program at the University of California. Aubrey and J.R. watched the sports channel to get the details, but they were in a state of shock. The first one interviewed was "Bull" Ripley who talked about what a great person Coach Cook was and how he was a great recruiter and offensive genius. He also had some kind words for Coach Whitton although they had never worked together. The phone rang and it was Zack Winborn calling to see if the boys knew. Then came a call from Jamie Hiller who was terribly upset over the news. Aubrey immediately began to pray for their families and the families of all the passengers aboard the plane. He could not help but think about the last time he talked to Coach Whitton and how he saw the real human side of the gruff coach. He was thankful for the hugs the two exchanged. He only wished he had hung around to personally thank Coach Cook for everything he had meant to Aubrey instead of writing him a letter. Darcy Williams came over to see what was happening and told the boys how sorry he was to hear about the crash. He went back and turned on the sports channel at the party so everyone would know what had happened. When Christina saw the news, she was incredibly sad, and she knew Aubrey was torn apart by the news. She wanted to go to him and give him a big hug, but she knew that would not look good for her and him in front of Quez and Gwen. She had met Coach Cook once when he came to Empire for Aubrey and J.R.'s signing day. She had thought he was genuinely a good man and was glad Aubrey was going to play for someone like him. She would send a card to Aubrey later expressing her sympathy.

The next day all players got a call from the A.D. at Kentucky A&M informing them that a memorial service was being held later that week and if they wished to attend, they would be allowed to move back into their dorm rooms earlier than anticipated. It would be about a week earlier than normal. So, the Durrells, Zack Winborn, and Jamie Hiller would be going back to Florence for the memorial service. All but a couple of players attended the service, and it was a sad affair as Coach Whitton's son Alex spoke about his father. He told some funny stories about how his blunt attitude had offended some of his high school friends, but they soon learned that if he was blunt or even somewhat rude to you, it meant he liked you. If he refused to say anything to you at all, he did not like you. Aubrey thought that he must have loved him since he was constantly cussing him out. The A.D. announced that the road in front of the stadium was to be renamed Jerry Cook Drive and the stadium renovations which included a new dressing room, and 15,000 new seats would by dedicated in honor of Coach Cook and Coach Whitton. The new team meeting room would be named the Frank Whitton meeting room. He expressed a heartfelt thank you to the two men who had led the Eagles back to prominence in college football.

The new coaching staff was there also as well as Coach Max Ellison who spoke about how easy it was working with Coach Cook and being able to share athletes. He said that Jerry Cook was a man of his word and someone you could trust to do what he said he would do. He also said that was a trait that was missing in the coaching world in many cases today. When the service was over, the boys went to eat at the pizza parlor, and they were joined by Cedric Gooch, Montez Robinson, and Paul Kersey. It was a sad day but as the players began sharing stories about the coaches, the mood lightened up a little bit.

The players spent the week hanging out at the weight room and playing pick-up basketball games. One night they went to a local bar, which was a new experience for Aubrey and J.R. However, they noticed that they had an amateur night for entertainers every Tuesday, so they decided to dust off Aubrey's guitar and loosen up J.R.'s vocal cords to see how they could do. The first Tuesday they performed James Taylor,

Bob Seger, and The Eagles. Most of the team came out to support them and they were a hit. As usual, some of the women made suggestive comments to them and J.R. spent some time with a beautiful young lady he met there. Aubrey continued to be loyal to Gwen, who came down to watch them play one Tuesday night in January. She spent part of her time fending off advances of drunks who tried to convince her to leave with them. She told them she was with the guitar player and some of them backed off, but a couple did not. Aubrey had to get rude with one gentleman one night who wanted to fight him for Gwen's affection. Aubrey told him in no uncertain terms what would happen to him if he proceeded with his intentions, so the man eventually backed down. Other than that, it was a good place to play music and the club owner offered them a job playing on weekends for $100 apiece plus tips. They decided to take the job until baseball season started in a few weeks. The boys would make another $700-$800 each. However, baseball season for the Durrells came into doubt in mid-January.

CHAPTER SEVENTY-TWO

Coach Roy Burns called the Durrells into his office and told them he did not want them to play baseball, saying his offense was so sophisticated that he wanted them at spring practice to learn it. Aubrey respectfully told him that parr of his deal when he signed to play at Kentucky A&M was that he would be able to play both sports. Coach Burns replied, "Well, that was not a deal made with me, so I don't feel obligated to honor it." J.R. asked what Coach Ellison thought about this new philosophy and Roy Burns told him that it did not matter what he thought since football was the biggest moneymaker at the university. J.R. said, "If it is all the same with you coach, I still want to know what he thinks about this." "Fine," said Burns, "but if you two are not at spring practice, I will assume you have made your choice. With that he dismissed them from his office. They immediately went to the baseball field to see Coach Ellison. He was not happy with this news, and he told them he would fight for them, but he did not know which side the administration would support. He also told them that baseball was paying half their scholarships so maybe that would make a difference. The baseball coach had agreed to pay half the scholarships so Coach Cook could offer Hiller a scholarship.

The next morning, he went to see Coach Burns and expressed his displeasure at his recent decision. He also informed the football coach that he was paying half the Durrell boys' scholarships, so he had a right to speak his mind. Burns repeated what he had told the players, that his system was too complicated for them to miss spring practice. Coach Ellison told him that last season the Durrells had come in at 6 am for meetings with their position coaches to catch up on anything they missed, and it did not seem to hurt them. After all, Aubrey had rushed for over 1,000 yards and J.R. had made All-American. "Sounds to me like you are trying to run those boys off Coach, and that would be a big mistake," Max Ellison stated. "Coach, I am trying to bring this university into the modern age of football, and I need to know my players are buying into what I have to offer, so I will need those two guys to make a decision soon," said Burns. "We are going to have to see what the A.D. says about that," said Ellison. "That will be fine Coach," said Burns, "I get paid a lot of money to win football games here and I don't believe the school would make such an investment just to mess with the decisions I make concerning the football program." Ellison wanted to tell him where to put his lucrative contract, but he restrained himself. Deep down inside he thought this cocky asshole was in over his head and had no idea how to treat people, and he believed that the football program was in trouble.

Max Ellison went immediately to the A.D.'s office but was told that he was busy and could not see him at that time. Max knew better and told the secretary that he would wait for a while and if she could let him know he was out there he would appreciate it. After waiting for about an hour, he got up and told the secretary to have the A.D. call him as soon as possible. She said she would relay the message. Aubrey and J.R. talked about the possibility of transferring to another school if this decision was upheld. Neither of them went to class but they did go to baseball practice that afternoon.

Max Ellison was at the office door the next morning at 7 am to catch the A.D. before he 'got too busy to talk'. When the A.D. saw Max waiting on him, he nearly turned around and walked out but he did not Instead, he told Max that he knew why he was there and that he did not know if he could help him. Max told him he could help by honoring the deal made with the Durrells by himself and Coach Cook. He reminded him that the Durrells had committed to Kentucky A&M over Penn State, Michigan, USC, and even Alabama Tech to name a few simply because of the deal made that would allow them to play both sports. He implored him to honor Coach Cook's memory by keeping his promise to the boys. "It won't sit well with Burns, "said the A.D. Max Ellison did not care whether it sat well with him or not. "I don't think that is what is important right now," he said. "I have coached and played ball for a long time, and I have seen a lot of Roy Burns' come and go. I know what it feels like to believe you know the secret for winning and everyone around you is an idiot. Maybe he does have it all figured out, but he needs to understand that alienating kids like the Durrells is not smart and he cannot win without kids like them. You would be doing him a favor by letting the boys continue to play two sports no matter what he says publicly, he won't give back TD's or booming punts next season." He also reminded the A.D. that he was paying half of those two scholarships, so he had a say in what happened. The A.D. called a meeting with Ellison and Burns for the next morning to render his decision. Aubrey and J.R. would make their decisions based on the outcome of this meeting. Around 10:30 am Coach Ellison called and informed the boys that a compromise had been reached allowing them to continue playing both sports but that in the future, no one else would be allowed to do this. He also told them to expect some payback from the football staff since Burns was not happy about this decision.

The first indication that things were not right was when Coach Burns announced that there would be not early morning workouts and that the team workouts would from 4-6:30 pm three days per week. When Aubrey and J.R. asked to be allowed to lift weights early in the morning, he told them that would not be possible since no coach would be present to supervise them. They had been lifting weights since seventh grade together and this clown thought they needed supervision. He was the boss however, and they would have to join a local gym just to stay in shape for football because this jackass wanted to have a pissing contest with a couple of players. A pissing contest that neither of them wanted.

Aubrey took comfort in Gwen's arms while J.R. played the field. The boys' parents were not too happy to hear the news either and Wyll offered his advice saying, "Son, my daddy told me long ago that if you work for someone, you respect their position and authority; when it gets to where you can no longer do that, then it is time to change jobs. If you need to transfer, then we will cross that bridge when we get there." He also advised Aubrey to pray for guidance and pray for Coach Burns because it sounds like he is going to need it. Eli Durrell wanted to come up there and slap some sense into this idiot but was talked down by his wife and oldest son. Finally, he told J.R. that he could go punt for anyone in the country so if he got ready to transfer, just let him know and he would pack him up and move him across the country if necessary.

Luckily, the baseball season was about to start, and games always got Aubrey's mind off his problems.

CHAPTER SEVENTY-THREE

The Durrells flourished on the baseball diamond and so did the team. Aubrey would hit leadoff for the first time and would respond with a .357 batting average and hit 6 homeruns; 16 for 16 on stolen bases and scored 41 runs for the season. J.R. would hit third and have a .349 average with 13 homeruns and 57 RBI. The Eagles would go 53-9 and would make it to Omaha for the college world series where they would lose to Miami and South Carolina in two straight games. Not a good ending but it was still progress.

It was home to Empire for the summer and working for Mr. Wardell again and working out with the Knights. For the first time, Aubrey did not feel like he was working for a purpose since he felt like an outsider on his own football team. When he and J.R. asked for a playbook so they could study up on the offense, they were told that they would get one when they showed up for practice. At the spring game, they were allowed on the field to watch the game, but they had to stand in the end zone and were not allowed in the locker room before or during the game. It was as if they were pariahs or had slapped the coach's mama. They had never seen a grown man act so immature as Coach Burns was acting. The offense struggled mightily during the spring as the Eagles had been built as a power run team and throwing the ball two-thirds of the time was not something the team could get used to overnight. Zack Winborn had expressed concern that they only had contact four days during the whole month of practice and he worried that the team may get soft. So, they went into the summer blind as to what the offense was trying to do or what their role would be, or even if they had a role on the team. Yet, they worked out as hard as usual so they would be prepared for whatever was to come their way.

Aubrey went to visit Gwen as often as possible with his work schedule being so hectic. He and J.R. had to take watermelons to Atlanta and Cordele to the market, so there was not a lot of time to spend with anyone not associated with melons. Nevertheless, they did get some quality time together. Aubrey even introduced her to Chicken Road a couple of times although it did seem weird the first time, he went there with anyone other than Christina. Gwen seemed to like coming to Empire and that let Aubrey know that deep down inside she was a country girl at heart. If by some chance, they ended up married, it was good to know that she would not object to life in Aubrey's idea of paradise. He had run into Jamie Dickinson who invited him and Gwen over to their house for a cookout one weekend in June and Aubrey accepted the invitation. Gwen and Jamie's wife Cheryl hit it off right away and Aubrey and Jamie talked about the good old days and how it started out a little rough. They talked about Tony Finch and Aubrey found out that he had started going to church at the Pentecostal Church had changed his life for the better. "I guess Coach Kelly's prayers were answered," said Aubrey. "Yeah, I believe they were," added Jamie. After supper, Cheryl announced to her guests that she was pregnant and was due in February. Gwen was ecstatic as if she had known Cheryl all her life. Aubrey was happy too, but he could not help but think about he and Christina's aborted pregnancy and he got a little big depressed.

Gwen would spend the night at Aubrey's house in his bed while he slept on the couch. She was in love so much and she longed for the day when they would be expecting their own child. She fell asleep thinking about that. Aubrey prayed for everyone he knew and tried to sleep but mostly tossed and turned all night. He kept thinking about how Quez Bailey would get to experience the miracle of life with the girl he still loved.

As the summer ended, the Durrells, Winborn, and Hiller headed back to Florence with two of the boys not knowing what to expect. Jamie had tried to show Aubrey as much as he could about the offense, but all he really knew was his route tree and his responsibilities on most plays. Aubrey understood that most of the pass routes were option routes and the QB and receivers had to read the same thing on the fly or else the play was a disaster. It would have been nice to get a playbook to study, but that was not to be, so he would be in catch-up mode from the get-go. Maybe Nate Jolly would return the favor Aubrey had done for him last season and work with him after practice. Jolly was a good guy so Aubrey felt sure it would not be a problem.

There was a new QB in town, a transfer who had played at UCLA until he ran into grade problems and had to go to Junior College for a year to get eligible. His name was Jake Hatcher, and he was talented but a little too cocky for the Middle Georgia crew. This meant that last year's backup Rodney Drew was probably on the bench again. Drew was a hard worker but was never going to be a great drop back passer. His strength was play-action and sprint out passing and just being a good leader and mechanic of the offense. He saw the handwriting on the wall too and just tried to put up a good front. He would never complain about any of this stuff going on, but he was no fan of Roy Burns.

When they got to Florence, Aubrey immediately went to see Jolly and talk to him about the offense. Jolly told Aubrey that it was more complicated than anything he had ever done but he thought he had a decent spring practice and some of it was starting to make sense. He told Aubrey that he would gladly help him after practice to catch him up and he was sure that Aubrey would catch on quick and have another great year. He told Aubrey that he was his placeholder during the spring, but Aubrey was not so sure.

There was a team meeting at 7 pm and maybe playbooks would be handed out then. They would do summer testing Monday morning at 8 am. This was about two hours later than Coach Cook and his staff had started the day's activities but that was then, and this was now. After greeting all his teammates, Aubrey and J.R. settled in for the meeting, The new QB was introduced, and he acted like a celebrity with long blonde hair like a California surfer. He was a big kid standing about 6' 4" tall and weighing about 220 pounds. He had a big arm as well according to Jamie Hiller. He said that Hatcher threw the ball so hard it took his fingerprints off. Of course, he was joking, but Aubrey could tell that this kid would probably play on Sundays someday. Coach Burns speech was about how last year did not matter anymore and how they were going to bring modern football to Florence, Kentucky. He listed his coaching accomplishments and stated that, "I have won everywhere I have ever been, and I will win here provided every player buys in to my system and gives 100% to football." He added, "I know how to put the ball in the end zone, and I have done it hundreds of times over the last few seasons. I know that you guys think you had an offense last season, but I am here to tell you all that you ain't seen nothing yet." Aubrey thought to himself, 'that was surely a lot of I and me. He was reminded of the verse in the Bible that said, "Pride cometh before the fall", but maybe this guy was right, and they were about to experience a new way to play an old game. He surely hoped so.

The next morning Aubrey ran a 4.34 time in the 40-yard dash / got 22 reps at 225 pounds on the bench press / and had a vertical leap of 39 inches. He weighed in at 194 pounds and stood 5'11" tall. He was proud that his work during the summer had paid off and that it should be obvious to the coaches. J.R. ran a 4.67 time in the 40 / had 19 reps on the bench press / and had a vertical leap of 34 inches at 6'5" tall and 230 pounds. He again proved to be the most athletic punter in America, although there was some talk about using him at receiver some this season. There were meetings with position coaches followed by the first practice of the day at 10 am. Aubrey's position coach was a slick young coach from California named Art Slater. He was the opposite of Frank Whitton. No more cussing indiscriminately or tobacco chewing, and he looked like a tailor dressed him for practice. Everything matched and his clothes looked like they had been pressed neatly every practice. Nate Jolly called him "Mr. GQ" and it fit him perfectly. They went over the plays that they would be running in practice today and it was an extensive list, but Aubrey had studied hard last night, and he felt like he knew enough to get through practice.

After the meeting, Coach Slater asked Aubrey to hang around for a few minutes. He told him that he was impressed with his numbers this morning and he thought he would have a great season if he learned the offense quickly. Aubrey explained that he had asked for a playbook last spring, but Coach Burns had refused to give him one. He told Coach Slater that he would give it all he had to learn quickly. The coach told him that Coach Burns would come around once he saw Aubrey play and that he was just upset about the A.D. not backing him. He also said that if Aubrey needed to know anything, just ask and he would help him out. Aubrey's first impression of "Mr. GQ" was a good one.

At practice he noticed a more lackadaisical attitude and he was not used to that, but he was willing to keep an open mind and see if this new way would work. He also noticed that all players had helmets on when between the lines except new QB Jake Hatcher who was sporting a ball cap and was constantly tousling his hair and worried about how he looked, but boy could he throw a football! First was group work where the running backs worked on pass protection which always was a challenge for Aubrey, but this was an especially difficult system to learn. There were too many adjustments based on what happened after the snap, so he hoped the coaches had patience with him. They went to a pass pro drill next and, as expected, Aubrey struggled but so did the rest of the backs include Nate Jolly. During a 'routes on air' session, Aubrey found out how Coach Burns felt about him when he got in the huddle with the first group at Jolly's urging. Burns had a meltdown and asked Aubrey" just who in the hell do you think you are? You do not just bounce in here off the street and pick up where you left off. Jolly, get your ass in this huddle." This was terribly embarrassing to Aubrey and when the QB chuckled about it, this made it worse. When he finally did get in for a couple of plays, the first call was 'Brown Right 74 Halfback Corner / X Smash', which required Aubrey to align at left halfback and run a corner route on the snap. When the ball was snapped, Aubrey took off like he was shot out of a cannon and was wide open on the play. Jake Hatcher threw a perfect pass and Aubrey caught the ball for a 38-yard TD completion. Aubrey was happy with this play and so was Nate Jolly and Jamie Hiller and Coach Slater. But Coach Burns was not overly impressed. He glared at Aubrey the whole way back to the huddle and called the next play, which was a play where Aubrey had an either / or responsibility. If the outside linebacker blitzed, Aubrey was to pick him up, but it he dropped into coverage, then his route would be a flair to the right. 'Red Right Slot 184 Double Slant' was the call and when the ball was snapped, Aubrey went right and saw the linebacker in a hardnose blitz position, so he set up to block him. However, the linebacker never came and instead dropped late into coverage. Aubrey was confused and tried to get to his flare route, but he was late in getting to it. Jake Hatcher unleashed a fastball and hit Aubrey in the back of his head almost knocking him down which caused some of the new guys to laugh at him and Hatcher called out. "Hey dumbass, you need to get your head around." Aubrey felt himself losing it, but he prayed for self-control. He also felt a terrible headache coming on and nausea setting in. He had a concussion but never came off the field until Burns ordered him off. He really had no memory of anything that occurred that day. J.R. stayed with him that night to make sure he was okay. He and Jamie Hiller discussed how Burns was an idiot for not recognizing talent when he saw it and how Aubrey would never give him the satisfaction of letting him run him off. As for the new QB, J.R. said he would get what was coming to him soon enough.

CHAPTER SEVENTY-FOUR

Over the next few weeks, it became obvious to Aubrey and everyone else on the team that Nate Jolly would start when the season started. For some reason Boy Burns did not like Aubrey Durrell and it had to be something other than the lack of the A.D.'s support over the baseball issue. One day after practice when Jolly and Aubrey were working on the pass protection scheme, Burns called Jolly into his office and told him that he was to meet with his position coach after every practice to prepare for the season opener at Idaho. Jolly told Aubrey about this and apologized for not being able to help him, but Aubrey told him not to worry about it. Aubrey knew what the real reason was for the meeting with Slater and so did Jolly, but what can you do about it?

The Durrells had been playing and singing with the house band at the local bar on Friday nights and the crowds were big on Fridays, especially the young ladies. The name of the band was the Kentucky Rhythm Aces, they were not as good as the R.C. Gold Band, but they were some good guys and they played good country music and some good rock and roll. The boys were making $50 plus tips which kept them going financially. As word got out that they were playing at the local college hangout, some of their teammates came down for moral support and looking for girls. One Friday night two weeks before the first game, Jake Hatcher and his crew of freshmen and transfer players came in but not to enjoy the music. From the opening song, Hatcher started yelling out, "Hey, play some real rock and roll, play some Motley Crue" or "How about something from this decade?" The more he drank, the louder he got. The boys and their band members did not even know what a "Motley Crue" was as they had just been started out in Los Angeles, California earlier that year, but Hatcher had seen them at the Whiskey- a- Go-Go and he was a fan. During a break, the Durrells came out and greeted their teammates including Jake Hatcher. J.R. got preoccupied with a cute little brunette, but Aubrey went to talk to the guys on the team. "How is it going Jake?" asked Aubrey. "Pal I am doing fine. How's your head by the way?" answered Hatcher with a crazy giggle. Aubrey said, "My head is fine, and I am doing just swell Jake. Thanks for asking and caring." As he was turning to walk away, he heard Jake tell one of the freshmen, "There goes a dinosaur, a kid who thinks the only way to win is by running the ball 50 times per game. That is why he will not be on the field much this year. Burns would be happy if he got lost." Aubrey turned and looked Hatcher in the eye and said, "Buddy while you were trying to get eligible at junior college, I was helping this team go 10-2 and win a bowl game. I ran for over 1300 yards and was a second team All-American, and through it all I did whatever the coaches told me to do. If they had said throw the ball, we would have thrown it. But they were smart enough to know that the secret to winning was to run the ball and stop the other team from running it. And we played great defense too. So, I think before you come in here and try to re-invent the game, you might want to have a little bit of experience under your belt first and I don't mean in some no-name Junior college in Kansas." As Aubrey waited for some type of response, Hatcher just stood there and fumed. When Aubrey turned to walk away, Hatcher lunged toward him, but Zack Winborn and Jamie Hiller grabbed him and Zack told him, "Son, you better be ready before jumping on either one of the Durrell boys. I promise you they will whip your ass quicker than you can spit." He then told the guys he came in with to get his drunk tail home and in the bed. Hatcher talked about how he was not scared of either one of those dumb-ass Georgia boys and he would show them before it was over with. Later that night, Aubrey went and spent the night with Gwen who had an apartment near campus. Aubrey had decided to major in history and education so that he could teach and coach and hopefully influence young lives the same way he had been influence by great coaches all during his playing days; that is until now. Gwen was happy to hear this since she was going to be an English teacher. She thought they would be happy together for many years if she could convince Aubrey to marry her someday. Aubrey was growing fonder of Gwen every day, but marriage was the farthest thing from his mind at the time. He was just trying to figure out what had gone wrong with his football career. He tried not to burden Gwen with his problems, but she was good to talk to and she loved him so much and that was comforting to him.

CHAPTER SEVENTY-FIVE

The next day was picture day and Aubrey was shocked when he was handed number 13. When he asked what was going on, he was told that Jake Hatcher was given number 5. He approached Coach Burns about it and was told that players who had been at spring practice were given priority on jersey numbers. He almost quit at that moment, but he remembered what Hatcher had said last night, "Burns would be happy if he just disappeared." No, he would not give Burns the satisfaction of telling the world that Aubrey Durrell had quit the team. When he came out wearing number 13, Hatcher started laughing and calling him 'Bad Luck Schleprock', a character from the old Flintstones cartoon. Aubrey could feel himself boiling inside but J.R. came up to him and told him to "be cool and remember, every dog has his day." There was a growing sentiment among the players from last year's team that Burns was not very smart. After all, they all knew what Aubrey was capable of and he was a great teammate, so they were talking amongst themselves about how they would handle it if it were them that were getting screwed over. Nate Jolly, who stood to gain the most from this ostracizing even contemplated going to talk to Coach Burns about it but had not gotten up the nerve to do it yet. Most of the guys were gaining more respect for Aubrey because of the way he was handling the situation. Most of them were coming up to Aubrey and telling him to hang in there and that they had his back. Aubrey did not want any dissension on this team, and he did not want it to be about him. The first game was next week and if he got a chance to play, he would show Burns what he could do.

The Idaho Vandals would come into Florence as huge underdogs and the Eagles faithful showed up early to tailgate and prepare for the victory. This would surely be a warmup game for the tougher schedule that lay ahead with home games versus Georgia Tech and Mississippi State as well as road games versus Notre Dame, LSU, and the rivalry game at Louisville. So, the crowd settled in to watch their beloved Kentucky A&M Eagles destroy lowly Idaho. Someone forgot to tell Idaho to play along. Toward the end of the first half, the Vandals had a slim lead 14-13 and Jake Hatcher had thrown two TD passes but had also thrown two interceptions, which he had blamed on the receivers making wrong reads. Aubrey had played five plays on offense and had one carry for 11 yards and no passes thrown his way. The only way he was contributing was a punt and kickoff returner. He had two punts returned for 43 yards and one kickoff return for 23 yards. However, with 1:34 left in the second quarter, he would receive an Idaho punt at his own 35-yard line and never look back on his way to a 65-yard TD return. A two- point conversion gave A&M a 21-14 halftime lead. He would take the opening kickoff of the second half at his own 4-yard line and return it back past midfield where the Eagles would move into the red zone before stalling out at the Idaho 14-yard line. Instead of running the ball on 3rd and one to go for a first down, they called a pass play that was intercepted in the end zone. Again, it was not Hatcher's fault even though he threw the ball early to avoid a hit from a blitzing linebacker. As Idaho drove the ball downfield methodically mixing runs and short passes, it was obvious that they were going to score. When they ran the ball across the goal line for the game-tying score, the fans had seen enough, and the boos rang down. When the Vandals recovered a surprise onside kick a few seconds later, the fans started leaving the stadium. A long pass for a TD gave Idaho a 28-21 lead at the end of the third quarter. A&M would kick 48-yard field goal to cut the lead to 28-24 with 6:12 remaining in the game. After a three and out on their next possession, J.R. punted the Vandals deep inside their own territory at their own 9-yard line and time was running out. The Eagles defense would rise to the occasion led by Zack Winborn who made a crushing hit on the Idaho running back for a two-yard loss on a third and one forcing them to punt the ball back to A&M with 2:03 left to play but it would not come down to Jake Hatcher winning the game, because number 13, Aubrey Durrell was back to return the punt. He fielded the ball at his own 42-yard line and set sail down the right sideline for the game-winning TD.

The Eagles had escaped an embarrassing loss to an inferior team in the season opener, and every reporter wanted to ask Roy Burns the same question, 'why was Aubrey Durrell not starting in the offensive backfield?' Burns did not appreciate the question, so he eventually said, "Nate Jolly is our starter right now based on the fact that he knows the offense better than any other back because he was around during spring practice while Aubrey Durrell was representing Kentucky A&M on the baseball field." Reporters also asked Aubrey what he thought about not starting and about being number 13. Aubrey simply answered that he would be ready when and if Coach Burns felt confident about putting him in on offense and as for the number change, he said he was proud to be wearing lucky 13.

The next week was another home game versus Indiana State and A&M handled this one easily winning 42-14. Nate Jolly had a good game rushing for 78 yards on just 12 carries and catching 4 passes for 64 yards and two TD's. Aubrey had 3 carries for 45 yards and a TD run of 22 yards in the fourth quarter. As a team they only ran the ball 21 times and threw it 45 times for 357 yards, Jake Hatcher would throw five TD passes and two more interceptions. His TD passes came to Nate Jolly, Jamie Hiller, and the last one to J.R. Durrell who had been inserted as a wideout for this game because he was a big target, and he was fast enough to run by defensive backs who tried to play tight man coverage on him. After two games, Aubrey's stats read 4 carries for 66 yards and one rushing TD. He continued to shine on special teams however, returning 5 punts for a total of 134 yards and two kickoffs for 43 yards. Meanwhile, fans were getting anxious to see him running out with the starting offense and every time he came on the field, they started to chant his name. He was sure this would not help him out with Coach Burns.

The Eagles would lose the next week at Annapolis versus the Naval Academy 28-13, and the offense struggled to move the ball running it only 14 times and attempting 56 pass plays completing only 28 for 332 yards and a TD to go along with 3 more interceptions. Reporters were anxious to ask why they were not trying to run the ball a little more with a second-team All-American sitting on the bench. Roy Burns blew his cool at the press telling them that he was hired at Kentucky A&M to bring them into the modern era and throwing the football was the future of the game and that he would not stop until he had his players who could run his high-tech offense. With that statement, he lost the locker room. He basically threw all the returning players under the bus saying they were not capable of performing up to his expectations, and that he would recruit his kind of players soon enough. When Zack Winborn heard about that statement, he told a reporter that his team was good enough to win 10 games and the Liberty Bowl last season, so he did not understand what his coach's problem was with the current roster. He also said that Aubrey Durrell could help the situation if he were given the chance.

It was a tense week at practice followed by a loss to Georgia Tech at home by a score of 43-26. Again, only attempting 21 running plays and throwing the ball another 47 times. Hatcher was completing only 52% of his passes with 13 TD passes and 10 interceptions. He was shielded from the press and only gave interviews after speaking with Roy Burns first. Anything off the cuff would be a disaster since Hatcher had no filter between his brain and his mouth and he was always blaming someone else for his failures.

Next was a blowout loss at Notre Dame by a score of 55-21. It got so bad that backup QB Rodney Drew was asked to finish the game for Jake Hatcher whose frustration had gotten the better of him and he was fussing with his offensive linemen, receivers, and running backs who were not worthy of playing with a QB as talented as he was. Rodney Drew calmly led the offense down the field for their last TD hitting Jamie Hiller on a 24-yard strike with just over a minute left in the game. Aubrey had seen only 6 plays on offense, all pass plays. After the game in the locker room, Jake Hatcher was overheard talking about how it was a mistake to come to this god-forsaken school and Zack Winborn went off on him. "Why don't you do us all a favor and transfer somewhere where your talent can be maximized. I for one will not miss you," said Zack. "Screw you jerk," replied Hatcher, "your sorry ass defense just gave up 55 points, so I don't care what you think." As Zack headed across the room to confront the QB, he was stopped by Nate Jolly who said, "I got this one big guy." He got in Jake

Hatcher's face and told him that he was also tired of the superstar act. He said, "Hatcher, you do have a lot of talent, but you have no class. I have heard you blame others for your screwups till I am sick of it. And why Aubrey Durrell has not kicked your sorry ass is a testament to his character, because believe me, he owes you a good one." "Yeah, I figured Durrell is behind this. I told Burns he needed to get rid of him, but he wouldn't listen," said Hatcher. About that time Aubrey came over and the crowd gave the two boys room. "Come on Durrell," said Hatcher challenging Aubrey to a fight. Aubrey knew if he fought this kid, his career at Kentucky A&M would be over with, but sometimes you just must stand your ground, so he squared off with the big QB. Hatcher threw a wild right hand that Aubrey sidestepped and counter with a right cross of his own that landed on the big QB's jaw. He followed that up with a combination of left hooks and right upper cuts that Muhmmed Ali would have been proud of. With the big Kid laying on the locker room floor, Aubrey could not help but say, "hey dumbass, you gotta get you head around." He would ask forgiveness for that remark later but at the time it felt great to say it. By the time Coach Burns got there and started to give Aubrey the devil for starting a fight, the rest of the team told him that Aubrey did not start the fight, but he defended himself against Hatcher's threat. Aubrey told him that he understood if he wanted him off the team but that he would have to kick him off because he would never quit. Burns told him that this would be his last trip with the team. Upon hearing that, Nate Jolly said, "If that is the case Coach, consider this my last trip as well." "Me too," said Zack Winborn. One by one most of last year's team echoed the same sentiments. Finally, J.R. stood up and said," Coach Burns, I was raised to respect authority, but you are in over your head, and you have totally screwed up a good football team. And you bring this clown in here to QB because he can throw a football. But as a leader, he couldn't lead a hog to slop, and I will never play another down for you if he is still on this team when we get back to Florence." Burns would resign effective immediately the next day and Jake Hatcher announced that he would be leaving as well. Art Slater would be named the interim head coach and he would immediately re-insert Aubrey as the starting halfback. Perhaps they could still salvage this season. In his press conference, Roy Burns stated that unwillingness to change by certain players had caused him to realize it was time to step down. When asked about Aubrey Durrell he said, "I don't believe in bowing down to any one player, especially one with limited skills, so I think it was time for me to go and the good folks at Kentucky A&M can continue with their hero worship." Asked to comment on the coach's statement, Aubrey took the high road saying, "Coach Burns is a good football coach with a proven track record, and I am sure he will land on his feet somewhere, but Kentucky A&M is all that is on my mind right now. We have got to get right in a hurry." And with that the Roy Burns experiment ended. He tried to return to BYU, but it turns out that they were not hat fond of him either and he was not rehired there. He ended up as a position coach at the University of Delaware running the Wing-T. He got out of coaching three years later and never was heard from again. Pride cometh before the fall!

CHAPTER SEVENTY-SIX

Christina had seen the story on the national sports report and college football highlight show, and she had seen the interviews with the coach and Aubrey. She wondered how he was doing and how he was handling the controversy, but she knew the answer to that already, he would handle it with class and dignity. She wished him the best and wished she could talk to him, but Quez would probably not understand that, and neither would Gwen.

She was preparing to graduate and apply to law school. Quez had already been admitted to Florida State University Law School so she would apply there also. She had met with Rod Hickey shortly after Dorothy Simmons suicide and told him about her letter and that if he mentioned a word about her abortion, she would go public with the letter. He had begged her to go with him and had apologized about the hotel room incident. He told her that he was in love with her and in time she would see that he was the best option for her future. She told him that she never wanted to see him again and that he should seek help.

In Coach Slater's first team meeting, he told the team, "Men there is a lot I could say about Coach Burns, but what purpose would that serve. He gave me a job and for that I will always be grateful. Now my job is to save what is left of this season. I hope you guys are up for the challenge, and from what I have seen looking at last year's films, I believe you guys are ready to put the bad stuff behind us and carry on." He added, "we are going to keep the offense that has been installed, but we are going to run the football and we will be in the I-formation more because I believe that is what you guys are more comfortable with. Aubrey Durrell, I hope you are ready to run because I intend to ride you hard my friend. By the way, I also played football and baseball in college, so that is no longer an issue, understood men?" "We have another road game this week versus Tulsa, and if we do not win, you will probably have another man making this speech next week. So, if you guys don't mind, how about helping me keep this job for at least another week," he said only half-jokingly.

Rodney Drew was excited to finally be getting his shot to lead the team, and the team would rally around him. Surely, he would make some mistakes, but he knew his job was to protect the football and get it to the playmakers. He was not there to win the game so much as he was not to lose it. A&M would defeat Tulsa 28-17 and Aubrey would tally 103 yards on 19 carries and would catch a TD pass from Drew in the third quarter. Nate Jolly would also rush for 57 yards on 12 carries and would also have a TD reception in the second quarter. Drew would finish with 246 yards passing on 17 completions and three TD passes. Better yet, no interceptions. As a team, they ran the ball 39 times and threw it 33 times. At 3-3 it was time to get rolling and they would do just that. Darcy Williams and hie wife Jeannie were there to see their Empire boys do their thing Darcy had just finished a good season for the AA Tulsa Drillers, a Texas Rangers' farm team. The boys had just enough time to take a picture with the Williams' and then it was time to go.

Next up was a road game at Mississippi State and the Eagles would win a close contest by a score of 32-29 on a late field goal set up by a great punt return by Aubrey who caught the ball at his own 25-yard line and took it all the way back to the Bulldog 37-yard line with 3:12 left in the game. Three plays later, a chip shot field goal game them the victory. Aubrey would rush for 110 yards on 25 carries and score two TD's J.R. also had a big day punting fives for a 42-yard average and caught a TD pass early in the game. Again, the Eagles were balanced on offense, running the ball 38 times, and throwing it 28 times completing 18 passes for 253 yards two TD passes, both to Jamie Hiller, and two interceptions. at 5-3 they still had an outside shot at a bowl game.

After three straight road games, it was good to be at home versus Missouri. The home crowd was back after the early season debacle, and they were all fans of Aubrey Durrell. There was lots of number 13 jerseys in the crowd from young kids to young ladies. The game would be tight until the fourth quarter when the Eagle offense finally found its groove and went on an 88-yard game-winning drive with 4:03 left to play and Missouri holding on to a slim 24-20 lead. On the final drive, the coaches decided to play Aubrey and Nate Jolly in the backfield together at the same time for the first time all season. They would align in their BYU look with Aubrey at left halfback and Jolly at fullback. The first call was 'Brown Right 18 Bob'—a running play where Aubrey got the handoff behind Jolly and the pulling right guard. It went for 13 yards and a first down at their own 25-yard line. They only had one timeout remaining, so they had to move quickly. Next was Red Right Slot 184 Double Slant', the play where Aubrey had an either / or responsibility depending on what the outside linebacker did. On his way to block the outside linebacker, Aubrey noticed that he was in coverage, so he ran his flair route and Rodney Drew reading the same thing lobbed a nice floater to Aubrey in the flats and he took it for 37 yards to the Missouri 38-yard line before being run out of bounds. Again, they ran 'Brown Right 18 Bob' for another 14 yards down to the Missouri 24-yard line. On first down, Drew would hit J.R. on an 8-yard out route on the left sideline and J.R. would step out of bounds to save the timeout. With 2:13 left to play and a second and two, Rodney Drew would drop back to pass but would be forced to scramble for the first down. He would gain 7 yards to set the offense up with a first down and goal to go from the Missouri 9-yard line. Coach Slater called his last timeout to set up the next couple of plays if needed, but it would take only one play—Brown Right fake 18 Bob—fullback option pass'. On the play QB Drew would fake 18 Bob to Aubrey and half roll behind the fake and look for the fullback Nate Jolly who would break in or out depending on the coverage. Again, the QB and receiver had to read the same thing, or it could end up in a disaster. Jolly broke inside and Drew hit him at the one-yard line where he caught the ball and walked into the end zone untouched for the game-winner with 1:36 left to play. Drew would run a QB draw for the two-point conversion to make it 28-24, ensuring that Missouri would have to score a TD to win the game. The defense would hold on for the victory when Zack Winborn knocked down a fourth down desperation pass attempt.

Next up was a road trip to Baton Rouge on a Saturday night for a nationally televised contest with LSU and the rowdy 'Death Valley' crowd. LSU was in the midst of a 3-7-1 season, but that crowd was hellacious to play in front of. Maybe it was the Cajun accent, but Aubrey was called names that he had never heard of before and they did not sound nice. Kentucky A&M took the opening kickoff and unleashed a Jolly / Durrell play that the coaches put in that week after noticing that the LSU contain men always flew to the ball instead of guarding the sideline. If Jolly fielded the ball, he would sprint right for about 8-10 steps; them he would hand the ball off to Aubrey who would be reversing behind him. This was the play the Dallas Cowboys used with Thomas "Hollywood" Henderson on a couple of occasions. When the coaches saw Jolly settling under the kick, they knew they were about to see something special. Aubrey came around behind Jolly and took the handoff and saw nothing but green grass between himself and paydirt. As he headed down the A&M sideline, he felt faster than he had ever felt. Suddenly the LSU kicker was in his way and as the kicker dove for his feet, Aubrey hurdled him on the way for the game's first score, a 73-yard kickoff return. That play set the pace for a route of the Bayou Bengals by a score of 46-14. In addition to his kickoff return, Aubrey would rush for 157 yards and two more TD's and would catch 4 passes for another 59 yards. Nate Jolly would rush for an additional 93 yards and a TD and Drew would throw for 356 yards on 26 for 38 passing and two TD passes—one each to Jamie Hiller and J.R. who basically had the day off from punting as the offense never had to punt—and one TD on the ground. He had two interceptions, one a pick six which bothered him until the next game. He was careless with the ball, and it could have cost them in a closed game, so he vowed to be better next week versus Louisville.

Since this game was on national television, all of Empire, Union Hill, and surrounding areas were tuned in to see their local heroes play. At Pickett's Barber Shop the old men gathered around the tv ready to see how good Aubrey Durrell really was/ they were not disappointed. Tony Finch rented a big screen tv and hosted a watch party at the Pentecostal Church and about 75 people showed up, including Jamie and Cheryl Dickinson and Darcy and Jeannie Williams. The Church of God in Hawkinsville where Wyll Durrell's family were now members also had a watch party and about 35-40 people showed up. The Durrell families, Wyll and Eli's, watched the game together at Wyll's house, but the phone rang off the hook all night long. Kenny Dudley watched the game with his basketball teammates at Albany State and could not contain his excitement when his best friend ram the opening kickoff back for a TD. In Union Hill, Coach Tony Rogers held a party with his coaches, some ex-players, board members, and current players to watch Zack Winborn play and marvel at how he had turned his life around. It is a safe bet to say that anyone with a television in Empire, Georgia was watching this game even if they were not football fans. The chance to watch someone you know on television was enough to get people interested. The last time anything close to this took place was when Cedric "Sugar Bear" Watson's Washington Bullets won the NBA championship for the 1977-78 season, but Watson rarely entered a game and was cut at the end of that season and signed to play with the Harlem Globetrotters after that. The Durrell boys would have a big impact on this game, so love them or hate them, you had to watch.

Rod Hickey hated Aubrey and even he watched at a bar in Macon all alone. He realized about halfway through the game that he and Aubrey had something in common other than both being from Empire. That was that they both loved the same girl and had been rejected by her. And by the way, he had to admit to himself that Aubrey Durrell could really play ball.

In Daytona, Florida at the Bethune-Cookman chapter house of the Alpha Kappa Alpha Sorority, Christina Dudley was going crazy watching the game and watching her ex-boyfriend show out on national tv. When one of her sorority sisters asked her why she was so excited, she told them that she had dated number 13 in high school. As the other girls started paying attention to the game, they all commenced on how good-looking Aubrey was and how Christina must have been crazy to break up with something so fine. Deep down inside, she agreed with them, but she simply said there was more to it than they would ever know.

One other man who watched this game was Red Hogan, the ex-official who exposed Sammy Barnhill's crooked attempt to screw Aubrey over watched the game and then went to bed after his nightly prayers. He would not wake up the next morning as he suffered a massive heart attack in his sleep. He daughter found him with his Bible next to him in his bed.

CHAPTER SEVENTY-SEVEN

The last home game of the season was homecoming versus Vanderbilt University who was having a bad season. A&M would win easily by a score of 44-7. Aubrey would rush 25 times for 184 yards and three TD's and catch 4 passes for 46 yards. Rodney Drew would throw for 357 yards on a 26 for 38 effort and three TD passes—two to Jamie Hiller and one to J.R. He would have no interceptions on the day. The Eagles now stood at 7-3 heading into their last regular season game at Louisville. Aubrey had accumulated 629 yards rushing on 135 carries with 10 total TD's. There would be no All-American honors this year with stats as low as his, but he had only played in 5 games on offense and they had won all five of those games, so there was no doubt who the team MVP was, unless you asked Aubrey. A reporter did just that after the Vanderbilt game and Aubrey answered quickly that Rodney Drew should be the team MVP. He accurately pointed out that Drew had started the same number of games as he had and had cut down dramatically on the turnovers and that he was hard-working and tough as nails. Many would appear to be ingenuous when saying something like this, but Aubrey believed what he was saying, and it showed.

Louisville would enter this game at 5-5 and would need to beat the Eagles to post a winning season. It would be a hard-fought game and the outcome would remain in doubt until late in the third quarter when A&M would pull away for a 35-21 victory. Again, it would be Aubrey's duties as a punt returner that would swing momentum in the Eagles' favor. With the game tied at 21 and 3:25 left in the third quarter, Louisville would be forced to punt from their own 23-yard line. Aubrey would settle under the kick at his own 42-yard line and made the first tackler miss before weaving his way through the middle of the field own his way to a 46-yard return down to the Cardinal 12-Yard line setting the offense up with a first and ten from there. On first down, Rodney Drew would throw to a wide-open Aubrey on a flag route giving A&M a lead they would not relinquish. Louisville would drive down to the A&M 14-yard line, but J.R.'s roommate Cedric Gooch; from Louisville, Kentucky; would break through the line and hit the Cardinal tailback causing him to drop the ball and Gooch would recover the ball as well. The offense would take the ball and drive 81 yards to seal the deal. Aubrey would figure heavily in this drive carrying the ball six times for 53 yards. On a second and ten from the Cardinal 26-yard line, Aubrey and J.R. would team up again like they had done in high school a couple of times on a halfback pass. Aubrey would fake a sweep right for about 4 or 5 steps before pulling up and launching a perfect pass to his cousin on a backside post route. He would finish this game with 143 yards rushing on 29 carries and one TD rushing; one receiving; and one passing. Not bad for a player with limited skills according to Roy Burns. Nate Jolly would rush for 57 yards on 9 carries and one TD. Rodney Drew would throw for 279 yards on 22 for 40 and two TD passes—one to Aubrey and one to Jamie Hiller. He would throw one interception on a 'Hail Mary' play at the end of the first half. J.R. would also punt 4 times for a 42-yard average. And pinning Louisville deep inside their own 10-yard line twice. After the game the Eagles would accept a bid from the Astro-Bluebonnet Bowl in Houston on December 31st to meet the UCLA Bruins. Aubrey would finish the regular season with 772 yards rushing on 164 carries and 12 TD's.

The players would get to go home for three days for Christmas and the Durrells were not expecting the welcome they received. As they came to the city limits sign, they saw the blue lights and thought they were coming upon a wreck, but the officer told them to follow them please. When they got to the Roddy Road, they saw the Empire Knights football team, cheerleaders, and the band lining the road. As they travelled farther, they saw probably 200 citizens or more lining the road to and forcing them to travel to the high school gym. When they got to the gym, they found a packed house waiting for them to arrive. They were met at the gym door by Coach Kelly who informed them that he was so proud of the way they represented Empire at the college level. Aubrey started to protest the star treatment, but Coach Kelly told him that they had given a sleepy little Georgia town so much to be proud of and the townspeople just wanted to show them a little appreciation. In other words, just shut up and accept it no matter how embarrassing it might be. When they walked into the gym lobby, they saw most of their old teammates there to greet them. There was Darcy, Jamie, Hondo, Bullfrog Mullins, Howell Emerson, Randy Stafford, Teddy Robertson, Josh and Lester Beasley, Kenny Dudley, Ashley Stacey, Bobby Parton, Ronnie Dobbs, Dwayne Hollis, Stevie Wilbur, Daryl Winston, and Johnny Pickens. Even Pooh Bear Winston showed up. Coach Kelly told them that they would be introduced one at a time and that Ashley Stacey, Darcy Williams, J.R. Durrell and Aubrey Durrell would be the last ones to go out. Of course, Donnie Durrell was there, in fact he had helped organize the whole thing. As Principal Bass stepped to the microphone and started his introductions the crowd got louder in anticipation of the biggest stars this place had ever seen. "Next is a young man that left Empire High School as one of the greatest all-around athletes we have ever seen and helped Empire to eight state championships in three years. He is now starting at cornerback for the Florida State Seminoles. Please welcome him back home; ladies and gentlemen Ashley Stacey," said Principal Bass. He then introduced Darcy Williams as a future star of the Texas Rangers. Next up was J.R. Durrell who Principal Bass called the most dangerous two-way threat in America as a punter who leads the nation in punting and plays wide receiver also. Finally, it was Aubrey's turn. Principal Bass jokingly said, "that's all of them, right coach? Oh, I almost forgot one—this young man is responsible for the 'play of the year' as voted on by the fans of college football. Ladies and gentlemen, I give you Mr. Aubrey Durrell." When he came out, he got a standing ovation. But the biggest surprise of them all was Doug Hall, Terry Lampkin and Billy Dobbs were standing at midcourt to greet the Durrells. The R.C. Gold Band was back together, and a stage was set up. After welcome speeches from Coach Kelly and Principal Bass, the boys took the stage and played just like they had never been apart for about an hour and a half. Aubrey noticed that Gwen had settled in backstage, obviously she had been in on this whole setup, and she had never seen this band play.

She enjoyed herself immensely. After the show, Christina Dudley had planned to go up to Aubrey and tell him congratulations on his season and how much she enjoyed the show and she got to the stage when she saw Gwen come out and hug Aubrey tightly, so she thought better of it and just went home.

After the show, the group of ex-Knights went to Nubby' s where they continued to draw a crowd of people all telling them how much they enjoyed watching them play for Empire and wishing them all luck in the future. Gwen thought it was great that a small community had so much pride in the accomplishments of these guys and how lucky she was to be dating the biggest star of them all. She still could not believe that the whole town practically showed up for the celebration. After a couple of hours of reminiscing the crowd dispersed and went home to be with their families. Billy Dobbs was the last to leave and he told Aubrey and J.R. that he was working as a studio musician in Nashville and was playing in bars on the weekends. He said he was about to go on tour as a band member with an up-and-coming singer from Texas named George Strait, but he did not know how that would go. He said he just wanted to see what life on the road was like for a while. The boys wished him the best and said goodbye. Aubrey and Gwen went to Aubrey's house and visited with his family for a while before Gwen had to leave for Barnesville. She told Aubrey she loved him so much when she went to get into her car, and he finally told her he loved her too. He had finally gotten over Christina he thought the minute the words came out of his mouth. He promised to see her again soon after the bowl game and off she went on top of the world.

The boys had to be back in Florence by Saturday morning at 11:00 as the plane was leaving for Houston at 2 pm. They made it back at 10:15 and went to the field house to get their equipment ready to go. It was approximately a three-hour flight from Cincinnati to Houston and they gained an hour crossing time zones, so they arrived at approximately 4:45 Texas time. They checked into their hotel and had supper at 6 pm and a team meeting at 7:30. At the team meeting, Coach Slater told them that he did not know if he would be hired as the permanent head coach after this game, but if not, he wanted them to know that he had enjoyed this season more than any other in his career. He thanked them for believing in him and responding like the winners he knew they were when he got to Florence. He told them that they would win this game by continuing to play great defense and stopping UCLA from running the ball and on offense, they would have to continue to run the ball and protect the football like they had done for most of the season. He laid out the practice schedule which was mostly just reviewing what they had installed before Christmas. They would practice from 9:00 am till 11:30 every morning for the next four days at Rice University. The afternoons would be spent sightseeing and doing chamber of commerce stuff. He reminded them to be nice and gracious no matter how disinterested they might be in whatever activity they were involved in, and above all else, keep their eyes focused on the prize and do not get involved in any foolishness or miss curfews and bed checks. "Remember men, you represent your hometowns, your families, the city of Florence, and Kentucky A&M University. So be on your best behavior and take care of business while you are here," he told them. When he finished speaking, Zack Winborn asked for permission to speak. Zack stood and delivered a great speech saying, "Men, trust me when I tell you that not many people thought I would be here a few years ago; I didn't even think I would ever be in this position. If any of you doubt what I am about to tell you, just ask the Durrells, they know what a scumbag loser I was. But the Lord works in mysterious ways, and he sent a few good men to help me see the light. One was my high school coach Tony Rogers who took an interest in me that few have ever bothered to do. Next was my junior college coach and mentor Jack Sullivan who made me to the line and showed me how a real man is supposed to act. Then there was Coach Cook who..." Zack said while choking back the tears. "Who showed me how to prepare like a winner and never lost faith in any of us no matter how bad we played. And now I have to say the Coach Slater, you were the right man for this job this season and I believe that you are the right man for the job permanently. I hope and pray that the university will do the right thing and hire you immediately after we take care of UCLA, and fellows, that is what we have to do so they have no choice." Zack got a standing ovation for his speech and "Mr. GQ" was even moved to tears and he gave Zack a great big hug and dismissed the team for the night.

Pizzas were delivered to the players around 10 pm and Zack came to see Aubrey and ended up telling him about his plan to harm and possibly kill him. He told him that miraculously Coach Sullivan had called him the night he made the plan and filed his chinstrap buckles. He told Aubrey that he had wanted to tell him for the longest time but never felt the time was right. "I hope you don't think badly of me Aubrey, I just had to come clean and let you know that football save my life and possibly yours too," said Zack. Aubrey was a little bit taken aback by Zack's admission and had to gather his thoughts before responding. Aubrey knew who to thank for the change in Zack Winbon, the Lord Jesus Christ. He told Zack that the Lord was responsible for saving both their lives and that he knew the night Zack had saved his life on Chicken Road that he had changed for the better and he told Zack, "I believe all things happen for a reason and I know that you are a good man Zack and I knew the last time we played against you in high school that you had the potential to be a heckuva football player. I appreciate you telling me about what you had planned on doing and if you are worried about what I am going to think about it, don't worry about that. The way I see it is that I have found a great friend through football, and I try to judge a man by his actions and not what he thinks about doing in a moment of despair. We have become teammates, friends, and brothers and I will always appreciate what you have gone through and the man you have become. "He asked Zack if he minded him praying for him and with him and Zack said no, he would like that. Aubrey prayed thanking God for saving both of their lives and for the friendship that had developed because of football. He thanked God for the great game of football and for blessing them with great coaches along the way. He thanked him for the good fortune that had brought them to this bowl game, and he asked for his blessings for their health and safety and for them to be able to play their best. When both of these young men went to sleep that night, they did so with a peace of mind unlike any they any had before.

CHAPTER SEVENTY-EIGHT

Kentucky A&M would defeat UCLA by a score of 33-17 pulling away with two fourth quarter TD'—one a 35-yard run by Nate Jolly and another on a 13-yard QB keeper by Rodney Drew. Aubrey would finish the game with 98 yards on 16 carries and two TD's. Nate Jolly would add 83 yards on 9 carries and a TD. Rodney Drew would be the bowl MVP after passing for 357 yards on 25 for 38 passing with no TD passes and no interceptions and a rushing TD. The administration would offer Art Slater the job as head coach after the game and he gladly accepted. Aubrey would finish the season with 870 yards on 183 carries and 14 TD's. This would be an average of 4.75 yards per carry and he made it easier for Rodney Drew to function in the play-action passing game throwing for 1,907 yards on 132 for 208 passing (66%) with 12 TD's and only six interceptions. As Aubrey predicted earlier in the season, Rodney Drew was voted as the team MVP. He was only a sophomore, so he had two seasons left to play for A&M. J.R. would lead the nation again in punting with a 42.4-yard average and 11 punts downed inside the opponents' 10-yard line. He was named first team All-American for the second year in a row. Zack Winborn would graduate in May with a degree in Physical Education and would have the satisfaction of knowing that he led his team to two straight bowl victories. Coach Slater would offer him a chance to be a graduate assistant coach explaining that if he took the job offer, he would be able to get a high school coaching job anywhere in the southeast whenever he got ready. Zack would end up taking the job and get his master's degree in physical education in two and a half years.

Aubrey and J.R. headed home for about a week before spring semester classes started. J.R. was majoring in agri-business as he had fallen in love with the idea of running a large farm around Empire after college, or a possible pro sports career. Working the farm for Mr. Wardell had sparked this love of farming. They two boys would do the baseball camp again this year for Coach Wilson and the Empire Knights. Kelcey Durrell would be a junior pitching prospect this season and he had also become a good running QB leading Empire to the state semi-finals this past season and an 11-3 record losing the region to Hartford and losing in the semi-finals to eventual state champions Montezuma. Kelcey was now standing about 6' 1" tall and weighed about 185 pounds. He was clocked at a 4.57 time in the 40-yard dash. He was now the plow puller for Wyll Durrell, and it was paying off again. Kelcey was doing great, and Aubrey was proud of the year he had put together with over 1000 passing yards and about 700 rushing yards on the veer option game Coach Kelly had installed to take advantage of his skills. Gerry Durrell, who now stood 6'9" and weighed 385 pounds was a dominant defensive tackle who was getting looks from all the division I schools around the southeast. Gerry was also a first baseman who could hit a baseball a country mile when he made contact. Aubrey had told Coach Slater about the two younger Durrells and he said he would check them out.

When Aubrey and J.R. got to Empire, they went in and hugged their mamas then were off to see their friends at Nubby' s. That is where they saw Ella Pipkin and she was looking great. She came to speak to the boys, and she told Aubrey to give her a call while he was in town and maybe they could do something together. Aubrey had to admit he was tempted to do just that, but he was loyal to Gwen. While Aubrey was at Nubby' s, Kelcey rode through with his girlfriend Dina Saunders and when Aubrey tried to flag him down, he just kept on riding through the parking lot as if he did not even see his older brother. Aubrey was confused and a little bit embarrassed by this snub. He would have to get to the bottom of this a little bit later that night. After leaving Nubby' s, Aubrey and J.R. went to wait on the train and talked about life in general. They discussed the fact that they had only one more year of college left and how time really flew by. They also talked about some of their friends and how their lives were playing out.

It seemed that every player from the championship years was doing okay and preparing to be successful in whatever field they chose to go into. Stevie Wilbur had started his own building contractor's business and was doing well. "Hondo" Winston was working out west on oil rigs and making good money. Darcy Williams was doing well in the Rangers farm system going 9-4 this season at Tulsa with an E.R.A. of 3.14 and would be at least at the AAA level next season if not in the major leagues. Kenny Dudley was averaging 18 points per game to go with 21 rebounds and 4 blocks per game. He said he was probably going to play professionally in Europe. Ashley Stacey was finishing up at FSU next season and would be majoring in business if not playing in the NFL. Teddy Robertson was playing division III football in North Carolina and majoring in education and winning two conferenced championships in a row. They both agreed that they had been blessed to have played at Empire with such great guys and great athletes. They felt fortunate to have been born where and when they were born. The train came on time and Aubrey felt more at home than ever before.

When Aubrey got home, he noticed Kelcey was already in bed, so he left him alone. Kelcey was not asleep however, and he heard Aubrey come in, but he did not feel like talking right now so he pretended to be asleep. He knew he would have to speak to his big brother sooner or later but for now, he chose later. The next morning, Aubrey was up early and asked Kelcey if he wanted to ride together to the camp, but Kelcey told him, "No, I have my own ride." As the two boys went to get into their vehicles, Aubrey suggested that he could ride with Kelcey and Kelcey told him, "Suit yourself but I may not be coming straight home after camp." He said nothing else on the way to the ball field. Aubrey was confused but did not push the conversation other than to say congratulations on a great football season. Kelcey simply nodded his head to the compliment given him by his big brother. At the camp there was over 100 kids there again and every kid enjoyed themselves for three days being instructed by two bona fide stars. A couple of the single moms hung around and watched camp or rather watched the coaches. One of these moms was Tamra Saunders, the mom of Kelsey's girlfriend Dina. She made a point to shake Aubrey's hand and introduce herself as Kelcey's future mother-in-law. She told him that he should come over to her house with Kelcey so they could cookout by her pool. Aubrey thanked her for the invitation and told her that he might take her up on the offer. He did not intend to, but he wanted to be nice to her considering she might end up being Kelcey's mother-in-law someday. She was a good-looking woman, and she filled out her jeans like a woman much younger than she was. Aubrey figured she was at least 42-43 years old, but she had aged well. Her husband had died a couple of years earlier because of a heart attack suffered at work at a cement factory in Perry, Georgia. She had not dated anyone since then, but she had needs and she thought Aubrey would be a good remedy for her needs. Aubrey thought he just may have figured out what was wrong with Kelcey, but he was not sure.

When he got in the car with Kelcey, he asked him if everything was okay. Kelcey did not say anything until Aubrey tried to talk to him about the season and how he felt about next year's football team. Kelcey said, "Aubrey, don't go over to Mrs. Saunders' house okay." Aubrey responded, "I don't intend to Kelcey, I was just trying to be nice. But what does it matter to you if I did?" Kelcey told him, "I don't want you to be around me because when you are near me, I disappear. You don't know what it is like being the little brother of the 'great legend' Aubrey Durrell. I can't win a championship like my brother did, and I can't play a guitar like Aubrey did. Even mama and daddy hold you up to comparison to me and I am sick of it. Now, my girlfriend's mom has the hots for you, and you already have the most beautiful girlfriend in the world. I sometimes wish that I had been born in another town to another family and I would not have to live up to your legacy." Aubrey felt badly for his little brother, and he did not know what to say but he offered this to help his brother out, "Kelcey, I can't help that I came along when Empire was loaded with talent, and I also can't help how people act and what they say about the team's performance. I just want you to know that I am so proud of you and the athlete and young man you have become. I promise you it was not easy winning those championships, but it was also not easy hearing some of the things said about me either, especially when I started dating Christina, but you must keep your focus and pray a lot. God will never let you down. You know that I believe." Kelcey started to tear up and felt a little bit ashamed of himself for telling Aubrey how he felt. Aubrey told him to drive to Nubby' s and he would buy him a milkshake. When they got to Nubby' s a couple of young ladies came up to ask for Aubrey's autograph and he reluctantly obliged. He asked Kelcey if he remembered when Big-Mouth Barry Kennedy threw him out of the ball game and what happened when Empire played Union Hill the next week? Kelcey said that he remembered it well and that he thought old Big-Mouth was going to kill him when he told him to 'go home and ice down his little barrys'. "Naw, we were not going to let him get near you," said Aubrey. "I will tell you something—right then and there you earned respect from all the guys including me," said Aubrey. "I can't tell you how many guys told me that you were going to be a bad joker when you got to high school. And they were right," he added. He told his little brother that he did a lot of the things he did on the ball fields and courts because he wanted to be a role model for him and Paula. He expressed to Kelcey that he never meant to put him in a bad situation, but after next season it would all be over, and he would be off in college making a name for himself without any comparisons to him or anyone else. Kelcey told Aubrey he understood, but he could not bring himself to tell his older brother the truth. Mrs. Tamra Saunders was very flirtatious and Kelcey had become infatuated with her. He thought she liked him too until she mentioned to him, in front of Dina, that she would like to meet his brother. Dina, who was a younger version of her mother and was a beautiful and had no idea how Kelcey felt towards her mother, thought it would be a good idea that her mother meets Aubrey. Kelcey was confused and angry at Tamra and Aubrey and everyone now. He felt badly for thinking that his brother could not leave town fast enough. Aubrey called J.R. and asked him if he was busy and J.R. told him he was not so Aubrey went to see him to talk to him about what Kelcey had said to him. J.R. told him that Gerry also felt the pressure to live up to the Durrell legacy, but he had told him to just do what he can and let the rest take care of itself. Aubrey said he had never thought about it, and he wished there was something they could do to relieve the pressure somewhat. J.R. said, "Unless we can go back in time and lose a couple of those championship games, I'm afraid they will just have to deal with it the best way they can." He added, "I think there is something else you need to understand about Kelcey." "What do you mean?" asked Aubrey. "Well, you did not hear this from me, but some of the guys were talking about how Kelcey was going to get that at the camp today," said J.R. "They were talking about how he was lucky to be getting the mom and the daughter," added J.R. Aubrey knew now that what he had thought earlier was correct and he thought about his own situation with Cathy Dehoff. He decided to tell J.R. about this for the first time. He apologized for keeping this from him for all these years, but he had promised Ms. Dehoff not to tell anyone and he had to keep his promise. He also told J.R. that had he not overheard a conversation between Coach Lord and Coach Jones, that he probably would have given in to temptation. He said he had prayed for help and that the Lord had allowed him to hear that conversation and that he had gone to see Ms. Dehoff and told her to please leave him alone. He wondered if Tamra Saunders had offered herself to Kelcey or if he had just imagined it. Either way he felt as though he needed to talk to her and see what her take on things was. When he got to her house, she answered the door in her cutoff shorts, and she was stunning. She was pleasantly surprised to see him and invited him in telling him that Dina was out with friends. She asked him what brought him to her house, and she was hoping for an answer to her liking. But instead, Aubrey told her about Kelcey's feelings toward her and wanted to know if she had done anything to encourage those feelings. She acted as if she was shocked saying, "I don't think so. Besides I want a man not a boy," she said and rubbed Aubrey's arm. Aubrey asked, "Do you consider yourself to be a sexy woman and a bit flirtatious?" "I am a hugger and I show affection. Perhaps he misunderstood my actions," said Tamra. "What about now Ms. Saunders? Are you just being nice or is there something else you would like to have?" asked Aubrey. "Oh, I think you know what I want Aubrey," she said as she reached over and kissed Aubrey passionately. He found himself not wanting to pull away, but he knew he had to. He tried to explain that he was in a relationship and should leave. But for some reason, he could not bring himself to leave. He gave in to temptation and she was not a disappointment. She had years of frustration built up inside her and she let it all loose. As soon as it was over, Aubrey felt terrible for what he had done to Gwen, to Kelcey, and to his own psyche. He had to pray really hard for forgiveness and just hoped he could live with himself after this night.

CHAPTER SEVENTY-NINE

After a week in Empire, the boys had to go back to Florence. Gwen and Aubrey rode back together while Jamie and Zack rode back with J.R. Aubrey was uncharacteristically quiet on the ride back. His conscience was bothering him terribly bad. Gwen was such a good person and he loved her, but he had cheated on her with Tamra Saunders, and he was having a hard time with this fact. Coach Slater re-instated the 6 am workouts three days per week and brought back the February mat drills. Baseball started up in early February as well and Aubrey and J.R. picked up where they left off the year before. Aubrey hit leadoff again and would hit .384 with 9 homeruns / 39 RBI / 22 stolen bases on 24 attempts. J.R. would hit for a .357 average with 15 homeruns and 48 RBI. The team would advance to the college world series again where they would lose in the semi-finals to eventual champions the University of Miami. A&M would finish the season at 55-15 and ranked number 7 in the country. In the June major league draft, Aubrey would be taken in the 5th round by the Minnesota Twins and J.R. was taken by the Chicago Cubs in the 10th round. Neither team was doing very well at the time, so the boys decided to decline the offers in favor of another college football season.

Gwen would graduate in December of the next year and she would hang around Florence until Aubrey graduated in May, then hopefully they would make some wedding plans. In the meantime, they were falling more in love every day, but Aubrey was not quite ready for wedding bells. Perhaps in the next couple of years he would be ready, but not now. Gwen would marry him at the drop of a hat if he popped the question. She did not know what Aubrey's future held; she just knew that she wanted to be a part of it.

Back to Empire for the summer and Aubrey did not look forward to seeing Ms. Saunders anytime soon. He would try to avoid her but with Kelcey still dating her daughter Dina, he had a steady reminder every time she came around. One day when Kelcey was out of earshot, Dina told Aubrey that her mom would like to see him again. He immediately knew that Tamra had told Dina about him coming over that night. Kelcey was acting a little better since he had an outstanding season in baseball leading the Knights to the state championship series where they lost two games to one to Ocilla. He had pitched great as a left-hander who threw about 88 mph and had a changeup and a slider that was just plain nasty. He had compiled a 12-1 record with an E.R.A. of 1.13 and 132 strikeouts, including 15 in the last regular season game versus Roddy. He was getting attention from several division I schools, and a few scouts were all over him, so he was forging his own way and was no longer Aubrey Durrell's little brother. Aubrey was very proud of his brother, but the feeling would not be mutual if he found out about Aubrey and his girlfriend's mom. Dina, sensing his uneasiness, told him, "Don't worry, Kelcey does not know about it, and he won't unless you tell him." "Are you insane?" asked Aubrey, "I will never tell him about it," said Aubrey. "Please, just call my mom. She really likes you Aubrey," said Dina. Aubrey wanted to tell her that he had a girlfriend, but he had one when he went to see Tamra that night, so he didn't think it wise to bring that up. He just got in his car and left riding around Empire to clear his mind. He ended up in front of the Dudley house where he saw Christina's car out front. He wondered if it would have happened if he had been dating Christina and honestly, he did not think so. He wondered if he really loved Gwen the way he should. He had made a mistake, but it was a mistake that was tearing him up inside. He had never cheated on any girl before, but now he had done it and it felt terrible. He ended up on Chicken Road where he prayed for forgiveness for the thousandth time and prayed for an end to this nightmare.

He and J.R. started to work for Mr. Wardell the next day so Aubrey was able to stay busy and, on the weekends, he was either at the farmers' market in Cordele or Atlanta or in Barnesville with Gwen. He and J.R.

also worked out at the Empire weight room each night, so he had very little free time to spend with anyone much less Tamra Saunders.

About three weeks after he had been home, Tamra showed up at the weight room one night just as Aubrey and J.R. were finishing up and she had been drinking a little bit. She came up to Aubrey and hugged him telling him she wanted to see him again. J.R. just kept walking to his car but Aubrey felt his disappointment anyway. He would have to explain all this to his cousin, but for now he had to tell Tamra to leave him alone. He tried to explain to her that he had made a terrible mistake and he felt terrible and that he had a girlfriend that he loved very much, but she didn't care to hear any of that. She told him that she only wanted him for a fling and that he could keep his girlfriend, but Aubrey told her that he could not ever see her again and he wanted her to leave him alone. She started to cry, and Aubrey felt terrible. He told her, "Look Tamra, you are a beautiful woman and if I did not have a girlfriend, I would date you in a heartbeat. You need to get out and meet someone who will treat you like you deserve to be treated, but that person is not me. There has to be a man more your age that you could date." She answered, "I am not a slut Aubrey please understand that, but I just haven't had a date since my husband died. I just needed a man in my life, and I saw you and wanted you immediately. I am sorry that I came here tonight and embarrassed you and myself. I am going home now." "No, I don't think you should be driving. Let me get my cousin to follow me and I will drive your car home," Aubrey said. He went over to J.R. and asked him to follow him and J.R. said, "You got it hoss, but I need to hear the story." "I'll fill you in when we get her home," answered Aubrey.

After seeing Tamra to her room, Aubrey came out to J.R.'s car and got in and said, "I messed up Cuz." J.R. told him, "I don't know how it happened but she's a real looker and I can't really say that I blame you." I went to see her about Kelcey having a crush on her and before I knew it, she was all over me, and I gave in. I have felt terrible about it since it happened and what I did to Gwen," said Aubrey. J.R. replied, "Hey look man, you ain't married yet and better that something like this happens now than after you are married. I mean how do you know whether or not you really love someone until you are challenged to prove it, even if you are just proving it to yourself." "I do love her, and I know that now, but I have almost told her a couple of times just to clear my conscience," said Aubrey. "Cuz, I don't think that would be wise. Some things you just must take to your grave, and this is one of them unless you want to hurt Gwen and possibly cause her to break up with you. Naw, I don't think I would let her know about this," J.R. said. "Yeah, I know you are right and thanks for understanding man. I feel better just talking to you about it," said Aubrey. "Now if I can keep Kelcey from finding out I will feel much better, but his girlfriend knows so it is just a matter of time before he finds out," added Aubrey. "Well," said J.R., "if he finds out, so be it. He can't say too much without letting his girlfriend know he has the hots for her mama. I wouldn't worry too much about that unless he is screwing the mom and the daughter now. I would shake his hand if I found out he was doing that." Aubrey knew that was not the case, so he trusted that J.R. was right.

CHAPTER EIGHTY

Aubrey took Gwen out that weekend to a nice restaurant in Macon, Leo's in the Cherry Street alley. It was expensive and Gwen wanted to know what the occasion was, but Aubrey just told her that she was worth it and that he wanted to take her out to some place nice. He could not help but notice the other men in the room stealing glances at Gwen. She was obviously the most beautiful woman in the place, and he felt lucky to be with her. He also felt guilty over his indiscretion and hoped and prayed that she would never find out. He took her back home to Barnesville and they spent some time alone in her bedroom before he had to go home. He told her he loved her dearly before he left, and she told him the same thing. He did not want to leave her, but he had to get back home soon, or his mama would be worried about him.

When he pulled up in his front yard, he saw Kelcey waiting for him. Aubrey spoke to his little brother, "Hey buddy, how is it going?" Kelcey answered, "Did you tell Gwen about Ms. Saunders?" "Man, I screwed up Kelcey. I don't know what else to say. I am sorry for what I did, and I feel terrible. I have prayed for forgiveness from the Lord, but I also would like for you to forgive me too," stated Aubrey. Seemingly perplexed, Kelcey asked, "What do I need to forgive you for?" Aubrey told him that he knew that he had a crush on her and that is why he went over there in the first place. "Who told that garbage?" asked Kelcey. "I do not have a crush on her. That is sick to even think that" he said. At that moment, Aubrey felt terrible about having listened to J.R.'s account from teenaged boys or perhaps Kelcey was just too embarrassed to admit it. Kelcey told Aubrey, "I know you are a good person and a great big brother; and I know how Dina's mama is since her husband died. I just don't want to see her or Gwen, or you get hurt in the process." Aubrey did not know when little Kelcey turned into such a wise young man, but it felt funny to me getting a lecture from his little brother. He did not know what to say so he just said, "Kelcey, I am truly sorry that I let myself get into this situation, but I really love Gwen and I love you too, so I hope you can forgive me and not think worse of me. I am continuing to pray to God for forgiveness and strength to never get in a situation like that again." Kelcey told him not to worry about it that it was over with as far as he was concerned. The boys went inside where Aubrey prayed to God for guidance while Kelcey also prayed for forgiveness for lying to his big brother about his feelings for Tamra Saunders.

After work each day, Aubrey and J.R. would watch the last thirty minutes or so of football practice at Empire High School before hitting the weights. They both thought that the Knights looked pretty good and may have a chance to win it all this season. As it turned out, they were right, and Empire would win the region over Hartford which put them in a great bracket for the state playoffs. They would ride this good fortune and momentum to a state championship victory over Sandersville High School. They would go undefeated at 15-0 in what turned out to be Coach Kelly's last season in Empire. He would take most of his coaches with him to Metro Atlanta and the ones that did not go with him went elsewhere. Kelcey would make first team All-Region and All-State rushing for 843 yards and 9 TD's and threw for 1194 yards and 14 TD passes. He had scholarship offers from option teams from across the country like Nebraska, Oklahoma, Texas, and Notre Dame. He was definitely out of Aubrey's shadow. Coach Kelly's son Quan was the workhorse running back rushing for over 1400 yards and 21 TD's and he would sign with Florida after high school. Ronald Paisley was a two-way player who really starred as a defensive back and a kick returner. Gerry Durrell was a huge defensive tackle who would sign with Kentucky A&M after meeting Coach Art "Mr. GQ" Slater. He tried to convince Kelcey to come to Florence as well and he met with him a couple of times, the second of which was at Dina Saunders' house where Coach Slater also met Tamra Saunders. He would not get Kelcey Durrell, but he would get Tamra Saunders. She finally found her a man about her age that would treat her nice and take care of her needs. Kelcey would end up signing with Nebraska. He would also lead Empire to another baseball state championship and would be drafted in the 9th round by Boston, but he wanted to play college football and baseball, so he passed on their offer. Tamra would be moving to Florence as soon as she sold her house in Empire. Dina would stay with her grandparents until she graduated in June. Tamra and Coach Slater would be married the following June. Things were somewhat strange between her and Aubrey until she told him the following spring that she was sorry that she seduced him and hoped that he could forgive her. She explained that she had never done anything like that before and that she had never been with anyone other than her deceased husband until that night. She had hoped to find a good man and she finally did in Art Slater. She also thanked him for not telling anyone about it and asked him if she could trust J.R. not to say anything. Aubrey assured her she had nothing to worry about from J.R. or himself ever saying a thing to anyone and that he was glad she was finally happy.

Aubrey's cousin Renee Thomas called Aubrey and told him that Earl Rabun had proposed to her, and they were going to be married in December and she hoped that he and J.R. could be there and be in the wedding. Earl had walked on at Georgia to play basketball and got a little bit of playing time last season. Renee enrolled at UGA as well, so they were going to be together in Athens. Aubrey got Earl's number from her and called to congratulate him and so did J.R. In early June the news came out that Kentucky A&M was going to be playing in Athens in the third game of the season versus the great Herschel Walker and his Georgia Bulldogs. The game was an add-on when Georgia needed a game because of a cancellation and A&M had an open week and needed a game. Aubrey figured the old drunk at the New Year's Eve party at Gwen's sister Judy's workplace would finally get to see if he was correct and that Aubrey Durrell could not hold Herschel's jock strap. Most people in Empire were Georgia fans but they told the boys that they would be cheering for them to do well but for the Dawgs to prevail. Aubrey and J.R. understood thar having grown up Dawgs fans themselves. Not that they needed it, but they just received extra motivation.

It was the Friday before the boys were to report for camp and Gwen was in Empire to visit with Aubrey's family and Kelcey and Dina were there. They were cooking out and Aubrey was on the grill while Dina and Gwen were talking. Aubrey hoped and prayed that Dina would not say anything to make Gwen suspicious. Kelcey told Aubrey not to worry; that Dina was happy because her mama was happy and that she did not know anything that happened between them anyway. She is also happy that when her mama marries Coach Slater, she gets to attend Kentucky A&M tuition-free since she will be the stepdaughter of a school employee. Aubrey had not thought about that aspect of things yet. He asked his little brother if he had considered life without Dina, and he said he and Diana knew that they would be breaking up at the end of the school year anyway and that they were just enjoying themselves until that time. He also told Aubrey that he was sorry that he acted like a jerk and that he loved Aubrey very much and was proud to be his little brother, He also admitted to Aubrey that he had been correct in his assumption about him having a crush on Ms. Saunders. He told Aubrey that he was confused around that time and thought he had a chance to get with this older woman. He admitted that his hormones were controlling his thinking and it was not until he saw how she looked at Coach Slater that he realized he was fooling himself. Aubrey told him, "We are all guilty of letting the 'little head' think for the 'big head'. Kelcey laughed at that comment and said, "I guess that is man's curse, isn't it?"

Later that night, Aubrey took Gwen to Chicken Road before she left for Barnesville. As Aubrey sat waiting on the train, he thought about all the romance and weddings going on and wondered if it was time for him to make a move. He would pray on that tonight when he talked to Jesus.

CHAPTER EIGHTY-ONE

On Saturday the boys headed back to Florence with Gwen and Aubrey riding together and J.R., Zack, and Jamie following close behind. As they stopped for gas somewhere in Tennessee, Aubrey told Gwen that he had something he wanted to ask her. She told him that he could ask her anything, but she never expected what happened next. Aubrey got down on one knee and asked, "Gwen Parker, will you do me the honor of marrying me?" Gwen started jumping up and down screaming so loudly that an elderly couple parked next to them asked her if she was okay. When they found out why she was screaming, they congratulated them and then recognizing Aubrey, they asked for his autograph and paid for their gas. J.R. and the boys were shocked as well, but they were proud for their friends and promised to have the best bachelor party ever. They set the date tentatively for next August after Aubrey would know whether his future involved the NFL or MLB. It would depend on where he was drafted and by whom. If it happened to be the Dallas Cowboys, it would be the toughest decision of his life since he had been a lifelong fan. As soon as they got to Florence and got settled in their dorm rooms, Gwen called her sister Judy and told her the news and they both screamed with excitement a little more. Aubrey called and told his daddy who said, "Son, I think Gwen is a wonderful girl and she will make you a good wife." His mama, who had taken a while to warm up to Gwen also congratulated him and started to cry tears of joy saying, "I can't believe my little boy is getting married. It seems like just yesterday we were watching you play Tee-Ball." As the news spread around Empire, Christina Dudley heard about it, and she was saddened by the fact that the true love of her life would now belong to another till death did them part. Kenny tried to comfort her, but she just cried uncontrollably. He wanted to tell his best friend about the fact that his sister still loved him dearly, but she made him promise to never mention it to anyone. She had made this bed and now she would have to lay in it. Perhaps Aubrey would be happy with Gwen and maybe she could be happy with Quek Bailey if he ever popped the question.

As soon as all his teammates and coaches found out about it, they kept teasing him about it, all in good fun of course. Aubrey just wanted to have a good year and see where it would lead him, but at least he knew he had someone who would gladly share in whatever the Lord had in store for him.

When practice started the coaches had to constantly remind the team that they had two games against very tough opponents—Navy and Oklahoma State— to open the season and they had better not focus of the Georgia Bulldogs to much or they would be 0-2 going into that game and it would lose its luster on a national scale. They heard them loud and clear, but still could not get their minds off facing the greatest football player the world had ever seen in Herschel Walker and the rest of the team was pretty good as well.

Just as the coaches had feared, the team looked distracted in their first game on the road at Annapolis. Aubrey had been chosen as a team captain and was immediately rendered speechless when his hero Roger Staubach came out as an honorary captain. My gosh, thought Aubrey, the man looks like he could still play, and he probably could have. The Midshipmen got out to an early 10-0 lead and would lead 13-7 at halftime. The coaches chewed the team out hard and challenged them to play up to their capabilities in the second half. Aubrey was singled out by Coach Slater who reminded him that Roger Staubach was pulling for him to lose "so how about getting over the hero worship and disappoint his ass today." Aubrey would respond with 110 yards rushing in the second half on 17 carries and two TDs in leading A&M to a 32-17 victory. In the second game of the season, a home game versus Oklahoma State, Rodney Drew would lead the way to a 49-7 victory throwing for 368 yards on 33 for 49 passing and 4 TD's and one interception. Aubrey would have 98 yards rushing and one TD rushing and 133 receiving yards and two TD receptions. J.R. would have 5 receptions and a TD reception as well as punting twice for a 39-yard average. Next was the trip to Athens and a regionally televised game versus the sixth ranked Georgia Bulldogs.

The gameday atmosphere in Athens, Georgia is amazing with tailgaters every five feet, and drunks yelling 'GO DAWGS!' and proceeding to bark like a mad dog. Kentucky A&M was supposed to be the lambs led to a slaughter, but they had one thing going for them—Herschel Walker had broken a finger before the season-opener and had only run the ball 11 times versus Clemson in their first game. No one wished any harm on Herschel, but if he could not play in this game then it made the game a little more manageable. As it turned out, the Georgia coaches had not planned on using the great running back too much if they did not need him, but they did need him as Kentucky A&M took a 14-7 lead into the locker room at halftime thanks to a 54-yard interception return for a TD by a sophomore defensive back from Jackson, Mississippi. Herschel would play more in the second half, and he would be the difference in this game as he would finish the game with 32 carries for 135 yards and two TD's allowing Georgia to pull off a 24-21 victory as Kevin Butler would hit the game-winning field goal from 45 yards out as time expired. It was a great game for the fans but for Aubrey Durrell he would leave the game in the third quarter with what was described as a hip-pointer. He would end his day with 102 yards on 23 carries and a 28-yard TD run in the first quarter. And who knows, perhaps if he had stayed in the game, maybe he would have outgained the eventual Heisman Trophy winner, but it was not meant to be. In fact, Aubrey would experience something he had never had to endure before—he would miss the next game because of injury and would be evaluated on a day-to day basis. He felt like he had let the team down, but he could not help it. This was the most pain he had ever had to deal with. It hurt to sit, stand, to lay down, and even taking deep breaths hurt. He was told that he may be out for two or three games depending on how his recovery went. When he went down after a 12-yard run he knew he had been hit hard, but he instinctively tried to get up but when he fell back to the ground, he knew it was serious, so he began praying. The Lord evidently heard his prayers as he was told that a hip pointer was merely a bad bruise that if not treated properly, could result in a more serious injury. When he was carted off the Sanford Stadium field, he was given a standing ovation by the crowd of Georgia faithful. He knew his family would be in to check on him shortly and sure enough they were. They were relieved to find out that he would be okay. Next, he had to call Gwen who was beside herself with worry and fear until he assured her that he was okay and would see her soon. Next, was his teammates who had to finish the game not knowing the extent of his injury. J.R, was the first to come in to see him and one by one they all came in to wish him a speedy recovery.

In Tallahassee, Florida there was a young first-year law student who was also on pins and needles worrying about Aubrey's condition. Christina Dudley had to dismiss herself from the party where she had been watching the game so no one would see her crying. She had to call Kenny and see if he could find out anything and let her know. He told her that he would call the Durrells as soon as he could but that it would probably be the next day before he would know anything. Kenny wanted to tell his sister to call Aubrey and just tell him that she still loved him, but he knew she would not that and mess up his life like that. He just wished that the two of them had never broken up.

Aubrey did not sleep at all when the team got back to Florence. There was no position he could lay in that did not hurt. The trainers would have to give him something for pain so he could sleep at night. Early the next morning, he had to be in the training room for treatment at 8:00 am and it was brutal. He had to get into, and ice whirlpool for 15 minutes then get into a hot whirlpool for 15 minutes. He had to do 5 rotations. He thought it was going to kill him, but he had to admit, it did ease his pain a little bit. After this torture session he had to do movement exercises to get the blood flowing. This would happen for the next five days. When he got back to his room, he had a message to call Kenny Dudley. He returned the call and Kenny asked him if he was okay. Aubrey told him what the prognosis was, and Kenny was relieved. He also told Aubrey that Christina had called and asked about him and Aubrey was happy to hear that she was doing great in law school. Kenny told him that he probably should not say anything, but his sister still cared deeply for him. Aubrey said he still cared for her too and wished her nothing but the best. Kenny decided to leave it at that and tell his good friend that he loved him like a brother.

Tulsa came to Florence with a good football team and defeated the Eagles 28-10 as the offense could get nothing going. Rodney Drew would have his worst game as a starter throwing three interceptions and no TD's. He was trying to do too much knowing that the running game would be lacking. The next week the Eagles would travel to Memphis State without Aubrey for a second game in a row. He tried to talk the coaches into allowing him to play, but they thought it best to give him another week to heal completely. A&M would win a close contest by a score of 17- 14 with Nate Jolly rushing for 136 yards and two TD's on 32 carries. J.R. would be the player of the game however, with 6 punts for a 42-yard average and two punts dead inside the Memphis State five-yard line.

Aubrey would return for a road game at Indians and would rush for 83 yards on 19 carries in a limited workload and Nate Jolly would add another 97 yards on 23 carries. Each would score twice in a 41-19 victory. Jamie Hiller would be the player of the game with 9 receptions for 119 yards and two TD's. A home win versus a tough Mississippi State team left A&M with a 5-2 record heading into the home stretch with a chance for a third consecutive bowl appearance if they could win at least two more ball games. The score was 24-22 with the difference being missed extra points by Mississippi State. Aubrey would run for a season-high 173 yards on 32 carries and three TD's.

Next up was a road trip to Missouri where the Eagles would win 35-13 with Aubrey going for 143 yards on 35 carries and two more TD's proving once and for all that Aubrey was completely recovered from his injury. At 6-2 the Eagled needed one more win for a good chance at a bowl bid, but it would not be easy with LSU coming to Florence followed by a trip to Notre Dame and finishing the regular season at home versus Louisville. Aubrey had tallied 707 yards and 13 TD's on 173 carries and with potentially four games left to play, he had a good chance of breaking 1,000 yards on the season for the second time. The team was ranked 12th in the nation as well.

LSU would avenge last season's loss in Baton Rouge, winning 20-10 as Aubrey and the Eagle offense found the going tough versus one of the Southeastern Conference's better defenses. Aubrey would only rush for 88 yards on 25 carries and would not see the end zone, and they would not kick to him all day after the great day he had the year before.

Rodney Drew would leave the game early in the second half after taking a ferocious hit on a sack. Backup QB Jimmy Haskins would play okay, but he was not ready for this stage yet. A&M had no time to fret over this loss as they were travelling to South Bend, Indiana to play Notre Dame who was ranked number 13 at the time and needing a win to secure a bowl bid themselves. Aubrey would bounce back with a terrific performance rushing for 118 yards on 24 carries and two TD's to lead the team to a 30-17 victory and give them their 7th victory of the season and a guaranteed bowl bid. They just did not know where it would be yet. In the final game of the season versus Louisville at home it was senior day, and the parents were in attendance. Before the game the seniors, escorted by their parents, were presented for the crowd. Aubrey was the last one introduced, and he got the loudest ovation of them all. As Wyll and Pattie walked out with him, Wyll told him he loved him and was proud of him and it almost brought tears to Aubrey's eyes. He had the best parents in the world, and he loved them so much, and he wished he could go back and relive some of the best days in Empire, but life goes on and Lord only knew what the future held.

The Eagles destroyed Louisville for the fourth year in a row by a score of 55-21 with Aubrey going for 175 yards on 32 carries and three TD's giving him 1,088 yards on 254 carries and 18 TD's for the season. Better yet, they accepted a bid to the Liberty Bowl in Memphis to play none other than Bull Ripley's Alabama Tech team in Bull's last game before he retired. He would be the star attraction and receive accolades from everyone, but Aubrey, Jamie Hiller, and their big lineman buddy from Lagrange, Georgia wanted to give him a special going-away present. The game was to be played on December 29, 1982, so the boys would not be back in Empire for Christmas. They talked Coach Slater into allowing them to have a few days the week of the 17th so they could watch the Empire Knights win a state championship over Sandersville in Empire and be in Renee Thomas' wedding to Earl Rabun on the 18th. Kelcey had a great night rushing for 125 yards and two TD's and passing for 102 and another TD as the Knights finished off a perfect season with a 28-10 victory. Quan Kelly rushed for 165 yards and a TD as well. Aubrey and J.R. were wished well all night as the hometown fans were glad to see them, but the night belonged to Kelcey, Gerry, and their teammates and they honored an old tradition by spending the night on the field. Aubrey was so proud of his little brother and after the game he went on the field to congratulate him. When Kelcey saw him, he hugged him tightly and told him he loved him. This made Aubrey feel good knowing that whatever animosity that had existed between them was long gone. Aubrey and Gwen went to Nubby's with a lot of ex-teammates and the current champs. The old guys sat and marveled at how the young players danced around with the trophy and Darcy Williams said, "It seems like just yesterday that was us dancing around." "Yep," said J.R., "we were on top of the world, and it sure felt good." Lester and Josh Beasley came up and everyone was glad to see them. The two of them had attended the Northrup-Grumman Apprentice School in Newport News, Virginia and had learned a trade while playing division III college football. And they were getting paid $12 per hour with benefits. It was a sweet deal, and they had a guaranteed job with the shipyard after graduation in a few months. They had both met girls up there and were planning to get married soon and stay up there and work. Gwen could tell how much his hometown meant to Aubrey and she loved that. She was a small-town girl at heart, even smaller than Barnesville, Georgia. She did not know whether life would lead her and Aubrey back to Empire, but it would be alright with her if it did. Aubrey told the guys that he hated to be a party pooper, but he had to be in a wedding tomorrow and head back for bowl practice the next day and he needed to get in the bed. He congratulated Kelcey, Gerry, and the rest of the team and he and Gwen left for Chicken Road first, then to the Durrell house where Gwen would sleep in Kelcey's bed tonight. Early the next morning, J.R. and Aubrey headed back to Florence with a stop in Warner Robins to pick up Jamie Hiller. On arrival back in Florence, the boys went to eat pizza then went to bed. The team would practice in Florence until Thursday when they would leave for Memphis.

Aubrey and Jamie talked about how life was full of surprises and how it almost seemed appropriate to finish their college careers versus Bull Ripley. Alabama Tech was not the juggernaut they once were, but they still played hard and would be well-coached, so it would take their best effort to come away with a win. On Thursday, December 23rd the team left for Memphis and would spend Christmas day with a local children's' home handing out gifts and trying to make their loads a little lighter. It made it more bearable to be away from home to know that you might be able to make some unfortunate child's day better. All the Eagles said that other than the game itself, this would be the highlight of the trip. On Sunday night the banquet was held with the two teams together. The coaches would speak briefly, and Art Slater stated how proud he was of his team and how proud they were to be in Memphis, and he thanked the Liberty Bowl for the invitation. Bull Ripley talked about himself and how he started out in coaching at the first Liberty Bowl in 1959 and now his career had come full circle and would end where it all began. He talked about his six national championships and all the great players he had coached and when he finished speaking, Aubrey could not help but feel like he had sat through a Bull Ripley tribute hour. Then the Liberty Bowl chairman got up and heaped more praise on "The Bull" and awarded him a plaque signifying induction into the Liberty Bowl Hall of Fame. No doubt it was well-deserved, but Aubrey could not help but think of the plot Gwen had exposed and the money sent to him and wondered if they knew about any of that when extending his membership to the Hall of Fame. He could tell them if he thought it would amount to anything, but he knew better. The best thing to do was to beat him in the game.

On Wednesday December 29, 1982, Aubrey Durrell would play his last college football game ever and he would have a good game rushing for 168 yards on 31 carries and two TD's rushing and a third TD on a second quarter punt return of 63 yards. He and Jamie Hiller would have the last laugh on Bull Ripley as Jamie would catch 7 passes for 157 yards and two TD's in leading Kentucky A&M to a 48-24 victory and a final record of 9-3 and Aubrey would be named the game's MVP. J.R. would catch 4 passes for 54 yards and a TD and would punt three times for a 52-yard average helped by a monster punt that rolled to a stop at the Alabama Tech 6-yard line after travelling 74 yards in the second quarter. This punt led to a fumble recovery by Cedric Gooch and a short TD drive that put the Eagles up by two TD's at halftime. Nate Jolly would finish the scoring with a 35-yard TD run in the fourth quarter. After the game, Aubrey went up to Coach Ripley and told him congratulations on a great career. "The Bull" looked him in the eye and told him that he wished he had played for him. Aubrey wanted to say he would have had he not been so stubborn about baseball, but instead he just said, "Thanks Coach" and walked away.

In the locker room after the game, Coach Slater told the team that he was humbled and proud to be their head coach. He also invoked the memory of Coach Cook and Coach Whitton and thanked them for their recruiting ability. He told the seniors how proud he was of them and wished them well in all life's endeavors almost coming to tears as he said those things, but he held it together like "Mr., GQ" should. Aubrey would finish his college career with 4,317 yards on 770 carries (average of 5.6 yards per carry) and 51 Td's. He would finish second all-time in school history in rushing yards and third in TD's scored. He would finally be named to the All-American Team along with J.R. and Jamie Hiller. Aubrey would also finish 8th in the Heisman Trophy balloting. The Eagles would win 34 games and lose 13 in four years and win three bowl games. All that was left to do was to see where he would be chosen in the NFL Draft in March and then see where he would be chosen in the MLB Draft and decide from there.

CHAPTER EIGHTY-TWO

The boys headed back to Empire for about a week before classes started for the second semester. Aubrey and Gwen went to the same New Year's Eve Party they had attended last year, and the drunk was there again, but this time he was all complementary to Aubrey and not quite as drunk as last year. He sat and talked to Aubrey like a decent person. Aubrey had found out that he had been a high school football star in Columbus, Georgia graduating in 1971 and was supposed to play in college at Samford in Alabama, until his girlfriend / wife turned up pregnant and he had to get married instead. He expressed a little regret about what might have been but did say that he loved his family and would not change a thing even if he could. Aubrey thought about his situation with Christina and wondered what would have happened if she had decided to have the baby. The man's name was Randy Jameson, and he was a nice guy who happened to be the biggest Georgia Bulldog fan in the world. But he had respect for Aubrey because he had stood toe to toe with his beloved Bulldogs and almost came out on top. "How does it feel to be on the same field with Herschel?" asked Randy, "Well I was happy that it was not my job to tackle him," said Aubrey. He added, "Herschel is the best player I have ever seen, and I am glad he won the Heisman. I am just proud to be mentioned in the same sentence with him." "Hey, you are really good too my friend," said Randy. Aubrey thanked him for the compliment and got ready for the stroke of midnight.

When the clock struck midnight, Gwen grabbed Aubrey and kissed him passionately and told him that this time next year, they would be married. Aubrey had not thought about that, and he was taken aback a little bit which prompted Gwen to ask him if he was alright. He assured her that he was and that he could not wait to marry her, and he meant it. God had been very kind to Aubrey Durrell, giving him a wonderful girl to fall in love with when he desperately needed someone.

On January 10th classes started for the last semester for the Durrells. Aubrey would have to do nine weeks of student teaching at a local high school so he would be busy preparing lesson plans and playing baseball while waiting on the NFL Draft. Coach Ellison told the Durrells to be prepared for agents harassing them trying to sign them, but he told them that if they signed with an agent, they would lose their amateur status and could be disqualified from baseball. Sure enough, the calls came daily and some of them posed as students, trying to get close to the boys. They even announced at a press conference that they were going to play baseball and then decide no matter where or by whom they were drafted in the NFL. This seemed to lessen the harassment to a certain degree.

Once the season started, the boys were able to relax and just play ball and that was something they had always been able to do—shut out all outside noise so long as they had a game to play. Coach Kelly had called them 'gamers' and that was an appropriate moniker. Aubrey, hitting leadoff again would bat .369 with 11 homeruns and 39 RBI. He was 19 for 22 in stolen base attempts and scored 48 runs. J.R. would hit for a .343 average with 16 homeruns and 55 RBI. The team would make it back to Omaha where they would lose in the championship game to Texas by a score of 4-3. Their record was 63-10 and they finished the season ranked number two.

In the NFL Draft, Jamie Hiller was drafted in the third round by Dallas, while Aubrey was a fifth-round pick of Green Bay. J.R. was taken in the ninth round by San Francisco. The big lineman from Lagrange, Georgia was chosen in the third round by Minnesota. In the MLB Draft, Aubrey was a second-round pick of the Houston Astros and was offered a $75,000 signing bonus compared to $25,000 by Green Bay of the NFL. J. R. however was offered $30,000 to sign with San Francisco to punt while he was drafted in the twelfth round by the Baltimore Orioles for a signing bonus offer of $10,000 so it was off to the NFL for him. Aubrey would take the baseball offer.

After graduation in May, the boys went home for a while. Aubrey would wait for the MLB Draft in June while J.R. was waiting until camp started for San Francisco. They would spend a lot of time together fishing, working out, and talking about life and how this would be the first time they would not be together playing ball on the same team. Even if Aubrey took Green Bay's offer, they still would be separated for the first time since first grade. J.R. asked Aubrey how he would feel without football in his life and expressed shock that Aubrey was not drafted earlier. It had been a down year for running backs in the draft and the ones taken high were from traditional powerhouse programs like Penn State and Clemson. It had been explained to Aubrey that if they took a chance on him at his size and from a school that did not play a tougher conference schedule that it would be their jobs if he did not work out, whereas if a bigger back from a traditional big-time school was less risk for them. While Aubrey appreciated his honesty, he thought it was cowardly not to trust your eyes when you see a man playing his heart out and getting results. Either way, he was thankful he had baseball and the NFL's loss would be MLB's gain. He was more determined than ever to take advantage of any opportunity he was offered and make the best of the situation.

Aubrey and Gwen decided to wait on their wedding plans till December since they had no idea where Aubrey would be when this whole thing played out. When Houston drafted him in June and paid him $75,000 to sign, he was told that he had one week to report to Kissimmee, Florida for the Gulf Coast Rookie League. He gave his parents $5,000 and gave Kelcey and Paula $2,500 each before leaving for Kissimmee. Gwen would meet him down there after a couple of weeks to give him a chance to settle in. He rented a one-bedroom apartment for $150 per month. It was far from nice, but it was a place to lay his head at night and it had a decent pool, and it was only 4 miles from the ballpark. Gwen came down and saw the apartment and decided it would be okay for a while. Any place would be okay so long as she was with Aubrey. There were some long days with Aubrey reporting at 9 am and working until 5 pm. They would play 60 games over 12 weeks usually at 7 pm. He was working at shortstop and left field, so he had a lot to keep him busy. When he got home at night he was worn out and took a shower and went to bed sometimes without supper. He would lose 10 pounds in 12 weeks. Gwen tried to understand his situation, but it was lonely during the day, and he was too tired to give her much attention at night. Aubrey told her that it would only be for a little while and things would be back to normal. She would be glad to get somewhere and settle down and find a teaching job soon. At least that way she would have something to keep her busy. She went to every game played at Osceola County Stadium and from what she could tell, Aubrey was doing okay.

His first professional at bat came against the Atlanta Braves rookie and he was leading off the game for the Astros. He took the first pitch—a strike at the knees on the outer half of the plate. He noticed that the pitchers were bigger and stronger than at the college level for the most part. This also meant that their fastballs were better and had a little more pop on them. But Aubrey always believed that he could catch up to any fastball and he just wanted to see one more in this at bat. The next pitch was a slider for ball one. He suddenly remembered Coach Ellison's words about being able to predict the next pitch based on game circumstances. With a count of 2 balls and one strike and the pitcher missing with two breaking balls, he knew he would see a fastball since the pitcher would never want to walk the leadoff hitter. He got what he wanted, a fastball at around 93 mph. Aubrey put a good swing on it and hit a homerun to right-center field. He would not see a fastball the rest of the day and would end up with two strikeouts and a ground out to the second baseman. The Astros would win the game however, 3-1. He knew he had to learn to at least fight off breaking pitches until he could get the pitcher to give in and throw him a fastball or make a mistake and hang a breaking ball. He had to call home and give them the news, both good and bad, but his daddy only heard that his son had gone yard in his first at bat as a pro. After three weeks, the players were given a day off and Gwen was happy about that and so was Aubrey. They decided to go eat seafood and see a movie—'vacation' starring Chevy Chase. It was hilarious and they had a great time. When they got home, Aubrey gave Gwen the attention she had been denied for weeks. They were definitely in love and could not wait to be married in December.

Aubrey would finish the rookie season with a .258 batting average with 4 homeruns and 13 stolen bases in 16 attempts and 21 runs scored, but he had 21 strikeouts and that was not acceptable. Not too bad but nothing to write home about either. They left Kissimmee in early-October and headed back to Empire to plan their wedding.

He had spoken to J.R. a couple of times in August and found out that he was going to make the team as a punter. He spoke glowingly about Coach Bill Walsh and QB Joe Montana. He also told them that they would be playing in Atlanta on November 20th, and he expected to see them there. Aubrey assured him that they would be there. He gave J.R. the date for the wedding and asked him if he could be there. The wedding would be on December 17th and since the 49ers played on Monday the 19th at home versus Dallas, he said he would be there. The 49ers did not practice during the regular season on Saturdays so there would be no problem.

Living arrangements in Empire were a bit of a concern. Since he and Gwen had been living together in Florida, he saw no reason for that to end now, but since he was not getting paid after the season ended, he would have to seek out employment to make ends meet. They could stay at his parents' house until they could get their own place but sleeping together was out of the question while they were there. Both Aubrey and Gwen would get jobs substitute teaching in Empire and Aubrey would help out the new football coach a man named Zeke Hendrix from Warm Springs. He had been an assistant there for about ten years and remembered Aubrey from their playoff games a few years earlier. He was a good man, but Empire was in a rebuilding mode after the last championship athletes graduated and it would require exercising a lot of patience from the coaches and the fans. Unfortunately, that is not something fans are good at. Coach Hendrix installed his wing-t offense, and it took a while for the kids to grasp it, so the Knights got off to a rough start going 0-3 to start the season. They would right the ship a little bit and win their next two games, but Union Hill demolished them by a score of 47-14 and the natives were restless. At 2-4 it was time to dig down deep inside and find some Empire pride and Aubrey challenged them to do just that. He asked Coach Hendrix for permission to speak to the team and he was told "by all means say what you need to say." Aubrey told the team that they were standing on the shoulders of men who had come before them and had given it their all and that it did not matter what the fans thought, after all, the word "fan" is short for "fanatic" so you cannot expect a fanatic to be reasonable or rational. But the former players thoughts did matter and all they want to see is 100% effort every Friday night and every day at practice for that matter. "Whether you win a championship or not is irrelevant, so long as you represent Empire the right way. And since I was a part of a few championships here, I have a right to speak for all my former teammates and tell each of you that I don't think y'all are giving your best effort to Coach Hendrix, to your teammates, and to this community. Remember, y'all are standing on the shoulders of men who came before you, but future generations will be standing on your shoulders. Can you bear the load?" he said. "Men, when you leave the field there should be nothing left in your tank. If you have any ounce of energy left in your body, then you cheated your teammates. Hustle does not cost a dime and it is contagious. I don't care if we win another game; I simply want to see Empire pride on display the rest of this season. Do y'all understand men?" he added. Aubrey borrowed from Coach Eldridge Cooks and started making the running backs run an extra mile after practice and shine the linemen's cleats before each game and pretty soon, the other skilled players were running with the backs just as they did when he was playing. Apparently, the players bought into what Aubrey had said and it showed in practice and on Friday nights. Empire would win their next three games and go into the final game of the season with a chance to finish at 6-4 and in fourth place in the region. They would have to beat Roddy to accomplish this feat and the winner would be the fourth and final playoff team. Empire would make the short trip to Roddy and come home with a hard-fought 17-14 victory. The game was decided in the last minute of play as Empire had to drive 76 yards with one timeout trailing 14-10. The fullback Darrin Echols would run it in from 14 yards out with 32 second remaining in the game. The kids acted like they had just won a championship, even the ones who were on the team last season and had won one. Aubrey was as proud of them as he would have been had they won the state championship also because of the way they had responded when they had a chance to quit on the effort and quit on their community. They would have to travel to Hartford the next week to play the number one team in the region and who had destroyed Empire earlier in the season 42-21. This time the score would be 21-19 in favor of Hartford, but the boys had proven that Empire pride was alive and well. Aubrey received a call that weekend from Coach Kelly congratulating him on a good season and telling him about his own problems rebuilding his alma mater which had fallen on hard times but had managed to go 5-5 this season. Aubrey told him that he had no doubt that he would win big there just as he had done in Empire. Coach Kelly told him that it would be easier if he had another Aubrey Durrell on his team. Aubrey thanked him for the compliment and for everything he had done for him over the years, and he invited him to his wedding along with all the former Empire coaches who were working with him. Coach

J. R. left ten tickets at will call for his family members and they showed up on Sunday November 20th to watch San Francisco play at Atlanta. J.R. was looking good in his number 31 uniform and he had to punt 6 times for a 43-yard average, and he also held for extra points so he was on the field plenty, but on this day the Falcons would prevail 28-24. After the game, he spent about 30 minutes talking to everyone before he had to go. He was doing well financially signing a contract for the league minimum of $130,000 per year, but he also had written into his contract bonuses of $50,000 for leading the league in punting and another $100,000 if he made the Pro Bowl. Aubrey was proud of his cousin and secretly wondered if he had made the right choice picking baseball over football since he only made $2100 playing rookie ball and was still living off his signing bonus of $75,000 of which he had approximately $50,000 left. He would not make any money unless he made the major leagues and with the season he just had, he doubted he would ever make it to "The Show".

As their wedding day drew closer, Aubrey wondered if he would ever make it to the big leagues and whether Gwen would be happy with him if he did not. On the Friday before his wedding on Sunday, his wedding party took him out for a bachelor party. Kenny Dudley, Darcy Williams, Teddy Robertson, Jamie Dickinson, Ashley Stacey, and J.R decided to take him to a strip club in Warner Robins just to see his reaction. Aubrey was very appreciative of their efforts, but he did not wish to participate in any shenanigan's involving strippers, but he played along when a group of fine young ladies took him to the stage to give him a group lap dance to celebrate his last weekend as a free man. One of them offered to take him in a back room and show him a lot more fun, but Aubrey turned her down. Aubrey had never tasted alcohol, but he had to partake in a champagne toast with the guys. Darcy and Jamie were married men and stayed true to their vows, but the others had fun sampling the treats presented to them by these eager young ladies. Aubrey did blame them, nor did he judge them. They were his best friends on earth and if they were having fun, he saw little harm in it. After all, no one was getting hurt. He and Darcy talked about the rough life in minor league baseball and Darcy told him that the minor leagues were the big club's way of weeding out the pretenders and seeing who really wanted it. He said that if Jeannie didn't get a job, they would not be able to make it. He also told Aubrey that they had decided to give it five years and if he had not made it by then, he would give up the dream and come home and work for a living. He was about to start his fifth season so this would be his make-or-break year. He had been at Triple-A Oklahoma City most of last season and expected to start there again this year and that paid about $1200 per month during the season. If he could just get a call up from the big club all his financial worries would be over. Aubrey told him he was sure that he would make it to the big leagues as long the mule was still kicking.

Meanwhile, Gwen was with her sister Judy and some of their friends having a lingerie shower. They were also drinking and talking about the men in their lives. Gwen felt fortunate that she was marrying a perfect gentleman and she never could consider saying some of the things she heard said that night about their husband and boyfriends. As the wine flowed more frequently, Gwen heard stories of everything from general laziness to sexual dysfunction. They all laughed at what they were hearing but Gwen knew she could never look at some of these men the same way again and the poor guys would never know what had been said. If they did, there would surely be some divorces or breakups. No, she would never speak about Aubrey like that.

The following night was the rehearsal dinner in Barnesville and all the friends and relatives were there including Gwen's uncle Jim Tanner who would give the bride away. He had always looked after the girls and he was the only male in the family who gave two hoots in hell about them, so Gwen told him that she would be honored if he would walk her down the aisle. He gladly accepted. Of course, Wyll would be Aubrey's best man and Judy was Gwen's maid of honor. With the wedding party sufficiently recovered from the bachelor party at the strip club, the wedding was set to go off without a hitch. The couple would honeymoon in Gatlinburg, Tennessee for 4 days before resuming their lives together. Aubrey had made sure to save enough bonus money for the honeymoon so there were no worries there. The next day at 2 pm at a little Baptist church outside Barnesville, Aubrey said "I do" to his beautiful bride. After a brief reception, the couple left for Gatlinburg as Mr. and Mrs. Aubrey Durrell. As they drove off, Kenny Dudley knew one person who was sad at this occasion—his big sister Christina. She had wanted to see the wedding, but she knew she would not be able to handle it and she did not want to be a distraction, so she decided to pass on attending. She sincerely wanted Aubrey to be happy and hoped that he got everything out of life he ever wanted. She would try to forget about him and move on with her future husband Quez Bailey who had one more year of law school. She had two more so wedding bells would probably ring for her in two years.

In Gatlinburg, Aubrey would learn how to snow ski for the first time in his life. Being a great athlete, he took to it fairly easy and was soon zipping down the mountain like he had been doing it all his life. They shopped at all the local gift shops and spent much of their time in each other's arms by a fire in their mountain chalet. It was nice to have someone be so in love with you thought Aubrey, but they still had to figure out how to make it on a minor league salary. Aubrey asked Gwen what she thought about a five-year plan to make it to the big leagues. She told him that they would make it okay, and she had no doubt that he would make it before then. He told her he appreciated the confidence, but Darcy had not been called up yet and he was the best player Aubrey had ever seen, so they needed to prepare for the worst-case scenario. She reminded him that he had always prayed for the Lord's will to be done and now he should continue praying for guidance. She also told him not to worry about her because she got everything she would ever need when they said, "I do."

They would live with Judy for the month of January before spring training started in February. Gwen would stay with Judy until Aubrey found out where he would be assigned to start the season. He figured he would probably be assigned to single-A Asheville, North Carolina as a member of the Asheville Tourists in the Carolina League.

CHAPTER EIGHTY-THREE

Aubrey would live with a sponsor at spring training and when he reported in mid- February, he had no idea what to expect. He walked into a training facility and there was Nolan Ryan, Aubrey's jaw dropped when Nolan actually said "Hello". He could not think of anything else to say so he said, "Hey Mr. Ryan. It is an honor to meet you." "Nolan is my name, Mr. Ryan is my daddy," said the great pitcher. "We are teammates now and you obviously belong here, or we would not have drafted you, so no need to be so formal or starstruck kid," he added. He could not wait to call his daddy and tell him about this. This was the coolest thing that had ever happened to him, and he had to tell somebody. He would have to call J.R. too. His host family was a nice older couple named Fred and Hilda Warner and they hosted Aubrey and two more players—one from the Dominican Republic named Marco Pineda and another from Grand Prairie, Texas named Bobby Joe Burgess. He knew who Aubrey was from his football days in college. "Man, I can't believe I am rooming with the great Aubrey Durrell. That kickoff return you made versus LSU was a thing of beauty man," he said with his Texas drawl. He told Aubrey, "We was all hoping the Cowboys was gonna draft you, but they didn't. If they had, would you be here right now?" he asked. Aubrey honestly answered, "Probably not."

Marco was a second baseman and Bobby Joe an outfielder. At 23 years old, Aubrey was the oldest one of the three and the only one who was married. Bobby Joe had been drafted out of high school, so he was away from home for the first time and was ready to experience life. He wanted to go out every night and see what he could get into. Aubrey knew he could not keep up that pace and perform at the level the

Astros expected. As Coach Lord used to say, "You can't hoot with the owls and soar with Eagles," Marco was quiet mainly because he did not speak much English, but he was a nice guy, and he was a great fielder but a little weak with the bat.

The Warners laid down the house rules—no girls in the house; no drinking or drugs, no profanity, and the boys would have to attend at least one Sunday service with them. All agreed to these rules although Bobby Joe didn't seem so happy about it. At least he was a fan of Aubrey's so he could influence him perhaps.

As spring training went on, Aubrey felt good about his progress. He was playing with a split squad and travelling to different parks across Florida. Had he been getting paid, it would have been great fun, but minor leaguers did not get paid for spring training and his bonus money would not last forever. They did get two meals per day at the clubhouse and $10 per diem so Aubrey saved money on food. He hit .278 for the Grapefruit League season with 6 homeruns and 25 RBI and best of all—only six strikeouts. He was assigned to Asheville, North Carolina in the South Atlantic, or "Sally League". He called Gwen to give her the news and told her to be ready to leave in three days. He would have just enough time to visit his parents and Bobby Joe would be travelling with him so they would get to see Empire in all its glory. Marco would stay behind for extended spring training mainly to learn some English. They rented a U-Haul and picked Gwen up before travelling to the big city of Empire. They would spend one night at a motel then head to Asheville. His parents told him to save his money and stay with them, but he told them they did not have enough room for three more adults, but Wyll insisted they could make room for just one night. So, they decided to try to stay at Wyll and Pattie Durrell's house. Gwen and Aubrey slept in his old room while Bobby Joe would stay in Kelcey's bed. Paula would spend the night with a friend, so everything worked out fine and they all saved money. His sister, Paula was a junior this year and had grown into a very attractive young lady and a very good softball player. She looked a lot like Aubrey who had taken after his mother's side of the family and from all accounts he was the spitting image of his mom's dad William Addison. Aubrey had never known either of his grandparents on his mama's side because they had both died young from diseases that there were no vaccinations for at that time. Pattie and her two brothers had been raised by her grandmother. Kelcey had taken after the Durrells and especially Wyll's Uncle Jesse Durrell. Kelcey had blonde curly hair and was a good-looking kid as well. Kenny Dudley used to joke that with hair like Kelcey had, there had to be a black person in the family tree somewhere. Aubrey noticed that Bobby Joe was looking hard at Paula, and he thought he saw her looking at him too. He would have to make sure this never happened at least until Bobby Joe settled down. Pattie fed them fried chicken and mashed potatoes with butter beans, peas, and corn bread. Washed down with sweet tea, this was as good a meal as any of them had ever had. She made a homemade banana pudding to top it off.

Around 10:45 Aubrey got up and went outside to his car to go watch the 11:00 train come through. Bobby Joe asked if he could go with him, and Aubrey told him he could. When they got to the courthouse, Bobby Joe told Aubrey, "Thanks for letting me come to Empire with you. It reminds me a little bit of my original home. "I thought Grand Prairie was outside Dallas. How could it remind you of Empire?" asked Aubrey. "Not Grand Prairie," said Bobby Joe, "That is where I moved to when I was adopted. Originally, I lived in a little Podunk place called Mustang, Texas. I lived there until I was eight years old. That's when the state took me and my little sister away from my mama and we were adopted by the Burgess family in Grand prairie." Aubrey had to ask, "Why did the state take y'all away from your mama?" "Well," answered Bobby Joe, "she worked in the only business establishment in Mustang—a strip club called Whispers, and our daddy had abandoned us when we were babies, so she had to do something to make ends meet. Finally, a local pastor turned her in for not providing proper food and care for us and we went to a children's home near Dallas. That's where the Burgesses found us and adopted us both and took care of us. I got to play baseball and football for the Grand Prairie Gophers, and I was pretty good at both sports—not as good as you mind you—but good enough to get a couple of scholarship offers to small schools, but when Houston drafted me, I decided to take a chance on making to the big leagues. They signed me for $25,000 and off I went." "You have a backup plan in case that don't happen?" asked Aubrey. "Not really," answered Bobby Joe, "but the Lord looks after babies and fools and I ain't wearing no diaper so guess which one I am?" he said with a smile.

"Mr. Burgess tried to convince me to go to college, he even told me he would buy me a truck if I went to college, but I didn't want to," he added. Right then Aubrey said a silent prayer for his new friend and protégé. He would help this kid any way he could to realize his dream. Just like clockwork, the train came through Empire all 76 cars and a caboose. Afterwards, he and Bobby Joe went home and went to bed.

The season would not begin until April, but the players were to report to practice the second week in May. They had to find an apartment to live in and Bobby Joe would live with them to share expenses. They left Empire at 7 am for the approximate 5-hour trip to Asheville, North Carolina. Pattie fixed them a fine breakfast of bacon, eggs, grits, and biscuits to send them off with a full belly. Paula made sure to be back early enough to say goodbye to her brother, her sister-in-law, and even Bobby Joe. As Aubrey saw his hometown fade into his rear-view mirror, he wondered if he would ever come back there to stay. His parents were getting older and soon they would be alone when Paula left home in another year and a half. The Empire Knights were rebuilding with a new coaching staff. J.R. and Darcy may never come back to stay either. He started reminiscing about all the summer days walking the railroad tracks barefoot in the heat of the summer, picking blackberries and plums along the banks of the railroad tracks, riding his bike with Kelcey on the handlebars, picking up coke bottles and cashing them in at Ross' Store or Mattie Ella's store, playing ball growing up and then for the Empire Knights. He finally thought about pulling the plow and dating Christina. He wondered what she was doing right now. He was off to start his next phase of life and while there were no guarantees, one thing he knew for sure was that the Lord was in control and whatever came his way, he could handle. After all, he was Aubrey Durrell and God was good to his humble servant.

THE END OF PART ONE.